THE UVALDE RAIDER

A TEMPLAR FAMILY NOVEL

Creative Texts Publishers products are available at special discounts for bulk purchase for sale promotions, premiums, fund-raising, and educational needs. For details, write Creative Texts Publishers, PO Box 50, Barto, PA 19504, or visit www.creativetexts.com

WINTER EAGLES: THE UVALDE RAIDER
By Ben H. English
Published by Creative Texts Publishers
PO Box 50
Barto, PA 19504
www.creativetexts.com

ISBN: 978-1-64738-037-3

THE UVALDE RAIDER
A TEMPLAR FAMILY NOVEL

by BEN H. ENGLISH

CREATIVE TEXTS PUBLISHERS
Barto, Pennsylvania

TABLE OF CONTENTS

Dedicated to Captain Dean Amick Wadsworth, First Air Commando, USAF,
and to the Marines who died trying to get to him.
Declared MIA 08 October 1963
Body Recovered 07 June 1995
Interred Arlington National Cemetery 03 June 1999
"Lest we forget"...

"Circumstances do not make the man, they reveal him."
–James Allen

CHAPTER ONE

Trooper Micah Templar lazed in the cab of the sandstone colored Ramcharger, relaxing from what started as an early morning shift. He had the driver's seat run back as far as it would go, with both doors as well as the rear hatch opened wide in search of a cooling breeze. It was the time of year when the mornings would start off chilly, but by mid-afternoon could turn uncomfortably warm. This was one of those afternoons and the spacious greenhouse of the Dodge made it all the more so.

Micah had his DPS-issued felt hat pulled low over his eyes, trying to shut out the west Texas sun that was just now peeking below the top of the windshield. He was trying to doze a bit but his excitement, along with that burning orb overhead, was making his attempt nigh impossible. Tipping the hat back slightly with the tip of his right index finger, the highway patrolman glanced at his watch and noted it was near the top of the hour. With nothing better to do and little progress made as far as catching some shuteye, he leaned forward and turned on the vehicle's radio for the latest news.

"...at present officials for the Bush administration say an international coalition must be formed to push the Iraqi forces out of Kuwait. Other sources in the Pentagon are stating that plans for military action have been drawn up for a possible response to the crisis.

Meanwhile, the United Nations is also considering further action against Iraq. A resolution has already been passed condemning the invasion and demanding that Saddam Hussein withdraw his forces.

In other such news, negotiators remain hopeful for the release of American hostages still held in Lebanon. It is believed the recent release of Irish citizen Brian Keenan signals a new opportunity in that direction.

However, intelligence experts remain noncommittal following the murder of Marine Lieutenant Colonel William Higgins. Higgins was abducted February of last year by suspected Islamic terrorists. A videotape purporting to show his execution was released, but the American government did not officially declare him dead until two months ago.

This is TSN, the Texas State Network..."

"Should've known, nothing but bad news," Micah muttered to himself, shifting his weight in the seat and switching the radio off. He and his wife Abby had two sons, both of whom were currently serving in the Marine Corps. A former combat Marine himself, he had a better idea than most of what going to war really meant. It had been a long time since the thought was discussed so freely among those with the power to do so, and by all indicators those discussions were in dead earnest. And when war talk occurs in dead earnest among such people, that's a sign of what will most likely result: a lot of other dead people.

These disturbing thoughts banished any further hope of a short nap and Micah crawled out of the cab of the Dodge to stretch his legs. Slouching in the driver's seat had badly skewed the gig line for his uniform, and by habit he hitched the Sam Browne belt around to line everything back up.

Running his thumbs along the inside waistband of his issued trousers, he smoothed the bunched material of his long-sleeved gray wool shirt. The warming temperature of the afternoon made him want to remove the uniform's obligatory blue tie, as well as the frontal body armor that trapped and magnified his body heat. But Max Grephardt wanted a photograph of Micah in his highway patrol uniform for friends back in Germany, and a strong sense of professional pride made Micah want to look his very best when that photo was taken.

He checked his watch again and scanned the skies to the southeast from under the brim of his hat. They should be showing up any time now, if they were maintaining their schedule upon leaving Houston. He reached inside the Ramcharger, retrieving the Ray Ban Aviators sitting atop the dash of the Dodge. Tio Zeke had given those sunshades to Micah nearly twenty years ago, when the younger Templar graduated from the DPS academy. Micah had worn them almost daily ever since.

Putting the well-used sunglasses on his face, he caught a reflection of himself in the large side mirror. Much like the glasses, the intervening years and experiences had left their marks. What had once passed for an almost baby-faced countenance was now the image of a middle-aged man with crow's feet around his eyes, framed in turn by graying hair that had recently sprouted near his temples. Unseen beneath the uniform felt hat was the thinning of that same hair underneath.

Taking in his weather-beaten image made Micah realize that even in the best of future circumstances, his race was already half run. As in so many other mile markers in life it all seemed to have happened overnight, even when he thought he was paying attention. A few more years and the highway patrolman would be eligible for retirement. The idea struck him with a vague bittersweetness.

Micah stuck an index finger inside the collar of the shirt and ran it around, trying for a bit of relief from the wool material that irritated his neck. Somewhat exasperated, he removed the clip-on tie and unbuttoned the offending collar.

He had been inside this uniform for over ten hours now, having missed the chance for a break at lunch to handle a call concerning a stranded motorist. When his shift was over there had been no time to take the uniform off, even for a few minutes. He had hurriedly parked the black and white Mustang in front of his home and piled into the Ramcharger, having already packed the necessary gear for the trip.

Again, he studied the southeastern sky expectantly. Yet it was actually a sound before any image was seen, the sound of pounding radial engines being carried along in the West Texas wind. He cupped his right hand over his ear and scanned the general area as the droning momentarily drifted away and then came back, stronger than before. Micah's gray eyes probed the horizon, knowing the aircraft would be approaching at low altitude.

It took a few seconds more before he caught the reflection of polished aluminum in the midafternoon sky, and watched it grow larger as the multi-engined warbird drew nearer. The trooper glanced over to a pole across the runway, making doubly certain the bright orange sock was not fouled. Their present location was a long way from any real assistance if something went wrong, and the incoming flyers needed that flag to gauge the wind on their final approach.

He could hear those engines clearly now, all four Wright Cyclone 1820s at full song and filling the air with the throbbing, exhilarating tempo that made Micah feel more like a ten-year-old kid again, rather than a grown man nearing fifty. Enthralled, he watched as the Boeing Flying Fortress loomed larger, coming in and swooping over the main runway of what was once a World War II era emergency airfield. Micah felt an involuntary chill run along his spine, as if the time frame of the present had temporarily given way to the airborne ghosts of a near gone past.

As the B-17G cleared the field it banked gracefully to the left, setting up for its final approach and landing. Suddenly, from the point opposing the Boeing's path, another powerful engine made its presence known, coming in low and fast from the west. Micah whipped his head around just in time to see a beautifully restored Messerschmidt 109G streak in from the opposite direction. Crossing the field at better than 275 MPH, the pilot executed a snap roll as it shot past the lumbering Flying Fortress. Finishing the imaginary firing pass, the 109 Gustav pulled into a tight half Immelmann as Micah recovered from its stupefying appearance.

'*Max...*' Micah thought to himself. '*I should have expected something like that.*'

Standing on the worn tarmac and watching the two vintage military aircraft go about their business, Micah mused again over the circumstances that first brought Max and Tio Zeke together, and then so tightly bound them. Having been in his own war and tasted of the searing experiences attending to it, he still marveled how the former mortal enemies could have grown so close.

Nearly a half century prior during the darkest, bloodiest period in modern history, these two men had represented the opposing sides of the greatest catastrophic armed conflict man ever made record of. In it Zeke Templar had formed a singular goal to bomb Nazi Germany back into the Stone Age, while Max Grephardt tried to shoot down anything that had wings and Allied insignias. Both had been relatively successful in their respective endeavors.

But due to chance and shared fortunes of war friends they had become, enjoying a close relationship that existed since about the time Micah was born. As a young boy whose own father had fought the Japanese and still carried an intense animosity in regards to them, he had asked his uncle about this near implausible occurrence.

Tio Zeke had thought it over before answering, his memories returning to other times and other places. Finally, he responded.

"It was war, nephew. And in war you do things that you have to in order to survive and protect your own. You fight for your home, your loved ones and all that you hold dear in this life. It was that way for me and I know it was the same for him. And now, it's over with."

"Let me tell you something else," Micah's uncle continued. "Max Grephardt is as good a man as I have ever known and he honors me with his friendship. I hope that someday you can understand all this better and have the wisdom to know that God does work in mysterious ways, and in manners you least expect Him to."

Zeke Templar had smiled slightly to himself and added, "He might even make your worst enemies into your best friends." From that day forward it would take Micah a lot of years, along with his own life experiences, to fully appreciate what his Uncle Zeke had meant.

And now he was the sole beneficiary of this impromptu air show, put on by two graying winter eagles who had once fought in the skies above because they had to, and now flew in those same skies together because of their shared joy in doing so. Micah watched as the B-17 lowered its landing gear and lined up the concrete runway, side slipping a bit as the pilot worked the rudder against a slight gust in the crosswind.

Even from this distance, one could make out the bold yellow letters reading 'The Uvalde Raider' emblazoned on the bomber's nose. Beside the moniker was a large facsimile of the state of Texas painted in red and blue, enclosing a white star marking the location of the town of Uvalde. This community and its surrounding ranches and cow camps was where Ezekiel Templar had grown up, a local boy who had 'made good' as people around there were wont to say.

That same exact insignia had adorned each bomber that Uncle Zeke flew during the war.

With its flaps down and losing speed, the Boeing touched the tarmac with as perfect a landing as one could ever see in any World War II movie. Admiring the scene, Micah felt the glow of kinship in his uncle's long-polished flying skills. That inner pride lasted about as long as it took to realize that it was not Tio Zeke at the controls of the B-17 as it taxied past, but rather former Luftwaffe *hauptmann* and holder of the Knight's Cross of the Iron Cross with Oak Leaves, Maximillian Friedrich Grephardt.

Somewhat taken aback by what he had just seen, Micah snapped his head around and watched quizzically as the Messerschmitt made its own final approach. The fighter's awkward looking landing gear touched down with the same practiced precision as that just demonstrated by the Flying Fortress. When the Me109 began to taxi past, the side-hinged canopy opened and Micah saw the unmistakable features and grin of Ezekiel J. Templar, retired full bird colonel, United States Air Force.

Quickly rebuttoning his collar and putting the blue clip-on tie back in place, Micah checked his appearance in the outside mirror of the Dodge, adjusting the tie tac a bit to pass his own self inspection. Once satisfied and with one hand on his western hat to secure it from the blowing prop wash, the trooper walked toward the mottled-gray camouflaged Messerschmitt. The fighter braked to a halt, its Daimler 605A engine popping and crackling impatiently, much like a powerful attack dog snapping and growling while being barely restrained on a leash.

Tio Zeke revved the inverted V-12 one last time to keep it from loading up and then killed the engine. Unfastening the restraining straps, he climbed out of the cramped cockpit with the grace of a born athlete. Watching him step on to the wing root and then down to the ground, it was hard to believe that he had celebrated his sixty-fifth birthday a couple of years ago. Of average height and a slim, physically fit build, he could pass easily for a man twenty years younger.

"Hello, nephew, it's good to see you!" he exclaimed, removing his gloves and grasping Micah's outstretched hand with a firm grip. "How do you like my new ride?"

"*Tio!*," replied the still surprised highway patrolman, using the Mexican word for 'uncle.' "When and where did you ever learn to fly a Messerschmitt?"

"Aw, she's not that much different than the P-51s I checked out on after the war. The cockpit is not near as roomy and it's not as forgiving as the Mustang was, but it is a lot of fun."

"And what does Max think about the B-17?" asked Micah.

"Umph, that German can fly anything with wings on it. 'Course, all those years piloting Lockheed Super Stars and other passenger jobs for Lufthansa gives him an edge." He paused, looking to the Boeing. "Speaking of which, we better get over there and lend a hand. He's got a lot more machinery to shut down."

The two men walked side by side in the direction of the Flying Fort. The Templar family genes ran strong through the generations and people often commented on the resemblance between uncle and nephew. That resemblance was no more evident than now.

The elder Templar looked around as they strode along, obviously expecting someone else. "Where's Jack?" he asked.

Jack Albright had flown Douglas A-26 Invaders in Korea and owned the ranch where the old landing field was situated. A founding 'colonel' in the Confederate Air Force, Micah had first met the man through his uncle when he came to the county as a rookie trooper. Once Jack realized the familial link between the two Templars, Micah became a regular on the Bar JA Ranch. The self-professed 'colonels' of the Confederate Air Force were a close-knit bunch, looking after each other's kin as well as their fellows.

Over the years Jack had improved the bomber-sized emergency strip to a state of repair where CAF aircraft could layover for the night, or be kept for a longer stay if the situation required it. He was well known as a gracious host with his West Texas hospitality and good conversation. It had become an annual event for Tio Zeke and Max to pick up Micah and Jack while enroute to the Confederate Air Force show in Midland.

"He won't be coming with us this time," explained Micah. "They got a call late last night from Amarillo about an aunt being in a bad way. He and Sally packed their bags and are already up there. Said we're supposed to make ourselves at home and he might catch us later at the show."

"Sorry to hear that," replied Zeke. "Maybe she'll get better and we can still meet in Midland as planned. I'll put them in my prayers."

They reached the Boeing as Max Grephardt killed the power to the number four engine. Zeke grabbed the release handle along the bottom of the fuselage and dropped the access door. He stuck his head inside and yelled: "Anybody home?"

"Ja," came a loud voice from inside. "Wait there, I will be right out."

"Typical German efficiency," mused Zeke to Micah. "He must have already finished the post checks. Guess he's trying to show me up."

Movement could be heard inside the interior of the large craft before a short aluminum ladder eased its way out. Then a pair of highly-shined black western boots, followed by heavily starched Wranglers emerged from the open hatch.

With a natural ease Max Grephardt stepped off the last rung and onto the ground, stooping to move from under the forward fuselage. Like so many other Germans of his generation, he had an infatuation with the American West and everything to do with it. That explained the boots, jeans and the black western long-sleeved shirt he was wearing. On his closely-cropped head of silver hair perched a blue baseball cap displaying the CAF 'Ghost Squadron' logo.

"Hello Micah, it is very good to see you," said Max as the two men shook hands.

"Max, you look fit. How do you like flying the B-17?"

"Well, I guess I like it fine. However, I never believed I would be flying one," he grinned, an ironic twinkle in his ice blue eyes. "Do you mind being my passenger to the Midland Air Show?"

"No, sir, I certainly don't," replied the highway patrolman.

"Good!" Max replied in his typical enthusiasm. "Ezekiel and I plan to fly each other's aircraft when we come in. It should be a real surprise to anyone who knows us once they realize just who is in what."

Micah chuckled lightly, thinking of his own reaction only a few minutes before. "You certainly surprised me, twice" he admitted. Max and Tio Zeke glanced at each other in knowing fashion and laughed.

The German stepped back a bit, taking in a full view of Micah in his DPS uniform. "You look very professional, Micah, a credit to your agency and to your state."

"Well, Tio Zeke said you wanted to take a photo. Thought I'd look my best for the occasion." Some of Max's friends back home were anxious to see that peace officers in Texas, even in the year of 1990, still actually wore cowboy hats and boots. It was yet another example of their curious fascination with the American West, and especially with the enduring customs and traditions of the Lone Star state.

"Ja, I want to show everyone back in Germany what a real Texas Ranger looks like."

Tio Zeke snorted and Micah hastened to try to explain to Max that he was not a Texas Ranger, but rather a Texas Highway Patrolman. Yes, highway patrolmen were offered the chance to promote to ranger if they chose to, and both services were closely related elements of the same agency. But they were distinctly different in manners of dress, methods of operation and assigned responsibilities.

It was not the first time that Micah had attempted to explain this to Max, but for some unknown reason he just refused to grasp the concept. Sometimes Micah wondered if the whole affair was yet another one of those inside jokes that Max and Tio Zeke shared only with each other, like their idea of switching aircraft at the air show. They always seemed to be involved in hatching some sort of private plot or another.

The three men turned to the tasks that needed done, checking the aircraft over and making certain that both would be secure for the night and ready to go next morning. After Max had taken his photographs, Micah had removed both the offending tie and wool shirt, along with the uncomfortable body armor and placed them inside the Ramcharger. Before donning some gray overalls given to him by a License & Weight troop, he also secured his heavy Smith & Wesson .357 Magnum and Sam Browne belt in the Dodge's console.

As they worked together Max asked about Jack, as well as Abby and their two sons. In response, Micah said the boys were on deployment overseas and with the current world situation, would likely be so for some time. Abby had driven to Midland earlier that morning and would meet them in the designated CAF section of the airport tomorrow. She had never flown in *The Uvalde Raider,* yet had always wanted to. This was supposed to be the year, but with Jack and Sally having to rush to Amarillo she thought it best to take a vehicle to Midland, just in case.

Tio Zeke listened as Micah outlined the change in plans before commenting. "Better tell her not wait too much longer, Micah. Max and I aren't getting any younger."

Max nodded his head silently in agreement. It was the first time Micah had ever heard his uncle speak this way, and the remark made him pause and consider. He had always looked upon his uncle and Max as being as timeless and durable as the two aircraft now parked serenely around them.

To him, neither seemed to have changed much over the years. Perhaps an extra touch of gray in the thinning hair, deeper creases in their faces and a bit more leisurely in their gait and physical movements. But they were still the same men, still larger than life in everything they did. They were just a day or two older.

"Oh, come on Tio," protested Micah good naturedly. "You and Max are as good as you've ever been. Most men half your age can't hold a candle to you two."

"Perhaps." responded Zeke. "Perhaps I might be just vain enough to believe that, at least when it comes to our minds and what goes on inside them. But most men half our age haven't covered near the miles that Max and I have, or seen what we've seen. One day we won't be able to fly these birds anymore and it could be sooner than any of us might think."

Zeke motioned to Grephardt, who was checking the connections on the extra fuel tanks he had recently installed in the Messerschmitt. "Max knows it too, we've already talked about it. He's getting close to mandatory retirement at Lufthansa, even if he just flies a desk for them now. As for me, well, the aerospace industry ain't what it was before. After Challenger blew up, a lot of things changed down in Houston. A lot of the old NASA hands I started out with are gone now."

Micah's uncle paused again, then added slowly. "In fact, lately I've had some pretty lucrative offers on the company. Offers worth considering."

"Oh?" asked Micah. There was a real surprise, the only thing that had enough pull to get Tio Zeke out of the Air Force had been the space race. Zeke Templar had been in on most everything that occurred since near the end of the Mercury Program. When Tranquility Control announced to the world that "the Eagle had landed" in July of 1969, they could just as easily added Templar Aerospace Industries to their statement.

"Yeah, and I have to admit to being real tempted. It's a currently standing offer, too. Lately I've often thought about selling out and leaving Houston for good. There's some nice places south of Alpine up for sale and I want to go take a look. Matter of fact, I'd like to have you come along."

Now Tio Zeke had Micah's full attention. When anyone began talking about the Big Bend country, they always had the full measure of a Templar's mind, heart and spirit.

Ezekiel Templar nodded approvingly at the look on his nephew's face. "That's right, and I'd need someone to help with a small ranch if I made the move. If it came to that and I made it worth your while, would you be interested?"

Micah felt an inner surge of excitement. In a way, it would be like going home for him. He was not quite ready for retirement yet, but the boys had their own lives now and Abby always liked the area. For years they had talked half-seriously about a place somewhere in the Big Bend, and there was the chance of transferring to Alpine or Marfa and finishing out those last few years. His mind began considering the possibilities.

"Well..," he began, rubbing his chin in thought.

"Think about it, Micah" encouraged his uncle. "That's sure enough Templar country. After all, our family and kin has sweated and fought over enough of it. Presently you're the only one of us even remotely near, other than Wolf Zacatecas."

Micah grinned a bit and remarked, "Well, after that big dustup of his, some folks just might pack up and leave if any more Templars showed up."

"So much the better," responded Zeke. "When we get up to Midland, I'd like to discuss this more in depth with both you and Abby.'

His uncle's words trailed off and he frowned a bit, looking past Micah's shoulder. "Say, were we expecting any kind of company?"

"No, why?" asked Micah.

"Because we're about ready to get some" stated Zeke, pointing to the rising plumes of dust headed their direction.

CHAPTER TWO

Standing near the heavy four engine bomber, Micah felt a touch of uneasiness at the idea of unexpected visitors. It might be Jack and Sally returning from their sick aunt but considering the time frame, the trooper seriously doubted it. Also, Jack had not mentioned a word about other people on his property, and he was very unforgiving to anyone on the Bar JA uninvited. Finally, they were a long way from any public road or neighboring land owners, so the possibility of someone wandering through or simply lost was remote.

A person driving accidently up to the field itself was a real stretch, as the dirt lane dead ended at the airstrip and was blocked by a closed gate where it teed from the main ranch road. And judging from the rising dust there was more than one vehicle, which made the sudden appearance of these unexpected interlopers that much more disconcerting.

Yet whoever it might be was likely nothing more than an oilfield supervisor and some hands, or a surveying crew with access who happened to see the two airplanes and took it upon themselves to investigate. Or maybe someone else with an avid interest in World War II history and heard they would be out here this afternoon. Yet there was something more off-center, something that didn't feel right, and Micah wished he had his issued .357 Magnum still on his right hip.

The trooper idly considered easing over to the Ramcharger and putting his Sam Brown belt and the revolver back on. Or better yet, retrieving his Marlin .30-30 out of the lockbox in the cargo area of the Dodge.

But he fought down the urge and attributed it to too many years in his chosen profession, and to the attending abundance of caution that comes with such a line of work. Besides, presenting a gun at the arrival of a curious public was not in the best interests or goals of the Confederate Air Force or the Texas Highway Patrol. Nevertheless, that nagging angst continued to radiate from the back of his head and he did not like it.

Micah looked to where Max Grephardt continued to tinker on the Me109G, either unaware or ignoring the approach of the unknown vehicles. With Grephardt it was most likely the latter, as the past Luftwaffe fighter ace missed very little of anything that went on around him.

The dust plumes were just around a low-lying rise now, and then a tan three-quarter ton Suburban came into view. It did not take much longer to confirm the Suburban was not alone, two other vehicles followed close behind. The one in the middle was a light green crew cab Ford one-ton with a camper shell.

Bringing up the rear was another Suburban much like the first, save this one was white in color. Micah did not recognize any of them and he knew most every vehicle in the county.

In actuality the little caravan might have passed for a survey crew or some oil field hands, at least at first glance. However, near constant experience with both sorts afforded Micah a more discerning eye. Though all three bore the ever-present layer of dust typical to West Texas caliche roads, none reflected the use as well as abuse by someone who drove those roads daily.

There were no dents, dings or scrape marks on the vehicles from bump gates, mesquite branches or a rock thrown up at speed. Their bumpers were not pockmarked or bent, and none displayed the almost prerequisite heavy duty grill guards so popular in this part of the country. These were vehicles from a more semi-urban environment, far too clean and unmarked by the rugged life required of their type on a ranch or in the oil patch.

All three slowed as they approached, not so much in being unsure of what they were doing, rather than not being in any particular hurry to get it done. Micah also noted the vehicles had darkly tinted windows so that no one could see what was inside, or how many occupants there might be. Within his own thoughts, his misgivings continued to mount.

When they were about a hundred feet away the three swung out beside each other and came to a stop. Ezekiel glanced at his nephew and said, "Well, I guess we had better find out what they want." Behind them, Max had stopped working on the Messerschmitt and was cleaning his hands on a red rag, watching.

Micah and Tio Zeke had just started forward when doors began opening. Several men, armed with Kalashnikov-style assault rifles, sprang out and trained their weapons on the two Templars as well as Max. They shouted orders in a guttural manner, yelling in a language that Micah did not understand and at first could not place.

With the sudden display of armed men pointing guns their direction, both Ezekiel and Micah froze. Max abruptly stopped wiping his hands, the rag dropping from his fingers and landing on the tarmac. The three of them stared into the muzzles of those rifles held by the uninvited guests, and the heretofore normal movement of time slammed hard to a dead stop.

Micah's mind was racing wildly, searching for options. His Dodge Ramcharger and its available firepower were too far away to do him any good. From where he stood there was no available cover in moving quickly to, even if he had been armed. Beyond that would have been the less than desirable outcome of trying to take on multiple Kalashnikov-toting opponents in a standup gunfight, with nothing more than a six-shot Smith & Wesson.

Ignominiously, they had been taken completely by surprise and in the absolutely worst tactical position one could ever put themselves into. Micah felt the sickening taste of helplessness churn in the pit of his stomach and slowly, ever so slowly, he and Ezekiel began to raise their arms.

"Easy, easy now fellows," implored the elder Templar in a soft, calming drawl. He placed his outstretched hands before him in an unmistakable sign of submission. "Let's not do anything rash."

Micah was not sure if his uncle was speaking to the heavily armed newcomers, or to he and Max. Perhaps Tio Zeke's soothing words were more for the benefit of all present. Considering the circumstances, it seemed like good advice for everyone.

The interlopers continued to bark out commands and motion aggressively with their weapons. To the casual observer, their general physical appearance would make one suppose they were Mexican nationals. But their language was definitely not Spanish in any dialect, and Micah was still trying to come up with a possible fit to whatever language they were speaking.

Then it dawned on him. Their words sounded very much like some sort of Arabic. Micah cut his eyes over to Tio Zeke who responded in turn. Without a word spoken between them, he sensed that his uncle had already decided the same.

The men were fairly young, in their late twenties or perhaps right at thirty years of age. The weapons they carried appeared mostly to be different variants of the Soviet Kalashnikov AK47. Micah picked up on this almost immediately, as he was more than familiar with the Communist bloc assault rifle owing to his combat tours in Vietnam.

With a rising curiosity replacing the immediate shock of surprise, he further noted these men were dressed in a style of clothing usually worn by illegal immigrants trying to enter from Mexico. To complete this effect, each man was dark headed and with a matching complexion, and each scowled ominously at the highway patrolman and his two companions.

A previously unopened door on the lead Suburban swung wide and another young man stepped out amid the others. There was no doubt he was the leader of this group, he carried himself with the air of authority and appeared to be in complete control of himself as well as those around him. Somewhat lighter in skin color than his fellows but of a slightly taller stature, the man's features were well-defined and proportioned. Even in his shabby clothes many would have said he possessed a somewhat handsome appearance.

With active, highly intelligent eyes, he leisurely took the measure of the three prisoners before him. Then his gaze shifted, settling upon the gleaming aluminum skin of the Boeing B-17 perched in the background. The calculating eyes lingered on the old bomber with open appreciation and the man smiled thinly, nodding his head slightly in the manner of inner true satisfaction. He returned his attention to Micah and the others.

"Good afternoon, gentlemen" he spoke English in an educated, almost British-styled dialect. "Please do not make any sudden motions. My compatriots would not appreciate it."

The leader quietly issued an order in Arabic and six of the men moved forward, breaking into three groups of two each. While one of the pair acted as cover for his partner, the other did a physical search of his assigned detainee. The three captives were relieved of their personal effects including their watches, wallets, pocket knives and other such items. The process was detailed and professional, and pointed to some sort of special training.

Once satisfied, they shoved their charges into a position directly in front of the lighter complected man who had spoken such perfect English. While standing there, Micah did a mental head count. The six men who searched them were to his rear, and a seventh one busied himself while sitting in the front seat of the lead Suburban. The evident leader who had addressed them made for eight.

A ninth and final man had taken a ready position beside his commander. Easily taller than even the leader, this ninth man was in superb physical condition with broad shoulders, a muscular build and not an ounce of fat showing. His hatchet-like face was accentuated by a full goatee framed by long, raven black hair that fell to his shoulders. Most noticeable of all were his dark eyes burning with a peculiarly malevolent hatred, a hatred that was purposely being directed at Micah.

"I want you to know, you have my assurance that we mean you no harm personally" the leader continued. "Let me introduce myself: I am Yahla al-Qassam, a humble follower of the Prophet and fighter for the liberation of the Shi'a Lebanese people."

Qassam gestured with a sweeping motion in regard to the armed men around him. "These are my comrades. We serve the Lebanese resistance movement known as Hezbollah and you are our prisoners. Now that you know who we are, allow me to determine exactly who you might be."

His attention first settled upon Max. "You are former Luftwaffe *Hauptmann* Maximillian Friedrich Grephardt, holder of the Iron Cross with Oak Leaves with 79 confirmed aerial kills during the Second World War. You are currently a high-ranking executive for Lufthansa Airlines and live with your family on an estate near Frankfurt. At present you are visiting your very close friend Ezekiel Templar here in the United States and enroute to a memorial air show in Midland, Texas. That is your Messerschmitt, the same kind of fighter aircraft you flew in the war." Qassam pointed at the nearby 109G.

Max gazed serenely at Al-Qassam, mentally gauging the man. "Ja" he said slowly, "I am Max Grephardt."

"Thank you" replied Qassam, who seemed to revel in showing his knowledge of the German. "One thing I should mention, Herr Grephardt. Do not attempt another storied escape as you did from the Soviets during that war. We are not a mob of ignorant peasants and would not take well to such a distraction. Suffice to say, there are far more important tasks demanding our undivided attention."

He shifted his attention to Micah. "Let's see now, you must be Trooper Micah Templar. You have nearly twenty years of experience as a police officer and your wife's name is Abby, I believe. You have two sons currently in the United States Marines. Also, you served in the Marines yourself during your country's war in Vietnam. Am I correct?"

Micah tried to keep his best poker face and simply nodded in affirmation. Inside of himself, he was still trying to mentally deal with this abrupt change in circumstance, as well as the highly disconcerting fact that someone he had never met seemed to know a whole lot about both him and his family. Someone who also gave every indication of being an especially dangerous enemy.

Without a further word spoken the long-haired taller man stepped forward and struck Micah a vicious round house slap, his open right hand making impact directly over Micah's left ear. It sounded almost like a pistol shot and the report was loud enough to echo off the parked aircraft.

Caught completely by surprise, the blow staggered the trooper as the man's palm slammed full force into Micah's temple. The younger Templar managed to keep his footing, but his vision blurred while a galaxy of stars and planets exploded in bright flashes before his eyes. His left ear rang loudly from the air being compressed by the cupped hand, which in turn mixed with the pain and accompanying dizziness brought on by the impact itself.

Looking through his disjointed vision, the highway patrolman gave his assailant an angry glare as the man stepped back alongside Qassam. In return, Micah's tormentor stared back with reptilian eyes that lacked any promise of humanity. Then the man smiled and it occurred to Micah that if a rattlesnake could do so, it would probably look like this guy.

"I see that you make friends quickly, Officer Templar." Qassam said with an appreciable snicker. "Further introductions are evidently in order. This is my second-in-command, Mustafa Abbas." He gestured to the powerfully built man to his side.

"Another bit of business that needs noted," continued Qassam. "When I speak to you, you will respond verbally. Nodding is considered as disrespectful and will not be tolerated."

Smugly, the Hezbollah leader eyed Micah. "And I would be very careful around Mustafa. He is well-known in Hezbollah as being without peer in unarmed combat and does not need a gun to kill a man."

Leaning forward ever so slightly, Qassam added maliciously. "He also possesses a great hatred for all United States Marines. You see, some years ago his brother was killed by a Marine in Beirut. Unfortunately for you, I happened to inform him of your previous service in that organization. By the way, your last name does not help you in this regard, either."

Qassam's attention swiveled to Ezekiel. "Speaking of last names, I believe there are two Templars present today. One is already accounted for. So that would make you Ezekiel Templar, retired colonel, United States Air Force. You are a widower and your only son was killed in a bombing mission over North Vietnam. You are also the owner and chief executive officer of Templar Aerospace Industries, as well as the owner and pilot of that magnificent aircraft behind you." The terrorist leader pointed at the four engine heavy bomber and smiled thinly.

"I am," responded the elder Templar in a calm, even voice.

"May I say, colonel, it is a pleasure to meet someone with so many achievements in so many different fields of endeavor," Qassam said with apparent sincerity. "Your list of accomplishments speaks of a highly intelligent man with foresight and determination. In fact, there are those who would say we have much in common. I hope that we have some opportunity to visit before parting."

"And how long will that be, Qassam?" questioned Ezekiel in understated fashion.

For a moment the Hezbollah leader seemed a bit surprised. Then he tilted back his head and began laughing, showing a row of perfectly white, even teeth.

"Always the curious intelligence officer, aren't we colonel?" Qassam still smiled but his facial expression held no real mirth. "I have an interesting dossier on you, including your escapades against the Communists after the Second World War. Very impressive. We will certainly have to find some time to have a meaningful conversation."

"I'm already looking forward to it," dead panned Ezekiel in return.

"As am I, colonel, as am I." Qassam lowered his voice to a semi-conspiratory tone. "But the same warning applies to you as to your nephew and Herr Grephardt. Be very careful. Your continued well-being is a plus to us all, but not entirely essential."

Ezekiel Templar cut his eye over to the coiled and ready Mustafa. The second-in-command gave every indication of being primed to strike at the slightest provocation.

Choosing his words prudently, the retired colonel replied. "Believe me, Qassam. You have made your expectations clear."

CHAPTER THREE

The three captives sat in a small room, in the rear of what was once an operations shack for the emergency airfield. The door leading to the main room was partially open, and one of the Arabs stood just outside that door with an AK at the ready. They had been in the room for some time now, the sun had disappeared below the horizon and dusk was turning into night.

Inside the main room a steady stream of activity never seemed to let up, men came and went and one could hear vehicles being moved around outside. There was almost constant talking going on, and Micah tried hard to listen in for anything he could make of their conversations. But it was all in Arabic, and he could determine little beyond the changing inflections used to differentiate between orders, serious discussions and light banter.

All three men sat on the concrete floor, hands bound behind their backs in some manner or another. Micah had been secured with his own handcuffs from his Sam Browne belt, Uncle Zeke and Max were restrained by zip ties. No one had spoken a word since they had been placed in the room. Their captors had not specifically stated they could not talk among themselves, but Micah's bruised left temple was a reminder of how their captors often told you about the rules after you paid for breaking them.

However, that did not mean there was not any communication going on inside the room where they were held. Facial expressions, nods, shrugs and other types of body language were being used to talk in pantomime fashion between one another. Micah picked up early on that his uncle and Max were quite adept at this, and he was left quickly behind in their mute mode of conversation.

Interestingly enough, Tio Zeke seemed to be following quite a bit of the Arabic spoken in the main room. As he listened, he also appeared to become more and more concerned. Over the past few hours, Micah had learned some things about his uncle he had never really been fully aware of before. In such a dire situation and still with that real concern showing, Ezekiel Templar appeared remarkably calm. It was as if the man never stopped thinking in a critical manner, or considering available options.

Of course, Micah had heard a few stories about his uncle and had been aware of his personal reputation through the eyes of others. Micah's own father, Jeremiah Templar, had said that his younger brother was one of the most intelligent and naturally gifted men he had ever known.

His father regaled the son with exploits of when Jeremiah and Ezekiel were teenagers along the Nueces River, and how his brother never seemed to be at a loss for words, or contemplations, or a continuing fancy for adventure. In the many years to follow, Tio Zeke had disciplined those youthful attributes and lived the kind of life that most others could only dream of.

Ezekiel J. Templar was someone who, as the old timers used to say, had been up the creek and over the mountain, and had gone to see the elephant on many an occasion. That much was plainly evident during the first chaotic moments of their capture, as he appeared almost nonplussed while dealing with the precarious uncertainties swirling about him.

When the retired colonel spoke to the one who called himself Qassam, he seemed to know exactly what needed said and just how to say it. More so, the terrorist leader apparently knew things about Tio Zeke that brought forth a certain admiration, maybe even a grudging respect. All put together, it made Micah wonder just how much he didn't know about his own blood kin.

Looking back, he realized that Ezekiel had not been around much until Micah's father had passed on. It was really only after that had occurred, followed by the tragic deaths of his uncle's only son and soon afterward his wife, that they began spending more time together.

Tio Zeke seemed to thoroughly revel in being part of Micah's family, especially during the period when the younger Templar's own two sons were growing up. Abby, with a good woman's innate intuition, welcomed Ezekiel's pressing need to be included in the goings-on of their modest home. More so than anyone else, she grasped the essential reason for this change and explained it to Micah. Having lost his own family made Ezekiel treasure someone else's as never before, and more so because of the intrinsic kinship. Personal loss and a searing loneliness often had that sort of effect on those whose spirit had been so near broken.

When it came down to it, in some ways Micah knew more about Max Grephardt than he did Tio Zeke. If his uncle had been somewhat shy in recounting his own exploits as a younger man, he was more than ready to talk about those concerning the former Luftwaffe ace. This unusual imbalance dated back to when Micah was a small boy.

Many times Ezekiel had spoken of what his German friend had accomplished, and of the many challenges and dangers Max faced in his eventful life. Some forty-five years ago, he had been one of the most highly decorated fighter pilots in the German Luftwaffe. But that in itself was only the smallest fragment of the extraordinary mosaic which illustrated Grephardt's rather remarkable, even unique story.

Micah listened as his uncle reminisced of how he and Max first met, or rather the first time they had met and both been aware of it. The odds were the two men had done so ever so briefly before then, in the sub-zero temperatures of high altitude above Western Europe. Most likely the event was one measured in a scant second or maybe two, closing in upon each other at a combined speed of some 600 miles per hour while spewing fire, steel and destruction. This was the circumstance of their youth, and of their respective duties in a vast and horrendous world conflict.

Similar to their first anonymous meeting, the next was again the product of chance brought on by war. Max had been in a holding camp for the vanquished, only one of literally millions of German POWs who had chosen to surrender to the Western Allies, rather than the Soviet hordes advancing from the east. Ezekiel Templar had been in the company of the victors, involved in running the daily operations of a converted German airbase in that devastated land.

Then a day came along when an airplane had gone down, crashed and caught on fire with men trapped inside. Max was first on the scene and risked his own life to save those of others trapped in the burning flames and black, acrid smoke.

That the aircraft itself was American and the men inside so recently his enemies had meant little to Max Grephardt, what did matter was they were fellow human beings who were in mortal peril and unable to help themselves. As Max went inside the blazing plane and brought out men time and again, Ezekiel Templar had arrived to personally witness the metal within the man. The Air Force colonel would later tell the story at a rare family gathering, smile to himself, and shake his head in amazement.

When he first heard this as a small boy, Micah simply could not understand. In his child's mind of that time, it was impossible to grasp the concept of loving one's enemy enough to risk your own life. Besides, everyone who had ever watched a Hollywood war movie knew that all the Germans were Nazis, and the Nazis were callous monsters incapable of such selfless acts. They had been the perennial villains pitted against the Americans in their proverbial white hats. Why would such an obvious bad guy do something so noble for some of the good guys? And that Knight's Cross with Silver Oak leaves, was that not presented in part to Max for fighting so well against the Americans, even in killing Americans?

Tio Zeke patiently tried to explain there was both good and evil in most men, and this was reflected in turn by the society in which they lived. Where good prevailed more in the hearts of the individuals who made up that society, the society was viewed in general as being such. The same thing happened when this went the opposite way and into the reaches of the state of evil. In Nazi Germany there had been many good men much like Max, but not enough to make that crucial difference. *Hauptmann* Max Grephardt had not flown into battle with the black heart of a villain; rather he went in harm's way only to defend his family, his home and his country as best as he knew how.

As far as the Knight's Cross, his uncle pointed out it was not the medal pinned to the outside of the man that so impressed him, but once again the metal of the man inside. That was how Ezekiel J. Templar went about choosing his inner circle of friends, the quality of the metal possessed within. To Tio Zeke, that metal was hardly burnished so brightly by any man as Max had done at the scene of the crashed American transport.

But the young Micah Templar remained puzzled and somewhat confused concerning this dichotomy during his growing years. Like so many other boys trying so hard to become young men, he tended to see the world in a starkly black and white manner. More so some men, some very good men, chose to go through their entire lives seeing that same world in mostly the same way. Ezekiel's own brother, Micah's father, had been that sort of man…

"Micah?" the softly spoken word on his uncle's lips brought the younger Templar back from the faraway fog of the past. As it was uttered, all three men looked expectantly in the direction of their Shi'a guard, anxiously awaiting any sort of reaction. The armed terrorist, still standing by the partially opened door, looked their direction with an expression of indifference as well as a bit of boredom. Apparently, he was far more interested in what was happening in the adjoining room and returned his main attention there.

Tio Zeke continued speaking in a voice now just a bit louder and more distinct than needed. "They missed the blade I keep hidden. When I get the chance, I'll cut myself loose."

Micah stared at Ezekiel Templar with an incredulous expression, wondering what in the world his uncle was blabbering about. "Watch the guard," he added, "and get ready, Jake keeps a revolver in a cubby hole above us."

The younger Templar doubted that Tio Zeke could have kept any knife secreted through that search and there was certainly no loaded revolver handy. At first baffled by his uncle's words and behavior, it took several moments before the true intent became clear. The older man was not even looking in the direction of his nephew when he spoke, but rather their Hezbollah guard. Ezekiel was testing for the slightest hint of comprehension or associated response from the Lebanese.

The Hezbollah sentry made a half-hearted effort to glance over his shoulder, and then returned to listening to what was being said among his comrades. Zeke watched him carefully, waiting. There was no change in the man's demeanor. Once satisfied Zeke looked over to his nephew, winked and nodded. In his peripheral vision, Micah noted that Max nodded in return.

Tio Zeke spoke again but now keeping his voice down as much as possible. "Keep it low and short, no need irking this guy with chatter."

Max Grephardt nodded again in agreement. Once more, the guard glanced unmindfully their direction and returned to what was occurring in the next room. Ezekiel waited a bit more before saying anything else.

"These fellas are into something big, really big, and they're using The Raider to get it done," murmured the elder Templar.

Micah was a bit startled at the announcement. Evidently his uncle could understand Arabic but Micah had no idea of where or how that ability came into being. Ezekiel noted the further puzzlement on his nephew's face and instinctively sensed why.

"Much like Spanish," Tio Zeke hissed for emphasis. "Often same words but sounded differently. They pronounce from the throat, not the tongue." Ezekiel paused again and looked over to their Hezbollah guard, gauging him.

The man did not acknowledge them this time with as much as a fleeting look. What was happening next door was of far greater interest and the Lebanese was observing the process intently. After all, his intimacy with that process had been his primary reason for existence for several months now.

The Hezbollah guard knew that in a few more hours history would take a drastic, irreversible turn. The years of planning, the months of repetitious training, the long journey from his homeland into the heart of the Great Satan, all coming to fruition as it unfolded before his very eyes.

It did not matter to him if his prisoners spoke a few cryptic words to each other. They were securely restrained, their sounds mere murmurs making for no interference to the voices of his fellows. Forcing them to be totally quiet would cause more disruption than just letting them whisper on occasion. His comrades were on a strict schedule, any distractions would eat into their remaining time and prevent him the enjoyment of seeing all their hard work finally come together.

The success of the continuing struggle in their holy jihad, their reputations among their likeminded peers, their enhanced ability to inflict a given amount of death and destruction, all were about to take on a completely new dimension in their perceived lethality. The Hezbollah member smiled grimly, savoring the knowledge of what was about to transpire.

At the same moment Micah was observing the Shi'a Lebanese, looking for those telltale signs of any possible intent. He took note of that unsettling smile and wondered at the why of it. One thing was for certain: it had the aura of evil ambition and wherever it had come from, the implication the expression carried with it was worryingly obvious.

He glanced over to Ezekiel and breathed, "Anything in mind?"

His older kin replied in like manner. "Nothing now other than decipher more of their plan. Use your Mexican and do the same. *Comprendes*?"

Micah nodded in return and put everything he had as far as concentration into listening. Almost immediately, the highway patrolman began picking out a few phrases that sounded something like a Spanish counterpart. Having been raised on ranches and in cow camps of this region of Texas, one couldn't help but have some sort of background in the language. The trouble was the border slang usually spoken was not true Spanish nor was it even proper Mexican, making for yet another kink in attempting to draw meaning from the words.

Sitting there, Micah felt the nudge from a nearby foot and leaned forward slightly to hear better. "One more thing," advised Ezekiel in a low tone. "Qassam is no fool and neither are these men. They're dangerously keyed up. Let them wind down, we'll get our chance."

Ezekiel Templar returned to focusing on the voices from the adjoining area, and it was plain to Micah that his uncle was getting a whole lot more of what was being said than his nephew was. Still, Micah continued to pick out the odd word or expression and tried to fit it into what he already knew. It was an exasperating, near impossible task, much like trying to put a thousand-piece jigsaw puzzle together while wearing a blindfold.

By now it was night time, and Micah was growing stiff from sitting on the concrete floor. His hands were secured behind his back, the cuffs having been applied in haphazard fashion. There was a real skill involved in the proper use of handcuffs and evidently that was something their captors had not been schooled in. He could actually twist his wrists slightly within the stainless-steel enclosures.

Nevertheless, he was quite cautious in doing so as he was not certain whether the terrorists had double locked the devices. If they didn't, any further movement on his part stood the chance of making them clamp down that much tighter. Every once and a while he carefully repositioned himself to help alleviate the muscle strain and fatigue; trying to stem the dull aching that began gradually making its way up his arms, through both of his shoulders and into the neck area.

The three prisoners had not spoken to each other since that first exchange over an hour ago. Yet even with the falling of night, they were still able to see each other due to the large shaft of artificial light coming through the mostly opened door. Their guard kept an eye on them that way, and it precluded the chance of any movement going undetected inside the small room.

Being able to do so was something Micah wished more for than anything else at this particular moment, and it wasn't because of the increasing discomfort in his neck and shoulders. Though no one else knew of it other than Abby, he had a small handcuff key hidden in the inside waist band of his uniform trousers. It was such an important secret that he didn't dare mention it even to his uncle, for fear that in doing so he would somehow tip his hand to their captors. That small, odd shaped piece of chromed metal was likely their best chance in turning the tables in the style to which Ezekiel had bluffed about earlier.

The key's long-time presence was the result of an incident that occurred many years before in the history of the Texas Department of Public Safety. In the early part of May of 1969, a highway patrolman had been taken hostage by an ex-con and his wife following a high-speed pursuit that resulted in their vehicle breaking down in the wee hours of the morning. The two fugitives escaped on foot through nearby woods, and later managed to seize the officer when he responded to their fake phone call of being robbery victims at an isolated farm house.

After being taken hostage, the young highway patrolman was restrained with the use of his own handcuffs. Then the criminals, using the officer's marked patrol unit, led the responding authorities in a slow-moving procession throughout parts of Southeast Texas. The trailing caravan ultimately involved numerous police agencies and law enforcement organizations, and was reported at one point as numbering over a hundred assorted vehicles. Of course, such a large pursuing motorcade made the national news almost immediately.

Basking in their new found fame, the two hostage takers milked the evolving sensationalism for all that it was worth. Meanwhile the authorities, rightfully concerned with the safety of the kidnapped patrolman, patiently played for some sort of an advantage as the rolling standoff moved on for hundreds of miles. Ultimately the ex-con was shot and killed, and his wife captured while the officer escaped his predicament mostly unharmed.

However, the legacy of the story was only just beginning. With the assistance of the continuing mass media hoopla, the resulting reshaped saga grew legs of its own and was later made into a motion picture entitled *The Sugarland Express*. At the time of its release Micah was out of the Marines and now a highway patrolman himself, so he and Abby had gone to see the movie one night while in San Angelo. It did not take long to determine it had little to do with what had actually happened, and like most other such 'true' stories was more the creation of someone's Hollywood imagination than anything else.

About a year later Micah had been at his In-Service School in Austin and the subject of The Sugarland Express came up. A few of the older hands present were familiar with the real facts of the case and personally knew the trooper involved. One of those facts was that if the young officer had possessed a hidden handcuff key, he could have freed himself on several occasions during the standoff.

Being a man who wished to enjoy his retirement, Micah made a mental note about the idea of a hidden key. Other patrolmen already carried a spare on a key ring, or twist tied to a boot strap, or in a wallet or taped to the inside of their duty belt. The former Marine went a slightly different route, and it was Abby who sewed a small, nearly invisible pouch to the inside waistband area of his uniform trousers. Small and inconspicuous and positioned just so, even a full pat down would almost surely miss it. Micah had dutifully carried that small key on him ever since, though never having any need for it until now.

But having the key and being able to put it to successful use were two different things entirely, and manipulation was a chancy proposition. He would need a certain amount of time while not being observed to do anything with it, as well as a bit of luck. Fumbling around with numbed fingers to retrieve the small, irregular shaped piece of metal from the secreted pocket would be in itself a challenge.

Beyond that he would have to maneuver the key while in an awkward position, and that would only be possible if the securing terrorist had left one of the lock holes facing rearward. Otherwise, the highway patrolman would first have to free one of his fellow prisoners and have them work the key for him. That presented even more complications and the need for even more time.

Thinking about it, Micah cautiously felt around on the handcuff securing his left wrist. He moved slowly, gingerly, not wanting to have the cuffs tighten on his wrists in case they were not double locked. He carefully checked the rearward face of the steel enclosure with his fingertips once, then over the same spot again to be certain. His heart sank, the lock hole could not be found and must be facing forward.

Doggedly he set his mind back to the task and switched sides, checking around the perimeter of the other cuff with his left hand. For a moment he was not sure, and Micah lightly probed the area again with his thumb and fingers. Yes, he was certain he could feel it. This lock hole was definitely facing to the rear. His spirit lifted at the vital piece of knowledge, but was quickly tempered by the realization that he would now have to work the small key with his left hand, and not his natural right. Furthermore, there was still the biggest hurdle of all, the dire need for the proper opportunity and amount of time to free himself.

CHAPTER FOUR

It was an hour or so before midnight when the Hezbollah guard stepped into the room and began prodding them with the muzzle of his Kalashnikov. The Shi'a pointed with the business end of the AK in the direction of the adjoining larger room, making for an invitation that could not be ignored. For himself, Micah was more than ready to oblige after hours of trying to find a semi-comfortable spot on the unyieldingly hard concrete floor. He put one knee underneath him, braced and managed to make it to his feet without too much trouble. He stood there for a moment, savoring the relief from the change in position as Max and Tio Zeke struggled to do the same.

Once able to, they made their way through the opened door and into the larger space. Micah stopped and blinked repeatedly before squinting against the harsh artificial glare, his eyes adjusting to the sudden onslaught of bright lighting contained within the room.

The heretofore dominant sounds of activity now faded to the visage of their captors conducting different tasks, all evidently part of some grand scheme of which Micah still had no real idea of. Qassam and his malicious shadow, the one he called Mustafa, peered over an aerial map set upon a large desktop to one side.

Both looked up after a moment, Qassam smiling with his white, even teeth as if genuinely glad to see them. Mustafa gave off no expression of emotion whatsoever, he simply looked at them with his flat reptilian eyes as if he was sizing something up for a future meal. If the Lebanese ever had an ounce of human kindness within him, the emotion had apparently evaporated a long time before.

"Colonel Templar and company, good to see you again" the Hezbollah leader effused. "I hope your lodging quarters have not been too uncomfortable. You have my apologies for the lateness of the hour, but I did want the chance to visit with you further. Now I have the time to do so."

Ezekiel Templar cast a practiced eye on what was happening around him. There were aerial maps, flight charts, meteorological forecasts, assorted storage containers and color-coded notebooks placed neatly at different points in the room, all illustrating a well-executed attention to detail.

He had already picked up enough from his eavesdropping to realize this was no rag tag bunch of petty criminals. They were a disciplined, well-trained and highly motivated group of men who were working together to accomplish an overridingly important goal. He already had a fair idea of what that goal likely was, but had been silently praying that he was wrong.

"I don't know about that, Qassam, you look kind of busy. Perhaps we should come back at a better time" responded the elder Templar with a hint of dryness.

Qassam laughed out loud in apparent merriment. "Oh no, you could have not come at a more agreeable one. Most of the work has already been done, at least for my part. It has been said the mark of a successful organization is for each member to know their job and do it well, and without any real supervision. Such motivation and skills make my duties far less stressful and carries the greatest promise in achieving the objective. I handpicked each of these men precisely with that in mind."

"Evidently so" agreed Ezekiel. He looked beyond the confines of the room and out through the front window that faced the runway area. *The Uvalde Raider* sat there, the center of attention for the activities going on outside.

The Boeing was lit up by numerous portable lighting fixtures, and Qassam's men moved with purpose both inside and around her. The bomb bay doors had been cranked open, and they were working on some sort of hoist and pulley device that was being lifted up through the open belly of the aircraft. Off to the side was a group of ten fifty-gallon drums, arranged neatly in two rows. The containers appeared to be made of some sort of heavy plastic and were blue in color.

His worst fears confirmed, the elder Templar took another step forward, focused entirely on the scene outside. "What are you doing to my airplane?" he asked quietly.

"Preparing it for jihad, Colonel. You might say that your airplane is being brought back into active duty" replied the Hezbollah leader.

"If you are expecting me to fly it for you, you might first tell me exactly what you have planned." deadpanned Ezekiel.

"That would be quite understandable, Colonel Templar, if you were the one who was flying it. As I alluded to before, the mark of a successful organization is for each man to know his job and do it well." The Hezbollah commander leaned a bit forward, arms folded smugly. "You see, I already have a pilot and he is quite proficient."

"Flying a B-17 is not like crawling into a Cessna 172, Qassam. Your man may be a good pilot, but there are very few these days who happen to have much experience at the controls of a Flying Fortress." Templar glanced to both sides and then again to the large window as the young members of Qassam's team went about their duties. "Frankly, I don't see anyone around here who likely has that kind of experience."

"Do not equate age with the experience needed to fly your airplane, Colonel," warned Qassam. "Think about it this way: how old were you when you first flew the B-17 during your own war? Twenty-one, perhaps twenty-two years of age?"

The terrorist leader peered intently at the older man, as if relishing the thought of staying one step ahead of him. "I have the right man for the task. He is outside now, supervising the loading of your aircraft."

Ezekiel Templar turned and faced the Hezbollah leader. "Qassam, I don't know how much you know about a B-17, but that bird sitting outside is nearly a half century old. It does well enough to get itself off the ground these days running empty. I see several fifty gallon drums underneath and every indication that you plan to load them on that airplane. If you do, your pilot is liable to kill himself and everybody else on board before anyone realizes he's in trouble."

"Your concern for the safety of my men is touching, colonel," rejoined the Hezbollah leader. "But I do believe you are overstating your case, including the alleged frailty of your aircraft. In truth your B-17 was specifically selected for several reasons, including how well it has been cared for over the years. Some of my more knowledgeable sources claim your airplane is better than new in some respects."

Qassam gestured to the large sofa behind the three men. "Please, sit down. There is much I want to talk with you about before being forced to devote myself in other matters." The tone was still cordial yet there was also an obvious element of control in it. Whatever else Yahla al-Qassam might be, he was someone used to being in charge and in getting his own way.

The three hostages backed up and sat carefully on the overstuffed couch placed to their rear. Each positioned themselves on the lip of the cushions to avoid stressing their bound wrists any further, as well as the accompanying dose of added discomfort. Ezekiel Templar continued to study the scene of activity through the plate glass window, his curiosity mixed with a rising dread in what he reasoned was occurring. Qassam was quick to pick up on it.

"Your anxiety for your aircraft is understandable, Colonel Templar. I think I know how you must feel, and why. Yet believe me when I say no real harm will come to it by our hands if all goes well. We just plan on borrowing it for a day or so."

"Borrowing is an interesting term, Qassam, considering the circumstances," Ezekiel replied evenly. "But aside from that, I am actually more curious about what you plan to use the airplane for."

"And I told you before, Colonel, we are preparing it for jihad" said Yahla al-Qassam. "You would disappoint me mightily by not knowing the meaning of that word."

"I am familiar with the meaning" responded Ezkiel. "But what does it have to do with *The Uvalde Raider*, or with us? Are you just 'borrowing' the three of us as cavalierly as you are doing my property?

Qassam again smiled widely and nodded his head in shrewd fashion. "In regards to hostages I never thought of it in terms such as borrowing. However, we can call it that too. As I said before, no real harm will come to your aircraft or to you if all goes well. The same can be said for Herr Grepardt as well as your Marine Corps nephew."

The terrorist leader paused for a moment and then added for emphasis. "That is, if I can keep Mustafa from snapping his neck as if it were a twig." With that last remark the powerfully built Mustafa fixed his cold, intimidating eyes squarely upon the highway patrolman. Micah stared back hard in return, the two of them locked in a silent war of wills.

Qassam observed both for a long moment, taking in the muted conflict with a certain amount of obvious amusement. "Do not seek to antagonize him, Officer Templar. Like your uncle and his friend, at present you are worth more to me alive than you are dead."

Seeking to interrupt the silently building crescendo of mutual enmity, Ezekiel casually commented, "Evidently your concern for our continued well-being is as touching as my own for the safety of your men, Qassam."

Successfully distracted, the Hezbollah leader looked back to the retired colonel, another smile forming on his lips. He enjoyed a play on words as much as the next man, and somewhat begrudgingly found Ezekiel Templar as intriguing as what his lengthy dossier had led him to expect.

"Then we understand each other, Colonel."

"Well, I must admit to only being able to try to understand you, Qassam. You still haven't told me what this is all about." Changing his tact, Ezekiel Templar continued on. "I can see that a great deal of time and effort have been invested, and the planner had to have been a very intelligent as well as resourceful person."

Ezekiel knew instinctively that Qassam was most likely the principal author of what was happening around them, and his calculated appeal was aimed squarely at the other man's sense of pride and ego. His gambit took only the briefest time to bring fruit as the terrorist began nodding agreeably.

"Why thank you, Colonel" responded the Hezbollah leader. "I take that as a real compliment, as I am the one responsible for this project." Qassam seemed overly pleased with the recognition and Ezekiel made a mental note of the first chink discovered in his opponent's armor.

"Since you are apparently so determined to discover what this is about," added the commander, "I will explain exactly what is happening and what will happen in the very near future, for all the good it will do you."

"You mentioned knowing something about the word *jihad*" Qassam began. "Pardon my lack of confidence in your knowledge, yet I seriously doubt that any non-believer can fully appreciate this fundamental pillar of Islam. Your people often simply translate it as 'holy war.' However, it means so much more to those who devoutly follow the teachings of the Prophet, blessed be his name."

Yahla al-Qassam paused for a moment, putting his thoughts in proper order. "Yes, Colonel, I will indulge your ceaseless curiosity in this. After all, the three of you are playing a very small part in what will be a verifiably momentous event, and you should have the chance to comprehend it more fully. But first, a necessary lesson in history that has brought us all to where we are now.

"For some thirteen centuries my people have waged this conflict in not only a physical sense, but also in what encompasses the mind, the heart and the spirit. Their ceaseless struggling and faithful acts of purification led Islam to be the light of the world early on. While your ancestors were only one step beyond living in caves and dying from the Black Death, ours were recognized as the greatest mathematicians, architects, astronomers, scientists and scholars the world had ever seen. Our culture was without peer.

"During that time cities such as Baghdad, Cordova, Istanbul, Cairo, Tripoli and many others arose, each becoming a sphere of influence for those in search of enlightenment and knowledge. The largest known libraries on earth were found within their confines and buildings of breathtaking beauty lined their streets. This period became known as the Islamic Renaissance, or The Golden Age.

"For example did you know that Ibn Sina, the Persian whom your people call Avicenna, finished a fourteen volume work entitled *The Canon of Medicine* in 1025 and it remained the standard for many Western doctors until the early 1800s? And that he was also renowned as a poet, philosopher and astronomer, as well as a respected scholar of the holy Quran?

"Ibn Sina was only one of innumerous giants of our Islamic Golden Age. There were so many others, all anointed by Allah himself and led by the teachings of the Prophet, blessed be his name. These men in turn inspired others and Islam blossomed in the minds and hearts of the true believers, and these in turn were rewarded with riches beyond imagination for their devotion."

As Qassam pursued his course of thought, Ezekiel noted the fervency growing in the man's voice. Yet it was the look in his eyes that so forcefully underscored what would otherwise have been mere words, those eyes that were neither focused on him or anything else in the room. Their burning intensity gave away the countenance of a man who was looking to a faraway place and time, and yearning to go there. They were the eyes of someone driven half mad by the zealotry of his own fevered dreams and altered perceptions of greatness.

Still lost in the recollections of a world equally lost to the ravages of time, change and circumstance, the Hezbollah leader kept on with his ascending monologue.

"Then came the Christian Crusaders from the West as well as the Mongolian hordes of the East. We were a people of peace and believed that knowledge was the key to cure all ills, including those of greed, avarice and the corruptible qualities of conquest and power. We were wrong.

"With our enemies attacking from outside and the rot of the Zionist Jews from within, our Golden Age came to an ignominious end. One disaster befell another as the centuries passed, and those who were once chosen by Allah became little more than servants and slaves to all who occupied our lands. We ourselves had forgotten the importance of the Prophet's command to wage jihad and the associated sacrifices required in doing so.

"However, when those occupiers gave up our holy land of Palestine to the filthy Hebrew who had collaborated in our defeats and helped fetter our people, a new page was turned in the story of Islam. More so than any other one thing, this last dishonor reminded us of who we had once been and how low we had sunk since.

"At that humiliating realization, that odious nadir in the midst of an open sewer, we at last rediscovered our destiny. Our banners now fly high again. Our swords are lifted in unity while the sacred words of the Prophet overflow in our mouths as well as our hearts. Once again, we relearn the true meaning of jihad and the vital purification it entails. No matter how heavy the cost, we shall never return to the shame of licking any infidel's feet." Qassam fixed his full attention on Ezekiel Templar again, staring at him with a seething emotion barely controlled.

"By this time tomorrow, the United States will also fully understand the concept of jihad and to learn to live in fear of it. You will be confronted with a new kind of war that you have forced upon us. Man, woman or child, it will not matter as all will suffer in what is to come. The words of the Prophet command it."

A pregnant silence filled the room as each of the three captives beheld in full measure what they were presently captive of. It was at that very moment when each became cognizant of this human embodiment of a wholly metastasized, malignant, form of wickedness.

CHAPTER FIVE

"Qassam" began Ezekiel, searching delicately for the right words to reach something akin to a conscience inside this self-defined terrorist, on a self-described mission of mass murder. "Is it not written in your Quran that your Allah loves the kind and the compassionate, and that he does not forbid you to be kind and equitable to others? There is nothing holy or honorable or justified in the murdering of innocent people."

The Hezbollah operative gave Ezekiel a quizzical look, cocking his head to one side. "Your choice of phrasing shows you know something about the Quran, Colonel, or perhaps you were told something of it by others. How is that so?" Qassam pondered a moment more and then seized upon a thought, wagging his index finger emphatically.

"Yes, I remember now. You served as part of the American delegation sent by your President Eisenhower to help with negotiations during the Suez Crisis. You were in Nasser's Egypt for most of the year of 1957, weren't you?"

Qassam's question was rhetorical and phrased as more of a statement in fact than anything else. Ezekiel gazed blandly back at the Hezbollah leader with his best poker face intact. Yet inside he was wondering just how much Qassam actually did know, both about him and *The Uvalde Raider*. With a growing apprehension the elder Templar was discovering his opponent was not only in fact highly intelligent as well as resourceful, he also did his research thoroughly and had a keen mind for seemingly insignificant details.

"You have very good sources of information, Qassam" Ezekiel responded impassively.

"And you have a very good memory, Colonel. I am pleased that you evidently tried to learn more about our people and our beliefs all those years ago," stated Qassam.

"But be that as it may, in reality your recollection is both fragmentary and imprecise. You see, in jihad there are no innocents among infidels and non-believers. Unfortunately for you, that is how your people are divinely defined in the Quran. For it is written, 'Fight and kill the disbelievers wherever you find them, and seize them, beleaguer them and lie in wait for them in every stratagem of war.'"

Qassam raised his right hand and shook it in the empty air. "Beyond that it is also written: 'Against them make ready your strength to the utmost of your power, including steeds of war, to strike terror into the hearts of the enemies of Allah and your enemies, and others besides.'"

The Hezbollah leader's voice raised an octave or two in passion as he went on, "Please note the terms 'every stratagem of war' and "to strike terror into the hearts of the enemies of Allah.' You and your kind are our enemies and we are commanded to make war on you in every way possible." Pointing to the Flying Fortress parked outside he added emphatically, "There is our steed of war and it is how we will strike terror into those hearts!"

Qassam then paused to recollect himself and flashed a well-calculated, wolfish sort of smile. "Besides, I seem to recall a ghastly number of innocent people killed in your bombing raids of World War II. It is said that entire towns and cities ceased to exist. Now tell me, Colonel, how does that square with your professed love for the innocent?"

The features in Ezekiel's face tightened and his eyes glinted in response. "That was war, Qassam."

"As it is now, Colonel Templar" the terrorist replied self-assuredly. "And there are exactly 164 verses in the Quran to tell us how to fight it."

Calming himself internally and still groping to somehow reach common ground, Ezekiel tried a different approach.

"Then what kind of war are you fighting against those such as Saddam Hussein and others like him?" queried Ezekiel. "How can we be this great enemy when we stand with you against such a terrible menace to your fellow Muslims? Look at what he has done to the Iranians and the dissidents within his own land. Even nations such as Syria are making ready to join us against him."

"Colonel," Qassam scoffed, "you believe too much in those childish adages attributed to our culture such as 'the enemy of my enemy is my friend.' Do not take us for fools or simpletons, we are far more sophisticated than that in thought as well as action.

"Yes, the Syrians will assist you in ridding us of an outright apostate such as Saddam, much in the same manner as they have assisted us in our own cause for many years. They do what they can for our shared faith of Islam, as do we. But that does not make any two of us enemies to each other because of a temporary alliance of convenience to you. When you lived among us, did you not hear of the concept of Taqiyya? You take us as being backwards and simple minded, yet it is you who is being deceived. A true believer will never lie to another believer, but he will readily do so to non-believers to protect himself or to protect Islam.

"We Muslims have used Taqiyya since the time of the Prophet. For it is written, 'Let not the believers take the disbelievers as friends instead of the believers, and whoever does that, will never be helped by Allah in any way, unless you indeed fear a danger from them.' That feeling of danger is why many of my brothers may praise you with their words but secretly curse you to hell in their hearts.

"No matter what sort of scheme you may devise to separate us, in the end we are all followers of Allah and you are not. Much like a large family we have our arguments and disagreements, sometimes leading to the shedding of blood. But make no mistake, it is a shared blood and a shared faith. When you or your Zionist allies interfere with members of our large family, we will all turn against you with a fury you cannot even begin to comprehend.

"Shi'a and Sunni will ultimately come together as the brothers they are in Allah's eyes, and we will defeat you. The Western world constantly underestimates us, as well as that divine power that Allah has bestowed upon those loyal to him. As long as we hold true to his commands, we will once again rule all in a global caliphate.

"Are you aware of the prophecies concerning the Twelfth Imam? Allah willing, he will come in our generation's time and lead us to victory. Shi'a over Jew, Muslim over Christian, the Prophet Muhammad over your Jesus, Allah over your God. It is already written, all we must do is to remain faithful. It is our destiny. The symbol of Hezbollah itself is a globe with an upraised arm brandishing a Kalashnikov. It is symbolic of our total devotion to the imposition of Islam through jihad, by any means necessary."

Yahla al-Qassam's very being was now overflowing in a flood of theistic zeal, his words building upon each other in devoutness as well as intensity. With his three prisoners acting as a captive audience he was reaching a near frenetic zenith, pacing the floor before them and waving about his arms and hands for added effect. Then in mid-stride he abruptly stopped and pivoted about, gesturing again to the restored heavy bomber waiting outside.

"Your airplane will be the harbinger of a new kind of terror unheard of to this point, with a killing capacity unimagined by those who designed it in the 1930s or by anyone who ever flew it before. You have a great city in your state, a city that is home to a population of nearly one million people and five different American military bases. It is a thriving hub for commerce and travel, as well as a cherished landmark for your people's history and culture. You call it San Antonio.

"What will happen there tomorrow morning will be the beginning of what is to come. I chose my target carefully, Colonel, in the very same manner as everything else having to do with this mission. It has been said that the goal of war is not in how many people you kill but rather how one can break the will of a people to resist. Can you think of a better place to do so than at the very site and symbol of your Texas fight for independence, the very ground on which your venerated Alamo still stands?

"Think of the irony of it all, Colonel Templar. An antique bomber once used to destroy your enemies and now owned by a man first sired by some long–forgotten Crusader, being used to destroy a cherished mission and city that are near sanctified symbols of your beliefs and way of life. All done in the name of Islam, and all done to sweep in a more enlightened belief system and way of life. Can you think of a better example of the odd circumstances of destiny, Colonel?"

Qassam stood in front of them, his lips slightly curled and exposing his white, gleaming teeth in a sort of predatory animal-like snarl. The man's brows peaked in fierce assertion, and his eyes were flared wide and glowing with something beyond mere mortal malfeasance. His was the countenance of evil personified, an evil driven by something beyond the tangible realm. Every one of the captives before him had looked upon pure wickedness before, but nothing quite akin to what was in their presence now.

Yet through it all Ezekiel Templar gave every appearance of being unshaken by Qassam's vitriolic tirade, refusing to be emotionally distracted or dismayed in confirming what exactly the terrorist had in mind. Still angling for this knowledge and another chink in his opponent's armor, he decided to push a bit more.

With a feigned casualness, Ezekiel commented, "Qassam, you are putting a great deal of hope into a fifty-year-old bomber with some plastic drums slung into its belly. Because if you do manage to get it off the ground without killing yourself and manage to find San Antonio before being shot out of the sky, there's no amount of high explosives that you could conceivably stuff into that plane to make any real difference or change.

"Yes, you might be able to blow something up and kill some innocent people but you're not going to break their will. About all you can really accomplish is make them mad enough to track you and your organization down to do likewise, no matter what rock you decide to hide under or how long it takes. Now, for everybody involved, don't you think you'd better call this off while you still can?"

The Hezbollah leader, eyes still wide and ablaze with a fire sparked by a supernatural malignancy, stared intently at the elderly man for a long moment. His features began to soften ever so slightly as he regained control of the raging beast that had escaped from within.

"Your continuing concern for our welfare never ceases to amaze me, Colonel," Qassam remarked, "nor to amuse. We will get your airplane off the ground safely and we will accomplish our objective as planned. This is not a massed bomber mission over Berlin in the winter of 1944, but rather a pleasure flight in peaceful skies by an enduring relic of your victory in that war. No one will suspect otherwise until it is far too late.

"As far as the effectiveness of our weapons, who said it would be high explosives? Once again, you assume far too much and persist in underestimating our means." Qassam halted to both savor the moment and to properly pronounce what he was about to say. Then in the measured manner of speech one uses to recite difficult wording he asked, "Does the chemical compound Ethyl-bispropanyl-aminoethyl-sulfanyl-methylphosphinate mean something to you?"

Ezekiel Templar thought hard for several seconds, calling upon his knowledge of chemistry and the possible compounds of such when used for munitions. When his thinking process seized upon an answer; his own eyes widened involuntarily as a vague, cruel chill near enveloped him, sweeping through both body and spirit. It took longer still to wrap his mind around the enormity of what had just been said.

"That's some sort of weaponized chemical agent," Ezekiel managed to respond. He did so haltingly, losing temporary command of how he said it. Qassam was smiling again.

"Yes, Colonel Templar. VX to be exact." stated Qassam triumphantly. "By far, the deadliest weapon of its kind ever invented. A nerve agent both odorless and tasteless, and which possesses the advantage of being very slow to evaporate compared to other chemical compounds for warfare. It is said to be a hundred times more powerful than Sarin, and a mere fraction of a drop absorbed through the skin is enough to kill the average human being."

The terrorist leader nodded to the Boeing and the blue drums situated beside the bomber. "There are five hundred gallons of VX agent in those ten plastic containers. It is enough to allow about a twenty-three-kilometer swath from one end of San Antonio to the other, with a path approximately one hundred meters wide. If you look closely, you will see that we are finishing the installation of the portable pumps, as well as the high-pressure lines needed to disperse it from your airplane. Following that, my men will don the proper protective clothing to load and secure those drums."

"How…" Ezekiel Templar began, still trying to discipline his lurching mind against the near unimaginable horror his thought process had high centered upon.

"Do you mean how did we, a blissfully ignorant and uneducated people, obtain large quantities of such a fearsome weapon?" interrupted Yahla al-Qassam. "It is a long and involved story, Colonel. Too long and involved to tell here, and best left for the pages of future history books to describe in detail what happens tomorrow.

"But suffice to say that it was done with the assistance of both the Syrians as well as the Iraqis, along with many of our Islamic brothers in other places and countries." Qassam leaned forward ever so slightly to accentuate what he said next. "I am curious, though. What is your perspective now of your supposed allies and enemies in any war for or against any Muslim people?"

Qassam continued to press hard, noting how the color had drained from the older man's face. The gravity of his words were also sinking into the consciousness of the other two men before him, and their obvious discomfort and growing alarm fed his insatiable appetite to control as well as dominate.

"As Hiroshima had its Enola Gay and as Nagasaki had its Bockscar, so will San Antonio have its Uvalde Raider. Think about it Colonel, we are standing on the brink of a future that will change not only nations but the world itself. We have the weapon; we have the ability and we have the will to employ it to its full potential. Nothing will ever be the same for any of us, for the roles of the past millennium will change forever in the four- and one-half minutes it takes for that airplane of yours to cover twenty-three kilometers. Islam will begin its new ascent as has been foretold, and all our enemies will either die or be relegated to their rightful place of dhimmitude."

The terrorist commander leaned forward still further, forcing Ezekiel Templar to look up as the old man pondered the sheer moral awfulness of what had been revealed. Qassam was not boasting idly, nor was his an empty threat. One look into his euphoric eyes and every one of the captives sitting before him had no doubt whatsoever as to his absolute sincerity.

"What do you think of my plan now, Colonel Templar?" taunted the Hezbollah leader.

Ezekiel Templar shifted his position ever so slightly on the edge of the overstuffed couch. In the expectant atmosphere of the room, the aging Texan cocked his head resignedly and raised one eyebrow while lowering the other. He looked hard at the terrorist leader looming over, his hazel eyes turning black as coal as they stared at his younger antagonist with an unmistakable aura of open disgust.

Calmly, with a composed manner that belied the sea of rancor welling up inside of him, Ezekiel Templar replied. "I think it's the result of a twisted, too smart for his own good, mind of a murderous sonofabitch spawned by a mother who likely recoiled in horror at his birth. She should have stomped the life out of the little cockroach then, and chalked it up as a mercy killing for the betterment of all mankind."

Ezekiel now took his own pause for full effect. Then he added, "That is what I think of your little plan, Qassam, and of you."

CHAPTER SIX

Whatever the response that Yahla al-Qassam was expecting from Ezekiel Templar, the one he had just received was clearly not what he had in mind. The triumphant passion in the terrorist's face changed to open surprise followed quickly by an active, venomous anger. Unable to contain the boiling rage bubbling up from within, the Hezbollah leader shrieked in a loud, primitive manner that has no understandable meaning in any language, yet conveyed more than any words could ever describe.

Everyone within earshot froze in the middle of their assigned tasks, both the men inside the room as well as those outside working on the bomber. Even his human pit viper, Mustafa, seemed somewhat taken aback by the alarming display of emotion. The second-in-command stood there, primed to spring into action but unsure of what he should do or why. It was plainly evident that none of them had ever seen their commander behave like this before.

Qassam kept the long, piercing wail going and then in the midst of his overwrought fit lunged forward. He began pummeling the older man rapidly with open palms about the face and head. At this point Mustafa did make his move, grabbing Ezekiel with both of his powerful hands and jerking him to his feet.

The wail died away as Qassam expended all of the air left in his lungs. But in his blinding anger, the Hezbollah leader pushed his henchman away and shoved Ezekiel down on to the couch again. He resumed his attack with mostly ineffectual slaps at Ezekiel, who had hunched himself up to brace against the blows. No one else dared to interfere or try to pull Qassam off and calm him down.

The terrorist leader discontinued the indecisive slapping and then started a series of awkward kicks aimed at the older man's head and torso area. Twice he nearly lost his balance before he stepped back, chest heaving and with the tottering stance of someone in the midst of exhaustion. His eyes were partially unfocused and rolled ever so slightly as if he were experiencing some sort of physiological disorder. Looking down at his bound prisoner, they refocused and filled again with a peculiar brand of rage reserved only for the most inhumanly cruel or the certifiably insane.

Redirecting upon the origin of his rampage, the Hezbollah leader started forward again but stopped in mid-stride as some other idea entered his head. His right hand went into the front pocket of his trousers, producing a diminutive Beretta Bobcat .25 ACP pistol. He brought the blued steel handgun up, cocking the exposed hammer and pointed its muzzle squarely into Ezekiel's face, finger on the trigger. Mustafa stepped back and away, while everyone else in the room grimaced at what was most likely to come. Everyone except Ezekiel Templar, who stared down the barrel of the small pistol as if it was nothing more menacing than a number two lead pencil.

The terrorist leader stood there, chest heaving and breathing heavily with a crazed, disheveled look on his face. The lack of reaction from the older man seemed to stymie his murderous provocations, and indecision began to creep across his features. The pistol barrel wavered ever so slightly, as a sliver of a resurgent self-control came again to Yahla al-Qassam's consciousness.

Qassam slowly lowered the pistol, glowering at the retired colonel and now acutely aware of how his behavior must have been viewed by both captives as well as captors. Ezekiel Templar grimly held to his same piercing stare, a thin line of blood seeping from the corner of his mouth amongst the other cuts, bruises and welts that were beginning to dot his face.

"Well done, Colonel, very well done", the Hezbollah leader literally spat out the words. "Probe for your enemy's weak points, identify them and concentrate to exploit them. Your long-ago reputation as an intelligence operative is well deserved.

"Providentially enough for you, it came to me just now what you were attempting to do. Yes, I know what you were thinking: Let me see if I can put this man off balance, to so irritate or anger him as to make him cease thinking logically. That is when we all make our mistakes, isn't it? When we become so emotionally involved or distracted as to lose control of ourselves as well as our objectives."

As Qassam spoke the tiny Beretta hung loosely at his side, muzzle down. However, the pistol had not been returned to its prior hiding place and the hammer was still cocked back. Ezekiel Templar remained silent, never breaking his line of sight.

"You very nearly overplayed your hand, Colonel," the terrorist continued. "But I suppose if I had put a bullet between your eyes, it would have worked to your advantage. I would be missing one high profile hostage, and far more importantly would have shown my men that I am not the leader they believe me to be. Killing thousands as part of a plan to win a war is the mark of a strategist, killing one in a fit of rage is nothing more than the conduct of a common criminal, someone with no concept of strategy, discipline, or honor.

"Yet you have managed to make me lose face in front of my men, and I will have to deal with the reverberations from that as well as the resultant loss of any respect. For that, you will be punished. This will not be done in anger though, nor as part of some senseless personal vendetta." Turning to Mustafa, he communicated rapidly in Arabic. After receiving his instructions, the second-in-command nodded and quickly went out the door. Soon enough he had returned with the others who had been working on the bomber. The men crowded themselves into the room, and the close confines became thick with uncertainty and tension.

After everyone was present, Qassam began to address his compatriots using a slow, emphatic tone. As he did so, Micah Templar again tried to understand what was being said but could only pick out the occasional word or expression. In general though, it was obvious the terrorist leader was explaining what had occurred and was coincidentally painting himself in the most favorable light possible.

Micah looked over to his uncle, who sat there calmly with a nigh inscrutable presence about him. Beyond him the younger Templar could see Max Grephardt. The German perched on the edge of the couch exuding a quiet defiance, his blue eyes having turned cold as stone to match a jaw set as if made of granite. Whatever was to come, Micah drew a grim satisfaction in being among a rare breed of men who possessed abundant amounts of both courage and resolve.

Once finished with his speech, Qassam returned his attention to Ezekiel. "Colonel, I have explained to them what has occurred over the past few minutes and that punishment must be meted out for such disrespect, as well as why."

The Hezbollah leader raised the Beretta again, carefully aiming it between Ezekiel's eyes. "I could press this trigger right now and end your life in the next second, and not one of my men would think twice of it. They understand the concept of respect that is demanded from all non-believers as much I.

"Or…" and Qassam shifted his aim over to Max. "I could just as easily shoot your dear friend here. Personal anguish and a survivor's guilt for being the cause of his death would be a very hard thing to live with, don't you think?

"Or…" Qassam shifted the muzzle of the Beretta a third time, putting the tiny pistol's sight picture on the left eye of Micah Templar. "I might decide to kill your nephew. After all, what could be worse than the loss of a dear friend, other than the needless death of your closest living relative?

"But perhaps it is the other way around." The terrorist glanced back at Ezekiel and smiled in a manner of pure self-dramatizing enjoyment. "Who knows, maybe I should force you to make the choice. That would be an interesting play on one's sense of morality, would it not? No matter what the outcome, such a decision would haunt someone for the rest of their lives and beyond."

Qassam gave every appearance of idly considering the thought before adding, "However, you can rest easy concerning all three of these possibilities. A few minutes ago you made mention of how Allah favors the merciful, and how he values compassion and kindness among his followers. Allah is merciful indeed and I am prepared to do you a kindness, whether you deserve it or not."

Without warning the Beretta changed direction again, pointing back and down near where Ezekiel Templar was seated. The single shot sounded like an exploding cherry bomb inside the room, and Ezekiel choked back a scream as the .25 caliber bullet burrowed into his upper left leg. His entire body went rigid with pain following the initial shock from the impact. A seething sensation of physical torment swept through him like a fast-moving prairie fire, blossoming into a wrenching grimace on his face.

Seemingly with a mind of their own, Ezekiel's wrists struggled spasmodically against the plastic zip ties, bruising and cutting the skin in the process. Gasping for breath and fighting to regain control of his agonized body, the man moaned and grunted with animal-like effort to release what was consuming him inside. Blood oozed freely through the fabric of his trousers, and in turn smeared itself upon the sofa cushions while his body writhed about.

As Ezekiel continued to battle against the fiery throes engulfing him, Qassam leaned down and whispered conspiratorially, "You can go ahead and scream, Colonel. I hear that it is good for the soul."

The Hezbollah commander straightened back up and turned to address his men. His tone was matter-of-fact as he explained more about his reasons for the 'merciful' solution chosen. All nodded in agreement, some even smiled while one or two chuckled in regards to what had occurred. Once Qassam was finished they returned to their assigned tasks, save for Mustafa and the rifle-toting terrorist assigned as guard.

While simultaneously struggling against a rising inner fury, Micah had been observing Tio Zeke all the while. A gray pall covered the features of Ezekiel's face, underscored by tiny droplets of sweat. His breathing had eased somewhat and was more regular now, as the old man mentally willed himself into doing so. Most concerning was the continued free flow of blood down his uncle's leg that was spreading to the floor. It needed tending to, and soon.

When Qassam turned from his men and faced the captives again, he found himself subject to a biting, unyielding glare from the bristling highway patrolman.

"Qassam, my uncle needs medical attention" Micah said through set teeth. "Take these handcuffs off so that I can do something for him. You won't gain anything by letting him bleed to death."

The terrorist leader studied Micah carefully for several moments before replying, "I think not, Officer Templar. I see a certain wildness in your eyes that I do not like, and I do believe if I were to remove your shackles you might try something other than to help your uncle. Then Mustafa would be forced to kill you and I would still be missing one hostage."

Qassam spoke a few words to Mustafa in Arabic and the second-in-command stepped forward, jerking Max Grephardt to his feet. He spun the elderly German around and removed the zip ties that secured Max's wrists.

"I think it would be best for all involved if Herr Grephardt saw to Colonel Templar" advised the Hezbollah leader.

Max rubbed and flexed his hands and wrists, trying to work some life back into them. He knelt beside Ezekiel and gave the bullet wound a cursory examination. "I will need a medical kit, a good one, to do something about this," observed the German.

Again, Qassam spoke to Mustafa who walked over and grabbed a large orange bag stacked in a pile of other equipment. From several feet away, the terrorist halted and effortlessly tossed the heavy carryall toward the prisoners. The intended trajectory was deliberately aimed at Ezekiel's injured leg but Max saw it coming and reached out, deflecting the bag away where it landed against the foot of the couch.

Micah's eyes narrowed as that barely contained inner fury nearly boiled over, and he shot an ice-cold stare at Mustafa. The second-in-command returned in kind, wickedly lifting a corner of his mouth into a half smile as he strode away from the three men. Micah continued to bore visual bullet holes into the terrorist's back all the while.

'There will come a reckoning, you pitiless bastard,' Micah thought. 'Good Lord willing, there will come a reckoning.'

Grephardt opened the bag quickly, searching about and finding a pair of scissors. Working in deft fashion, he cut the fabric of Ezekiel's trouser leg away and gingerly examined the wound more carefully. Ezekiel Templar winced and groaned, but made no other sound save for his heavy breathing.

The German looked up at his friend. "It is a clean wound, Ezekiel, both in and out. I would imagine," he paused and looked over to the terrorist leader, "it was meant to be that way. A flesh wound calculated to cause the maximum in discomfort and pain."

Qassam nodded slightly in affirmation, bowing a bit from the waist in mocking formality. Max returned his attention to the bullet wound. "Our main concerns are to stop this bleeding and keep the area from becoming infected."

"You will find everything needed in that medical bag, Herr Grephardt" interjected the Hezbollah leader.

"I will need water, distilled water if you have it" responded Max, still concentrating on the bleeding wound. Qassam spoke this time to the guard, who brought over two gallons in plastic jugs. With them Max cleaned the wound and unscrewed the cap on a bottle of antiseptic gel. "Get ready Ezekiel, this is going to burn."

Ezekiel Templar gritted his teeth and nodded to Max. He grunted as the antiseptic was worked into the entry site, followed by an adhesive pad of clotting agent. Max cautiously rolled Ezekiel's injured leg to one side and treated the exit point. Micah marveled at his uncle's ability to withstand the pain and keep from calling out.

Grephardt began wrapping Ezekiel's thigh with a wide roll of gauze to help stabilize the area. Finding antibiotics inside the bag he gave some to his friend along with a couple of pain killers, which were washed down with a long drink from one of the plastic containers. Yahla al-Qassam looked on impassively. Once finished, Max placed the remaining contents back in the bag and shoved it across the floor in Qassam's direction.

"Excellent work, Herr Grephardt" mused the Hezbollah leader, "one might even think you had some latent talent in that area. But then again, it is said you were thinking about becoming a doctor before the war."

"That is true" agreed Max. "But that was all a long time ago and the plans for one's life often have to become something else." Changing the subject, the German added, "He will need more water to replenish the blood loss."

"It will be done" replied Qassam. "The guard will be instructed to provide him with water at regular intervals. And yes, I understand about one's future plans when young. I was going to be an architect but Allah had different plans for me. Such are the sacrifices we make for those things we hold dear."

The terrorist returned his attention to Ezekiel, studying him intently. Making certain that he had the older man's eye, he commented further. "Let me know if there is anything else that I can do for the colonel. His continued good health is of real importance to me. You see, his value as a hostage could mean a great deal to the welfare of all."

Still looking at the injured Texan, Qassam concluded with an ominous addendum. "But most importantly, I want him to live long enough to see what he helped bring upon his own people. That is what I wish for him more than anything else."

Qassam spoke to the guard again in Arabic, who slung his AK and produced more zip ties. Resignedly, Max turned around and crossed his wrists behind him.

As the guard secured his hands, Max contemplated Qassam keenly.

"You have something that you want to say, 'doctor'?" asked the terrorist leader, adding a slightly demeaning lilt to the last word.

Max ignored the intended insult as he kept looking into the other man's eyes. "No, not as in making a declaration or a judgement, Yahla al-Qassam. But perhaps as an observation." He paused and added mildly, "As well as a warning."

"I am somewhat surprised at you, Herr Grephardt. I had the police officer pegged as the threatening sort, not you."

"No, it is not a threat" countered Max. "Only a warning, an experienced perception from one human being shared with another for reflection."

"You arouse my sense of curiosity, 'doctor'" said Qassam, verbalizing that same lilt again. "Tell me, what would you warn me of?"

"I would warn you of your hate, Yahla al-Qassam" answered Max, "and what it will ultimately do to you. Many years ago I saw such hate. I was then only a young man, not near wise enough to realize the ruin ahead until it was far too late. You mentioned something about the things we hold dear. I saw most everything I held dear at that time destroyed because of such hate. It nearly destroyed me, also.

"No matter what you might believe you can gain through it, you will ultimately lose much more. Hate leads down a path of self-destruction and makes it far easier to ruin than it does to build. No two words stand in any starker contrast to each other than those, they lie at opposing ends in any language.

"Hate and its dependents will never build anything of lasting worth. All that hate will do is consume from the inside out, leaving nothing but burnt ashes where a man's soul once resided. For your sake as well as others, I hope you can somehow change your present course before it is too late."

Qassam sneered openly at the German. "That is quite an unusual speech from someone who once wore the Knight's Cross with Oak Leaves so proudly, Herr Grephardt. Your words sound much more like those uttered by some pious old Christian holy man, rather than an eagle in winter who once excelled in the slaughter of his enemies."

"My father was one of those Christian holy men," replied Max in a steady, nonconfrontational tone. "A Lutheran minister who tried in vain to make a headstrong son understand what I am now attempting to tell you. He was a better man than I, and far wiser. Remember my warning, Yahla al-Qassam, please think upon it with scrutiny and reason."

Pointedly ignoring Max's last remarks the terrorist leader said something to the guard, who began herding the three prisoners back into the adjoining smaller room. Ezekiel Templar stood on his own and hobbled slowly in that direction, grimacing with each painful step. Walking awkwardly, he limped over to a wall and managed to sit down in a semi-reclined manner.

Max Grephardt watched the retired Air Force colonel as he did so, alert to any further signs of bleeding or other complications. Once satisfied and knowing he could do nothing more to help Ezekiel at this time, Max sat near him and began losing himself in thoughts of both past and present.

The old German mused to himself how strange the workings of the human mind could be. The memories now spreading forth had not been considered in some time, nor the life lessons learned. There were things in a man's life which were just too hurtful to be explored too often, one tried to make some good of them in what was termed as experience and went on.

Yet briefly speaking of that past brought so much of it into the present, especially when one had time to examine such sad souvenirs in minute detail. More so, there was much to consider than just the memories themselves.There were the past evils so firmly enjoined to them, the evils that he had both looked upon and been a part of during his younger years.

And then there was the present evil he had just shared a conversation with, an evil that would never rest and could never be anything else.

CHAPTER SEVEN

Micah Templar sat on the cold concrete floor, doing his own thinking to size up the situation as best he could. He had seen more than his fair share of violence, and how some seemed to thirst for any opportunity to work the worst depravities imaginable on their fellow man. Between two years as a grunt in Vietnam and some twenty years in the highway patrol, he had seen all manner of human wickedness and what it was capable of. But in all those years, he had never seen someone with such an impossibly cruel and calculating intellect as Yahla al-Qassam.

The former Marine was not familiar with this nerve agent that Qassam possessed, and only had a general idea of how it would be distributed from *The Uvalde Raider*. He did know his uncle well enough to tell when he was concerned, and Tio Zeke became gravely so as the terrorist leader explained his plan. Moreover, Qassam had left Micah Templar with no doubts as to his intent to commit mass murder on a scale that boggled the mind. Nor could Micah entertain any doubts as to whether Qassam possessed the needed capabilities in carrying out such a monstrous act.

The trooper studied their guard, who again stood in the half-open doorway. It was the same terrorist as before, but the AK toting Arab was now at a heightened sense of alertness. Every time any of the three prisoners made an audible sound, the guard provided his full and suspicious attention.

Micah came to the grim realization that even Qassam's own men were somewhat afraid of him, with the possible exception of that two-legged rattlesnake called Mustafa. What had happened in the adjoining room was an abject lesson to those men as much as it was to anyone else. Their fear would keep them on their toes for as long as Qassam was anywhere around.

Up to this point, the highway patrolman had moved cautiously enough as to not disturb the tension on the handcuffs clamped to his wrists. If they weren't actually double locked, they still had not tightened up any further. In the semi-darkness he began slowly rotating and exercising his hands at intervals to keep the circulation and feeling in them. Micah was still looking for the opportunity to use his hidden key and he would need his hands as flexible and ready as possible for that, as well as whatever was to come afterward.

"Nephew?" murmured Ezekiel through thick, dry lips. The guard snapped his head around to determine the source. Micah moved as quickly as he could to his uncle's side, studiously examining Tio Zeke's wound as if he had been called for that purpose. At the same time, Max Grephardt pressed in from the other side. The guard relaxed and turned back around.

"Same guard?" the fevered man croaked out.

"Same one, but more alert and suspicious" replied Micah in a low voice while Max Grephardt nodded in agreement. "Qassam has them wired pretty tight," the younger Templar added.

"Yeah" replied Ezekiel slowly, "I think I can understand why." He managed to grin slightly.

"I'm pretty sure we can talk, as long as the guard thinks it has to do with this hole in your leg" remarked Micah quietly. "You sure pushed his button the hard way, Tio."

"Yeah, tell me about it." Ezekiel muttered in half humor. Then his voice turned grave, insistent. "We have to stop him. Somehow, some way, he has to be stopped, or a lot of innocent people are going to die a horrible death."

"We will, Tio" Micah cast a quick glance at the guard who had turned again and was looking square at them. The trooper made busy as if he was taking a closer look at the bandaging and continued to speak in low tone. "I can get loose, but I need a few minutes unobserved to get it done. Our friend at the doorway don't want to play ball right now."

Both of the older men shot quizzical looks at the younger one. Micah did not say anything else, he only nodded in affirmation to confirm his words.

"Can we help?" asked Max.

Micah shook his head slightly from side to side. "Not now, but be ready if that guard happens to wander off."

Ezekiel Templar spoke again, a driving earnestness in his hoarse voice. "Whatever it takes, Micah. Qassam is a monster, and a very intelligent and fervent one. He's dangerous and his zealotry makes him that much more so."

Micah nodded his understanding. "Tio, will his plan work?"

Ezekiel Templar looked up at his nephew. "It can and it will, unless we do something about it." The older man stared intently into his eyes, and Micah understood without another word how much depended on that small handcuff key secreted in his trousers.

"Okay" Micah replied. "Try to get some rest, it's the best thing you can do for right now."

"The pain killers should let you sleep awhile" murmured Max. "Let them work, Ezekiel."

It was Ezekiel Templar's turn to nod his head in affirmation. He fixed his gaze on the two other men, each in turn. His facial expression still bore the evidence of pain but it was also furrowed with the lines of an intense determination. "We have to stop him. We have to stop him cold."

The older Templar leaned back against the wall, searching for a position in which he could rest a bit. Max Grephardt and Micah Templar looked at each other for a moment, and then wiggled away from Ezekiel to find their own spots. When they began to move, Micah noted they had the guard's full attention and it held to the point their movement ceased.

'*Not now, not yet,*' Micah thought to himself. '*But soon. We need to make our move soon.*'

CHAPTER EIGHT

A few minutes had passed, and Ezekiel Templar's breathing smoothed out and grew deeper. As Max Grephardt had predicted the pain pills were taking effect, giving his friend respite from the quarter inch hole in his left thigh. The former Luftwaffe *hauptmann* sat in the half-lit gloom, wiggling about while trying to find something remotely akin to a comfortable position. When he did so, their unwanted chaperone gave the German his full attention. Max ignored the extra scrutiny and instead fixated on the opposite wall.

Micah was correct, the guard was far too alert at present for them to try much of anything. In the meantime, their cause was best served in resting as they could and being ready to move fast when the opportunity arose. Max was not sure of what Micah had in mind, but the younger man seemed confident that he could free himself if allowed just a few minutes of not being observed. When that time came, everything that followed would be happening at tremendous speed and coming from unexpected directions. Of that much Max was sure of. The three of them would have to make the most of their attempt as it happened, there would be no second chance.

As the minutes crept by, his mind went through a hundred different scenarios and ways he might respond to each one. After a while it became a mental jumble of 'ifs' 'buts' and 'maybes,' until Max shut it all down and distracted his mind on to other things. It was something he had learned to do long ago, and it called for a good deal of inner self-discipline and experience.

His father had often said that life was a matter of courage and faith: one used his personal courage to carry him as far as it could and then relied upon a trusted faith in God to do the rest. As he had grown older and seen the ironies of life mostly for what they were, Max Grephardt had found that advice a source of both strength as well as solace when facing the difficult times of his past.

And that was where his mind was now returning yet again, to his past. To another time and place, and of a world long gone and of people long dead. When Yahla al-Qassam had spoken derisively of a "pious old Christian holy man," Max had thought of his *vadi*, his father.

But the kind of man the Hezbollah leader had dismissed with nary a second thought had been just the kind of man one needed to remember. A gentle and loving husband and father, who viewed the world and those in it through wizened and knowing eyes. He had been a man whom Max had never learned to fully appreciate until it was too late. Max Grephardt knew that he was far from being alone when it came to fully understanding such men in their own time, but that knowledge did not take away any of the regret for not doing so.

Vadi had been the minister of a small rural Lutheran church near the medieval town of Meiningen, located in the central part of Germany along the Werra River. Meiningen was then considered the cultural, judicial and financial center of southern Thuringia, and the surrounding area was steeped in the traditions and philosophy of what was to become known as the German Enlightenment.

Famous personages such as Goethe and Schiller had walked along its picturesque streets only a century before, conversing with each other on subjects pertaining to history, poetry and philosophy. Together in Meiningen they would work on their collection of short satirical epigrams known as *Xenien,* an artistic form of thought attributed to the Roman poet Martial.

Not too far away, in the neighboring city of Weimar, Germany's first democratic constitution had been signed following what was then known to mankind as 'The Great War.' Few would have guessed during that historic event they would be fully engulfed in a second world war following so closely behind the first.

It was into this environment, at about the time that short-lived document was being finalized, that Maximillian Friedrich Grephardt was born. He was the middle son of five in the family, a situation making for ready playmates on hand to share his free time with. Together the five brothers would explore in and around the countryside, and all up and down the verdant banks of the nearby Werra.

But in their young minds the boys were high in the Himalayas or the Alps, or along the banks of the Congo or the Amazon. Each son in his own way yearned for adventure and Max possibly thirsted for it most of all. He would sometimes make up wild stories to fill the large gap between that constant thirst and the reality of their quiet existence, until Vadi would raise an eyebrow and wag his index finger. That would be all that it would take to gently remind young Max of the difference between fanciful dreams and factual circumstance.

His Mamma would come through the busy kitchen at such times, shaking her head and asking her husband where the middle son of a Lutheran minister could possibly come up with such thoughts.

Vadi would chuckle and reply, "Because he is a boy, Mamma! All boys think such thoughts, and certain boys like him just happen to give voice to what is imagined in their minds."

His father would reach across and pat his middle son's head affectionately, a joyful twinkle in his eye. "God has special plans for Max, but Max must first grow into a man to fulfill those plans. For now he is still a boy and boys need to fill their lives with adventure, imagined or otherwise.

"The time will come when he will be able to put such imagination into harness. All great men had great imagination, with which they were able to turn their dreams into reality." He would then look at Max and smile, putting his own imagination to work in regards to the future of his precocious son.

That future involved the dream of Max becoming a doctor, a man who would save lives and make the world a better place for all to be. Max did not know then, but Vadi had been an Imperial German Army *feld sanitater*, or medic, during the Great War. It had never been something he talked about much to anyone save his wife, who had seen first-hand how it had changed her husband over those despoiled years.

Max's two older brothers claimed to have seen a whole row of medals in a weather-stained trunk they were rummaging through one time, right before Mamma caught them and shooshed them away. They had stood their ground just long enough to find out the medals were Vadi's, before Mamma backed up her shooshing with a kitchen broom.

And so the years went by and Max and his brothers grew. As they changed into young men, the outside world around them changed also. The short-lived Weimar Republic, headed by the aged statesman and military hero President von Hindenberg, had come to an ignominious end. The ancient field marshal, failing in physical health and slipping into senility had appointed Adolph Hitler, leader of the German Nationalist Socialist Party, as chancellor of Germany. After a long, bitter political struggle that often devolved into mob violence as well as outright murder, the Nazis had at long last taken control of the *Vaterland*.

It was the first time he had seen Vadi become angry. Even isolated as they were, the jovial Lutheran minister followed world events as closely as possible and was a voracious reader. Max's father was respected in the surrounding area as an informed and passionate debater of history and religion, and oftentimes visitors would stop by just to have a conversation with him.

Upon first learning of the Nazi consolidation of power, the erstwhile composed minister had pounded his fist in exasperation upon the dinner table. As his startled family and visitors involuntarily jumped from the uncharacteristic outburst, he covered his face with both hands and shook his head from side to side. Massaging his forehead with the fingers of his right hand, he leaned back and said, "The Nazis and the Communists, two sides of the same sinful coin. God help us all, for they do not know what they have done."

In the stunned silence that followed Max's youngest brother, Paul, asked innocently, "Who, Vadi? Who does not know what they have done?"

His father slowly took his right hand from his face and looked at his youngest. The ignited flash that had burst from his outraged features had been replaced with an immensely sad look, a look that made him seem both worried and vulnerable. It was another emotion Max had never seen before in his father, and he did not know which of the two distressed him more.

Vadi sighed and replied, "My son, they are the people of Germany who do not know what they have set loose. They have sown the wind and we shall all pay in the reaping of it."

Looking around the table and cognizant of the air of uneasiness among those seated, he added, "Please forgive me of my anger, the last thing we need at this time is more anger. But what we do need is prayer, earnest prayer for Germany, for her people and for our families. As I have already said, only God can help us now."

From that day forward, most everything in their lives seemed to take on a different track. At first it appeared as if it was for the better, and many had questioned Vadi's dark vision for their collective future. That questioning ultimately included even members of his own household, and Max himself.

Hitler talked of a great aspiration, of an immensely strong new Germany and of a Third Reich that would last for a thousand years. He gave the German people a new self-respect for themselves and their nation, and banished much of the disgrace associated with the ruinous loss of the recent war. Men went back to work and vast new projects were undertaken to showcase Teutonic skill, knowledge and engineering expertise. Among those was a concentrated effort to expand the military, and the building of a powerful new German air force called the Luftwaffe.

Vadi still entertained a different dream for Max, and a different future for him in being a physician. But of all of Max's youthful desires, the most persistent and lasting was the one to fly. This led to several discussions that became heated on occasion, an unfortunate circumstance usually brought on by Max. He would become so exasperated with his father, as he could not make the elder Grephardt understand what the idea of flying meant to him. Yes, being a doctor was a noble and respected profession, and Max understood the vital need for good ones. It was just that being a doctor and saving lives did not hold any personal calling to him.

In the end and ironically enough, Max Grephardt would instead spend much of his younger years in the taking of lives during the war to come. Tragically for the five brothers, he was not the only son who heard the beguiling call of the sirens that sang the songs of military glory.

Heinrich, the oldest, was the first to don a uniform. He joined the *Kriegsmarine*, the resurgent German Navy and served aboard one of her dreaded *Unterseeboots*, or U-Boats. One dark night his submarine slipped out

THE UVALDE RAIDER | 53

from its base in Lorient, never to return. Somewhere in the vastness of the North Atlantic, it found an unmarked watery grave for all hands aboard.

The second one out the door was Rudolph. He had enlisted in the Panzers and became a tank commander on the Eastern Front. He and his crew were lost during the Battle of Kursk, when his Panzer Mark IV Ausf.G was turned into a fiery, exploding volcano due to a direct hit from a Soviet T-34. Rudolph and his fellows never even caught a glimpse of the enemy iron monster that killed them all.

After Max had joined the Luftwaffe, younger brother Willy signed up for the *Wehrmacht Heer* as a common infantryman. By that time the Grephardt family already had three sons committed to the Vaterland and knew all too well they were in a war in which the tides were turning. But Willy was still eager to go and do his part and dutifully marched on until January of 1944, when he was killed in action outside of Monte Cassino on the Italian front.

Paul was the youngest and the only one to not put on the uniform. A very bright, introspective young man of faith, he had decided to follow Vadi into the clergy, a decision that brought a collected sense of relief to what was left of the Grephardt family.

He had gone to study in Frankfurt, not too far away from Meiningen. In the black days of early 1944, he would become yet another civilian casualty to the Allied bombing campaigns. Paul was killed in the same raid that destroyed the historic Paulskirche, along with most of the renowned center area of the city that dated back to the Middle Ages.

When he received the word, Max had pondered upon the coincidence of his youngest brother losing his life within sight of the church named after the same apostle as he. The timing of this news had been devastating for both of his parents, as they would receive the official notice concerning Willy just days afterwards.

Yet for Max, he was living his dream and was quite good at what he had always been so keen to try. The tragedies of his own family, along with his personal exploits, found him recognized nationally as one of the true heroes of the Fatherland, and he wore the Knight's Cross medal proudly around his neck. Luftwaffe *Hauptmann* Grephardt seemed to lead a charmed life in the midst of a tidal wave of carnage and death that engulfed all around him. The fact that he was now the only surviving brother of five only heightened that assumptive perception.

The Nazi Party propaganda machine, desperate for such inspiring stories in the midst of so much bad news from so many fronts, ran full length feature articles on him. German magazines and newspapers carried his carefully crafted image, a jaunty young fighter ace with handsome features complete with the required perfectly blonde hair and piercing blue eyes. They had even brought him back from his badly needed presence on the Eastern Front, to portray himself on film while spending time in Berlin rubbing elbows with the powerful and privileged.

That trip to Berlin and being placed so close to the upper echelons of the Nazi Party was when he first discovered that all was not as it had first seemed. His boyish enthusiasms and patriotic dreams in this Third Reich were shocked to their very core, confronted with the reality of what he and so many others had been fighting for. So much blood spilt, so many lives lost and for what? For these pompous, self-serving *zecken* to strut about at the beck and call of their delusional leader?

Of course, he had already realized the war was an issue in serious doubt. Max had experienced firsthand the merciless hordes of the Red Army in the east, as well as the industrial might and resolve of the Allied forces to the west. But up to this point the reasons and goals for the struggle had been clear enough for him to follow without question.

But now, much like the war itself, the doubts and the needlessness of it all began to haunt him. In Berlin, his perspective began to change and the wisdom of his Vadi from years ago began to reveal itself in full. It was then that he first began to suspicion that Germany's true enemies were emplaced within as much as without.

He found himself wanting so badly to return to that little Lutheran Church along the banks of the Werra, and to speak with the minister who was so faithful to it and to all that it stood for. This time not as a young boy or a rebellious teenager, but as one man in search of truth from another. A man finding himself confronted with many more questions of essentiality than possible answers for them, and seeking wisdom from what he now saw as the wisest man he had ever known.

Instead he was hustled back to the front and to the cockpit of his waiting Messerschmitt, to do battle once more against the massed waves of Yaks, Migs, and Lavochkins, as well as the British made Hurricanes and American built Airacobras, Warhawks and Kingcobras. The Red Army was on the move, which meant the Red Air Force was fully deployed in providing the requisite close aerial cover. It was the largest and most brutally effective war machine the world had known up to that time, and it was methodically grinding its German adversaries into the icy, snow covered ground of Northern Europe.

The Luftwaffe mail routes were often sporadic and unreliable, but still occasionally he would receive a letter from his father. In them he noted an increasingly open disgust for the Nazi Party and its leadership, and the disastrous path they were leading Germany down. Max wrote back as much as he could yet wondered how many of his letters actually made it home.

He was very careful about what he said and how he said it. There was a joke going around that one would never find a Gestapo man anywhere near the front, as they were too busy sitting around post offices and reading other people's mail. Such was the dark humor that permeated among the men who were actually fighting, and dying, in this increasingly hopeless war. Max hoped that his father would hear that joke and take heed of the intent.

It was on his ninth mission after his return from Berlin, and what he had seen and experienced there was still fresh on his mind. Max never even saw the Yak-9U that slipped in from behind, directly astern and slightly lower in the classic fighter-on-fighter line of attack. His first hint of any real trouble was when the powerful 20 mm rapid fire cannon of the white camouflaged Yak ripped the guts out of his tried-and-true Me109, and turned it into a smoking piece of airborne junk that was rapidly falling out of the winter Lithuanian sky.

That smoke had quickly turned into an oil fire that filled the cockpit of the little fighter, and *Hauptmann* Grephardt still carried the burn scars to prove it. Max managed to hastily get the canopy back and the mortally-wounded Messerschmitt inverted, upon which he bailed out into the shockingly frigid slipstream.

With his heavy flying clothes still on fire he was able to deploy his chute, which led to another immediate problem: the victorious Soviet pilot had not only wanted the gray camouflaged 109, but he also wanted one *Hauptmann* Maximilian Friedrich Grephardt, holder of the Knight's Cross of the Iron Cross with Oak Leaves. Max had spent the rest of his slow ride down to the frozen ground side-slipping his parachute to spoil the Russian's aim, while still trying to put out the fires on his winterized uniform.

While ultimately successful on both counts, his rather precarious situation was compounded by the fact that he just happened to bail out over recently acquired Soviet territory. He also found himself unarmed, as he and his issued Walther PPK had evidently gone their separate ways sometime during the hasty exit from the Messerschmitt.

For two whole days Max led elements of Stalin's military machine on a not-so-merry chase, until he found himself between the proverbial rock and a hard place. On the third morning *Hauptmann* Grephardt awoke with the ominous muzzle of a Mosin-Nagant 91/30 mere inches from his face and his back against cold, unyielding stone.

Weak from exhaustion and pockmarked with burns as well as shivering from exposure, he must have not looked important enough to waste a rifle bullet on. Instead, the Red Army soldiers in attendance decided to pick up where the smoke inhalation, the flames, the brutal cold, and the lack of food and sleep had left off. Rather than just up and killing him, they had beaten the hapless *hauptmann* to the point where he was rapidly becoming more dead than alive. His only saving favor was the timely arrival of a Soviet propaganda officer, who recognized the Luftwaffe pilot for what he was and decided he just might know something of tactical or even strategic importance.

So Max was packed into a lend-lease American six-by truck, along with some other German prisoners who looked as if they had been given the same Communist warm welcome as he. But the young Luftwaffe officer had other ideas and a second dose of Russian hospitality was not among them.

Picking his moment, he literally rocketed out of the bed of the truck as it sped along, right under the noses of the guards who had let their own lack of sleep and attending complacency get the better of them. He had hit, skidded and then bounced down the side of a steep incline and into the thick forest below, closely pursued by shouts, cursing and a substantial amount of small arms fire attempting to seek him out.

Max had jounced hard through the brush line and came up sprinting, encouraged by the cracks and pops of bullets striking all about. He ran as far and as fast as he could until he could run no further. Then the beleaguered young man simply dropped in his tracks and laid there, unable to go another step.

It was the lowest point he could ever imagine in his entire life. He was shaking involuntarily from the cold, physically exhausted and spiritually spent, and surrounded by his enemies. His bid for freedom and the attending short euphoria of success had been quickly replaced with a realistic appraisal of his current situation, and an overwhelming dread of what might come next.

Huddled miserably in a snow drift, Max knew he was close to the end of the line. His was a situation beyond hope and beyond any definition of futile, and he found himself drowning in an all-encompassing sea of absolute despair. When Max Grephardt told this story to others many years later, he confided that it was the one time in his life when he actually considered suicide. He found himself wishing for that small Walther PPK that was lost when he bailed out, so that he might bring a swift end to his overpowering suffering and pain.

Yet deep inside himself, something still stirred. Call it a need or a fixation or perhaps unfinished business in trying to make some things right, but Max knew he couldn't let it all end here. He had to make it back to the banks of the Werra, to let a man better than himself know that he had been right all along. Vadi deserved that much and he deserved to hear it from his one surviving son. It wasn't all that Max needed to do, not by a long shot. But it would be a start.

Max tried to get up again, yet didn't have enough physical strength left to do even that. It was only then, in recognizing he had run out of the personal courage his father had so often used as an illustration, that he reached out in a way that was also a first in his young, eventful life. The once fearless and so prideful hero of the Fatherland cried out piteously in silent voice for help from a merciful God above.

With tears coursing down near frozen cheeks, he laid himself bare and begged forgiveness for all the years wasted upon things other than what had been truly important all along. He prayed for the strength that went beyond any of that found in the physical or mental, the kind that can only come through the blood of a crucified Savior who died for all of mankind's sins. He appealed to a far mightier power than what was merely numbered by men, guns and fighter planes.

And in that instant, Max Grephardt was saved by Grace and was never the same man again. The old Max died there in that cheerless snow drift on a freezing January morning and a new Max Grephardt got up and walked away, not once looking behind.

CHAPTER NINE

For the next few days Max moved west through the Soviet lines, taking sustenance and shelter where he could find it. Filled with his new faith and its attending resolve, he somehow managed to make his way undetected by those who wanted him so badly. In the continuing violence and confusion of small unit attacks and counterattacks, he was finally found by a German reconnaissance patrol and hustled to a field hospital. From there he was moved twice more due to the rapid advancement of the Soviet Army. Finally, he was taken back to Germany itself and placed in a hospital ward for his burns and other physical infirmities.

Lying there in bed with the sounds of a war growing closer every day, Max rested to regain his strength. He was able to obtain a Bible, devouring the words contained within in the manner of a starving man with a virtual feast set before him. If he noticed the questioning looks or occasional hard stare as he studied the passages, he paid the rejective onlookers little attention. Max Grephardt was trying to make for lost time, and read with a rapturous inner joy what before had never really made much sense to him.

As soon as he was able to, he left the hospital without any real official orders and started making his way home. In the middle of all the turmoil and endless flow of casualties, he was most likely not even going to be missed for some time. His bed would be filled quickly enough and by someone who was in far greater need than he. There was so much he wanted to talk to his father about, so many things he wanted to say and so many questions that needed asking. The little church along the Werra beckoned to him with the promise of a new beginning.

Germany was now a country completely wrecked. Soldiers and civilians alike wandered around aimlessly with no clear direction or thought in purpose. Communications and modern transportation were mostly nonexistent, there was no fuel or power. Rumors ran rampant and wild talk was everywhere, which further added to the growing chaos that gripped the nation by its collective throat. A mass migration, usually by foot or by cart was streaming west away from the advancing Red Army. If the German war machine continued to fight with any real goal at all, it was to keep the hated Bolsheviks at bay long enough for the Western Allies to occupy their homeland.

Along the way Max saw entire cities and populations that had been completely obliterated. It was said that Dresden itself was nothing more now than a burned-out corpse of ashes, while large population centers such as Hamburg, Mainz and Bochum had basically ceased to exist. Devastation raised its ugly head most every mile along his route, and made its presence felt in ways only known to those who have actually experienced the barbaric reality of total war. The Third Reich, once proclaimed as being destined to last a thousand years, was nothing more than a smoldering funeral pyre.

Undeterred, Max pushed on toward the Werra. He was still weak from his prior ordeals and as malnourished as most of the rest of the German population. The hills and valleys were bleak with the aching iciness of a begrudgingly resistant winter, judged to be one of worst in recent European history. Max's well-worn wool uniform did little to protect him from the biting cold, and his slowly healing burns were chaffed and irritated by the material. He walked when he had to and grabbed a lift with passing military vehicles when given the opportunity.

No one asked him about his papers or where he was going. It was obvious that the sickly, scar tissue splotched Luftwaffe *hauptmann* was in no condition to climb back into the cockpit of a fighter plane or do much of anything else. Some of them might have recognized him as the dashing young ace who had so recently been the darling of the German mass media, but no one said anything. Those days were dead and gone, and they had their own problems to deal with in their own hunger, inner doubts and ever-present miseries.

Finally, one crisp morning early in April he arrived at his destination. Max walked up the country lane, savoring the first tiny hints of spring and the culmination of a long, arduous journey. He was so close; each step was lighter now and he felt a resurgent strength sweeping through his being as the anticipation inside arose.

But what he saw after walking around that last bend was not what he had traveled so far for. The little white church was only a wasted skeleton of itself, charred and abandoned. The adjoining home where he grew up, the hearth for so many happy memories was empty and barren, its contents mostly either vanished or vandalized. Nothing stirred, no hearty cry of welcome was given from within. The site was like an open grave, silent and foreboding.

Beleaguered and beyond heartsick, Max sat on the steps that led up to the blackened structure, mind racing with what might have happened and what his plan of action was from here. He was still sitting there when an old man happened by, trudging along the lane pulling a hand cart. At first, he had not recognized Max and had only given a nervous, furtive glance as he started to scurry on by. But something caused him to take yet another look and through the dried mud, the pinkish burn scars and hollowed eyes he recognized who was in that blueish gray uniform.

"Max! Max Grephardt! Can that really be you?" the old man had blurted out, walking hesitantly toward the sitting figure.

The Luftwaffe *hauptmann* looked up, somewhat startled at the sound of his name carried by a familiar voice.

"It is you!" the aged neighbor exclaimed in recognition. "Welcome home my son, welcome home! We had all thought you lost in the war, there has been so much bad news lately."

The old man, one of those who had sat at their dinner table on so many occasions during Max's childhood, reached out and grabbed the German officer in a heartfelt hug. Grinning widely and giddy with unexpected happiness, he held the younger man in a vise-like embrace that belied his many years and slightly stooped stature.

"Herr Bekker, it has been a long time" Max managed to say in return. "Tell me, what has happened here? Where are my parents?"

Bekker ignored the questions and reached for Max's small, worn traveling bag. "Here, you must come home with me. So many times I shared a meal with your father and your family at their dinner table. Now is the time for me to repay that kindness."

"But my parents…" Max insisted.

The elderly German glanced pensively to each side, as if even the charred walls and scattered debris had ears with which to listen.

"I will explain it all to you Max," Bekker responded. "But not here, not now. These are dangerous times we live in, even at home. Come, do not tell me that you are not tired and hungry."

Max began to protest again, but the old man waved him off. Yet it was not the wave of the hand that had stymied any further questions, but the look of fear in the man's eyes. With each holding a handle on the decrepit cart, they started in the direction of Herr Bekker's home together.

Later that evening, in front of a warm fire that removed a lingering chill from his bones, Max sat with his benefactor staring into the flames. Frau Bekker worked busily clearing the dishes from the table, the end result of a meal like Max had not had in some time. Contemplating their own thoughts, neither man had said a word since the finishing of the dinner. It was Herr Bekker who finally broke the silence.

"It happened several weeks ago" he began, the words slowly working their way up through obvious hesitation and angst. "Your parents had received a message that you had been shot down and no one could say what happened beyond that. For some time, your father had been speaking of the futility of the war, of the wickedness of those who were leading our nation into further ruin. After he heard about you, he became quite open in those criticisms, even while speaking from the pulpit.

"Strangers began coming around, well dressed strangers with an air of authority about them. They were asking questions about your parents, your family, and especially your father. They even attended some of your father's services.

"We all knew they were Gestapo. We begged your father to not be so open in his beliefs, to be quiet until at least these strangers left. But your father..." he looked up at Max, tears welling in his eyes. He snorted a bit, rubbed his nose and smiled thinly.

"Well Max, what can I tell you about your own father? You know him as well as anyone. When we went to him, he told us 'I have lost four sons to Germany, perhaps five. I have lost friends and sons of friends to this useless war. But I will not lose my own soul, also. I will speak out and I will stay true to the teachings of my faith.'

"They came in the dead of night and ransacked the church and your home. We were told they were gathering 'evidence' that your parents were Communist agitators, enemies of the Reich who were being taken in for interrogation. I guess it was decided to burn the church and your home for good measure."

The old man lowered his chin into his chest, ashamed and speaking now with no more than a whisper. "And not one of us lifted a voice or a finger to stop them. May God forgive us all."

Max studied his father's ancient friend, slumped down in his chair and with his head hanging as tears of frustration and regret freely flowed. Some might have felt anger or betrayal, but all Max could do was feel pity and grieve with him. If there was any anger, it was an anger against a corrupt and tyrannical regime that would fall upon its own citizens like so many wolves among sheep.

"Herr Bekker" he asked gently. "Do you happen to know where they were taken?"

"No one knows," the old man replied ruefully. "If they do, they are too frightened to say anything." He looked at Max earnestly, his eyes reflecting in the flames. "Max, your father was a brave and wise man, and he was a true man of God. He tried to warn us all those years ago and no one would listen. Perhaps we deserve this fate, but he did not."

Bekker stared back into the fire and murmured. "What have we become, when our own government ensnares its people like rabbits in a trap and we stand idly by and do nothing. In the name of God, what have we become?" The old man sobbed and buried his face in his hands. He was still sitting there, wrestling mightily in his mind with a world gone mad, when Max finally went to bed.

The next morning Max dressed himself and enjoyed another meal at the Bekker table. Frau Bekker had taken his dirty Luftwaffe uniform and cleaned and brushed it vigorously, to the point of almost being presentable. His worn black boots reflected a fresh polish, as did his leather belt and hat bill. As he started to leave, he and Herr Bekker stood talking near the doorway.

"Are you certain you cannot stay? Anyone can see you are still hurt and weak," observed the elderly neighbor.

"It would not go well for you if I was found here. I have no orders, and I am the son of a man who the Gestapo considers a traitor to their Reich."

"Then where will you go, Max?" questioned Bekker.

The *hauptmann* considered Herr Becker's concern for a moment. "West, I think. Towards Fulda. The war cannot last much longer and I will not be captured by the Bolsheviks again."

The old man nodded and asked anxiously. "Do you think they will actually get this far west before the Americans arrive?"

"Not if the Wehrmacht has anything to do about it. From what I can tell, they are throwing everything they have left to blunt the Soviet advance. But they cannot last for long without air cover and the Luftwaffe is done, finished. We have no planes, no parts, and no fuel."

Max looked off to the west. "If I can make it into the Fulda area, I can surrender to the first Americans I come across. It is said they and the British treat captured Luftwaffe officers more than fairly. When I can, I will get word back to you."

"So, it is almost finished again?" asked Herr Bekker.

"Yes," replied the young officer. "This part of our long nightmare is almost over and the Third Reich will be gone. I only hope that Germany will not be totally obliterated along with it."

"Good luck, Max, and may God bless you." The old man extended his hand in a firm grip. "Remember we always have room for you under our roof."

"Thank you, Herr Bekker. If my parents come back, please tell them that I am alive. Tell my father I shall return and help rebuild his church."

"I will Max, I certainly will. And we will all help him rebuild that church, if he can still consider us worthy of doing so."

"He will," assured the younger man. "I know this, Herr Becker, because I know my father. I just never realized how rare of a man he really was until now. Someday, I am going to be able to tell him so."

Max began walking down the road and away from the Bekker home. Just before he went out of sight, he turned and waved. The elderly couple waved back.

It would not be until many years later that Max would learn of his parents' fate. The answer was found within the walls of a grim appearing stone building in the Westend-Nord of Frankfurt, which housed some of the Gestapo's records that survived the war.

Neatly noted were his parents' full names, ages, occupations and home of record. The entries went on to say they had been arrested as suspected spies and enemies of the Reich. There was a final notation, inscribed in bold letters, stating they had been "shot while trying to escape."

When Max read those last few words, he at first did not know whether to cry or to laugh. In the end, he did both.

CHAPTER TEN

Two days later Max Grephardt was still making his way along the road to Fulda, along with many others. A rumor had started that the Soviets were initiating a major offensive into the central part of Germany and were already west of Dresden. Whether the rumor was true or not did not really matter, no German desired to be under Bolshevik occupation. The stories of wholesale rape, plunder and outright murder of civilians by the Soviets were all real enough, and only grew in number and savagery as these accounts were repeated. Those who could move did, fleeing as quickly as they could in the direction of Patton's rapidly advancing Third Army.

On that second day, Max had crossed a small vehicular bridge choked with an endless flow of refugees heading toward Fulda. Tired and foot sore from the journey, he found a rickety chair under the overhang of a boarded-up café to sit upon. Resting there for a minute, he surveyed the heart wrenching spectacle of scared, lost and broken people.

While doing so Max also noted a small contingent of German soldiers arriving on the scene, led by an *obersturmführer* of the *Schutzstaffel*, or SS. The *obersturmführer* was dressed in his dreaded black livery, replete with the polished skull and crossbones insignia centered squarely above the brim of his hat.

He was a sallow faced man with a vicious, weasel-like appearance and matching demeanor, and yelled continually in a loud, high pitched voice at both the soldiers as well as the refugees. To accentuate his present authority, he waved about with a Luger Parabellum pistol tightly clinched in his right hand.

The men under his command were dressed in the common gray uniform of the Wehrmacht Heer. But once Max looked past those uniforms, he saw that they were nothing much more than young boys and old men. They carried their weapons in an unfamiliar, haphazard fashion, and the fear and uncertainty in their eyes was just as evident as in those of the refugees around them.

However, there was one, an *unterfeldwebel* or senior sergeant, who caught Max's attention while standing in front of the others. He had a seasoned, competent look to him, and carried both himself and his bolt action Mauser in an experienced, confident manner. The Luftwaffe *hauptmann* sized up the *unterfeldwebel* almost immediately as a professional fighting man.

Unnoticed by the newly arrived group, Max turned his attention to his aching feet and the growing holes in the bottom of both of his boot soles. He had placed some sheets from a newspaper inside his boots earlier in an attempt to protect them, but they were already worn through again. He looked around, trying to find some sort of material more resilient than mere paper. *Tar shingles, perhaps?* he thought to himself, his eyes searching along the edges of the overhang.

Suddenly, pandemonium broke out on the western approach to the bridge as the soldiers shut down passage across it. Those already on the span were being physically forced back against the following stream of other refugees behind them. As the civilians closest to the soldiers attempted to do so, some were knocked down and frantically scrambled about to regain their feet. In the increasing confusion, one man was pushed completely off the structure and into the freezing water below. The action taken by the soldiers had been unexpected, and a sense of growing panic swept through the unwieldy mass of tired, anxious people.

The long stream of human destitution wavered, and then was pressed forward again by those still pushing in from the rear. The SS officer screamed out an order and leveled his Luger at the crowd. Reluctantly, those under his command raised their rifles, pointing in the general direction of the hapless civilians. The sergeant Max had noticed earlier cast a questioning side glance at the SS officer, and kept the barrel of his weapon pointed into the air.

A deep, frothing hole formed fast in Max's gut and he knew he had to do something quickly. Bringing himself back to his feet, he knocked the dust from his uniform and the once polished black leather boots. Reaching into his pocket, he carefully pulled out a handkerchief and removed his Knight's Cross from within its folds. Max draped the medal and attending ribbon around his neck, checked its position by feel and stepped smartly from under the café overhang.

Meanwhile, the situation on the bridge was deteriorating rapidly. The SS *obersturmführer* was not only losing control of what was happening around him, but of himself. He screeched out another order and the soldiers slowly, reluctantly worked the bolts on their Mauser 98Ks. With the unmistakable metallic sound of rounds being chambered, an eerie hush fell over most of the crowd. Somewhere in their midst was the rising wail of a hungry infant.

Max squared his shoulders and picked up the pace. Mustering all of the military bearing that he had ever possessed, he marched toward the armed knot of men standing at the opening to the bridge.

In a powerful voice that carried above everything else Max addressed the SS man. *"Obersturmführer,* what is the meaning of this?" His words were in the structure of a question, but spoken as an obvious order requiring an immediate response.

The authority in Max's tone startled the SS officer, who spun on his heels to face the rapidly approaching Luftwaffe *hauptmann*. Instinctively, the black clad *obersturmführer* snapped to attention and gave a well-rehearsed Nazi Party arm gesture. Max responded with the older hand salute of the pre-Nazi German military, while simultaneously speaking to the soldiers.

"You men, put down those rifles!" Max commanded them. Instantly the soldiers did so, relief oozing from their every pore. Max redirected his attention to the *obersturmführer,* who had opened his mouth to argue with the interloping *hauptmann*'s order. But the Luftwaffe ace was quicker in speaking again.

"Well, *Obersturmführer*, I am waiting. Who are you and why are you pointing German weapons at citizens of the Fatherland?" He stood before the SS man, hands clasped behind him and leaning ever so slightly forward, scowling. Max was working hard to keep the psychological advantage. Unarmed and alone, it was all he had going for him.

"*Hauptmann*, I have orders to secure this bridge and prevent anyone from fleeing the area," the SS man replied. The *obersturmführer* was obviously taken aback by this gaunt, burned apparition of a Luftwaffe officer who seemed to have appeared out of thin air. His eyes were locked in near hypnotic manner on the highly esteemed Knight's Cross around Max's neck.

"You still have not identified yourself, *Obersturmführer*" retorted Max impatiently. "We will get to your orders in a moment."

"I am *Obersturmführer* Johannes Strieber, of the *Schutzstaffel Reichssicherheitshauptamt* for this sector, *Hauptmann*" stammered the SS officer.

"Ah, the security police that seeks out traitors and other enemies to the Reich," responded Max. "And just how many enemies of the Reich do we have here today?" he gestured with his left hand for emphasis to the pensive crowd of refugees silently observing the two protagonists.

"The Fuhrer has ordered that all Germans stand and fight, *Hauptmann*" replied the *obersturmführer*. "Anyone who does not do so, anyone who flees from the sound of battle, is to be shot."

Max looked hard at the SS man for a moment. "Just what are you planning to do, *Obersturmführer*?" he demanded. "Assist the Bolsheviks in exterminating more of our fellow Germans? My God, man, take a look at them. They are not traitors and they are not enemies of Germany. They are nothing more than helpless women, children and tired old men. They are our countrymen, or what is left of them."

The SS officer looked about, unsure and seemingly a bit confused. Max continued to talk to him in a lower, softer tone in an attempt to reach something human inside the black regalia.

"Strieber, the Americans and the British are to the west and approaching rapidly. The Soviets are doing the same from the east. We have lost this war, these people and those like them are all that is left of Germany. You shoot them down and you will be assisting in murdering what little hope remains of a future for our Fatherland."

"I have my orders, *Hauptmann*" warned the *obersturmführer* warily.

"Yes, you have your orders. We have all had our orders and as good Germans, we followed them without hesitation. But that time is past, the Third Reich is finished."

Max continued to quietly reason with Strieber, who still held tightly to the P08 Luger. "We have to do something to save what is left. Let these people go wherever they choose in peace; the Americans and the British can probably care for them far better than we can. It is over, *Obersturmführer*."

The sallow faced SS officer stood indecisively for a moment, the pistol dangling along his right side from a relaxing hand. He turned abruptly away from Max and took several steps toward the watching crowd, as if he was taking a closer look at them. Stopping, he turned back around, his mind now made up. Strieber stared back at Max and his features twisted into a half-crazed expression of a resounding, institutionalized hate.

He said only one word, which was spewed through clenched teeth. "Traitor."

The Luger came up smoothly as the *obersturmführer* worked its toggle action with his free hand, chambering a round. He calmly pointed it at the Luftwaffe *hauptmann*, who stood too far away to do much of anything about it. Of all of the ways there was to die in this war, Max found himself thinking this would have been the least likely he could have ever imagined. A short, final prayer began forming in his mind.

To his front the deciding blow and echoing shot came, but it was not the 9mm bullet that Max had resigned himself to. Instead, the small chunk of lead burrowed itself harmlessly into the dirt shoulder making up the approach to the bridge. Max remained standing, still very much alive and unharmed. It took him a moment to fully comprehend what had happened.

He refocused on the scene. Strieberer was sprawled out haphazardly in front of Max, the driving hate that dominated his face a second before now changed into sudden shock and sheer terror. His left hand was clasped tightly over the radial area of his lower right arm. The SS officer was crying out in pain and looking wild eyed at the Wehrmacht Herr senior sergeant looming above.

The *unterfeldwebel* had sprung forward in the manner of a large cat, swinging down hard with the fore end of his Mauser rifle. The weapon had smashed into the *obersturmführer*'s outstretched arm, deflecting the shot and knocking the pistol from Strieber's hand. Still moving forward in the aggressive fashion of a man well versed to close combat, the sergeant changed his angle of attack. The butt of his weapon knocked the SS officer to the ground in an awkward heap.

Standing over the stupefied, cowering figure in the black uniform, the senior sergeant looked down on him with a cold, ready-to-kill expression. This time he did work the bolt on his 98K, sending a steel cased 7.92mm round into the chamber. Its muzzle was pointed squarely in the SS man's face.

"I will not allow a German officer who wears the Knight's Cross with Oak Leaves to be murdered by the likes of you, *Obersturmführer*" spat out the sergeant. "There will be no shooting of anyone here today with the possible exception of you. The *Hauptmann* is right, we have lost. What you were preparing to order us to do is insanity."

"That will be enough, *Unterfeldwebel*" Max said emphatically. He walked over to stand beside the senior sergeant, who was still looking through his rifle sights at the cringing SS officer. The *unterfeldwebel*'s eyes were dark with fury, and his index finger had gathered up all the slack in the Mauser's trigger.

"He is nothing but a vicious thug, *Hauptmann*. Sewer vermin, and he was ready to murder you in cold blood" replied the sergeant, his words clipped with anger.

"Yes *Unterfeldwebel*, you are undoubtably correct. However, you have stopped him from doing so and killing him now would only complicate matters further. Besides, he is not much of anything without this." Max picked up Strieber's Luger from the muddy ground, inspecting it closely. He cleared the round from the chamber and wiped the pistol clean as best he could.

"I will take possession of this weapon though, for good measure." Max bent down, removing the leather gun belt from the waist of the grimacing SS officer. The *obersturmführer* gave no protest or resistance as Max inserted the Luger into the holster and put the belt and gear around his waist. Somewhat reluctantly, the senior sergeant brought the muzzle of the Mauser up and methodically made his own weapon safe. After doing so, he ordered the other soldiers to do the same.

Looking down on the SS officer, the Luftwaffe *hauptmann* spoke to him. "I have a suggestion for you, *Obersturmführer* Strieber. If you are so determined to shoot enemies of the Reich, you can begin walking to the east to meet them. They are called the Red Army and they are coming by the millions." Max paused a moment to let it all sink in for the other man. "Be forewarned, though. I can tell you from personal experience that unlike helpless civilians, they have the disconcerting habit of shooting back."

Max turned away from Strieber, confident the senior sergeant was still watching the *obersturmführer*. He moved closer to the mixed crowd of both civilians and soldiers who stood there, still processing what had occurred in their presence. Stepping up to the top of the dirt embankment, Max addressed them all in a loud, clear voice.

"I am Hauptmann Maximilian Friedrich Grephardt, lately of Jagdgeschwader 52 of the Luftwaffe." A murmur stirred through the throng as some recognized his name and accompanying fame from the recent past. Max motioned to the SS officer still sitting woodenly in the middle of the narrow road. "That man will no longer constitute a threat to any of you. You are free to come or go as you please. Do know the Bolsheviks are indeed behind us and the Western Allies are to our front. I would advise you to continue west if you are going anyplace, but that choice is yours.

"We Germans have lost this war," continued Max, "and in a far more telling way than we lost the last. The time for fighting is over and I pray it never comes to us again. What you must do now is take care of yourselves, your families and what is left of our Fatherland. Do not forget this because from this point forward, that is what it means to be a good German. *Mach's gut*, and may God go with each and every one of you."

The crowd milled around astray for a while more, undecided about their next move. Then slowly, gradually, the vast majority started trekking west again while others sought shelter nearby. Max made his way back to the rickety chair for a bit more rest, and to look around for that errant tar shingle before he continued on. He found his path blocked by the senior sergeant, who placed the Mauser butt down smartly to his side and saluted.

"Herr *Hauptmann*, what do you require of myself and my men?"

"The same as of our people, *Unterfeldwebel*," Max replied. "Your men can go as they please, individually or as a group. They may return to their unit, if they have a mind to do so. But whatever they do, remind them that as long as they wear the uniform of the Wehrmacht Herr, they will conduct themselves accordingly."

For the first time, the senior sergeant appeared a bit unsure of himself but persisted nonetheless. "*Hauptmann*, if I may be so bold, might I inquire into your own plans?"

Max studied the hardened veteran who had saved him from certain death only seconds before. "*Unterfeldwebel*, I plan to continue west and to surrender myself to the Americans at the earliest opportunity. For me, I am done with this war."

The senior sergeant was thoughtful for a moment, still standing at attention. "*Hauptmann*, if possible, it would be an honor to accompany you. I started as an *obersoldat* with Field Marshal Rommel in North Africa, in 1941, and it seems I have been fighting ever since. The time has come to stop."

Max quietly considered the request and then nodded affirmatively. "You are welcome to come along, *Unterfeldwebel*, as are any of your men who choose to do so. It will probably go better for them to surrender as a group than to try to go home at present.

"Tell the men who choose to accompany us to make ready. They will be required to keep their weapons for defensive purposes and are to behave as German soldiers. We are still in the middle of this wretched war and all which that entails. Moreover, I am certain there are more *Obersturmführer* Striebers lurking about." At the mention of the name, both men looked down the road. The SS officer had finally picked himself up and was walking unsteadily to the east against the rising tide of refugees.

"*Jawohl, Hauptmann.*" The senior sergeant saluted again, bringing his Mauser up to port arms. He conducted a sharp about face and started back to the other soldiers. The *unterfeldwebel* had gone no more than five paces when he stopped abruptly, did another about face and brought himself back to the position of attention.

"*Hauptmann*, if I may ask, would you by any chance be from the Meiningen area?" he queried respectfully.

"Yes, my home was north of there, along the banks of the Werra."

"Were you familiar with a Willy Grephardt, an officer in the 267th Regiment of the Wehrmacht Heer?"

"He was my brother, *Unterfeldwebel*." Max replied evenly.

"I knew him in Italy", the sergeant said. "He was a good soldier."

Max looked at the *unterfeldwebel*, his face an impassive mask. "Weren't we all, Senior Sergeant?" he asked. "Weren't we all?"

CHAPTER ELEVEN

As the end of the summer of 1945 drew near, Max was in a disarmed enemy forces camp in the western part of Germany. He had managed to safely surrender both himself and his inherited command to the first American soldiers they could find. The war ended soon thereafter and the long nightmare for tens of millions had finally come to an end. Hitler was dead, and his inhumanly ruinous Reich had joined him in his incinerated grave.

Being a former German officer, he and others like him were being held until an exact determination could be made as to who he was, and what was to become of him. Life was better than it had been for a long time; he ate well, he slept well, and in the meantime his burns had fully healed with the assistance of American medical care.

He also had ample time to read his small Lutheran Bible, and to think about what he should do with his life from this point forward. Max had even begun wearing a small silver cross around his neck, a reminder to himself as to his new path.

The detainee camp was on a former Luftwaffe airbase, one he had flown out of many times during the war. The Americans had appropriated it for their own use and situated the camp near the end of the longest runway, which was used primarily by multi-engine aircraft. Max and his fellow Germans would sit for hours and marvel at the sheer numbers and types of aircraft flying in and out, signifying the overwhelming might of their erstwhile enemy.

'How could we have ever hoped to defeat the British and the Bolsheviks at the same time?'' he had wondered. *'Much less these Americans with their endless stream of aircraft, men and equipment? Hitler and those closest to him must have been completely out of their minds.'*

And so time passed day by day; time to heal, time to reflect and time to ponder. Two years ago the younger Max Grephardt had been so assured of himself, believing that he alone possessed all the necessary answers. Now his older reincarnation realized that not only had he not possessed any of the answers, he had never posed any of the proper questions. This place, this environment, this situation finally allowed Max the opportunity to do so.

Security at the camp was rudimentary at best, the hard corps Nazi party types had already been identified and carted away in the weeks before. The remaining former members of the German war machine were pretty much given free rein of the area, as long as they stayed in the general vicinity and away from the parked aircraft, along with the command and control facilities. The Americans knew what these German officers also knew: the war was over,

Germany had lost. There was no reason to continue skirmishing in hopeless fashion against someone who no longer behaved as your enemy.

One obliging afternoon Max was sitting in a canvas folding chair, dozing after the noon meal. He had been watching the countless Allied aircraft coming and going until even that had become too much effort for him. The *hauptmann* pulled his uniform hat over his eyes, leaned back, and let the warmth of the sun and the surrounding peaceful sounds soak through his soul. Together, they served as a remembrance that just being alive was a very good thing indeed.

That was when he heard it, the noise of an airplane in trouble. Big trouble. The disconcerting sound shocked him rudely back into full consciousness, and he tipped his hat up to see a C-54 Skymaster trying to claw its way into the sky.

The C-54 had just become airborne and was struggling to gain altitude against an unseen giant hand that enveloped the transport craft, trying to shove it back to the ground. The plane slewed from side to side as the engines screamed futilely to keep it in the air. The young Luftwaffe pilot watched as the starboard wing began to dip, and he knew with a sickening certainty what was to occur next.

Max Grephardt was already out of the chair and bolting in the Skymaster's direction when that same wing dug into an earthen berm, and the American cargo plane began cartwheeling violently along the ground. He sprinted onward as hard as he could go, his legs propelling him at a speed he had not known since those Soviet bullets had cracked and hissed around him months before. That was when trying to save his own life, now he was trying to save the lives of others.

Nearing the scene of the horrific crash, Max was confronted with circumstances that would have prevented most men from going any further. A heavy acrid smoke assaulted his eyes and lungs, while the odor of melting rubber and electrical wiring filled his nostrils. A mostly solid sheet of flame from the ignited avgas blocked his way but he plunged on through, making for what was left of the cockpit and main fuselage ahead.

He could hear something of remaining life from inside, the sounds of confusion, of pain and of terror. Every man who had ever challenged the skies shares one thing in common with all others, the fear of fire and of being burned alive. This uncommon kinshmanship with those trapped within kept Max going, and he entered through a ruptured part of the fuselage near where the wings had once been.

In the smoke-filled interior of the shattered aircraft, the odors and the intense heat were all magnified to the level of being nigh unbearable. The first man Max came across was dead, eyes wide open but not seeing anything ever again. Max silently prayed the shortest of prayers for the man's soul and a slightly longer one for the strength to keep pushing forward, as he tried to shield his freshly healed face from the consuming flames.

The next American he came upon in the confines of this particular hell on earth was unconscious, his upper right leg bent at an awkward angle and marked by the broken bone protruding through his flight suit. But he was alive, and Max grabbed him under both armpits and began dragging him to safety. Once outside and away from the fire the Luftwaffe officer placed the man down as carefully as he could, gulped a few precious breaths of the fresh summer air and headed back into the fiery conflagration again.

Three more times the young German made that trip, each time bringing out another man from the clutches of a certain death. Max's lungs felt as if all the air had been sucked out and replaced by blackened soot and ash. His vision was blurred and the exposed parts of his hands and arms were red and blistered from the heat. The Luftwaffe captain's hair and eyebrows were singed or partially burned off, and his knees were wobbly and unsteady as he turned back toward the crashed Skymaster yet once again.

Max Grephardt took a couple of steps that direction and then stumbled, wondering why the grass was suddenly rushing up and forward to meet him. He hit hard face down on the ground and laid there, coughing and retching up a vile mixture of spit, phlegm, vomit and ash. Max tried to get back to his feet but strong hands had taken hold of him, easing him down again and rolling him over to his side.

"Easy now, fella, just take it easy," implored a voice that seemed faraway. "You've already done your part and then some, there's plenty of help now."

Max looked up, his vision cloudy and unfocused as his eyes tried to find the source of the faraway voice. He could barely make out a big man looming over him in the olive drab of an American Army Air Force uniform, and the bold tech sergeant stripes on both upper arms.

"Hey! How about it over here!" The burly tech sergeant bellowed over his shoulder, "This Kraut officer is about half dead himself!"

"How is he, sergeant?" another faraway voice asked. Max blinked several times, attempting to clear his vision and found himself staring into the greenish-grey eyes of an American major with pilot wings on his chest. He looked to be about Max's age.

"He's pretty bad off, major," the tech sergeant replied. "When we drove up, he was bringing the fourth guy out of what's left of that Skymaster. There's no telling how much smoke and trash he's breathed in."

"Did you see what happened?" asked the major.

The sergeant shook his head. "Not before the Skymaster went in, sir. But I did see this guy take off like he was shot out of a cannon. Major, he went through those flames like they weren't even there. He's a man, alright, Kraut or otherwise."

Amid the small crowd of medical personnel now gathering about to help, the young major knelt down, fingering the small silver cross on the exposed part of Max's blackened chest. To no one in particular he murmured the words: *"Let your light so shine before men, that they may see your good works, and glorify your Father which is in heaven."*

"What's that, major?"

"A quote from the Bible, Sergeant. It seems to fit the circumstance."

Looking up from the cross, Major Ezekiel Templar reached over and patted the German officer on his shoulder. "Thank you, my friend. You saved lives today."

Max stared again into those same greenish-gray eyes, now reflecting gratefulness and even admiration. The Luftwaffe *hauptmann* did not understand much English but he could tell from those eyes, as well as the American officer's tone of voice, that he had done well. With that lingering thought of having made a difference Max felt himself drifting, and the light from the bright sunny afternoon went away.

CHAPTER TWELVE

Sometime later he had awakened in one of the wards of the base hospital, his hands and arms freshly bandaged with a greasy salve for his burned ears and face. Each day he was held to a strict regimen of breathing treatments and bandage changes, accompanied by good food and plenty of rest. The bandage changes were especially painful. Yet each time the dressings were replaced it reminded him that he was still alive, and with the real promise of getting better.

The young American major who had been at the crash scene was also part of that daily routine. He became a regular fixture by checking in on Max and making certain he was being properly cared for. When the field ambulance had brought the Luftwaffe officer to the facility, the major had ridden alongside, speaking to him in words of encouragement.

Later, while going through Max's personal effects he had secured his identification papers, a few old photos and his small Lutheran Bible. With the assistance of the Army Counterintelligence Corps as well as his fellow German detainees, Major Templar learned more about the Luftwaffe *hauptmann*, including his many combat decorations. The Iron Cross with Oak Leaves made a real impression on everyone involved. Through an interpreter, the major returned those personal effects and thanked Max again.

Meanwhile, Max had found out the major's name was Ezekiel Templar and that he was from Texas. During the major's many visits they made small talk as best they could and, in the process, became better acquainted with each other. Max was fascinated with anything to do about the American West, so Ezekiel obtained numerous Western novels by Zane Grey, Max Brand and Will James printed in German, for the Luftwaffe officer to read during his convalescence.

During their many conversations Max would work on his English and Ezekiel would struggle in like form in German. The two men had many of the same interests: flying, hunting, literature and most importantly, an abiding faith in a Higher Power above. In this a deep, lifelong friendship was being born. From others at the base hospital, Max learned that his American counterpart was a well-regarded pilot himself who had flown numerous B-17 bombing missions over Germany. Max wondered if Ezekiel Templar saw the same irony in that as he did.

Several weeks later Major Templar was standing in the headquarters of his commanding officer, Colonel George Hapshell. They had already gone over a litany of subjects having to do with day-to-day operations at the base, as well as needed decisions about personnel and some swapping of the latest rumors.

Now the two men were reaching the juncture of their meeting that had been forefront in both minds: What could they, or would they, be able to do for their former Luftwaffe enemy who had likely saved four American lives in the risking his own.

"I want to do the right thing by him, Zeke" said the colonel, pouring himself and Ezekiel a cup of hot black coffee. He handed a steaming mug to the major, who sipped lightly at the contents. "What he did at that crash scene is all over the Allied Sector."

Hapshell motioned Templar over to an overstuffed leather chair and seated himself in an identical facing twin. "If he was one of my men" he continued, "I'd put him in for some sort of commendation like the Soldier's Medal."

"I think he already has plenty of medals, Colonel" observed Ezekiel.

"Yeah, the Knight's Cross with Silver Oak Leaves," mused Hapshell. "I'd have to work hard to beat that, wouldn't I?" The colonel paused, leaning forward and looking intently at Ezekiel. "You've gotten to know him well, Zeke, what do you think? What can we do for this man?"

Ezekiel looked straight back at Hapshell and said, "Give him a job."

"A job?" asked the colonel, half incredulously. "What kind of job do you have in mind, Zeke?"

"Well sir, we both know the Germans possessed some very technologically advanced weapons, and they conducted numerous experiments and studies into the feasibility of others. We already know something about the V1s and V2s, as well as those Messerschmitt jet and rocket fighters we came into contact with late in the war. But what we don't know would likely fill volumes and could be used against us by somebody else in the future."

A troubled countenance settled on the colonel's features. "You're right about that, Zeke. It's a big concern for most everyone in the upper echelons of command. Evidently the Soviets have been running ops to snap up German scientists, and whatever plans and equipment having to do with that technology. I would suspect we're doing the same thing."

Ezekiel Templar shifted his weight in the oversized chair and leaned forward. "Sir, I really think that Max Grephardt could help out substantially in that regard."

"Hmmmm?" the colonel questioned, caught about half off guard.

"Think about it, sir. He could open doors and reach people in ways we never could. Not more than a year ago his photograph was on the cover of all sorts of German magazines, lionized as a true son of their Fatherland and the only one of five brothers having survived. He was a hero, their hero, who fought for them with everything he possessed. They will remember that."

Hapshell placed his righthand fingers on his chin in thought, rubbing it slightly as he considered the idea. "I understand what you're saying, Zeke and agree with the potential of it. But the big question is, will he?" reasoned the colonel. "That's an awful lot to ask of a man. He might even see it as betraying his own country."

"Or maybe saving it," rejoined Ezekiel. "Colonel, Max Grephardt and I have had some serious conversations on this subject. He and many others like him have long considered communism as the biggest threat to their homeland, and they still do. That is why they fought so hard against the Soviets, and why everyone who could came west when the Third Reich collapsed."

"You feel that strongly about him, Zeke?" queried Hapshell. "Because if I go along, we could both end up as some politician's whipping boy over this."

"Yes sir, I do. Max Grephardt is an intelligent, brave and resourceful man. More so, he is a patriot. Not only for his country but for the entire human race. He proved that the moment he ran through those flames to get to our people."

Ezekiel could see he had Hapshell thinking, considering both sides of a fairly big decision. The Texan bulled ahead, pushing his point.

"Sir, the way I see it is this. If the German people, who were so well educated and so steeped in Western civilization could be so badly misled so quickly, then the very same thing could happen in our own country. We are not immune to what occurred here. All it would take is the right crisis, the right faction and the right fiend to take control. It's the oldest and most dangerous political con game known, give us your freedom and we will give you order and safety.

"In many ways there was very little difference between Hitler and Stalin. Both had the same goals, told the same lies and used the same ruthless tactics to achieve those goals. In the end, that's probably why they hated each other so much. Grephardt believes firmly that Stalin will now try to swallow this entire continent whole, if we just stand aside and let it happen."

Ezekiel Templar paused and studied the half empty cup in his hand, choosing his words. "What's more, Colonel, I tend to agree with him. If we don't take action and do something now, we'll be over here in another twenty-five more years, fighting in another world war."

He stopped again before looking his commanding officer square in the eye and adding, "And honestly, I really don't know if humanity can survive a third one."

"That could be construed as dangerous talk against a valued ally in our recent war, major." Hapshell stood and made his way to a nearby window, staring out for a few moments as he pondered Ezekiel's words.

"Our world is currently in a giant mixmaster, Zeke, even as we try to figure out what to do next. Washington wants us to roll out the red carpet for the Communists and placate them in any way possible. Cripes, we both know what happened to Patton when he made the mistake of being honest about our Soviet 'friends.' That remark about kicking their butts back into Russia and making it look like they started it just about finished him."

The Colonel paused again and then remarked. "Maybe the wrong words and the wrong methods but right in regard to what the Communists have in mind, same as suspicioned by your German friend. Washington may not like it and the American people may not even know it yet, but the Soviet Union will be the next great threat that we'll have to deal with. It's already beginning and we're going to need all the help we can get."

Hapshell turned and looked at Zeke, saying "I think I know where to place a bug in the right ear and I'm fairly certain they'll go for it. When I get the word, we'll see if we can make your man a job offer."

Ultimately, the word did make its way back from higher authority and when asked Max Grephardt jumped at the opportunity. In short order he had gathered like-minded former German military officers around him, selected from the detainees at his camp as well as others. Each were meticulously investigated and vetted, not only for any past Nazi sympathies but also for anything the Communists might offer or could use against them.

Once chosen, this developing cadre was formed into operational units that were paid, equipped and led by Allied intelligence organizations. Ezekiel Templar, chafing at the bit to be a part of this, managed to have himself detached from air operations and into one of these teams. Coincidentally, or likely more on purpose, he ended up in the same highly successful group that Max was working in.

Furthermore, it became the opinion of all concerned that Ezekiel Templar was not only a first rate combat pilot, but also had a natural inclination for intelligence work. With additional training and experience, the former bomber commander became an exemplary asset to whatever mission he happened to be involved in.

In those years much good work was done and a great deal of trust was fostered, trust that would be proven time and again in the years and decades to come. Friendships, both institutionally as well individually, were forged and fortified that would last a lifetime.

A new chapter was written in European history and although there were setbacks, disappointments, and lives lost, the next war that Ezekiel Templar warned of never came. In preventing yet another great cataclysmic conflict far worse than the two prior, men like he and Max would have their names printed large in the pages of that particular ledger.

Yet some of those setbacks, disappointments and lives lost weighed very heavily in the personal memories of Max Grephardt. At times between their intelligence endeavors and for many years afterward, Max would sometimes drive from Frankfurt and get as close to the border as he dared. The Iron

Curtain had fallen on Eastern Europe and Germany itself was divided into two different, opposing factions.

Across the heavily guarded line sat his old home now located in East Germany, a puppet government propped up and ruled by the Soviet Bear. He would sit there for hours and gaze toward the Werra, remembering better times before the entire world went stark, raving mad.

Each time he promised himself that someday he would return. Vadi, Mamma and the rest of his family were gone, but there was still a church that needed to be rebuilt and a generational past that needed reclaimed.

CHAPTER THIRTEEN

Ezekiel Templar lay in the shadows of the store room, unconscious and groaning occasionally in the way that only a suffering man could. He had lapsed into a deep sleep brought on by the pain medications, but then was partially roused from his slumber by a blossoming fever that kept his mind in a state of disjointed, fitful dreaming.

But they weren't really dreams at all, they were nightmares. For in them he was back in the war, once more leading formations of Flying Fortresses against the enemy. However, this time the aerial armada he was part of had Nazi insignias and were being targeted against American cities.

Messerschmitt 109s and Focke Wulf 190s, painted with American emblems and unit designators, would rise in a forlorn attempt to stop the incoming hordes of heavy bombers arrayed in their combat boxes. But there were far too few defenders to stem the continuing aerial onslaughts. The bombers would drone on and deliver their payloads upon the helpless civilian populations below, over and over again.

Far worse was what the massed formations of bombers were dropping. It was no longer high explosives or incendiaries, but rather every sort of sinister chemical or biological weapon known to man. They would make their runs, return to base, and go out yet once more as if they were part of a huge conveyor belt carrying devastation beyond description. There were no military targets, no complexes of industrial importance nor areas of strategic value. Each mission was specifically targeted only against the civilian populations, who died in hideously indescribable ways by the hundreds of thousands.

In his fevered mind's eye a man stood in the background above it all, waving his hands about and speaking to adulating crowds who cheered him on. His form was masked in dark shadow and his face was indiscernible. Even if the language he used could not be understood, his manner and inflection were eerily effective in preying upon the gamut of raw emotions emanating from his mesmerized audience.

He spoke earnestly, passionately, and the millions who listened to him would begin marching in every direction on the dial of a compass. They would continue on purposefully in the form of the military goosestep, holding their right arms up and forward in salute to the man who spoke so forcefully and eloquently. Their lines were ruler straight, each a perfect reflection of the others to either side as well as to the front and behind.

They would march in robot-like precision until they came to the waiting fleets of heavy bombers, which sat on airfields amazingly large in size stretching as far as the eye could see. Amid the countless ranks he could see himself marching alongside the others as if in a deep trance, knowing that what he was doing was beyond reprehensible but unable to stop himself all the same. He would climb into the pilot's seat, the engines would begin turning over one by one, and he and those with him would set out on yet another mission of mass murder.

All the while the sky grew a more lurid shade of red and the man, the one who controlled them all like some diabolical master of puppets watched their activity from afar, never stopping in his endless speech. No matter where they were going or how far, his presence loomed over the vast armada of killing machines and filled the heavens above them. When the bombs would drop the man would cease talking and gesticulating just long enough to smile widely and then hug himself in some sort of twisted self-rapture.

Then he would begin to speak again, faster and more emphatically. As he did so, his features became more distinguishable. He was in a uniform and was a person of rather small, frail stature with would have been, in another circumstance, a somewhat comical Chaplinesque moustache. In Ezekiel's personal nightmare, the figure became distinct enough to identify the man so idolized by the adoring crowds as the one they called 'Der Fuhrer,' the demented, murderous leader of Nazi Germany who loomed so large in so many other people's nightmares. It was the monster known to the world as Adolph Hitler.

But then another change came over the figure, it grew even larger and more ominous. The man, the uniform and everything around him slowly dissolved into multiple hues of red, purple and black, and the image of Hitler gave way to another form that could only be that of Satan himself. Through the transformation the voice continued on unabated; exhorting, encouraging, ordering and sometimes even using assorted threats to keep the masses focused on their horrifying, soul numbing task.

The cheering became ever wilder and more clamorous, as if the minds of a half billion people slipped the twin moorings of both sanity and common decency, and slid into the bottomless depths below. The visage, the prince of the power of the air who commanded it all began to transform again, and this time took on the features of the one known to Ezekiel Templar as Yahla al-Qassam.

Qassam…

The thought of the man, along with the mental image of the sinister shape in the nightmare, brought him to full consciousness. Ezekiel's eyes fluttered open and he shifted his body abruptly without thinking, bringing forth shooting pain from his injured leg.

But he had to stop Qassam.

Ezekiel's sudden movement startled the guard standing at the open doorway, who had apparently been watching the old colonel for some time now. He spoke quickly in Arabic to someone else in the adjoining room, which was followed by a brief pause and the sound of another voice giving out commands in return. It sounded like Qassam.

The Hezbollah guard remained at the door as one of the other terrorists stepped in, carrying an orange medical bag and a large canteen bladder. He walked over to Ezekiel and knelt down while reaching into a side pocket. Palming several pills in his right hand, he forced them into Ezekiel's mouth and then held it shut until the old man managed to swallow them. Then the Shi'a allowed the elder Templar a long, greedy swig out of the water container. Ezekiel took in all that he could, trying to wash the bitter taste of the pills from his mouth and quench the desert-like thirst that permeated his body.

After allowing him to take his fill, the Lebanese turned his attention to Micah and Max. He checked them both over briefly, as if he was getting a quick determination of their physical health and condition. Surprisingly enough, he let them drink some water out of the bladder also.

It was wet, cool and immensely satisfying. Micah looked up as he took the proffered canteen and noticed the man's eyes glowering at him with a cold and bitter hate. Evidently the terrorist was only carrying out orders, and he did not like them. For his part Micah really did not care, just as long as he could get a drink of water and that the Lebanese were looking after Tio Zeke.

Abruptly the terrorist jerked the container away and recapped it. Then he moved over and did the same for Max. Still scowling at Micah, he gathered up the medical bag and stood back up. Taking one last disdainful look at his hostages the Lebanese walked out the doorway, passing the guard without so much as a word.

Micah shifted around a bit, taking care as to not put any pressure on the handcuffs clasped around his wrists. He still had the idea of escape firmly on his mind, and of throwing the biggest monkey wrench he could come up with into the intricate machinery that made up Qassam's scheme. Thinking back, it was just as well the restraining devices had not been removed when Tio Zeke was shot with that .25 Beretta. The terrorist leader had been correct in thinking that Micah might have been entertaining other thoughts than in helping his uncle.

And if Micah Templar knew nothing else in this world, he knew himself and what his personal weak points were. He also knew the sum total of those weaknesses was headlined by a quick, sometimes all-consuming temper. For most of his adult life he had worked hard on controlling it, yet that temper had gotten away from him in the other room and nearly flared to a full boil.

As an experienced and self-aware man who had been between a rock and a hard place a few times before, he knew that when one allowed himself to become that angry, one quit thinking rationally. He also knew that such an essential failing could mean the loss of an argument, an advantage or even somebody's life.

Micah settled back, considering again his situation and possible options. They had to put Qassam and his bunch out of commission, that much was obvious. Whatever it took or whatever the sacrifice, fate had left them with no other choice.

But if they were to be successful in the attempt, they needed the proper time and place to make their play. Hours had passed since the new guard had been posted, yet this particular one showed no indication of any slacking in his attention to duty. The handcuff key was the hinge on making their present circumstance swing in another direction, but he needed some time unobserved to use it. Just a little bit of time and some attending luck.

Hungry, aching from the physical abuse and with life hanging in the balance, Micah's mind drifted off to another place. In it he began thinking of his wife, Abby, and how glad he was she had decided to drive to Midland rather than take the plane ride with him. At that time and true to his form, he had been disappointed and even a little testy when she had chosen to do so. They had planned for this trip together for some time and his selfish, willful side wanted things to go his way.

However, Abby knew the Albrights might need her more than she needed to ride in an old bomber, and had made her mind up accordingly. More so and true to her own form, she had dug in her heels when he appeared less than enthusiastic about her decision.

Now Micah found himself giving thanks that he had married such a caring, conscientious, yet willful woman and gave praise to a decision that he had first questioned due to his own shortcomings. Abby was safe, and with that knowledge he knew that his greatest Achilles heel remained out of reach of those just outside the doorway.

The younger Templar came back to the here and now, and what the near future most likely promised. There was no doubt in his mind that when the opportunity presented itself, it would be a brief, chancy thing for the three of them and very uncertain as to the final outcome. He'd seen too many good men die with the best of intentions perishing alongside to ever dissuade himself otherwise. So much depended on how he, Tio Zeke and Max Grephardt made use of those few, decisive moments.

In the gloom Micah found himself praying silently, earnestly. *'Lord, show me what I must do and give me strength to get it done. I doubt there'll be a second chance.'* Along with his own prayer came the memory of a far more eloquent one: *'Blessed be the Lord my Rock, who trains my hands for war, and my fingers for battle…'*

It was funny how one's memory worked, you only realize what's truly important when someone, or something, comes along to take it all away. Micah hadn't thought of that Bible verse since, well, since his last tour in Vietnam. At present he could not recall the rest and really wished he could. Tio Zeke would know that verse from beginning to end, he had always been gifted at that sort of thing. But just the few words that Micah could remember brought an inner peace and helped steel himself for whatever might come.

He peered into the semi darkness at his uncle, who appeared to be sleeping again. Whenever Micah made his move, he realized that in those first critical seconds Ezekiel probably wouldn't be of much help. Tio Zeke was a tough and capable man, even upon nearing some seventy years of age. Nevertheless, he would have to clear the mental fog brought on by the pain killers he'd been given, and the time needed for that would be far longer than what it took to start the ball rolling. That same calculation also didn't take into account the bullet hole in his uncle's leg, either.

The peace officer refocused his gaze beyond his uncle and at the unmoving form of Max Grephardt. The German appeared to be simply resting but Micah had the distinct feeling that in Max's case, looks were deceiving. He knew the story about the Luftwaffe *hauptmann*'s escape from the Soviets, and had known Max for too long not to notice and appreciate the sort of man he was.

Micah's own father, Jeremiah Templar, had once remarked "that German is a born fighting man, through and through." Such praise came very rarely from his father and he would have known as well as anybody. There was no doubt that Max Grephardt would be there in the clinch.

The memory of his father at that particular moment brought a wistful yearning, Jeremiah Templar was one man that his son wished was here. As a boy he had been in utter awe of his dad and that feeling had not dissipated much as the years passed by. Born in south Texas around the end of World War One, members of the family had often joked that Jeremiah Templar had arrived into this world with his boots and spurs already on. The same temper that Micah struggled with had come to him honestly, for in his own youth his father was known for such by both friend and foe alike.

As a young man that temperament, along with an easy way with the cards as well as the ladies, had led to more than one scrape which gave folks plenty to remember him by. One night it sparked an epic brawl in a San Antonio bar with a town bully, said to be the meanest man thereabouts. He might have been, but Jeremiah Templar proved to be the tougher and mopped the floor with his opponent. The small statured, wiry, full of fire Templar, not more than about nineteen, had left his mark and put the far bigger man in a local hospital.

Unfortunately and to his great chagrin, it was only then the Turkey Creek cowhand discovered the bully in question had plenty of kin, especially in some of the local higher elected offices. A warrant was put out for his arrest and the young Jeremiah, knowing a stacked deck when he saw one, hitched a ride on the first freight out of town.

That particular train had been heading east, so that was where Jeremiah Templar went next. After a couple of months of bouncing around and becoming hungrier and *mas flaco*, he began thinking about finding some honest work and fattening up a bit. However this was during the time of the Great Depression and jobs were hard to find on the East Coast; especially for south Texas cowboys who didn't know much more beyond horses, cattle, cards and creating occasional mayhem.

But one day Jeremiah ran into a likely looking gent who said he might be able to help, a no-nonsense sort of fellow in the spiffiest dark blue uniform the cowhand had ever seen, sitting at the desk of the local Marine Corps recruiting office. The rawhide and barbed wire tough Texan liked what he saw and what he heard, and so he signed on. And his world changed drastically yet once again.

The first thing he found out was although he might have had a partial claim to being the toughest man in San Antonio, this unratified title did not include the rank and file of the United States Marine Corps. His comeuppance occurred on his third day at Parris Island, and the eye-opening lesson was taught with finality by another man also made of barbed wire and rawhide, and who just happened to be Jeremiah's drill instructor.

It was the first time he had ever been whipped so soundly, but Jeremiah took it well enough and learned some of life's lessons from the drubbing. In the years to come that hard-boiled, fist slinging drill instructor would become his closest friend, and together they ended up being part of what was then termed as 'China Marines,' due to their pre-war service there.

Their friendship would endure until a particularly horrific day along a dusty road outside the Filipino town of Balanga, during a time of infamous sorrows and inhuman brutalities that became known as the Bataan Death March.

On that day three long years of a very personal war began in the mountains and jungles of Luzon, fighting an enemy who was seemingly without mercy or compassion for others than themselves. It was a grinding mill of days and nights of sickness, pain, near starvation and constant danger, interspersed with dozens of vicious ambushes and firefights that neither asked for or gave any quarter.

Jeremiah Templar fought eye for an eye through it all, and in the process obtained near legendary status in not only his own ragged band of guerillas but among the general civilian population. He also earned a special reputation among the Japanese invaders, and with good reason was both feared and hated by them.

It had been during some of the same years as Ezekiel's own war over occupied Europe, but in crucial ways Jeremiah's crucible was an entirely different kind of onslaught in primal savagery. He had experienced firsthand the unthinking, almost institutional, cruelty of the average Japanese soldier on a near daily basis. What he took with him from that soul-searing ordeal, was an active hate for anything having to do with the Japanese for the rest of his days.

After the liberation of the Philippines and the end of the war, Jeremiah returned to the upper Nueces River country a changed man. Gaunt and battle scarred, his easy ways and happy-go-lucky nature had been replaced by a grim maturity and frank appraisal of himself, as well as the world around him. The temper that often got the better of him as a younger man was now mostly chained down deep within. In the remaining years of his life the fire-eating centaur had escaped only rarely, but Micah had been present during one of those few occurrences and it was a sight to behold.

There were those who said that Jeremiah Templar was a war hero, and others who said he only did what had to be done and had paid a dear price for it. The former Marine had come back to his roots, gotten married and made a living for his family doing what he loved most, working with cattle and horses on a small place outside of Uvalde.

Like so many of his peers who had gone afar to help defeat an implacable foe, he now went about his duties in a simple, day-to-day existence. The fruits of his quiet labor could never be measured in dollars but rather the most priceless denomination of all, the respect of those around him. Micah remembered him as a loving and wise father, who spoke far more openly about his own shortcomings and faults than he ever did anyone else's.

One warm spring day when Micah was about nine years old a dusty gray, four door Ford sedan had pulled up in front of the ranch house. On the doors it bore the words "Department of the Navy", and a Marine major sat behind the wheel in his service khaki uniform. He had come to see if he could speak with the once Marine sergeant Jeremiah Templar.

Jeremiah's mother, always the gracious host and ready for company, had invited the major inside for some iced tea and a slice of pecan pie. She explained her husband was out checking on a leaking water trough in a nearby pasture, but should be in soon enough.

As she busied herself in the kitchen Micah sat down at the table with the major, admiring his crisp creases and the rows of ribbons on his chest. In turn, the Marine officer noticed the boy's interest and began visiting with him on an assortment of subjects such as school, sports and life in general on a south Texas ranch.

After an hour or so had passed, his dad came in and the major introduced himself, saying that he was from the Marine Corps historical section at Quantico, Virginia. He had come all this way to speak with Jeremiah Templar about his time in the Marines, particularly about those years spent in the Philippines during the war. Micah's dad listened intently to what the major had to say. In a measured tone, Jeremiah replied by commenting that he would try to help as best he could.

The two men began the interview on general topics, and his father answered the questions slowly and thoughtfully. He related names, dates and locations as exactly as possible or would simply say the estimation was only a guess, or that he could not remember. All the while, the major scribbled notes on a yellow legal pad with a pencil. Micah sat at the kitchen table and listened with rapt attention.

But as the questions became more focused on Jeremiah himself, the answers became shorter and more clouded. It was as if an unseen, impenetrable wall was rising slowly from the floor between him and everyone else in the room. Finally, the major began asking about a certain staff sergeant by the name of Vincent F. Pate. Then the conversation ground to a halt, as a pall of deep sadness and grief came over his father's features.

For several long moments there was absolute silence. Jeremiah put a calloused hand over his eyes and worked his temples with his thumb and middle fingers. Then he sighed heavily and finally responded, "Don't think I want to talk about that, major."

"Sergeant Templar, the Marine Corps needs to know what happened, as does Staff Sergeant Pate's family," persisted the major. "We have a fair approximation after speaking with some of the others present at that time, but every one of those men says that only you know the entire story."

"Major, I ain't no sergeant anymore. Just someone who's spent a lot of nights trying to forget most of what you've brought up today. Vince's family don't need to know everything that happened. And to be honest, I wish I didn't either."

"But..." the Marine officer began.

"Leave it be, major. It's enough to say that Vince Pate was one of the finest men I ever knew, and a Marine extraordinaire. He died in the service of his country after he gave every last bit of life left inside him. That's plenty enough to remember anybody by."

The room fell into an uneasy silence again, save for the steady ticking of the tall grandfather clock along the east wall. The major gazed steadily at Jeremiah Templar for some time, coming to the slow realization that this was one objective that he would never be able to obtain. Knowingly, tellingly, he nodded his head ever so slightly in appreciation of the man seated before him.

Jeremiah glanced over to his young son still seated at the table, listening in. "Micah" he asked gently, "don't you have some chores that still need to be done?" Knowing that it was past time to take his leave, Micah hurriedly excused himself and headed out the front screen door.

The adults stayed inside the ranch house for some time, before the Marine major appeared on the front wood porch alongside his dad. The two men spoke in low voices for a few more minutes and then shook hands. His dad turned and went back inside, and the major made his way to the waiting sedan.

Opening the door and climbing in, he cranked up the gray Ford's flathead V8. As he let the engine settle into an idle, he looked over and saw Micah sitting by the tack shed. The Marine officer smiled, as if maybe recollecting some of his own childhood and motioned the boy over.

Micah came at a run, skidding to a stop in the hard dirt beside the driver's door. Reaching inside his briefcase, the major produced a shiny brass casting of the Marine Corps emblem resembling the blackened ones on the lapels and cover of his uniform. He handed the crest to Micah, saying, "Son, I want you to have this. I'd like for it to be a reminder of what kind of Marine your dad was, and the kind of man he is now."

The officer peered into the young boy's face. "Ever known a real war hero?" he asked. Micah thought hard with his nose wrinkled up, and then shook his head slowly from side to side.

"Well, you do. And you probably never heard him utter a single word to make you think he was. But I'm going to tell you something that needs saying, your dad is a real hero whether he will ever admit to it or not. I imagine he's never been anything but. Don't ever forget that, son.

"Now you take care of yourself and be proud. Not every little boy has that kind of a dad." The major brought up the idle and eased the clutch out, and the Ford sedan pulled away. Micah stood there in the settling dust, studying the golden eagle, globe and fouled anchor clinched tightly in his small right hand. He looked up at the disappearing car and knew in his heart that one day, he would be a Marine, too. Bounding up the steps and across the front porch in his excitement, he pulled up short at the scene presented through the screen door.

His parents sat together, his dad with his head on his forearms resting on the brightly-patterned cloth covering the kitchen table. His mom was close beside, running her fingers through his hair and speaking to him in a soft, comforting tone. When she glanced up and saw Micah looking in, she shook her head from side to side rapidly and shooed her son away with her free hand.

It was the only time he could ever remember his father crying.

CHAPTER FOURTEEN

The sound of men working in the other room, as well as in the darkness beyond was quieting down. It was in the wee hours now, the hands on the clock that creep through the period between the departing lateness of night and the early morning yet to come. Ezekiel Templar began waking up in slow degrees, rising up to full consciousness through the enveloping malaise brought on by the hour and those pills the Shi'a had forced down him. He felt the sensation of having sweated profusely, which he took as a good sign that his fever was breaking.

Until encountering the mental fog that accompanied his rise from unconsciousness, Ezekiel had been dreaming again. But it was nothing like the disjointed nightmares before, in this sequence he relived precious thoughts of the past and of those who had meant so much to him. In it his wife, Sue, was still alive and Jacob but a rambunctious little boy again. They were at the ancestral Templar family home along the banks of the Nueces, during the coolness of late autumn when the leaves of those enormous old pecan trees begin to fall.

There was nothing really special about the circumstance the dream portrayed, he had spent so many days at that old place with his family. On several occasions, Sue spent time there before they were even married. She would drive out from Uvalde to stay with the Templars and though raised a town girl, she took to ranch life and was square in the middle of everything occurring on the premises. It quickly became her home as much as anyone else's. During his years in the Air Force, the two and then later three traveled across the world and back again. But home still remained where it was, and they returned to it every chance they had.

In the dream his family was simply spending time by the river, enjoying the late autumn afternoon as much as each other. They had walked from the ranch house and down to the rock-strewn riverbed, holding each other's hands as Jacob ran forward and examined every small thing that a growing boy's budding imagination could build upon.

"Jacob Templar! Now you be careful!' she warned emphatically to the small boy scrambling about.

"Aw, Maw" the little boy protested.

"You speak respectful to your mother, son, and do as she says" Ezekiel sternly added.

"Yes sir. Sorry Mom, I'll be careful." Jacob replied somewhat ruefully.

"Zeke, I tell you that boy is going to be the death of me," Sue confided. "I never know what he might do or say next. In fact," she added, looking at Ezekiel somewhat mischievously, "he reminds me a whole lot of you at about the same age."

"Dad often cautioned that I would pay for my raising," replied Ezekiel in good humor.

"But that doesn't mean I have to, also. I swear, you Templars are all the same. If there's trouble to be found, you will find it. And if there isn't, you won't rest until you manage to stir some up." Her voice had the slightest hint of exasperation, yet Sue was grinning up at him as she said it.

"Yes ma'am, and since you are now part of the clan, we fully expect you to do your part."

Sue half-snorted in glee and gave that special giggle, the same one she had since she was Jacob's age and then they walked on together.

The scene had changed again almost immediately in the dream, and that was when the sleeping Ezekiel finally recognized it for what it was. The cold chill of reality kept trying to intrude upon this shortest of spans of happiness, forcing him to accept that Sue and Jacob were gone and he was now alone in life.

He needed not the heartbreaking reminder, as he already knew this was nothing more than the journey of a mind and soul that so desperately ached for those whom he loved most. Yet he enjoyed it all the same, as it brought back something immeasurably precious that had been missing over the long, lonely years.

Toward the end of the dream Ezekiel knew he would have to leave soon enough, though he wanted so badly to not have to go. Like so many times before he yearned to stay, to do nothing more than be with her and Jacob and let the rest of the world just pass on by. But duty of some sort would always call, and he would pack his bags and head out the door.

Sue never said much about it. Yet he knew that she not only understood but in her own way encouraged him to go and try to make that difference, be it big or small. At times, she seemed to realize even better than he the kind of man he was and his role in this life. Ezekiel had treasured her for that and for so many other things.

Even in the dream, she knew it was time for him to go again. Sue smiled and they had kissed as he held her so very close, soaking up the love and warmth now missing for so long. Wistfully, he turned away and faced his awakening consciousness as the scene around him evaporated like the dew of a late summer night, when exposed to the unsparing sun of morning.

All that was left was the fading, final taste of that same life-giving dew in a still grieving heart, and the reawakening dread of something horrific beyond imagination about to occur. For there would be many other mothers and small sons walking along another river in San Antonio this morning, and they would never see another day unless he somehow stopped Qassam.

Lying there recouping in the semi-darkness, Ezekiel Templar allowed himself a moment to take stock of his present physical condition. The hole in his left leg still throbbed, but nothing like before and nothing that he could not put up with. It occurred to him that he needed a clear head far more than he needed any more of the pain killers, and the old Texan resolved to avoid any more of those if at all possible.

From long habit, Ezekiel did not move until he brought himself out of the fog in which he had awakened. He strained his ears to listen outside of the room in which they were being held, but could not catch more than the occasional low word spoken in Arabic or the muffled sound of someone moving about outside. When he opened his eyes, most of what he could see was limited to the ceiling and the upper part of the opposing wall.

Wanting to take in more of what was around him, he shifted his position slightly. Ezekiel moved with care, not wanting to cause any more trauma to his injured leg, or his bruised and lacerated wrists. The large zip ties had dug deeply into the skin when he writhed around on the sofa, battling to control himself against the searing pain of the bullet. His mouth was dry again and the colonel found himself wishing for some more water from that bladder canteen. He worked his mouth and tongue against each other, trying to get some semblance of moisture going.

Turning his head, he first looked over at Max. His movement had almost been imperceptible, yet the German acknowledged him with a slight nod from among the shadows. Rolling his head the other direction he saw Micah, who had positioned himself best to observe their guard. The previous one had been replaced and another stood just outside the door. The man appeared fresh and alert, his Kalashnikov AK slung at an angle across his chest.

The older Templar pondered on his nephew saying he had a way of getting loose, that he just needed some time away from watchful eyes to do so. But as in most things time was a valuable resource, and they were quickly running out of what was left. As long as that guard was alert and paying attention, Micah could not make whatever move he had planned.

And if Micah could get loose, what then? He would have to overpower the guard, free Ezekiel and Max, obtain weapons and only then could they try to take control of *The Uvalde Raider*, along with its deadly payload.

Ezekiel Templar had been involved in plenty of dicey situations and knew that such ad-libbed assaults usually had one way only to success, and about a hundred other ways where it could go from really bad to much worse. Really bad in itself meant a failure and there was no way they could allow that. They had to stop the Flying Fortress from completing its mission as a biological incubus.

He racked his brain, trying to remember everything that Qassam had said, along with his own surmising of the viability as well as possible weak points in the terrorist's plan. The VX nerve agent possessed was reportedly the most potent chemical substance of its type ever put into mass production. It was the kind of rabidly murderous weapon that kept world leaders up at night developing ulcers, and put other men tasked with responding to such into an icy cold sweat.

Bizarrely enough, VX had been developed by British scientists in the mid-1950s, building upon German research conducted during the Third Reich. Ezekiel remembered a decades old conversation with a British MI5 security officer, discussing the then-current Klaus Fuchs affair as well as the attending discovery of the Cambridge Spy Ring. While lamenting over the damage caused by these scandals and the accompanying compromise of state secrets, the MI5 man had gone on to speak of other intelligence concerns that bothered him even more.

These included the possible pilfering of classified information involving other highly sensitive projects, including work done in the development of a new super nerve agent family known as the V-series. Among these laboratory spawned nightmares, VX was the most advanced and potent concoction of them all.

The secrets for developing this devastating killer were later traded to the United States in exchange for thermonuclear technology. From there, the information was somehow leaked to the Soviet Union, just as Ezekiel's MI5 contact had worryingly predicted.

Following true to form, the nerve agent began appearing in the research facilities of some of the Communist superpower's client states. These included Cuba, who in the early 1980s was embroiled as a major participant in the Angolan Civil War. Beginning in 1984, regional hospitals reported the existence of patients who had apparently been exposed to a chemical weapon that was ultimately confirmed as VX. Some four years later, a UN commission determined this barbaric act to be part of Cuba's anti-insurgency activities in the strife torn African country.

Nevertheless, the most publicly identifiable of those client states had been Sadaam Hussein's Iraq. At about the same time as the United Nations established Cuban culpability in Angola, rumors began to swirl about the use of VX by Hussein in the ongoing Iran-Iraq war. Furthermore, it was highly suspicioned the ruthless dictator had gone so far as to employ it against his own Kurdish civilian population in the city of Halabja. The results were described by witnesses as being stunningly horrific.

Yahla al-Qassam claimed to have five hundred gallons of this diabolical mixture. From what Ezekiel had seen and heard earlier, the terrorists were installing portable pumps on *The Uvalde Raider* as a technique of dispersal. If that was the case, it would turn the old bomber into some sort of improvised aerial spreader, much like a crop duster but on a far larger comparative scale. However, the objective would not be some farmer's field for the betterment of his crops. This effort would be a devastating terrorist attack on a major city in the United States.

The ensuing environmental damage and casualty rates would be unimaginable to most, even Ezekiel with his specialized knowledge had difficulty in calculating just how bad it could be. He knew the inherent qualities of the agent were made to order for the kind of application that Qassam envisioned. Following the aerial release of the deadly substance, the population of San Antonio would be exposed to it through skin contact, absorption through the eye, or by breathing in the settling mist.

Unlike many other weaponized chemicals, it was heavier than air and would tend to settle in areas of lower elevation. It was also odorless and tasteless, and its consistency was said to be much like a light motor oil. VX was astonishingly lethal, any droplet large enough to be seen with the human eye was enough to kill the average human being.

Furthermore, the agent's likeness to a thin motor oil meant it evaporated slowly, and in a cooler climate could remain for days or even weeks. Experts in the field of chemical warfare had a clinical term for such useful abilities, they referred to it as an agent with 'high persistence.'

Ezekiel wondered if that characteristic was why Qassam had chosen this particular season to carry out his plot. The weather would be cool compared to the blazingly hot days of summer, but not so much as to keep people indoors during the morning hours. As a general rule, October was considered to be the nicest time of the year for the San Antonio area. There would be more people outside, thus a greater number of highly vulnerable targets.

As far as any indirectly attributing lethal effects, Ezekiel recalled reading that VX could also mix with water, although not as easily as other nerve agents. The San Antonio River bisected the city running roughly north to south, and then joined with other rivers before exiting into the Gulf of Mexico some 250 miles away. Any runoff would be yet another means to introduce the substance to populations downstream, and yet another opportunity for the substance to wreak death and devastation upon all who came into contact with it.

The retired colonel turned his thoughts to the logistics involved, to further gauge objectively those same chances of success. He calculated the total weight of the nerve agent and its attending ancillary equipment to be in the neighborhood of three tons, a weight *The Uvalde Raider* was easily capable of accommodating.

Any chance of mechanical difficulties on the part of the Boeing ran from extremely small to none, Ezekiel knew that better than anyone else. His professed doubts to Qassam concerning the airplane's current state of repair and capabilities had only been a ruse, a red herring to dissuade as well as learn more. He had personally seen to every small detail of the Flying Fort's restoration; it was presently a better aircraft than any B-17 that flew during World War Two.

The next link in this potentially catastrophic chain was the identity of whoever Qassam had chosen to fly the Boeing. Piloting a Flying Fortress was no mean feat, and there were not many pilots still alive who had any real seat time in that type of multi-engine aircraft.

Yet Qassam seemed to be supremely confident in his choice for the task. The terrorist leader was not the sort to run a bluff, and putting a bullet hole in Ezekiel's upper left leg signaled that he had no need for the colonel's flying abilities. Evidently all that was required of Ezekiel was to witness what was to come, as well as being a hostage who might prove himself useful in the future. But who had Qassam picked to fly *The Uvalde Raider*? The identity of this mystery pilot gnawed at him.

With no defining answer to that essential question, the elder Templar rechanneled his thinking into other aspects of Qassam's scheme. There was plenty of avgas in the Boeing's tanks, enough to get it to San Antonio as well as a good ways beyond. Ezekiel had always believed in the experienced pilot's rule of keeping plenty of fuel aboard, one never knew if there might be a diversion due to need or circumstance. The present range for the heavy bomber would not be an issue as far as available fuel.

The flying time in getting to San Antonio was not much more than about an hour, once the aircraft reached a correct heading and cruising altitude. Ezekiel figured that would be no more than around 5,000 feet, which also dovetailed nicely into what the Hezbollah leader had in mind. To power the portable pumps needed for the agent dispersal, Qassam would most likely use small gasoline engines like the type found on large lawn mowers. Such two stroke powerplants worked best at lower altitudes, where there was sufficiently dense air to run reliably.

From long habit, the elder Templar recalled the prevailing regional weather conditions that he committed to memory before starting from Houston. A high-pressure system was sitting over most of western and central Texas, and the forecast called for a bright, sunny day with no chance of precipitation or any sort of cloud cover during the morning hours. Visibility would be unlimited, and at 5,000 feet the average Boy Scout could find San Antonio with little more than a folding road map from a convenience store.

Qassam had spoken of covering a path with the agent some twenty-three kilometers long and a hundred meters wide, or by the more familiar English measurement about fifteen miles in length by a hundred and ten-yard width. From an estimated 5,000-foot altitude while traveling around 200 miles an hour, Ezekiel calculated that covering the targeted area was completely doable and likely Qassam's estimate was conservative. There were four Wright Cyclone 1,200 horsepower radial engines powering *The Uvalde Raider*, and each one of them turned a large three blade Hamilton Standard propeller. That made for a lot of air turbulence.

His own calculations were also dependent upon the on board equipment used to distribute the chemical for maximum effect, but Ezekiel was forced to give the devil his due in that, too. Yahla al-Qassam would not stump his toe in the choosing of that equipment, considering the other meticulous research and planning that had been done.

The terrorists would probably pump the agent at high pressure out both sides of the Boeing, angling the sprayer tips down and to the rear from the aircraft itself. To further enhance the improvised system, it would be simple enough to affix some style of aerator on the nozzles. This would churn the nerve agent into a finer mist as the ghastly mixture spewed from the aircraft.

Any sort of crosswind would carry the deadly substance over a still wider area as it drifted down to the ground. From those same weather forecasts Ezekiel had noted a projected breeze from the east at some five to ten miles an hour. If Qassam and his team arrived over the city at any time past ten in the morning, that wind would be present.

His best guess was that Qassam would make his run roughly north to south over the targeted area. This would be partly for the forecasted breeze, as well as several other tactical reasons. Coming in from the northwest, a north to south course would call for little more than gentle pressure on the controls to line up for the attack. There were plenty of easily discernable landmarks on the northern side of the city to facilitate such an approach.

Flying in from that direction would make for a downhill run due to the higher terrain located north of San Antonio. This in turn would allow them to drop some of their altitude in a smooth, natural manner, making it easier to pick out a prominent point to aim the aircraft towards. The slightly lower approach would also allow for a more effective dispersal pattern. Finally, that particular course would have them headed to their closest likely escape route, the Rio Grande and Mexico.

Ezekiel had already judged the Hezbollah leader as not being kin to the suicidal type. Like many of his kind he was quite capable of ordering others to their deaths, yet considered his own mortal existence far more precious. His escape would be just as carefully planned and attended to as the mission itself.

It was obvious the terrorists had entered Texas from Mexico, and returning there would be far more logical than an attempt to remain in the United States. It was just as obvious this group possessed a fully functioning and capable support network there. Once south of the river their available options would widen dramatically, as would their chances of successfully evading any pursuit.

All in all the entire scope of the operation was as gifted in design as it was utterly damnable in nature. More important in practical terms was its execution, and everything appeared to be working in Qassam's favor so far. It was one of those plaintively tragic instances that made one marvel at human determination and ingenuity, while at the same time being horrified by the homicidal baseness and innate cruelty.

But if there was one weak point to the plan, one element that could bring near instantaneous disaster to all involved, it was the VX itself. The effectiveness of a weapon is sometimes mirrored by the inherent danger to the user, and this nerve agent the terrorists possessed was the best example that Ezekiel could think of. The formulation of the deadly chemical along with its storage, transportation and handling was fraught with catastrophe if the smallest mistake was made at any juncture in the process.

One could look upon those involved in these stages as being some sort of snake charmers, interacting with a supremely venomous serpent that was never completely controlled, and searching for a way incessantly to kill them as well as any other living thing in the general vicinity. There was no room for error when dealing with VX, no safe zone in which one could take a respite and relax. Laxity in any form sorely tempted fate and in the most grievous manner imaginable.

Ezekiel recalled how this particular serpent had already struck inside the United States, and not that long ago. An airborne military test drop in Utah involving VX had gone ever so slightly awry, and the substance killed thousands of head of livestock in the appropriately named location of Skull Valley. Though the Army at first vehemently denied responsibility in the face of accusations made by furious area ranchers, it was that one single incident that led President Nixon to ban all open air chemical weapons testing in 1969.

Yet somehow Qassam, in that same dreadful example of human determination and ingenuity for the worst of all possible goals, had managed to charm this monstrously poisonous snake, and he and his team were still alive and doing well in the final stage of delivery. They had transported the insidious killer nearly halfway around the world, and were now maneuvering it into the position needed to display its full, utterly horrendous potential.

That accomplishment, more than any other one thing, proved to Ezekiel just how resourceful and capable this individual terrorist leader really was. It also stood as irrefutable evidence as to how incredibly dangerous the Hezbollah operative could be when loosed in a world teeming with innocent people, masses of human beings unaware of the reckoning evil that lurked among them.

As in so many other feats, once one had the means and the power everything else became a mere question of logistics and will. Qassam had given ample attention to the logistics, and there remained no question whatsoever of his will to see this appalling plot of mass murder to fruition. Neither was there any doubt that when given the opportunity, he would do so again at another time and place.

The retired colonel thought hard, trying to come up with some improbable angle or weak point in what Qassam had said, or in what Ezekiel had personally observed. No matter how he tried, he still ended up drawing a blank. The plan was completely doable and there was precious little time left to stop it, save for a sudden and complete act of gross incompetence on the part of Qassam and his peers. Either that or some sort of Divine Intervention on the part of the unknowing multitudes, who would soon become the decimated ranks of dead or dying.

It is said that Divine Intervention is only brought on by prayer driven by faith. With nothing else that could be done at present, that was exactly what Ezekiel Templar did now. He began praying as fervently and earnestly as he had ever done before in his life, and hoping that an all-powerful God on high, with His own plan, was listening in.

CHAPTER FIFTEEN

It was somewhere after five in the morning when two of the Hezbollah terrorists joined the guard at the door and made their way into the small room. They kicked and prodded the three hostages to their feet, but one allowed himself the simple humanity of assisting Ezekiel as the captives moved into the larger adjoining room. Micah suspected this was due to specific orders from Qassam, and for reasons other than those akin to any real sort of good intentions.

Standing there and blinking against the harsh artificial light, Micah immediately noticed that the previous pile of equipment and supplies were now absent. The maps were removed from the table, as were the assorted papers and ring binders. Save for an odd plastic bag or empty food container, it was much in the same condition as it had been in when he first arrived, and before Qassam and his Hezbollah terrorists came on the scene. In short, the place had been basically sanitized.

Independently but at the same time, the two other captives were glancing about and coming to the same conclusion. Whatever those assorted maps, guides, notes and supplies had to do with their captors' assigned mission, that phase of the operation where they were useful had passed. Most likely they were now packed away for transportation to another location and/or destroyed for security purposes. That meant that preparations were coming to an end, the next phase would be the beginning of the flight to launch the attack itself.

Qassam stood in the middle of the room with a large smile on his face, evidently more pleased with himself and his evolving situation than he had ever been before. Mustafa stood nearby, arms folded and leaning against a large desk. There was not a hint of merriment appearing anywhere on his features and Micah was not in the least surprised. Rattlesnakes, be they human or otherwise, are incapable of emotion. All they exist for is the opportunity to destroy some other of God's creatures.

"Good morning, gentlemen" Qassam began. "I hope you were able to get a bit of rest. This is going to be a memorable day for all, and each of us should have a clear head to remember the details."

He motioned them over to the same overstuffed couch and Micah sat down, again careful in how he placed his handcuffed wrists and trying to avoid any tension on the devices. Max sat down next to him and Uncle Zeke joined them last of all, hobbling painfully across the room on his wounded leg.

"So that you may follow along for purposes of documentation to what is occurring, you need to know that we have completed the preparatory phase of our assignment. Actually, we made faster progress than hoped for and our timeline is now ahead of schedule. As you can readily imagine, transferring the VX was of particular concern; yet we accomplished it without incident."

Outside, they heard an engine start on one of the Chevrolet Suburbans parked near the Boeing. It began pulling away, using nothing but its parking lamps to maneuver by. The Hezbollah leader turned and watched the vehicle go.

"Things have gone so well that I am sending my support team to get some well-deserved rest at the Albright residence. Once they have done so, they will return here. Together, both they and you will leave this area later in the morning and make your way to a rendezvous point. Following the completion of our mission, the elements of our group will join them as we begin the long journey back to where we came from.

I wanted to speak with you one more time before the next phase commences. As I have said before, no harm will come to you if you behave in a manner as to not cause any undue concern or difficulties. After all, you three will be able to give first-hand accounts as to the preparations for this event as they took place. You will be able to relate the story far better than most anyone else, and it will be a story worthy of the retelling."

Sitting there Ezekiel Templar considered one last try in reasoning with the Hezbollah leader, one last attempt to change the man's mind in some way or manner. But he knew that he would be wasting his breath. People like Qassam never second guessed themselves or questioned their perceived righteousness, especially on something they had labored so hard and so long for. Qassam was a zealot of fanatical proportions, and fanatical zealots can never change their minds or their self-determined reasons for whatever wrong they do to others. Even including mass murder.

The Hezbollah leader seemed to be reading Ezekiel's mind. "What, Colonel? No last ditch plea for the sake of humanity or for the imagined innocent lives that will be lost? No stirring appeal to my intelligence or inner conscience, nor an attempt to influence through some corrupted interpretation of my religion? You do surprise me."

Ezekiel looked up at the terrorist leader with a resigned gaze. "Would it do any good?" he asked.

"Of course not," Qassam chuckled drily in a way that contained no mirth. "But I expected you to try, all the same. Perhaps my reprimand to your left thigh had more effect than I first estimated. Still, I must admit that I am somewhat disappointed.

"Yet be that as it may, I am looking forward to a more leisurely visit with you in the future, under less pressing time restraints. There are events in your past that people of mutual acquaintance would assuredly like to know more about." Looking over at Max, Qassam continued. "In addition, perhaps Herr Grephardt can help sort out a few of the murkier details."

Refocusing back on Ezekiel, the Hezbollah leader remarked, "By the way, I almost forgot to tell you how pleased my pilot is with the condition of your aircraft. He is almost beside himself with the opportunity to fly such an enduring example of American technology from fifty years ago."

Qassam paused for a moment more, and then added in a particularly malicious tone. "It makes one wonder if there will be much of anything concerning the United States of any value, fifty years into the future."

The terrorist smiled again widely, taking full pleasure in the verbal cajoling of his captive audience. Leering over them in an expansive manner, he turned his attention to Micah Templar. Yahla al-Qassam considered himself a man of patience and of disciplined mind, so he had saved the best for last.

"Officer Templar, you might be interested in knowing that Mustafa will be in charge of your little entourage, and will also serve as your guard for the next few hours. I mention this in the hope that you do not give him any excuse to kill you. Do you understand me?"

Micah scowled up at the Hezbollah leader, mentally struggling to keep his temper and tongue in check. Too much was riding on what he said or did at this juncture, and he couldn't tip his hand with any unusual inflection in his voice. Nor could he now let that temper get the best of him. The trooper swallowed the hot anger rushing up through him and responded with a monotoned "I understand."

"Excellent" said Qassam. "It is truly unfortunate your wife chose not to accompany you on your uncle's planned flight to Midland. After all, we did make arrangements for the taking of four hostages. Her presence among us would have suited my plan even better." Glancing over to his second-in-command, he added "I know that Mustafa was looking forward to meeting her. But as they say, *c'est la guerre*."

Micah bit down harder still on the mixture of shock, fear and evolving rage bubbling up from within. Recognizing that Qassam was deliberately trying to bait him into something foolish helped maintain his quaking self-control, along with the knowledge that he literally possessed the key needed in turning Qassam's world upside down. That thought helped him focus beyond the interfering mental confusion of how Qassam knew so much about his family, and the appalling realization the terrorist commander had not only expected Abby to be here, but had planned for it.

Bringing forth every last vestige of calmness that he could muster inside of himself, the highway patrolman looked evenly at the Hezbollah leader. Then Micah quietly replied, "Things have a way of working out, Qassam. One way or the other."

Qassam paused for the merest of moments, glancing at Micah a bit quizzically. The highway patrolman's ability to contain himself and his response were not what the terrorist leader had been expecting. Of the three men before him, every experience in Qassam's life guided him to hold this rural police officer in total disdain. The Hezbollah leader came from a culture where there was very little rule of any law not trumped by the rule of certain ruthless men. Law enforcement officials were corrupt, cruel and bullies of dull intellect who were either manipulated, paid off or done away with.

But Micah Templar posed an enigma to him, a peace officer who was respected and admired in the community that he served for his sense of fairness, integrity and honor in all things. He was also not a simpleton by any means, and possessed a reputation for competence and professionalism that did not reflect in those from Qassam's part of the world.

Shaking himself from this slightest hiatus for contemplation, the terrorist leader proceeded on. "As with the other group my team will rest for the next few hours by your aircraft, so this is the last chance I have to speak with you prior to take off. I see no reason to attempt our flight in darkness, or to deal with the inherent difficulties of navigating in it. San Antonio will still be there in the morning, and our plan calls for a certain time period over target to ensure maximum effectiveness.

"Our schedule is to leave at sunrise and be on our way. Again, I am telling you this is so you can relate the story to others when the time comes. If all goes well, we shall have other discussions following the completion of our mission. My men have been instructed to treat you well, as long as you do not cause any problems. You will be provided with adequate food and water; among other needs you may have."

Leaning forward, he addressed Ezekiel Templar in a slightly conspiratorial tone. "That includes medical treatment for you, Colonel. So like you Americans are fond of saying, please don't screw it up."

Qassam straightened again, a malignant self-satisfaction oozing from every pore. "My team is waiting outside, there are a few minor items needing review before we rest for our launch. So, I will take my leave now and join them. I would say wish me luck, but I seriously doubt you would wish me much of the right kind. Instead, I will share a verse from the Quran that speaks of what is to come this day. For it is written, *'And the True Promise draweth nigh; then behold them, staring wide in terror, the eyes of those who disbelieve!'* Allah'u Akhbar!"

The three captives watched as the Hezbollah leader turned and nodded to Mustafa, who had repeated the obligatory "Allah'u Akhbar" when he heard Qassam utter the religious phrase. The two men stood looking at each other for a moment and then embraced. The terrorist leader took a step back and slapped his second-in-command on the left upper arm, smiling broadly. Mustafa came to attention with a facial expression as impassive as stone, his reptilian eyes brittle and soulless. The two men exchanged their verbal farewells in Arabic, and Qassam stepped briskly out the door.

Mustafa observed his leader through the large plate glass window, making his way to the old bomber. After a long minute he turned his attention to the hostages before him. If his eyes had appeared soulless before, they were now gleaming in a burning hatred mixed with utter contempt. When the terrorist stared directly at him, Micah slowly looked down and away. Starting a contest of personal will at present would accomplish nothing, and could possibly ruin any chance of stopping this madness before it was too late.

Since it did not appear they would be placed in the adjoining room again, the three men began to position themselves on the sofa for individual comfort. Micah noted that his uncle did not say a word and neither did Max. This was probably due to them sharing the same suspicions that he harbored about Mustafa, that the terrorist could understand at least a bit of English. That meant they could no longer risk any verbal communication.

The Hezbollah terrorist glared at the three men from across the room for a bit more, then he made his way over to the chair behind the large metal desk and sat down. From time to time, he would stand up again to look out the window, or walk about the room. Whatever he was doing, he continued to keep a close eye on his prisoners and made note of every single physical move made by any of them.

For his part Micah leaned back in the overstuffed sofa while Ezekiel slowly, painfully eased himself into a standing position. As the old man did so Mustafa gave him his full and undivided attention, following the motion with his reptilian eyes smoldering in hate and disgust. To Micah, the terrorist reminded him of an agitated western diamondback, already coiled and prepared to strike.

Tio Zeke must have noted the same response, because he froze where he stood. In cautious fashion, he made eye contact with Mustafa and then looked over to the chair placed beside the sofa. He let the terrorist follow his line of sight to the piece of furniture, and then cautiously began to sidestep toward it in a hobbling, uneven fashion. Mustafa seemed to relax, but still followed Ezekiel with cold, calculating eyes. The old colonel made it over to the chair and sat down, stretching his aching leg in front of him.

Micah shifted to one side of the sofa for the extra room, while Max did the same against the other. When Mustafa took another long look out the window, the younger Templar studied his uncle to better gauge his condition. In return, Ezekiel locked eyes with him in pointed fashion. The older Templar nodded his head ever so lightly and began shutting his eyelids in a deliberate manner.

The message was clear, for now at least act as if you were resting. Do not give away any signs of animation or possible thoughts of resistance.

Out of the corner of his eye the highway patrolman noted that Max had evidently received the same message, and was already finding a more comfortable position. Admiring again how the two other men communicated so well Micah did the same, but not before settling where he could keep Mustafa in full view through barely opened eyelids. Allowing his head to roll back against the top of the sofa made it that much easier.

Micah reclined there, stretched out with his handcuffed wrists tucked in the open space between his lower back and the sofa itself. He turned his thoughts to what Qassam had said, trying to pick out something that might prove useful or important. The terrorist leader was making a real effort in keeping them informed as to what was occurring, as well as why. Obviously, how his reasoning and actions would be remembered by history were very important to the cell commander.

And exactly what would be remembered? What would the history books say if Qassam's nightmarish plot was allowed to blossom in full fruition? Micah was still trying to get his mind around the staggering devastation that would result if the nerve agent was successfully employed. The younger Templar had seen much of death and destruction in his life, but not anything remotely akin on the scale of what could happen today.

How many would die? Ten thousand? One hundred thousand? Or even more than that? The enormity of it all brought to mind a quote attributed to Robert Kennedy. *"Killing one man is murder,"* Kennedy had proclaimed. *"Killing millions is a statistic."* There was a hard, bitter truth to that revelation. The human mind becomes numb to the boundless horrors attending such overwhelming death tolls of one's own kind. It was simply beyond the intellectual comprehension and emotional cognizance of most people.

In a world where more and more placated themselves with the mistaken belief that all things were relative, such sheer depravity flew in the face of their freshly coined 'new age' philosophies. The idea of good and evil was mentally and emotionally uncomfortable for most and intuitively challenged this kinder, gentler narrative. Their journey through life found them professing little belief in either and blissfully ignoring any evidence to the contrary.

Micah Templar knew better. He had lived a life where both existed in tandem, often enough on a day-to-day basis. Man's unbridled inhumanity to his fellow man was not some feckless byproduct of chance or circumstance, it was a real and enduring primal drive engendering all the vilest elements that lie at some depth in the soul of the species.

This perversely strong passion ran through one conduit or another to ultimately whatever destination where it could do the most harm. It was known as hate, and hate is the byproduct of the evil that occupies some corner, be it small or large, admitted or denied, in all men's hearts.

The seed for such a somber epiphany into the shades and shadows of all men's souls had been planted by his own father, during the time Micah was preparing for his first combat tour to the Republic of South Vietnam. The year was 1966, and the Tonkin Gulf resolution had paved the way for a large-scale Marine Corps involvement into that unhappy land. Micah had come home on leave prior to shipping out and as he stood there waiting for the Greyhound bus, Jeremiah Templar stood with him.

In the interim they had talked of many of the usual things, of livestock, of family and of the need for rain. Yet it was only at the sight of the bus itself that Jeremiah Templar appeared to become more apprehensive as to what was occurring, and perhaps even vulnerable. The idea of his father being vulnerable in the slightest to anything of mortal man's hand was something new to his son, and Micah had found it a bit unsettling. Seeing the bus approach, the elder Templar's countenance darkened with a great sadness mixed with resignation to the bitter remembrances of earlier perilous times.

With the noise of people bustling about and the odor of spent diesel fumes hanging in the air, Jeremiah Templar took Micah's hand in a calloused grip that was stronger than any other his son had known before or since. In that strength was not only the barbed wire and rawhide physical toughness of the man, but also an impassioned yearning from the inner spirit to pass along the hardest-won lesson of all. It was at that moment, in front of that terminal, when Jeremiah Templar cautioned about hate and what it could do to a man.

Peering out from under the brim of his sweat stained, weathered felt hat, his father had said; "Son, you do your duty and stay true to your raising. But whatever you do, try real hard not to hate your enemy. Hate is the mother for most all of the evils in this world. The man you are looking at through rifle sights will probably be fighting for what he believes in, same as you. That don't make him right but it don't make him evil, either.

"There'll come a time when you will confront an evil, and that is the only thing on this earth that you should hate with all your heart. But when you do, keep in mind there is some sort of evil in us all, just looking for an excuse to up and break out. Keep a tight rein on it and on that hate. Because if you ever let that hate start controlling you, the evil within us all will set itself loose. And it will burn hotter than the fires of hell, and consume most everything else good found inside."

With his greenish gray eyes shining with emotion and the gift of hindsight, Jeremiah Templar added, "I know, because I rode that black trail myself for too long. For God's sake, son, as well as your own, you do better than your old man. You come back home whole and in one piece."

As he finished, the bus came to a stop behind them and the door swung open wide. Micah managed to get out a "Yes sir," and picked up the sea bag at his side. Releasing the elder Templar's hand, he turned and tossed it into the bin beneath the passenger compartment. Facing his father again, Micah found there was so much he wanted to say but just could not find the words.

Standing there in his faded blue jeans and long sleeve khaki work shirt, Jeremiah Templar found them for him. "I know son, I know. Now get on that bus."

The young Marine clambered aboard the Greyhound and found a window seat. As it sat idling, he watched his dad standing on the sidewalk with his arms folded. When the bus began moving, Jeremiah Templar raised his right hand above his head, palm out. He kept it that way for as long as the bus remained in view.

Not more than about a year and a half later, Jeremiah Templar breathed his last and passed on into the next world. Weakened and now bereft of his trademark physical toughness, his mind and spirit continued on undaunted to the very end. When the preacher stopped by to pay his respects, by necessity the subject of eternal salvation or damnation came up.

"I have sinned greatly, Reverend, you can be sure on that. It was kill or be killed and for some unknown reason the Lord saw fit that I should survive. Since then, the two of us have had many a serious conversation about all that."

The old man paused, coughing up some of the phlegm that would soon kill him. "I figure myself saved as much as any man can. But if those gates are made of sharpened bamboo and a Jap soldier is standing guard with an Arisaka, I'll know I figured it wrong."

It had taken Micah two tours in Vietnam to fully understand how his father must have felt, fighting his own war against a cunning, implacable and far more numerous enemy. From there, it had taken still longer with a Bible to fully appreciate Tio Zeke's viewpoint. Yet in the end, Micah Templar considered himself a better man for both experiences.

CHAPTER SIXTEEN

Occupying the other side of the sofa, Max Grephardt considered options and actions from behind his obscuring screen of closed eyelids. The old Luftwaffe *hauptmann* realized too well the three of them were going to have to try something, anything, before the time for doing so went completely away.

Thinking upon the potential personal risks involved, there was not one soul among the millions who lived in the city of San Antonio whom he could call friend, or even say they were some sort of close acquaintance. He was nothing more than a brief visitor to this part of the world, some place he came to occasionally because of a desire to spend time with the unlikeliest of old friends and once more be among those of his own kind.

It did not matter so much if they were German or American or whatever, they shared his passion for flying and he appreciated their same enduring passion in return. More so, he had more in common with some of these men than he did with many of those from his own home land, even if they had been on the other side of a terrible war during an incomparably heartbreaking period of his life.

Though they had once been enemies he harbored a great admiration for both them and this grand country called America, that had birthed and nurtured such men. With his own eyes he had seen time and again this young, sometimes childlike nation from the New World at its very best, as well at its most formidable.

When at its most formidable, this upstart country had proven to be an awe inspiring engine of destruction, sweeping away all attempts to stop or deny it from the goal of unconditional surrender on the part of its opponents. Yet when that hard won victory had been realized, he was even more awed in seeing this melting pot of humanity when at its very best.

He had heard knowledgeable scholars say the military forces of the United States of America has seized more enemy territory than any other armed force that ever existed.

What made them unique, though, in their martial accomplishments among the great powers of the world was their open discomfort to any notion of empire building. That exceptionalism and singular system of beliefs had, in turn, led them to give back more conquered territory than any other sovereign power in recorded history, often leaving the vanquished land and populace in better circumstance than first found.

So had it been in his own country and with his own life. Max Grephardt bore personal witness to the astonishing rebirth of what had been little more than an utterly defeated collection of burnt ashes. West Germany had risen from a physical and psychological obliteration to take its place among the major manufacturing and financial forces on the planet. Yet it had not managed to accomplish this miraculous reconstitution alone.

During this arduous rebuilding process, the people of the United States did not stand idly by and let their struggling former enemy fend for themselves. This remarkable nation had shared in the expenditure of planning, effort and treasure to make Germany's phenomenal rise from those same pitiful ashes a heretofore unheard-of reality.

It was the Americans who had developed and employed the Marshall Plan, and it was the Americans who had helped most in standing against the mammoth Soviet menace that loomed over the new Germany. When the Communists tried to choke the life out of a resurging Berlin, it was the Americans who provided the brunt of assistance in the ensuing airlift to keep the Soviets from doing so.

When the Communists erected their infamous wall and attending death strips, it had been an American president who had stood at that wall and proclaimed, *"Ich bin ein Berliner."* A quarter of a century later, it was another American president who stood at the Brandenburg Gate and demanded, *"Mr. Gorbachev, tear down this wall!"* The force and conviction of these two great leaders of a great people made the rest of the world pause and take notice.

That wall did come down, and Germany at present was becoming one nation again after decades of forced division and immeasurable human miseries. No other one power was more responsible for this long-anticipated achievement than the United States of America.

In the midst of this decades' long struggle, Max Grephardt had gone on like so many others to make a new life for himself in his revitalized *Vaterland*. He had invested everything he had in the future of Germany, including his own heart, mind and backbone.

Like his father, he and his wife Anna had raised five sons and now were grandparents several times over. His family lived in a free country as a free people in a nation now prosperous, respected, and with the real possibilities of an even brighter future ahead. With the coming reunification, who knew what heights the people of this new Germany might soar to?

However, such expectant optimism was blunted by a disturbing and equally vital, unanswered question. What human depravities would also be a part of that same future? Because within his lifespan there had already been two great evils, which under the same guise of a brighter future had nearly devoured not only himself, but everything else that he ever cared about.

Both of these evils corrupted and laid waste to the very best qualities that constitute humankind, and left it with a pried open Pandora's Box bubbling with a potent brew made of the darkest elements of man's inner self. Max Grephardt had experienced great personal pain and sorrow due to that pried open box, and walked with the severe knowledge that the most important lessons in life often come at the highest price.

The first great evil of Nazism had nearly obliterated both family and country. It had been so insidious and deceiving that he and tens of millions of others had blindly followed it without question, at least beyond the point of impending catastrophe. In turn the second one, Communism, had tried to kill him and had taken up where Nazism left off in destroying his home as well as his birthright. Both had only been defeated after a long and difficult contention, documented in near immeasurable quantities of human tears, human sorrows and human blood.

Now there was a third great evil to be reckoned with and Max had been acutely aware of its exponential growth for some time. He had first watched it wantonly murder innocent people at Munich in 1972, while still in its fitfully malicious infancy. As the years went by and this third evil cast its ominous shadow on the Western world like some mythical monster of darkness, Max Grephardt realized it was destined to join the ranks of both Nazism and Communism.

Over the intervening decades it had morphed into something superbly cruel and dangerous, an implacable wickedness that hid behind a corrupted religious doctrine to do its filthy business. The result was something intrinsically vile with no real sense of conscience or decency, as it involved deistic fanatics who could explain away any atrocity with a serene sense of divine self-righteousness.

That one difference, separating it from the prior two great evils, could make this cancerous phenomenon far more ominous than the others put together.

When Max looked into the eyes of Yahla al-Qassam, the elderly German recognized the obscene promise being fulfilled by the fanatical malevolence shining from within. This aberrant mutation of a seventh century prophet had reached its full maturity, and a world some fourteen centuries later was being forced to deal with the resultant raging beast. If allowed to go unchecked, that beast would continue to procreate in ways the other two great evils never contemplated.

Max Grephardt had already made his peace with this unsettling conclusion, and the things that must be done to combat it. No one desires to stand in the path of an unrelenting enemy, an enemy who has been driven absolutely insane by the inner demons that permeated a blackened soul. Such a conflict could never end in any real truce, or be allowed to stalemate with the warring factions agreeing to return to their own homes and keep to themselves. By necessity it would be a fight to the death, and on occasion would continue even beyond there.

Max would always be grateful to America, one only had to be aware of the effects of Soviet rule in Eastern Europe to fully appreciate American idealism and beliefs. Yet in this fight, his desire to be allied with those who had done so much for him and what he held dearest was only part. It went far deeper than that, and carried a rippling effect beyond the individual, the family, the community or the body politic. It even went beyond the continued existence of sovereign powers such as Germany or the United States.

For this would be a battle for the hearts and minds of humankind itself, wherever they came from and whatever their station in life might be. There would be no neutral countries, no diplomatic resolutions and no safe havens for those who wished to remain uninvolved. Max knew there was no good war, but there were definitely necessary ones. And in a necessary war it was the duty of every person to do what they could to defeat the common enemy, no matter what the cost.

In Max Grephardt's mind a decaying airstrip in the vast, arid expanses of West Texas was indeed a long way from that small Lutheran church along the banks of the Werra, but it was where he would make his stand. The enemy was here, the time was now. The silver-haired holder of the Knight's Cross of the Iron Cross with Oak Leaves prepared himself as any good soldier would, steeling both heart and spirit to act when called upon. All that he needed was the slimmest chance and briefest of openings to make the crucial difference.

CHAPTER SEVENTEEN

Micah Templar watched Mustafa through almost closed eyes. Yahla al-Qassam had repeatedly referred to the big Lebanese as his best man, and that his second in command did not need a gun to kill someone. However, the terrorist had one now, a blued Smith & Wesson Model 59 9mm shoved down inside the front of his pants. There appeared to be no extra magazines for it, or evidence of other weapons seen on Mustafa's person.

The former Marine sized the terrorist up and tried to recall anything else he might have heard or noticed about Mustafa over the past few hours. From what Qassam had said, the long-haired Hezbollah member was some sort of martial arts fighter and he certainly looked the part. With a broad, hawkish nose that had obviously been broken before, Micah had noted he was appreciably taller than the other Arabs, even more so than himself and with a fine, muscular build.

Everything about the man, from the way he carried himself to the smoldering disdain displayed for his prisoners, exuded an entrenched confidence that pointed to much more than misplaced arrogance.

There was something else also, a special kind of essential cruelty that oozed out of every pore of Mustafa's body. When he looked at Micah, the terrorist's eyes smoldered with a hate that went beyond what any semi-sane person could convey. Micah had seen that kind of look before, but never in such heaping portions of undisguised intensity and singleness in purpose. From his experiences as a peace officer as well as a combat veteran, he knew all too well what kind of person their lives were presently balanced upon.

Outside a thin ray of sunshine began peeking through the window facing the airstrip, and one of the Wright Cyclones on *The Uvalde Raider* began to turn over. The engine rotated slowly, coughing once or twice, and then roared to mechanical life. Looking out of the corner of his eye, Micah saw that neither Max nor Tio Zeke stirred at the sound. Either they were so tired from the drawn out night they had actually dozed off, or they were lost in their own thoughts of how to stop this madness in the critically short time remaining. Whichever it was, Micah's very being strained ferociously to make the most of those same disappearing minutes.

Lured by the crescendo of throbbing radial engines starting up one by one, Mustafa moved to the large picture window in an attempt to see what was occurring outside. He tried several positions from different angles but none were evidently to his satisfaction. Plainly aggravated, he turned away and for a long moment suspiciously eyed his three prisoners. Micah stilled everything in his body except for his slow, steady breathing as if asleep.

Finally, much like the proverbial cat overcome by his own curiosity, the terrorist turned again and made his way to the door. He placed his hand on the knob, took one more look over his shoulder at the three restrained men, and stepped outside on the porch to watch the old bomber warming up.

This was what Micah had been waiting for, praying for. As Mustafa stepped to the side and away from the open doorway, Micah began fumbling frenetically with the inside of the waistband of his uniform trousers, near the center of his back. The terrorists had searched him thoroughly and removed his pocket knife, wallet, keys, belt, and even the small change in his front pocket. But there was one unusually shaped piece of metal they did not take, because they never found it.

As his fingers groped and clawed at the hidden enclosure securing the key, he glanced around to see both Max and his uncle fully awake and observing him intently. *"Watch the door,"* he hissed under his breath, as the key came out and into his hand. Working with swollen, half-numbed digits from the lack of blood flow, he strained blindly to find the tiny lock hole in the right cuff face. By sense of touch Micah finally found what he was looking for, inserted the key and twisted it clumsily. The cuff came loose.

Quickly he brought his hands to the front and removed the other handcuff, noiselessly placing the devices on a nearby sofa cushion. Coming up to a crouch, he vigorously rubbed his raw and inflamed wrists to bring some kind of life back into them. At the same time, he divided his attention between the door and looking for something to cut the zip ties on the wrists of Tio Zeke and Max, who had meantime struggled to their feet.

The younger Templar made his way to the large steel desk sitting near the back wall of the office, rummaging frantically through the drawers in search of something to remove the zip ties. The room began vibrating with the deafening roar of the Wright R-1820s revving up outside. The sound changed into a massive bellow as the Flying Fortress began moving, slowly gathering speed as it accelerated down the runway. Micah knew they were running out of those few remaining minutes, and fast.

"Look out, Nephew!" Ezekiel yelled, and the highway patrolman looked up to the see Mustafa looming in the doorway. Their eyes met and the Lebanese grabbed for the Smith & Wesson nine-millimeter in his waistband. Instinctively, Micah charged the terrorist from across the room. Even as he began to move, he knew his effort was futile. He was simply too slow, too far away, and the steel desk partially blocked his angle of attack.

It was as if everything had gone into the slow-motion sequence of a Sam Peckinpah movie as he propelled himself forward. The pistol cleared

Mustafa's waistband, and Micah saw the muzzle coming up and pointing squarely at his face. The barrel spit flame and he heard the first-round crack by his left ear. The long, heavy double action trigger pull, along with the terrorist's surprise and haste, had caused the jacketed hollow point to miss Micah's head by scant fractions of an inch.

Still in his perceived slow-motion mode and totally focused on the threat posed by the pistol, somewhere in a detached part of his mind Micah marveled at his ability to clearly see Mustafa's trigger finger start to move back again for the second shot. The muzzle was now centered on Micah's chest, and the trooper willed himself forward even faster, mentally bracing for what was to come.

And then the muzzle was no longer there, blocked from view by the back of the black pearl snap western shirt worn by Max Grephardt. The former German Luftwaffe officer, still cuffed with zip ties, had rushed in from the side and interposed himself between Micah and the pistol in Mustafa's right hand. Neither of the two protagonists had seen him move, having been completely absorbed in the tunnel vision created by the threat of the other.

The sound of the nine-millimeter exploded again in the confines of the room, followed immediately by two more quick, panicky shots as Max's body slammed into both the terrorist and the pistol he was holding. The two interlocked men hit the open-door frame and bounced back inside together. Micah, still focused on the threat, grabbed at the Smith & Wesson with both hands and forced it up and away as Grephardt crumpled to the floor at their feet.

Recovering from the suddenness of his evolving situation, the terrorist fought savagely to maintain control of the weapon still clenched in his right hand. The muzzle pointed skyward as the two men shoved, grappled, elbowed and swore at each other in a primeval fury driven by desperation. The trooper could hear the Lebanese screaming something unintelligible in Arabic into his ear, and he could feel as well as smell the hot, stinking breath and spittle that accompanied it.

Realizing quickly the longer the fight lasted; the more likely the younger, more physically fit Mustafa would gain ultimate control of the pistol, the highway patrolman shifted his death grip on the Smith & Wesson and pushed the magazine release. The fully loaded magazine fell away from the Model 59 and clattered loudly on the concrete floor, automatically engaging the factory safety that would not allow the weapon to fire again.

As they struggled, the terrorist managed to bring the pistol back down to chest level between the two men. Bracing his back against the retaining wall and with both hands wrapped around the Smith & Wesson itself, Mustafa shoved hard against Micah. The trooper was sent reeling backwards, losing his own grip on the pistol and nearly falling over.

Mustafa took a classic two-handed stance with the Model 59 and smiled grimly at his enemy, pressing the weapon's trigger as Micah lunged forward again. Through the haze of close combat, Micah gave a quick prayer of thanks when the trigger went to the rear and nothing happened. The terrorist's face changed to a puzzled look of astonishment, and then changed again as Micah hit him square in the mouth with a hard right fist. Mustafa's head snapped back from the punch, and blood began flowing between loosened teeth and spread into his mouth.

But if anything else, the Hezbollah terrorist was a seasoned fighter and the taste of his own blood was a familiar one. In return he swung down hard with the pistol in his outstretched right hand. The butt of the Smith & Wesson struck a solid blow to the top of the highway patrolman's head, sending an erupting shower of crimson into the air and leaving an ugly gash almost to the bone.

The impact stunned Micah to his very core, and he staggered drunkenly backwards as he tried to keep sight of the terrorist through the stars, planets and galaxies bursting in his head and clouding his vision. Fighting to maintain his balance, not to mention his consciousness, he watched as Mustafa nonchalantly cast the pistol aside and assume some sort of martial arts fighting stance. Somewhat disconcertedly he gave Micah that same grim, smug smile, but now with scarlet tinged teeth.

Micah set himself for a moment, breathing with large gulps and feeling the warm flow of his own blood running down the side of his face. With his right forearm, he wiped the red mist away to clear his vision as his legs steadied. Taking his own fighting position while eyeing his opponent, Micah Templar slung his head like a wild Brahma bull and charged forward once more.

But as he tried to close with the terrorist, he found himself attempting to make contact with a ghost. Qassam had not exaggerated about Mustafa's formidable fighting skills, Micah's best punches were either deflected or found nothing but empty air. The highway patrolman simply could not put knuckles against the longer reach of the Lebanese. Every move he made was countered by hand strikes and kicks that found their mark much of the time.

Doggedly Micah battled on, trying to find a part of his enemy that he could either grasp or strike in return. An elbow slam came out of no place, hitting Micah hard just above the left eye which began swelling rapidly. A kick caught him high on the right side of his torso, and he felt at least one rib crack from the impact. Another kick caught him full on the left side of his lower thigh, striking the peroneal nerve area and threatening to buckle his leg underneath him. Through the growing murkiness of pain and anguished gasps for air Micah realized that he was in the fight of his life, and that he was losing.

Again, the dazed and bloodied Texan staggered back, every fiber in his being just wanting to lay down and call it a day. He was some twenty years beyond his prime and about the same over his fighting weight, and Micah felt every bit of both like a crushing weight upon his shoulders, trying to force him down to the cold cement floor beneath his boot soles.

The highway patrolman could only see through his right eye now, as the left one had swelled mostly shut. His fists hung loosely at his sides like heavy stones, and he moved his head slowly to the side and spit out a mixture of blood, chipped tooth, and saliva. He was tired, hurt and wore down more than he could ever have imagined being before. He was done. He knew it and Mustafa, still with his smug little smile, knew it too.

Through the enveloping fog of physical injury and mental despair oozing through him, he heard a voice saying something loudly, urgently. It was a voice he had known since childhood, speaking words that had carried down in his family from generation to generation. The voice belonged to Tio Zeke, who was hobbling forward with everything he had left as he attempted to rouse his spent and near defeated kinsman.

"Micah Templar, remember who you are and where you come from!" Ezekiel bellowed. Moving much too fast for his own condition, the wounded leg gave out from under the old colonel. With his hands tied behind and nothing to soften the impact, the elderly man landed hard with his face on the unyielding concrete floor. Ezekiel Templar shrugged off the bone jarring fall and rolled to his side, trying to get a knee underneath and regain his footing.

"Don't you give up, he'll kill you" Ezekiel implored in a loud, rasping breath. "You're the one chance for a lot of innocent people. We've got to stop that plane!"

Ezekiel's call to arms also carried into the ears of Micah's tormentor. Mustafa shifted his dark eyes, still glowing with certain victory, over to the old man struggling vainly to get back to his feet. Those eyes narrowed into the focused visage of the near supernatural cruelty seething from within. The Hezbollah terrorist began moving toward Ezekiel Templar with the look and manner of someone preparing to squash an unwanted bug beneath their shoe.

At that precise moment, Micah felt something strange and powerful stirring inside him. Perhaps it was the legacy of a hundred and seventy years of Templars in Texas, coupled with the Marine Corps pride that still coursed through his veins. Perhaps it was the silver badge on his chest that read "Texas Department of Public Safety--Trooper" and everything of worth that carried with it.

Perhaps it was the limitless grace of an all-powerful God who does listen when mortal man calls upon Him for the strength to continue on. Whatever it was, it all came together and took the form of something totally inexplicable to most anybody else, unless they have made that same journey into the stygian breach themselves.

The overwhelming wave of agony and despair began to roll back, along with the physical as well as inner exhaustion accompanying those sensations. Call it a second wind, or the will to survive, or divine inspiration or even darkest desperation. Call it what you will, but Micah Templar was feeling it sweep through both body and spirit like a furiously wild, west Texas thunderstorm that boils and blows and wreaks havoc on whatever lies below.

Down in one's semi-subconscious where memories met substance Micah not only heard Tio Zeke yelling at him, but also his own father along with the shouting choruses of a thousand other voices from cow camps along the Nueces to Parris Island to the Republic of South Vietnam and back to DPS Recruit School. They were all encouraging him, cajoling him, shaming him to keep pushing forward and through the challenges each had faced themselves, in their own times.

No. Not now, not ever. This was a fight to the finish and if he was going to go down, he was going to go down game and still swinging.

"Hey, *Crotalo!*" Micah growled through split, swollen lips. "Don't crawl off now. We ain't through yet, not by a long shot."

The animal-like intimation in Micah's voice halted the terrorist in his tracks. Mustafa did not understand the words themselves so much as he understood the tone, and what it meant. There was still some fight left in this man, this hated Marine. He apparently did not realize how badly outclassed and already defeated he was, at least not yet. The Hezbollah terrorist turned to face Micah again, and to begin the lesson anew.

Micah stood there, battered and bruised but with the glint of unbroken defiance in his grayish-green eyes. The Texan knew he could not stand and go heel-to-toe with Qassam's second in command, he would be fighting the Shi'a Lebanese to his own liking where he could best use his martial arts skills. What Micah needed was a game changer, something unexpected to even the odds stacked so perilously against him. The trooper set his jaw, ducked his head and charged forward one more time.

As he closed the distance, he picked his mark and concentrated on the waist of the Hezbollah operative. The lawman already carried the bitter experience in just how quick and formidable Mustafa was while on his feet. Micah intended to take him off those feet and knew that no matter how quickly the Arab could move or feint, the man would still be where his waist was. Like any good linebacker who takes a bead on a crazy-legged ball carrier, the key to bringing him down was to focus on the waist.

Boring in, Micah felt the impact of the strikes as he bulled his way through his opponent's defenses. The younger, more agile terrorist had been expecting the older man to try to throw a punch or pull up short for some sort of kick. He was not expecting the semi-crouched Texan to come at him like some sort of maddened feral hog, smashing his way through high grass and tangled undergrowth as if they were nothing more than small clumps of summer daisies.

At the last moment the terrorist realized what was about to happen, and tried to sidestep the oncoming freight train. As the Lebanese began to shift his body the trooper cut the distance, noticing the movement in Mustafa's waist and adjusting his angle to make up the difference. Micah's arms and hands, until now tucked in tight against his head and body to help deflect the blows, opened up and wrapped around as the two men collided. The trooper drove his right shoulder deep into the Arab's right torso, just below the rib cage. Pumping his legs rapidly with everything he had left, Micah lifted the terrorist off his feet and carried him backwards across the room.

The lawman's newly found momentum powered both to the opposite end, only dissipating itself when the highway patrolman slammed the Lebanese into the bare cinder block wall. He took heart at the sound of air being knocked from the man's lungs, as well as a loud thud as the back of Mustafa's head smacked against the painted surface. Keeping his stunned adversary pinned and unable to move away, Micah began hooking the terrorist in the lower torso with a series of vicious, achingly effective uppercuts and crosses. Powerful elbows and fists rocketed into Mustafa's lower gut, floating ribs and both kidneys.

Enraged beyond reason or care, Micah continued to pound the Hezbollah terrorist unmercifully. As he felt the man begin to wilt against him, the Texan grabbed one arm and a fistful of blue jeans near the belly button. Using his own strength and weight as leverage he took a step to the side and spun on the balls of both feet, flinging the terrorist across the room and sending him crashing into and over the large steel desk. The highway patrolman promptly followed in pursuit, scrambling over the desk and on top of the sprawled body below him. When Micah came down, he landed with both knees squarely in Mustafa's chest.

Reaching over and intertwining the fingers of his left hand in the Arab's long black hair, Micah dallied off and began rapidly striking the man in the face with his right fist. With each punch, he'd give a bit of slack and the back of the terrorist's head would bounce off the concrete floor. Methodically, Micah would then pull Mustafa's head back up and hit him again with all the inner fury remaining.

Finally, Micah stopped and untwined his fingers from Mustafa's hair, letting his head bang against the floor one final time. Dead, dying or simply beat unconscious, the Hezbollah second in command was no longer a threat. Micah braced against the prostate body and staggered unsteadily to his feet, peering through a film of blood with his one good eye at Tio Zeke and the deathly still form of Max Grephardt.

Leaning on trembling legs upon the desk, Micah reached over and fumbled through the top drawer with bruised, shaking fingers that seemed to have a mind of their own. He found an old pair of nail clippers and as quickly as he could, made his way over to Ezekiel. The trooper knelt down and laboriously cut the zip ties from the elder Templar's swollen, bloody wrists. Immediately the old colonel began half stumbling, half crawling toward the body by the door, calling out Max's name all the while.

With Micah's help, the two men rolled the German over and into Ezekiel's lap. Tio Zeke sat there on the floor, supporting his friend's upper torso as Micah began examining the ugly nine-millimeter holes in Max's chest and stomach. The German's breathing was uneven and punctuated with a sickening, rattling wheeze. Bright red, frothy fluid bubbled out the corner of Grephardt's mouth each time he exhaled.

The movement brought Max back to a dreamy state of semi-consciousness. He opened his eyes to blurry images above him; talking to him, consoling him, trying to help him. Though they were hard to see through the gathering darkness, he knew who they were. He reached out weakly, haltingly to the one who was holding him. A warm, familiar clasp met his hand more than halfway. He could feel other hands frantically trying to staunch the steady flow of blood, along with the air escaping from his perforated lung.

"Easy Max, just take it easy", the familiar voice was saying. "You're going to be all right. Stay with me, Max."

Another voice was speaking in a lower tone, worried and obviously flustered. "He's in really bad shape. I don't know of anything else to do."

"I know, nephew."

"Tio, he saved my life and I can't help him."

"I know, Micah. I know."

The first voice moved closer to his ear. "Hear that, Max? You made the difference, Micah did for the one who shot you and we'll get the rest. You've got my word on that, Max, every last mother's son of them."

Yes, he knew that voice. He understood the words and wanted to smile in response, to show them that he was still in the fight. But the blurry figures were growing dimmer and their voices kept fading away. Max tried to concentrate on taking air in and breathing it out, but it was as if a tremendously heavy boulder was sitting on his chest, crushing the life out of him.

As the pale rider came nearer and his mind continued to drift, he was no longer laying on a concrete floor in west Texas, but rather in the late summer grass of Germany back in 1945. He could almost feel the blistering heat from the burning Skymaster, and he was struggling again to breathe with the acrid smoke and sooty debris lodged deep in his lungs.

Max Grephardt could feel fingers upon the small silver cross that had hung around his neck over all the intervening years. That same voice was in his ear again, thanking him. Telling him how much he valued his friendship and for being there for him so many times. The voice was talking about saving other lives today. Then a few words that he heard in clarity.

"Don't die on me, Max! Please don't die!"

He tried once more to smile, to reassure his friend that he would be all right. But he couldn't, he was just too tired. And from the other side of the vanishing veil other loving, long gone hands were reaching out for him. They were lifting him up as if he weighed no more than a feather, and beginning to pull him through that veil to what lay beyond.

Ezekiel's voice was going away, he felt so sorry for him in his great grief. The last few words that he could discern came to his ears.

"...*Gute reise, mein freund.* God be with you..."

And Max knew that God was.

Secure in that knowledge, Maximillian Friedrich Grephardt, holder of the Knight's Cross of the Iron Cross with Oak Leaf Cluster, a warrior among warriors and a man among men, felt himself drifting even further.

And the light from the bright sunny morning in this world went away, while another shined far more brightly just ahead.

CHAPTER EIGHTEEN

"Tio, he's gone." Micah continued to search for a pulse yet knew the effort was useless.

With his nephew's help, Ezekiel Templar eased out from under Max's body and gently laid his friend's head upon the floor. Carefully, haltingly, the old colonel forced himself to stand up. His head felt woozy and his left leg ached and trembled, while his eyes started watering in a gathering wave of near unbearable sorrow. He struggled mightily to remember what was paramount now and blinked hard to stem the tide, there was no time for that.

Then the anguish transformed into a deep, dutiful anger, mixed with a deadly sense of purpose that came welling up from within.

"We have to stop the Raider," Zeke rasped as he started hobbling through the doorway and on to the porch.

"With what?" asked Micah.

"With that," Ezekiel Templar said, raising his arm and pointing to the gray camouflaged Messerschmitt fighter. "Qassam never did figure I could fly the 109, too. Time for him to find out different."

"Tio, that plane has no guns and I'm not even sure they left it flyable." Micah did not want to say it, but he was wondering if Ezekiel Templar was in any condition for much of the same.

"Just get me in the cockpit and give me something to shoot with," spat back the elder Templar. "And you had better make it fast, before the rest of that bunch shows up to rendezvous with their buddy Mustafa."

Both men knew the clock was running out as Ezekiel trudged in painful, halting steps toward the Messerschmitt. Micah, unsure of Mustafa's condition and with no time to make a real determination, simply dragged the Hezbollah member to the metal rail at the front of flight shack and handcuffed him to it. After a quick search of the terrorist, he returned inside and retrieved the dropped Smith & Wesson Model 59, easing the slide back and checking for a loaded chamber. Stepping over to the weapon's discarded magazine, he reached down and slammed it home.

By now Ezekiel had managed to make it to the little fighter and was limping around the outside of the 109, conducting a quick once over. His left leg burned like fire as he moved about, but he only gritted his teeth and kept at the task. Everything looked serviceable exterior wise and since the Messerschmidt's inverted vee engine had been run just yesterday afternoon, there wasn't a possible problem with the traditional bugaboo of oil drainage into the combustion chambers. They were still in business.

Micah shuffled over to help his uncle on to the wing root and into the cockpit. Settling himself inside, the first thing Zeke noticed was the instrument panel. Someone had smashed several of the gauges and other assorted ancillary equipment in a clumsy, amateurish attempt to disable the airplane.

The most critical damage had been done to the radio, effectively cancelling any communications for outside assistance. Beyond not being able to broadcast a warning about *The Uvalde Raider* and its deadly cargo, the harm done did not bother Ezekiel Templar much. He had flown with shot out instruments and no radio before.

As the older Templar began a hasty check of the flight systems and control surfaces of the Messerschmidt, Micah started hunting around for something, anything for his uncle to fight with beyond a nine-millimeter pistol with maybe eleven rounds left in the mag. Mustering as much speed as his aching ribs would allow, he made his way over to where the vehicles were parked.

His first stop was his Dodge Ramcharger. A quick examination revealed the terrorists had ransacked the vehicle, and made confetti of the electrical wiring beneath the dash as well as under the hood. He also noted the opened top of his lock box behind the rear seat, showing they had found his Marlin .30/30.

Disgusted, he moved over to the tan Suburban sitting next to the Dodge and looked inside. In plain view was his Marlin laying on the front seat, along with his holstered Model 28 .357 Magnum and a collapsible stocked AK47. Micah tried to open the driver's door but it was locked. He had found no keys in his hasty pat down of the handcuffed Hezbollah second in command, so he moved back about five steps and put a round of nine-millimeter through the side window glass.

At the report of the unexpected shot, Ezekiel whipped his head around and then relaxed as he realized what his nephew was doing. He returned to completing his checks and pressed the master switch for the upgraded starting system Max had installed. He hand-primed the fuel system, activated the generator and fuel pumps, and let his hand pause over the starter handle for a moment. Taking a deep breath to confirm the sequence, he pulled the handle.

Micah heard the starter drive whine and then engage as the Daimler Benz 605A began turning over. Slowly, reluctantly at first, the three big propeller blades began to rotate, followed by a cough and belch of blackish smoke out the exhaust stacks. The engine ignited, and the surrounding area was filled with the deafening crescendo of an inverted V-12 as Zeke busied himself with the fuel mixture and prop settings. He revved it up quickly, bracing against the open hinged canopy to keep it from being slammed shut by the kicked-up cyclone of wind.

Moving to the mottled gray fighter, Micah placed his right foot in the spring-loaded step embedded in the Messerschmitt's fuselage, and placed his left on the root of the port wing. Leaning as far as he could into the cockpit to escape the exhaust noise and prop wash, he handed Zeke the loaded AK47. The trooper also gave his uncle a scrounged canteen of water.

"Thirty round mag with one in the tube!" he yelled into Zeke's left ear. "This is safe, this is full auto and this is semi!" Micah continued, working the weapon's safety lever for emphasis as Zeke looked on. "Sights are on battle sight zero! Keep the muzzle up in the cockpit!"

Ezekiel Templar nodded his head in affirmation, signaling that he understood. He opened the canteen and took a long, filling draught of water and followed up with another. His thirst satisfied, he capped the container and handed it back to Micah.

For a long second the two men stared intently into the other's eyes. Not a word was spoken, but each took a long look into their kinsman's soul. As far back as he could remember, Micah had heard stories about this man and what he faced over the skies of Europe, and of his many accomplishments after the war. Now, at an age where most were living off past glories and thinking of a retirement home, United States Air Force Colonel Ezekiel J. Templar was flying one last mission. They both knew it was the most important one of his life.

"*Buena Suerte*, Tio Zeke." Micah mouthed the words. Ezekiel did not answer, but rather held his left hand high and gave a thumbs up. Micah stepped off the wing root as Zeke pulled the canopy over and down, securing it. The highway patrolman ducked his head and turned away as the Messerschmitt's engine revved again, sending back a biting blast of dirt, gravel, grit and assorted debris.

The Me109 began rolling, making its turn to the southeast as it entered the runway. The pitch of the engine changed into a howling rage as Ezekiel advanced the throttle as far as he dared. The lithe fighter plane gained speed quickly, and Micah watched as it retracted its awkward looking landing gear even as the wheels lifted off the tarmac. Once in its natural element, the German fighter rocketed up and away, toward where the Flying Fortress had disappeared some than twenty minutes before.

Micah stood there listening, as the usual sounds of a West Texas October morning began to come back to his ears and the snarling echo of the DB 605A faded away.

"God speed, Tio Zeke" he murmured to himself. "God speed, and good hunting."

Snapping his mindset forward to what lay at hand, Micah began buckling on the DPS issued Sam Brown belt and checking the loads in his Smith and Wesson .357 magnum. Holstering the big revolver, the peace officer topped off the magazine of the Marlin after jacking a round into the chamber. Setting the hammer on the rifle at half cock, he moved off to the side and toward concealment as he eyed the dirt road leading to the Albright Ranch headquarters.

They would be coming now. If not to pick up Mustafa, then to investigate the pistol shots, and the unexpected sight and sound of the Messerschmitt revving up and leaving. Taking a long swig from the canteen he had his fill of what remained, sloshed the last bit around in his mouth and spit it back out. The paltry remains still inside the container he poured over his head, wiping it with his left hand to wash away some of the blood in his hair and on his face. Gingerly he probed the ugly gash in his skull with his fingertips, it was still bleeding slightly and hurt like the blazes when touched.

Pitching the empty canteen away, Micah began working his bruised and battered fingers, shifting the rifle from one hand to the other as he did so. His cartridge loops were full of 125 grain hollow point ammunition, and extra rounds for the .30/30 were riding loose in his front trouser pockets. In the distance, he could see a plume of dust rising in the direction of the ranch house, and he caught the drifting sound of a vehicle's engine going through the gears, moving fast.

'Bring it on, boys,' he thought to himself, *'Time is short and Hell's a waitin'.'*

CHAPTER NINETEEN

Ezekiel Templar was back where he belonged, and he was pushing the mottled gray Me 109 Gustav for all it was worth. He had jammed the folding stock AK up against the right side of the cramped cockpit, away from his throbbing left thigh. Moving around on the leg back at the airstrip and then using it to work the rudder had started the bleeding again, and Zeke could feel the warm red seepage oozing slowly down his thigh and soaking into the fighter's seat cushion.

With no compass, no radio, and precious little other instrumentation, he was literally flying by the bloodstained seat of his pants. But he did have decades of experience in his favor, and an innate feel for an aircraft which few other men could ever equal or even really understand. From the very beginning, flying had come as naturally for him as breathing.

That beginning, nearly a half century before, had taken place in the same area he was now racing above. From the very start of his primary flight training, the retired colonel had flown over this part of Texas. Before then, he had grown up in this general area as had other generations of his family. Ezekiel had driven it, rode it by horseback and walked many a mile on the land below for one reason or another. The canyons, creek beds, high ground and flats that made up much of the Hill Country were well known landmarks to him, guiding him along his present blazing pace to San Antonio.

Because of his need to impress others, as well as having his horrific plan well documented, Yahla al-Qassam had given Ezekiel Templar much of the information needed to find the hijacked Flying Fortress. The parts missing were filled in easily enough by Ezekiel's own intimate knowledge of what *The Uvalde Raider* was capable of, as well as the terrain features and flyover routes of the targeted area. Furthermore, and owing to his military background, he also possessed some knowledge of weaponized chemical agents and their favored employment.

Pushing the Messerschmidt onward for all that it was worth, more perceptions and details entered Zeke's thinking as to the consequences hanging in the balance. Giving the monster his proper credit, Qassam was an intelligent, well-educated and fanatically devoted man who had formulated a scheme possessing a very high chance of success. Presently, every mile *The Uvalde Raider* traveled in the direction of San Antonio made that chance for success even more of a reality.

VX was the most lethal nerve agent ever synthesized by any known weapons laboratory, a hundred times more deadly than its closest counterpart Sarin.

With a properly designed and functioning system to dispense the nerve agent, those 500 gallons could cut a swath of devastation that would be mind boggling. The death toll would be heartbreaking and parts of San Antonio uninhabitable for months to come.

Not only that, but the VX would spread throughout the encompassing region with its innate high persistency. A vehicle with the smallest smudge of VX could travel hundreds of miles away in a day, its driver completely unaware of having fulfilled the unwitting role of transporter for the fiendish compound.

The substance could stay there for days, even weeks, until someone brushed against it or inadvertently placed a hand in the wrong spot. Then the sleeping cycle of death would reawaken anew and the ensuing panic could spread throughout the nation. Local and state emergency response units and law enforcement agencies would be completely overwhelmed, and the federal government itself likely hard pressed to maintain some semblance of order.

As Ezekiel Templar thought the evolving possibilities through, it became more obvious how important it was to stop *The Uvalde Raider* from completing its last mission. What Qassam had planned could not be allowed to happen with his airplane. Whatever had to be done and whatever the attending cost, would by necessity have to be the price paid.

Yet the how in all this was a real question, as well as the where. All Ezekiel was armed with was a short-barreled assault weapon firing an intermediate rifle cartridge with no special elements or abilities. It was well suited for a close firefight with men out in the open, but was never designed to knock a twenty-ton, four engine bomber out of the sky. He also had only one magazine for it, so whatever he did would have to be accomplished at close range with as much surprise as possible.

Beyond that was the other question of where. There were numerous small and mid-sized communities along the way to San Antonio, and if the heavy bomber could be brought down it couldn't be anywhere near those population centers. Furthermore, if even one of his rounds were to strike a nerve gas container, the result could be a trail of death for a hundred miles.

Zeke shook his head and tried to concentrate on what he knew and what his options might be. The Texan was tired, hungry and had already developed another real thirst due to his wound and attending loss of blood. The leg ached with a dull, constant pounding and every time he moved, it brought forth a burning pain that ignited up his body. His eyes were bloodshot and felt gritty, and his vision was not what it should be. There was a time when…

Immediately he willed his mind back into the present and left the past where it belonged. This was the here and the now, and he had to keep his focus on what had been forced upon him by circumstance. Those days past were dead, and many innocent human beings would follow if he failed in keeping his concentration.

Gingerly bending his left leg inward and moving his right one off the rudder pedal, he wedged the stick between his knees. Ezekiel took his right hand and vigorously rubbed his eyes and face, feeling the sandpaper-like surface of his day-old stubble. He put his hand back on the stick and relaxed his legs, the left one protesting every fraction of an inch that it moved.

By habit he scanned the mostly useless instrument panel. The RPM gauge was destroyed as well as the artificial horizon/bank indicator, the clock, the compass, the air speed indicator, and the altimeter. The gauge he wished he had most, the Ata, or manifold pressure gauge, wiggled and flopped around intermittently, making itself an annoyance more than anything else.

About all he had left was the fuel indicator and the combination fuel/oil pressure gauges. They had evidently escaped damage in being placed so low on the instrument panel. With the extra tanks Max had installed in the Messerschmitt, sufficient aviation gas was not a problem. However, the fuel/oil pressure gauge was more useful and it showed the inverted V-12 was getting plenty of both.

By the sound of the Daimler V-12 coupled with his decades of experience, Ezekiel experimented with different settings for the liquid cooled engine. He was shooting for around 2700 RPM at nearly 60 inches of manifold pressure, and all those measurements were being made by an educated guess based on gut feel. At the low altitude he was flying that would equate to just under 300 knots, which was nearly double the cruising speed of the Boeing B-17.

The Uvalde Raider would be traveling even slower as long as it was climbing to altitude, which Ezekiel had already figured to be about 5,000 feet. There was no need to go any higher, and much lower would tend to spook most inexperienced men at the controls of something as massive as a Flying Fortress. Besides, between 4,000 to 5,000 feet was the prime altitude for delivery of the nerve agent. He was certain that Al-Qassam had calculated for the same.

The Me 109 Gustav streaked through the clear blue sky, eating up better than five and a half miles every minute. If it was not for the grave nature of the flight and his throbbing left leg, the retired Air Force colonel would have been enjoying himself immensely. Keeping the powerful fighter as close to the deck as he dared, at times they cleared canyon walls and high points with only feet to spare.

Occasionally a person going about their business down below would look up, startled by the sudden thunder of the V-12 in full song shattering their morning calm. One even started to wave, but the mottled gray fighter with the black cross insignias was already past them before they could get their hand fully up.

Ezekiel continued to pour on the power, squeezing out every last ounce of energy that German engineering from that era had to offer. He wanted to stay low and let the Messerschmitt's wartime camouflage scheme blend in with the terrain beneath him. If anything else, such an approach would give him an edge in surprising the terrorists and in keeping them off-balance at the initial point of contact.

Everything depended on that, because if they felt their mission was endangered by the pursuing Me 109, there was no telling what they might do as far as an alternative plan. And if he knew anything about this man called Yahla al-Qassam, Ezekiel Templar was sure the terrorist leader had at least one.

As the remaining minutes ticked away, those two words that encapsulated his success or failure worked upon the colonel's consciousness with a growing urgency: Where and how?

His eyes scanned through the cockpit glass above and to the front, they darted to any perceived reflection within his field of vision. It was a typically bright, sunny southwest Texas day, and the sun's rays made any reflective surface shine and dance about as if it had a life of its own. Ezekiel squinted hard against the magnified brilliance and brought his eye lashes closer together in an attempt to cut some of the glare. He found himself wishing for a pair of Ray Ban Aviators more so than any other time of his life.

Then he saw it. A reflection in the sky off to the northeast and somewhat higher, and about spot on for altitude. It had to be the Boeing. Ezekiel looked away for a brief moment to rest his eyes and then brought them back on target. Yes, he was sure of it now. He was certain it was *The Uvalde Raider*, still several miles ahead and off in the distance. The highly polished aluminum surfaces served as a signal fire to her rightful master, beckoning to rid her of the deadly blight now concealed within her airframe.

Ezekiel eased the control stick ever so slightly to the left and toward him, and the speeding Messerschmitt responded as if it could read his mind. The 'where' was beginning to shape up, but the odds involving the 'how' was still anyone's guess.

CHAPTER TWENTY

Micah Templar crouched in the shade of an overhanging mesquite tree, looking through tall pasture grass and eyeing the lay of the land to his front. There was a steep shouldered draw, averaging some eight to ten feet deep, which snaked around to the west and south of the old airstrip. It was this draw, along with the numerous fingers running into it, that Micah decided would make the best area to launch his attack from. For years during deer season the trooper had worked as a hunting guide on the Albright, and he had walked and scouted the surrounding terrain to the point of knowing it as others might know their own back yard.

From his vantage point he watched the four Hezbollah members disembark from the late model Chevy Suburban. Smelling trouble, the men had stopped the truck well before reaching the airstrip and began moving forward on foot. They were well within the range of the Marlin cradled in the crook of Micah's left arm, and he had been tempted to start the ball rolling right then and there.

But the fact was he really needed that Suburban in the worst way. Furthermore, Micah needed it to be in fully operable condition. The former Marine wanted them completely away from the vehicle when the shooting started, and have the terrorists in a position where they could not easily retreat back to it.

While making his way around to his current location, Micah had idly entertained the thought of just taking off across country on foot and maybe flagging someone down for assistance. But it was a good five miles to the nearest pavement and at least twelve miles back to town from the airstrip. Besides, he was not too keen about walking away from at least four heavily armed killers still running loose and unchallenged. Things were not going according to their plans, which made them that much more dangerous to anyone else whose path they might cross.

Finally, there was the fact that he didn't know how far he could travel in his present physical condition. Micah knew he was hurt inside, but wasn't sure how badly. Better to fight now than try moving fast on foot for miles across country, and perhaps being caught out in the open by a larger and far more mobile pursuing force.

The highway patrolman began easing sideways again, circling around behind the terrorists as they cautiously made their way toward the landing field. He looked over in the direction of the Suburban and wondered if the driver had been careless enough to leave the keys in the ignition. He decided against that possibility, the men he now faced had as of yet shown no signs of rank stupidity. And again, even if he was able to drive away it still left them free and unfettered to do whatever they wanted. He knew that he couldn't allow that to happen.

Climbing through one of the numerous fingers for the draw, Micah grunted in pain as his foot slipped on a loose rock and caused his chest muscles to tense. Any sudden movement that used those muscles triggered a searing wave of fire on the right side of his rib cage. Occasionally the pain was accompanied by the sickening sensation of fractured bone and cartilage rubbing up against one another.

It was not a good sign, and made the injured Texan even more aware that what was to come would be a fight to the finish. There would be no chance of disengaging and moving away at a rapid pace.

Staying low and as much as he could in the shadows of the surrounding mesquite, Micah carefully made his way toward an area closer to the road and to the rear of the terrorists. The scattered clumps of tall grass and cedar brush helped conceal him from the scanning eye. As he moved, he checked his background repeatedly, making every effort to blend in with the mesitas to his west. Micah Templar had hunted men before, and knew how the slightest inattention could spin the balance between who was doing the hunting and who was supposed to be the prey.

The trooper found himself wishing he had thought to check for the Bushnell binoculars inside the Ramcharger's console. In the haste to get Uncle Zeke armed and airborne, he had forgotten about them. Micah had already noted that one of the four terrorists had some sort of scoped self-loading rifle, possibly a Dragunov SVD. This put him at a disadvantage for any sort of distance shooting, or for long range observation.

His thoughts wandered back to Ezekiel Templar and how his uncle planned to stop *The Uvalde Raider*, as well as deal with the deadly cargo emplaced within. Micah did not know much about nerve agents but he had seen the deep concern, along with real fear, in his uncle's face when Qassam spoke of it earlier.

What was it called? VX? Yeah, that was it. That was a very important thing to remember once he was able to get the word out. For a moment his inner determination slipped, and for the merest fraction of a second he found himself thinking '*if I get the word out.*'

Micah immediately shook off that briefest lapse into despondency, mentally castigating himself for losing focus on what lay at hand. He paused again in the splotched and scattered shade, flexing his hands and fingers to keep them from stiffening up so much. He knew he would need to do some fast snap shooting soon enough, and he wanted his hands and fingers as ready as possible. The beating they had taken in the fight with Mustafa had left them swollen, battered and with the sensation of clumsiness.

He could see the four terrorists intermittently through the undergrowth and brush that he was utilizing in screening his movement. They were still warily walking in the direction of the airfield, as well as the cinder block operations shack where Mustafa was handcuffed to the front railing. The Hezbollah operatives would not be able to see their second in command until they were nearly abreast of the structure, and could see around the corner to the three tiered steel rail.

Micah could not let them get to that building. The structure would give the terrorists excellent cover, and once finding Max's body would realize there was most likely only one man they had to contend with. Plus there was the very real chance the unconscious Mustafa might revive and be able to give them more information on what happened. The less they knew, the better it was for Micah.

Dropping to his elbows, Micah stared through the intervening foliage to his adversaries beyond. He began making mental notes on each one individually, their tactical proficiency and how they were armed. The former Marine took grim satisfaction when he saw how they stayed mostly within the road's right-of-way and did not spread themselves out further.

It was natural instinct for humans to bunch together in the face of an unknown danger and even seasoned infantrymen had to guard themselves from doing so. These Hezbollah Lebanese were certainly capable of killing and undoubtedly highly dangerous when in their own element, but they were certainly not well-trained light infantry.

Micah watched as one of the Hezbollah operatives used hand and arm signals in an attempt to control the movement of the other three. All four were dressed similarly except for this one, who was armed with some sort of submachine gun along the lines of an Uzi and wore a blue t-shirt. His gesturing and general demeanor left Micah with the opinion that Blue Shirt must be their defacto leader.

The next man he studied was the one with the scoped rifle the trooper had taken note of earlier. That particular rifle represented the biggest threat that Micah could determine at present. It appeared to be an SVD or like type, and that meant it had far more range and inherent accuracy than Micah's .30/30. The scope was the real deal breaker, and the terrorist who carried it knew enough to stop from time to time and glass the encompassing area. Whatever else happened, that particular shooter would have to go down first.

The other two were acting as flankers, slightly off the road on opposite sides forward of their group leader as well as the marksman with the SVD. Both were armed with AK47s, much like the one he had given Uncle Zeke. From prior experience Micah knew that good accuracy was not the AK's forte, he was relatively safe from their aimed fire at this distance. After sizing up the two AK carriers briefly, the former Marine returned his attention to Blue Shirt and the Lebanese with the SVD. Both were still moving slowly along the confines of the caliche roadway.

Micah understood that now was the point of no return. The armed group was still some 300 yards away from the building and he was right at 200 yards to their rear. Taking a deep breath, he sat up and took a modified kneeling position, running his left arm through the Marlin's sling. As he did so, his right thumb eased the rifle's hammer back to full cock.

He let out half a breath and mentally forced his body to relax at the prospect of shooting another human being. The .30/30 was set for a 200 yard zero and there was no real crosswind, so Micah placed the front sight square on the marksman's back and centered the post in the Williams rear aperture. The tip of his right index finger pressed against the trigger, taking up the slack. He paused for a moment, double checked his sight picture and began pressing again.

The doomed terrorist had stopped and was glassing the area once more when the Marlin boomed. The 150-grain soft tip bullet took him slightly off center as he turned, slamming into his upper right back and driving deep into his vitals. The scoped rifle fell from his hands and he dropped to both knees, then toppled over flat on his face against the surface of the dirt road. The man uttered no sound as he fell, there was only the puff of dust on either side of his upper body as he hit the ground.

The Hezbollah rifleman was still falling as Micah hurriedly worked the Marlin's lever, chambering another round while shifting the front sight in search of their leader in the blue t-shirt. In his peripheral vision, he could see the other two scattering like quail, both seeking some sort of cover. He ignored them and picked up the flash of blue heading away from the road, fleeing into a line of scrub and brush.

As the Muslim terrorist scrambled madly for safe haven, a disparate part of Micah was oddly fascinated at how fast a man can move when consumed with fear. There was no time to fire another aimed round as if he were on a target range, so he tracked the fleeing blue shirt with his rifle's front sight and gave it a bit of a lead as it entered the brush. This time he gently popped the trigger and rode the recoil back down just in time to see the Hezbollah leader knocked spinning, and then disappear into the scrub.

Now it was his turn to move quickly. Micah slung the Marlin over his left shoulder and scrambled on his hands and knees back to the finger of the draw he had come out of. As he did so, the stabbing sensations in his right rib cage flared up once more. Yet the angry buzz of projectiles in his general direction hurried him along.

The other two terrorists with the AKs were returning fire blindly, shooting into the area where he had fired from. Both of their assault weapons were set on full auto, and the gunmen were spraying rounds wildly. He dropped down into the finger and out of the line of direct fire, coming up to his feet while topping off the Marlin's tube magazine. The firing lessened, and then stopped as Micah eased the rifle's hammer forward to half cock.

Remaining still for a moment, he strained his ears and listened intently. Off and away where he had engaged the Hezbollah terrorists, he heard words in Arabic drift in and out. Micah did not know what they meant, however they sounded like some sort of heartfelt cursing muttered on his behalf. The Texas lawman found himself smiling thinly at the prospect. Then there was nothing but the sound of silence.

Moving as quickly as he dared, Micah began a recon shuffle down the finger and toward the main draw from where he had first come. He knew he had a few moments of respite as the remaining terrorists regrouped, recalculated on their present status and came up with some sort of plan of action.

The trooper was going to make the most out of that little window of time, and change his location to come at them from a different direction. The Hezbollah terrorists would be very hesitant in attempting to make their way back to the Suburban. Beyond the fact they had been fired upon from the rear, the Lebanese had no real way of knowing exactly where his rounds had come from or how many shooters there were.

These unknowns in their tactical situation, along with not knowing the terrain around them, would play to his advantage. Most likely they would circle wide and try to continue on to the cinder block building. He would be waiting for them when they did.

Micah Templar slowed down to a walk, breathing hard while trying to step as lightly as possible. His broken ribs had been protesting in agony each time his right foot touched ground when jogging along, and he was concerned that he might be making enough noise to catch an attentive ear. He turned his thoughts to the two armed and still ambulatory Hezbollah Lebanese out there, and what might be going through their minds. Most likely they would separate now while still keeping each other in sight, probing hesitantly in a circling motion in the direction of the operations shack.

The former Marine also began to consider the condition of their leader in the blue shirt. Micah did not feel confident that his rushed second shot had anchored Blue Shirt for good. The Texan had seen the man spin away into the brush and nothing more, and he had done more than enough work with a rifle to know when a shot did not feel quite right.

Bringing it all together, Micah figured he was bracing himself against the two shooters with AKs and a possibly wounded third one carrying that submachine gun. He tried to form the mental picture of that second shot but shook his head in exasperation.

If he had only gotten his front sight on Blue Shirt a split second earlier, he would be a lot surer of where exactly that bullet went. Then he put it out of his mind, he needed to be thinking ahead and not of what was behind. And he needed to be thinking quickly, while giving his opponents every doubt as to his own strength and capabilities.

The highway patrolman picked a likely spot against the north wall of the draw and moved up just high enough to peek through some dropseed grass growing along its edge. From here the draw turned south, roughly paralleling the airstrip. Some of the undergrowth had been cut as a rough right-of-way for the nearby landing surface, but there was still enough to fool someone into thinking the terrain was nothing more than flat, undefined ground for hundreds of yards.

From where he watched he could see the front of the operations shack and the handcuffed Mustafa, still firmly secured to the railing. The body of the Lebanese Shi'a had changed position from the one Micah had left him in. Most likely the badly beaten Arab was not only partially conscious at present, but perhaps even aware as to what was going on. That was something else for the Texas lawman to keep in mind.

A slight movement in Micah's peripheral vision diverted his attention. Off to the left, about 150 yards from him and west of the structure, he picked up something unusual in the brush line. Keeping his eyes trained on the spot, Micah gradually made out the form of one of the two Hezbollah gunmen armed with an AK47. The terrorist was studying the operations shack closely, trying to discern whatever secrets that might be concealed within.

Micah briefly considered trying to get a round off from his present position, but it was at the wrong angle and unsuitable for firing accurately from. If he changed to a better one, the movement could attract the gunman's eye. Laying perfectly still he decided to continue observing the Shi'a, looking for any clue the terrorist might inadvertently give in locating the others.

For his own part the Lebanese continued to scrutinize the area around the cinder block building intently. His body language told Micah that he was thinking about getting closer to the structure, but there was too much open ground to do so safely. After nearly a minute, the gunman began backing away into the brush.

Suddenly, the shooter stopped and looked toward his north. Micah followed the man's line of sight and saw the second AK-wielding Hezbollah terrorist, standing atop a limestone boulder and motioning the first one to move forward to the operations shack.

The two men appeared to be in a silent conflict of wills. The first terrorist was stubbornly shaking his head back and forth, and pointing to the open ground before him. The second man kept motioning him onward. Apparently this impasse had been going on for some time, and in a fit of impatience the second terrorist had stepped on top of the large rock to better illustrate his emphatic gesturing.

Seeing that both were currently preoccupied with his fellow traveler, Micah inched back down the sharply inclined face of the draw until he was out of sight. From there he moved quickly to a better shooting position some fifty feet to his left. Up to the present none of the Hezbollah gunmen had done anything recklessly stupid. But now they had, and Micah meant to cash in on the offered opportunity.

Micah came to the spot he had in mind and made his way cautiously up the bank of the creek. Bellying down in the dirt and looking through a cedar shrub, he could see both men still engaged in their muted dispute, their respective hand gestures and body language becoming more insistent in regard to the other.

The first terrorist was within 150 yards and a sure mark from Micah's semi-prone position. He shifted to contemplate the other terrorist, still standing on the boulder. That man was every bit of 350 yards away, making for a chancy shot for most lever action deer rifles and very much so for an iron-sighted .30/30.

From this slightly different vantage point, Micah could see something else too. It was a sliver of blue cloth on the other side of the boulder where the second terrorist was standing, the very same shade of blue as the t-shirt worn by the Hezbollah leader he had shot at before. As he watched, the sliver of blue disappeared behind the rock.

So Blue Shirt, their leader, was still alive. Now the mime–like argument between the two others became clearer. Blue Shirt was most probably telling the other terrorist accompanying him to have the first gunman advance on the nearby building, while he and the second terrorist stayed pat to provide any needed cover fire. However, the first terrorist was more than a little hesitant to walk out into that open ground.

For Micah that realization settled the decision for the next round nestled in the Marlin's chamber. Blue Shirt was still able to give orders, but apparently could not get around too well. Due to his wounded condition he had to have someone to relay his orders for him. As long as he stayed where he was, Blue Shirt was safe behind that large rock. Yet if Micah could remove the Hezbollah leader's ability to transmit those orders, his command and control role was useless.

Taking care to not let the polished blue barrel of his Marlin reflect any sunlight, Micah stealthily slung up the rifle and wiggled ever so slightly to his right to get the best firing position. He grunted in spite of himself, the protesting ribs sending a clear message that they did not like the contortions that he was putting them through. He picked up the front sight of the rifle inside the rear aperture and paused to check the airstrip's orange wind sock for any needed change in windage. The sock hung limp and still.

Micah measured the distance in his mind once more, still coming up with his target being a full 350 yards away. He had to be absolutely sure of everything about this shot to connect with the Shi'a Muslim standing on the boulder. At this range, the trajectory of the .30/30's flat nose bullet was much akin to that of a tossed grapefruit. The trooper thumbed the Marlin's hammer to full cock as he took in a full breath, let it halfway out and put the tip of the front sight exactly a foot and a half over the second terrorist's head. Gently, ever so gently, he began squeezing the trigger.

The second Hezbollah gunman was starting to get the upper hand over the first one in their frenzied arm waving dispute. The first terrorist, cowed by the continual prodding, had moved ever so cautiously into the fringe of the open area when Micah's .30/30 went off. The triumphant second gunman, still waving his hesitant comrade on, lurched a bit forward as the bullet impacted his chest. He toppled from the face of the rock, landing hard on the sloping ground below him. The Arab's body slid a bit on impact but did not move again.

All of this was happening out of the corner of Micah's right eye, as he fought against the Marlin's recoil and shifted his aim to where the first terrorist had been standing. The man was no longer there. The highway patrolman saw movement among the low hanging branches and surrounding undergrowth where the Lebanese terrorist had run back through the brush line. Micah rose up on one knee and levered three more quick rounds to keep the fleeing gunman in high gear.

It was past time for the trooper to vacate, too. The four rounds he had fired were more than enough to give away his own position. Micah half turned and slid from the lip of the draw, making his way down the steep incline and back into the bed of the meandering cut itself. From there the law officer began working his way west back up the washout, and to the general vicinity where he had been before.

Stopping briefly he cupped his left hand to his ear, straining with everything inside of him to listen. He heard nothing. No yelling, no muttering, nor any sound of anything to do with any other man or the weapon he might possess.

An eerie stillness had settled in, as if the last four rounds had never been fired. Only the cessation of activity on the part of the land's natural inhabitants revealed that something deadly had just occurred.

Micah's mind raced at the onslaught of options and probabilities. The first gunman had not retreated back into the brush line, he had fled as fast as his feet could carry him. Once there he had made no attempt to turn to either side and try to return fire. He was in a panic, and panic kept one from thinking of what they should be doing next. More so, there was no return fire from the area where Blue Shirt had been, which meant his injuries did not allow him to do so or that he had nothing to return fire with. Either that, or Blue Shirt had no idea where the bullet that killed his companion came from.

Any of these possibilities put Micah in a stronger position. He had narrowed the odds down from four armed assailants to two dead, one wounded, and one who was not thinking clearly. The thought gave him confidence. However, at the same time he tempered that rising level of certitude with the knowledge that he could well be only one bullet away from catastrophe himself. This deal was not even close to being over and he was running out of time.

Micah began picking his way up the steep shouldered draw again, looking for a protected spot where he could get a little respite and a bit of reloading done. Another fifty yards and he found what he needed, a depression in the north face that would protect him from observation either up or down the dry wash.

Putting his back to the dirt wall, he flattened out against it and tried to reach inside his right front trouser pocket for some fresh .30/30 cartridges. But all of the walking, shuffling and crawling had caused the tightly-cut uniform trousers to settle down low on Micah's waist. He simply could not get his raw and swollen right hand into the cramped pocket and his fingers around the loose riding ammunition.

Begrudgingly, he propped the Marlin rifle against the arroyo wall and took a step away. Clasping the front of the Sam Brown belt with his left hand, he pulled both it and the trousers up as he reached inside the offending pocket with his right. Micah had just touched the brass casings when he heard someone at the top the draw and behind, closing in fast.

The trooper hastily brought his hand out of the pocket and stepped to the rear, freezing with his back pressed again into the embankment. His right hand had gone automatically to his side, fingers resting lightly on the butt of his issued Model 28 revolver. He cut his eyes longingly to the resting Marlin, but the rifle might as well been a hundred miles away.

The sounds of the unexpected interloper running through the brush stopped. Evidently, whoever it was could now see the unanticipated gulch before them and was figuring on what to do next. Micah found himself momentarily squeezing his eyes shut, focusing his remaining senses to concentrate on the unknown from behind and above. Then he heard it, the sound of a twig brushing up against clothing as whoever it was moved nearer. They were now so close that Micah could literally feel them in the small of his back.

Micah studied the ground around him, searching for the slightest shadow. But it was late October and any human silhouette created by the sun would be to his rear, not the front. He then gauged the rough ground at the bottom of the cut closely, all the way to the opposite wall of the arroyo. If he decided to move, it would have to be fast and he needed the certainty of firm footing.

The trooper's heart was pounding in his chest, and the accompanying adrenaline coursed through his veins like a raging flood crashing through a narrow mountain canyon. The man was so close that none of Micah's five normal senses had him located so exactly as that unnamed sixth sense, the one perfected over eons of man being both hunter and hunted. That primeval instinct for self-preservation was screaming that at any moment, the man above would look over the edge and see Micah below.

It was now or never.

CHAPTER TWENTY-ONE

The battered highway patrolman propelled himself away from the vertical face, his right thumb busting the retention snap on the DPS regulation holster. He palmed the .357 Magnum, turning as he did so. Micah looked up and saw the Hezbollah gunman who had fled through the brush just seconds before looming over him, holding his weapon muzzle high and framed by the perfectly blue sky.

The Lebanese was leaning forward, slightly off balance, trying to look into the small gorge beneath him. The lawman continued to draw, forcing himself to be as smooth as possible with his bruised and swollen right hand. The Hezbollah terrorist, startled at first, recovered rapidly and began to bring the muzzle of the AK down and on to the trooper.

Micah's left hand met his right and both enveloped the black Pachmayr grip of the revolver, locking it into a vise like grip. Forcing himself to take another fraction of a second, the trooper picked up the front sight and centered it squarely on the shooter's chest. The AK muzzle continued to swing down while the hammer of the Smith & Wesson started back as if it had a life of its own. The Model 28 roared and dust kicked up on the front of the Arab's khaki shirt, slightly off the second button from the top.

But the AK muzzle continued its arc, unfettered by the blast of the magnum and still seeking its own target to engage in return. Methodically, Micah sidestepped to the right as the hammer of the S&W came back again. He had trained for decades with the big double action revolver, and had carried it from the time of recruit school. It was like a part of him, and everything he was doing now he had practiced untold times before.

The magnum blasted again, and another puff of dust kicked up on the terrorist's shirt. His rhythm now set, Micah took one more step to the side as he fought the front sight back into line, and triggered another round. He was rewarded by a third impact on the man's chest, even as the flash hider of the assault rifle continued bearing down on him.

Awkwardly, the AK's muzzle swept past the Texan, now pointing straight down. Micah was looking directly into the man's eyes and saw the light had gone out of them. The Hezbollah terrorist tottered forward and fell in a lifeless heap at Micah's feet. The man twitched once and lay still, and the ground around him turned into a deep, rich color of red.

The highway patrolman reached down with his left hand and picked up the dropped AK, still clutching the magnum in his right. Glancing quickly up and down the draw, he moved back to where he had been before, his back locked against the wall of the arroyo. Checking the Kalashnikov, he flipped the safety on and placed it to the side. Then he picked up his own rifle and resumed the interrupted reloading.

Micah had finished with the Marlin and was trying to reload the Smith & Wesson when it started. At first there was only a slight tremor in his right fingers, and then both of his hands started shaking. They shook so badly that it was almost impossible to pull the cartridges from his belt slide and put them in the chambers of the revolver.

One round from his fumbling fingers fell to the sandy ground, followed by another. He thought of the younger troops in his area who were now carrying speed loaders, and promised himself that he would get a pair for his own duty belt; the bulky, untraditional appearance be damned.

Finally getting the Smith & Wesson reloaded, he shoved it back into the holster and reset the snap. Squatting down, the trooper picked up the dropped .357 cartridges and reinserted them in the loops of his belt slide. He had gone through the shakes before, but not since the Da Krong Valley in Vietnam. They were already starting to subside as they had done all those many years ago. At the time, he had hoped he would never experience that sort of sensation again.

Yet here he was. Fear, exhaustion and raw adrenaline made for inexplicable human body responses, and Micah's body was running on nothing but a straight mixture of all three.

After getting control of himself again and formulating the next move in his head, Micah moved away from the embankment and to the body of the dead terrorist. He began patting the corpse down, looking for anything of use but especially for a key fitting the ignition of that Chevrolet Suburban. It was a scant chance, and like most scant chances Micah came up with nothing.

His thoughts turned again to Blue Shirt behind that large rock. As the evident leader of this Hezbollah group, Blue Shirt was the most likely to have that ignition key. Thinking of what must be done to confirm that and the risk involved, the highway patrolman sighed deeply. He straightened up, checked his gear, and began moving up the draw once more.

Blue Shirt was the last remaining part of his getting out of here, and needed to be located and dealt with. Also, the Shi'a Lebanese had to have the keys to that Suburban and Micah knew that he was pulling negative numbers in the minutes needed to stop the Raider.

Going up another two hundred yards or so, the Texas lawman left the main draw and entered one of the numerous small fingers leading off to the northwest. Carefully selecting a proper observation spot from cover, Micah moved on cat's feet to that location and scrutinized the area where Blue Shirt had last been seen.

From his new vantage point he could see the dead terrorist lying at the foot of the boulder, sunlight reflecting off the man's dropped AK47. More surprisingly, and far more importantly, he could see Blue Shirt in a semi-sitting position, back propped up against the large rock. Micah raised the .30/30, running his left arm through the rifle sling again. But something stopped him and he took the Marlin out of his shoulder for a second look. Blue Shirt was not moving, and that was not the sort of position any man would take to fight from or try to hide in.

Micah raised up slightly to get a better view, his own features blending with the shade from a large live oak tree branching out overhead. No weapon could be seen anywhere around other than the dropped AK in front of the boulder. There was still no sign of any movement from Blue Shirt himself. The former Marine found himself wishing for those binoculars again, or anything else that would help him observe the immobile Hezbollah leader in greater detail.

But if he was going to get a better look, he was going to have to get a lot closer. Skirting the back of the live oak and the brush around it, Micah picked his way through the undergrowth, pausing every now and then to make certain that Blue Shirt had not changed position. Crisscrossing the terrain between them, the Texan found a spot in the road's right-of-way where he could cross unseen from the boulder's location. As he prepared to do so, he doublechecked the dead Lebanese who had been carrying the SVD still lying nearby, as was the scoped rifle. Neither had moved from where they first fell.

Shaking off the lingering pang of guilt for having taken any human life, Micah reset his mind to what he was doing next. He peered searchingly around his position before exposing himself, and crossed the road at a rapid pace to more concealment. From there he began circling, continuing to pause at favorable spots to see if Blue Shirt was still there. He was. Soon enough, Micah had come up on the far side of the unmoving terrorist and was scant yards away.

From there it was plainly evident why Blue Shirt had not moved. A large part of his right shoulder, torso and right leg was soaked in blood. Looking closer Micah could see the large, gaping wound torn through muscle and bone by the flat-nosed .30 caliber bullet.

The passing chunk of lead had turned just about everything in the man's right shoulder into a grisly mixture of shattered bone fragments, gristle and pulp. The Arab's shoulder was beyond useless, its only present worth an oozing testament of probable finality for someone who was perilously close to dying.

The terrorist's dark eyes shifted about from time to time, slightly out of focus and radiating with agony as well as an attendant deepening shock. His breathing came in uneven gasps and lines of pain crossed his pasty face that mixed with a disoriented expression, all of which combined to give the full definition of a badly injured man. Micah had to give an inner nod to Blue Shirt, most men would not have had the grit to make it this far. The highway patrolman moved in with the Marlin at the ready, making certain that both of Blue Shirt's hands remained empty and in plain view.

The half-closed eyes of the terrorist continued to wander about aimlessly, a process of an oncoming delirium more than any real sign of alertness. But they opened wide and regained their focus at the distinct sound of the hammer of a Marlin .30-30 coming to full cock. The Hezbollah leader rolled his head slightly to the right, and looked down the gaping muzzle of the same rifle that had ruined his shoulder and killed his men. The hands holding the rifle were rock steady, and the eyes which met his were cold and hard.

"Don't move a muscle, Mohammed," Micah growled.

The Hezbollah Lebanese did not understand English but he did understand the obvious warning in the words. More so, even through his all-encompassing clouds of agony, he understood those two cold, hard eyes.

"I ought to kill you right where you sit" the trooper said. "But murdering someone with that kind of hole would bother me some, and I'm still wearing a badge. It's just not our way." Micah eased up near the man's feet, his rifle still aimed squarely in Blue Shirt's face. "I guess you wouldn't understand that, would you?"

The Texan scrutinized the shoulder again, and lowered the hammer slowly on the lever action Marlin. "Then again, I might be just wasting another bullet. That first one is liable to get the job done all by itself." The highway patrolman paused. "Here, let me take a fast look. You're probably worth more alive than dead to someone else, anyways."

CHAPTER TWENTY-TWO

Yahla al-Qassam leaned back slightly in the co-pilot's seat, trying to relax as much as his excitement and the demands of *The Uvalde Raider* would allow. It was as if the infernal machine had a mind of its own, and was protesting in every way it knew how against those who now controlled it. Whoever had said the B-17 Flying Fortress was an easy plane to fly had never flown one, or was a fairly remarkable liar.

If it was not for the presence of Gholam Javad, Al-Qassam did not see how he could have gotten the recalcitrant bomber even this far. But working together they had managed to do so and their ambitious mission was going exactly as first envisioned. That growing realization and the excitement accompanying it was something that he was presently trying to keep tamped down inside himself. Things had gone far too well to be jeopardized by a careless mistake brought on by sheer giddiness.

But as far as Gholam Javad was concerned, he was having the time of his life. For most of his entire existence, this Iranian air force veteran had dreamed of sitting in the pilot's seat of a Boeing B-17G Flying Fortress. His uncle, who once bore the high responsibility as a chosen chief pilot for the royal family of the Shah and had commanded a converted Trans World Airlines B-17 in that capacity, would have been so proud of him.

It did not matter in Javad's mind that his uncle, an avowed secularist supremely loyal to the throne, would most likely have been summarily tortured and executed in the modern Islamic Republic of Iran. Nor did it ever enter Javad's unusual sense of reality that his uncle would have recoiled in utter horror of who Gholam was flying for now, and why.

No, those thoughts had never entered his head. All he cared about was the realization of an often dreamed of opportunity to fly his one obsession in life. He was finally at the controls of a real Boeing B-17 Flying Fortress, just like the American actor Steve McQueen in *The War Lover*.

Yahla al-Qassam wondered about Gholam Javad from time to time, but allowed his peculiar companion to savor his present flying experience with minimal interruptions. They had all struggled so hard to get to this point and Al-Qassam had by far driven himself the hardest. There had been so much along the way to overcome, so many things in his own life that guided him to this defining moment. So many sacrifices that had been made.

To his own way of thinking, the Iranian leader understood far better than most what the word 'sacrifice' really meant. After all, Yahla al-Qassam was not even his real name, he had not let his birth name cross his own lips for several years now. There were others who knew but they were very few in number and mostly in the very highest echelons of the Iranian Revolutionary Guard, and could keep a secret as well as Qassam could. Furthermore, they had more than a passing interest in his continued well-being and made every effort possible to protect one of their most valuable human assets.

The one now called Yahla al-Qassam had been born in the mountainous northern reaches of Qazvin Province, in an area close to the fading remnants of the ancient fortress known as Alamut. It was where Hassan-i Sabbah, the leader of the Order of the Assassins and also known in medieval history as the 'Old Man of the Mountains,' once ruled from.

As a young boy Yahla had been known as a sort of child prodigy possessing a rare mixture of inner determination, leadership abilities and a very high intelligence. His parents were both devout Shi'a, who in turn came from a long lineage of other devout Shi'a going back to the time of Ali ibn Abi Talib. Zealously faithful in their beliefs they made certain this son of theirs, so blessed by Allah and The Prophet Muhammad, would be as well versed in his religious upbringing as he was in other matters involving a more formal education.

During his childhood and this deep immersion into his family's theology, combined with the imagination of an adventurous boy living in the middle of so much history, the one now called Yahla al-Qassam became increasingly aware that he was linked to some sort of important destiny.

After all his family could claim direct lineage to the Prophet himself, along with many others who had shaped the surrounding world in which he lived in. He had been told repeatedly that he was especially blessed for as long as he could remember, and had become quite conscious as well as comfortable in that fact. Yet in his mind, a question remained as to exactly what that important destiny might be.

Some years later, while studying architectural engineering at the prestigious University of Tehran, he had finally come to the full understanding of what that predetermination must be. The year was 1978 and Iran was engulfed in the ongoing struggle between a secular head of state and the Shi'a cleric known as the Ayatollah Khomeini. Like so many of his fellow students, the young man from Qazvin Province found himself in the streets far more often than in the classroom, protesting against the ruling Shah and supporting the exiled ayatollah.

When Shah Pahlavi abdicated his throne a few months later and departed the country in disgrace, the ayatollah returned from his forced exile in sacrosanct triumph. Millions of Iranians watched as their proclaimed religious messiah stepped off a chartered Air France passenger jet, and Yahla had been in that crowd when they exploded instantaneously with an indescribable shared joy at the ayatollah's return.

But the fight for an Islamist Republic of Iran was far from over. There were many betrayers to be dealt with internally as well as the venting of long-held external animosities toward The Great Satan, the despised United States of America. The young man raised under the shadow of Alamut had been there from the very beginning, from the sacking of military armories and dealing with government forces still loyal to the Shah, to the execution of those same traitors.

Then came the day when he and 500 other 'students,' marching under the banner of The Muslim Students of the Imam Khomeini Line, took over the American Embassy in downtown Tehran. With the implicit assistance of the newly-formed Islamic republic, they had collectively thumbed their noses at the Great Satan for 444 days by continually brutalizing their hostages and costing President Jimmy Carter any chance of being elected to a second term.

Within another year following the release of the American hostages, the fledging Islamist Republic of Iran was embroiled in a devastating war with the neighboring country of Iraq. The Iranians were pushed back by the well-trained Iraqi military forces and the Iranian Army, long at war with itself, was showing every sign of collapsing. As a member of the Iranian Revolutionary Guards, who remained fanatically loyal to the Ayatollah, the man now called Yahla al-Qassam had been one of many in taking drastic measures to turn their precarious situation around.

One of the most desperate of those drastic measures involved the creation of the *Basij Mostazafan*, or 'Mobilization of the Oppressed.' What became commonly referred to as the *Basij* was the brainchild of the Ayatollah Khomeini himself, and was seized upon by the Revolutionary Guards to combat the superior military advantages of their Iraqi foes.

Made up mostly of a corps of teenaged boys between the ages of twelve and seventeen, the Basij became a symbol of Iranian theological resolve. Best known for their human wave style of attacks, they were sacrificed by the hundreds of thousands to clear the way for the far better equipped, professional Iranian military units, including many elements of the Revolutionary Guards themselves.

Thus was the symbiotic relationship between the Basij and the IRG, or *Sephah*. Iranian Revolutionary Guardsmen would recruit male youth for the Basij, usually from the ranks of the very poorest and downtrodden. The pauperized families of these martyrs-to-be were promised financial compensation, as well as other opportunities that to this juncture had never existed for them.

Their sons, many little more than children, were given a rudimentary training course of some two weeks and sent to the front. Each was issued a key by their Sephah superiors, a key that would supposedly unlock the doors of heaven to enjoy divine blessings. Sometimes, almost as an afterthought, they might be hastily armed. Often times they were not.

Their recruitment was done by the Sephah, their training was conducted by the Sephah and in the field they were commanded by the Sephah. To complete this wretchedly pathetic symbiosis, they willingly sacrificed their lives upon the express orders of those very same mentors.

Early in the war, the Iranians attempted to use donkeys and other animals to clear the innumerable minefields in which the Iraqi forces excelled with markedly deadly effect. However, this experiment was soon deemed unsuccessful, as the animals would scatter in every direction after one or two of them detonated a mine. What was needed were sweepers who would follow orders, staying in perfect lines even as others that they called friends were blown apart on either side.

The Basij's initial reason for existence was to provide a ready supply of such mine sweepers. The widespread utilization of these child volunteers became so refined that the young boys would wrap themselves in funeral shrouds before starting their advance, making it easier to give what was left of their bodies a proper burial after detonating a mine. There was never a shortage of these volunteers.

The man called Yahla al-Qassam had experienced a heady rise in his prominence during this ghastly period. As an IRG member he recruited, trained and then ordered innumerable Basij youth to their deaths. He took great pride in these units, among all others his were always the most highly motivated and ready to die. Often enough his biggest difficulty was keeping them reined in until the proper time. The young boys often wanted to run to their deaths instead of purposely walking forward, keeping those ever important perfect lines in their near suicidal formations.

His superiors noted al-Qassam's innate leadership abilities and loyalty to the cause, and soon earmarked him for bigger and better things. Within two more years he was in southern Lebanon, advising a ragtag bunch of mostly Shi'a Lebanese militants who called themselves the Hezbollah. The assignment had been a herculean task in the wholesale killing zones of southern Lebanon. Whoever the opposing militias did not manage to dispose of, the Israeli Defense Forces summarily finished off.

Nevertheless, that hard fact also served as a major culling effect in improving the Hezbollah ranks. Combined with proper training and guidance from Sephah, along with tacit supply and logistics links furnished by the neighboring Syrians, this formerly vagabond group rapidly morphed into the premier terrorist organization of their kind.

It was during this period that al-Qassam assumed his current name. It had a far more local ring than his old one of Persian lineage, and his Shi'a Lebanese comrades appreciated the lengths that he took in proving worthy of their loyalty and trust. The IRG operative made it a point to learn their local dialect of Arabic, rather than speaking to them in his native Farsi as many of his Sephah peers had done. His new comrades responded in kind, and soon enough he found himself firmly emplaced as not only one of the golden ones in the Iranian Revolutionary Guards, but also in the eyes of the increasingly dangerous Hezbollah terrorist movement.

After the successful completion of several operations of limited scope, Yahla al-Qassam soon found himself involved in bigger, far more lethal schemes. When others thought in terms of car bombs, he came up with the idea of trucks packed with high explosives. While others were content to murder select individuals, he instead saw the real value of not only kidnapping them for some sort of renumeration but also in using the event as a major propaganda coup.

Deftly playing the psychological shock involved in abduction for maximum effect, al-Qassam would dangle the hapless hostage's continued well-being like so much red meat in front of ravenous mass media outlets. The right date, the right time, the right circumstance, the right pronouncement, all figured into a complicated game of human perception, human feeling and human frailties. And each time he proved himself a master in each.

Lastly, when he did decide to commit outright murder, the Iranian thought in much grander terms than one or even a few victims. If the truth be known, it was his innovation and operational skills that led to the deaths of hundreds of foreign troops assigned to Lebanon as peacekeepers. Some of these operations were so well planned and executed they occurred near simultaneously, including certain suicide bombings in Beirut that left behind massed piles of dead and broken bodies.

These rabid attacks ultimately led to the evacuation of those American, French and Italian forces that had been sent to that unhappy land, to keep a peace no one else really seemed to want. Their removal, along with the growing disarray of the official Lebanese government, allowed Hezbollah to expand exponentially in both size and capability, becoming a de facto shadow government on its own. Yahla al-Qassam could take a large amount of credit in that emergence.

Sometime later this rising obelisk amid a sea of human horrors returned to Iran, toying with a germ of an idea that by far eclipsed anything that any terrorist cell had ever attempted before. Ironically enough he owed much of this evolving brainchild to his Iraqi enemies, against whom his countrymen were still fighting.

The Iran-Iraq conflict had seen the first massive use of chemical weapons since World War One. The Iranians suffered tens of thousands of casualties when exposed to Saddam Hussein's weaponized stockpiles, and the overall effectiveness of this hellish style of wholesale killing captured both al-Qassam's eye as well as his imagination.

A nerve agent could be a spectacular tool in the maturing arsenal of international terrorism, and would be an act that would not only potentially cause tens of thousands of casualties, but would also spread fear and panic among millions of other human beings not otherwise affected. The actual employment and rippling aftereffects from this type of attack was sure to send far reaching shockwaves through any nation's economic, medical, governmental and societal infrastructures. This would be true for even the most powerful nation on earth, the hated Great Satan of the United States of America.

Yahla al-Qassam had proposed his evolving succubus to his superiors in Sephah, who were enthusiastic of this intriguing plan from one of their best and brightest. They in turn took the idea to their ruling council of mullahs who considered it a divination from Allah himself, an assured way to strike a fearsome blow to the very heart and soul of the infidels who stood against them. More information was requested.

More information was given. Have whatever nerve agent chosen for the mission shipped into a port in Mexico, a third world country not well-versed in physical security measures or imported goods enforcement. Use freighters with Cuban registries for the transport of personnel and equipment, a nation with which Mexico shared close diplomatic as well as economic ties. Befittingly enough, Cuba was also quite friendly with the Islamic Republic of Iran as well as various terrorist groups, and had been willingly utilized for such activities before.

As in standard operating procedure for these sorts of strikes, three teams would be created to get the job done. One would be a reconnaissance group, the first to arrive to choose the best routes, set up safe houses and gather the needed human intelligence. Once they completed their task, they would be withdrawn for debriefing and a support team inserted to set up for the coming strike group, who would conduct the attack itself.

The nerve agent as well as the apparatus needed for dispersal would go in with the support team, then situated at a pre-chosen location along with the supplies and equipment needed for the strike group. While being moved, the weaponized chemicals and attending ancillaries would have every appearance of typical crop dusting implements bound for northern Mexico.

Each team would consist of proven Sephah and Hezbollah operatives, specifically selected for their skills and knowledge as well as physical characteristics to blend more easily into the general Mexican population. Their target would be a major city just inside the long, porous border with the United States; a city selected for size, significance, and the availability of surrounding remote areas.

The delivery of the agent would come from an aircraft capable of lifting and dispersing the considerable chemical payload. Finally, the strike team would escape back across the border in the ensuing confusion and panic, and arrive in friendly territory along with the support group within 72 hours of completing their mission.

Soon enough al-Qassam was working diligently to bring his personal *angra mainyu* into reality. At first he had calculated on using Sarin as the nerve agent, but his well-placed contacts in the Syrian intelligence services told him of a recent success that changed his mind. Aided and abetted by scientists working in Saddam Hussein's Iraq, they had combined their resources to produce the chemical concoction known as VX.

VX was a more advanced compound than Sarin and had a far better shelf life, as well as a much longer persistence once distributed on target. Far more importantly for his intent and purposes, it was estimated to be one hundred times more powerful than the older Sarin agent. Following a good deal of bargaining and political maneuvering, a deal was struck with the Assad regime and the necessary arrangements made for delivery.

Now Yahla al-Qassam had his nerve agent, but then faced the problem of determining and procuring the proper means for delivery. Automatically his mind went to a large civilian airliner, yet there were a myriad of difficulties in using that sort of aircraft for such a purpose.

To begin with, it flew too fast and was not amenable to the modifications needed to properly spread the substance. More so, the taking of one would bring an immediate call for alarm. Prior terrorist acts had made the security around any commercial jetliner more formidable than ever before. Plus there was the likelihood of having passengers and a crew involved. The more one inserted the human element into such a complicated scenario, the higher were the odds for something to go wrong.

With the formation of contacts in Cuba and Mexico through mutual acquaintances, he came up with a thick folder detailing the types of civilian aircraft found in the Southwestern United States.

Most of the smaller civilian types of one or two engines were completely unsuitable, by his figures the airplane chosen must be able to lift at least 6,000 pounds. He then looked at the models used as crop dusters, designed specifically to spray farm fields with insecticides. However, he ruled them out in needing to carry more agent further than any of them were capable of. Plus, he figured he would need a crew of four and these crop dusters were single seat craft.

The utilization of a large, multi-engine aircraft like those used for fighting forest fires was a possibility, but almost all of them were located several hundreds of miles from the three potential targets topping his list. Coincidentally, most were also stationed at larger airfields where any suspicious activity could be quickly reported to the authorities. Something else was needed, something fairly local yet out of the normal mix of the three large cities he had circled on an old Rand McNally road atlas.

CHAPTER TWENTY-THREE

One morning while in the midst of his growing frustrations, an old acquaintance happened to stop by. This welcomed visitor was a man in whom he put a good deal of trust in, and who was also a fervent follower of the Ayatollah. As a point of fact his comrade had been in the fight alongside him from the very beginning, from the street demonstrations to the government armory sackings to the taking over of the American Embassy.

Not only that, he was also a member of the Iranian Revolutionary Guards and a fellow instructor in the training of the Basij. Recently he had moved over into politics, and Yahla al-Qassam believed his old ally had great possibilities in that area. The acquaintance's name was Mahmoud Ahmadinejad and he possessed information that would solve several of Yahla's remaining difficulties.

During his visit, Mahmoud listened intently to the current crop of problems involved in Al-Qassam's monumental undertaking. As a trusted member of the Sephah and a quickly rising political force supported by the ruling Mujtahids, Ahmadinejad was already aware of the plan and had given it much thought. A very bright individual with a master's degree in civil engineering from the Iranian University of Science and Technology, Mahmoud Ahmadinejad understood instinctively how successful this operation could be. He also understood the breadth and depth of the attending difficulties requiring resolution to ensure that success.

Qassam's trusted friend had a suggestion. Ahmadinejad had heard of and confirmed the existence of a few old World War II era heavy bombers still operational in America, and that were in private hands. These airplanes were used for living history exhibitions and air shows, and were mainly based in the American Southwest, specifically the state of Texas.

Furthermore, there was an organization for such aircraft enthusiasts known as the Confederate Air Force, headquartered in the very southern tip of Texas within twenty kilometers of the Mexican border. Among the airplanes still being flown were a couple of Boeing B-17 Flying Fortresses.

Mahmoud laid a thick binder with yellow tab markers in front of Yahla al-Qassam. Inside was a gold mine of information concerning these aircraft, their capabilities, where they were based in this region of the United States and some background notes on their present caretakers.

Yahla immediately grasped how several of his problems were being solved in one fell swoop. Nevertheless, the resolution of so many at once still necessarily led to other ones. Who could fly such a craft and how could they be persuaded to do so? These planes were nearing a half century in age, and the knowledge of how to operate them must be as rare as the aircraft themselves.

Mahmoud had an answer for that, too. It came in the form of the person who had helped in collecting this information for him, and who was a walking encyclopedia on this particular type of vintage American heavy bomber. Mahmoud Ahmadinejad related how he had first met this young man while still a student at the university in Tehran, just before the return of the exiled Ayatollah.

At first, he struck Ahmadinejad as being a bit 'different.' Yet he was full of religious fervency and professed loyalty for the Ayatollah, and proudly bore the description of an utterly committed Shi'a Islamist. Possessing a high intelligence, his behavior occasionally bordered on being obsessive in nature. He was never a leader but rather the gifted loner completely dedicated to his cause with little room for anything else in his life, including the people around him.

Yet in this strange young radical Ahmadinejad saw real promise, and had taken the necessary steps to recruit him into Sephah. As Mahmoud had gotten to know this individual better, he had learned that his peculiarly geared recent recruit had one other great obsession in life: the American Boeing B-17 heavy bomber.

The young man's uncle had once been in charge of the converted B-17G given to the Shah by Trans World Airlines after the Second World War. As the uncle's favorite nephew, the little boy was regaled with the stories of his flying adventures and of this magnificent airplane that served as the royal family's official aerial transportation. Finding a mesmerized audience the uncle enjoyed reliving his past experiences in flying the four engine craft, speaking in detail as well as acting out at great length.

This was followed by assorted learning aids being given to the boy, as the uncle began to realize just how fascinated and technically adept his nephew was. Books, models, manuals, posters, and the like soon crowded every available nook and space in the boy's room.

His uncle went as far as to come up with an instrument panel from a cannibalized B-17, and would quiz the boy as to what instrument did what and why. Not only that, the nephew memorized proper fuel mixtures, RPM settings, performance graphs and flight characteristics of the Boeing at different altitudes.

The young boy soaked it all up like a sponge; he was destined to fly. That destiny reached its full realization during the harsh years of the Iran-Iraq War, a chaotic, unforgiving environment that he not only survived but managed to thrive in. Now a reputably experienced as well as exceptional combat pilot in an array of different aircraft, that same young boy was presently sitting in the pilot's seat of *The Uvalde Raider*. His name was Gholam Javad.

As he had done with the others in his handpicked strike team, Yahla al-Qassam had learned from Gholam the rudimentary things necessary as far as piloting duties for the completion of their mission. That was something a good leader did as a role model for any group. It also allowed him to better understand the difficulties associated with each task assigned and prove himself as not only the driving force in command, but as someone who was also part of the team.

It had been deemed imperative that someone assist Gholam with flying the antique Boeing. Yahla had accepted that assignment due to its importance and steep learning curve, but did not share in the enthusiasm and almost rapturous involvement that Gholam heaped upon this infernal machine. The Sephah commander only wanted the operation completed, so that he could remove himself from this incredibly complicated and cantankerous metal beast.

The terrorist leader reached down beside the seat for his operational checklist, consulting it yet once again after scanning the bewildering multitude of switches, levers and instruments before him. The compass heading was good, as well as the altitude and speed. Gholam was a rather strange type, but there was no denying that he was doing a very good job at flying the heavy bomber.

Any minute now they should pick up the meandering bed of the Guadalupe River to the east. Yahla glanced over to the south, seeing in the distance the well-defined right-of way that marked the traffic lanes for Interstate 10. Once over the river, they would follow its general course to a point just short of Canyon Lake where U.S. Highway 281 ran south to San Antonio. At that juncture, they would turn to the right and follow U.S. 281 into the very northern edges of the city.

At some three minutes out, the two Hezbollah Shi'a sitting behind him would start a pair of portable air compressors, pressuring up their respective tanks to deliver the necessary PSI. Upon reaching the required air poundage, the tandem mounted centrifugal force pumps rated at approximately 65 gallons per minute would be made ready.

The Boeing would start a shallow descent from their current altitude of 5,000 feet as they crossed Loop 1604, picking up speed to 185 knots while banking gently east over the San Antonio International Airport. Just north of the airport, the pumps would engage and the oily droplets of the nerve agent would start their lethal decent to the unsuspecting population below.

Qassam had wanted to come in at a higher altitude, but there was some concern about the small gasoline engines for the compressors having fuel mixture problems at such heights. Still, the two pumps would be able to project the amber tinted VX agent about 75 feet out from either side of the plane, and the turbulence from the four rotating propellers would help further distribute the substance.

The Hezbollah leader had also taken the trouble to locate and install controlled droplet applicators, which would take the liquid stream and separate it into a more uniform mist, thus making for even better dispersion. The release was timed for the middle part of the morning, after the predicted easterly wind had a better chance to pick up. Latest weather reports forecasted this breeze at about seven miles per hour, which would assist in spreading the deadly mixture not only on the land itself, but into the nearby San Antonio River. This would allow the agent to be transported by the waterway.

Continuing south along their course they would ease back over U.S. 281 and aim for the very heart of downtown San Antonio, using the numerous tall buildings located at its center to guide upon. Once over downtown, the hijacked B-17 would fly south along Roosevelt Avenue, crossing just west of Stinson Municipal Airport. Yahla al-Qassam had calculated they would run out of agent near the intersection of Roosevelt Avenue and Loop 410. The portable gasoline engines would shut down, and the historic city of San Antonio would start to wither and die.

With the release of the five hundred gallons of VX, the Boeing bomber would be appreciably lighter. That fact, combined with their continued slight descent would increase the airplane's speed still further.

After another half hour they should be landing at an old auxiliary airstrip situated roughly south of Carrizo Springs, on a cattle ranch known as the Chupadera. This remote paved strip, built during the Second World War, was about 4,000 feet long and originally constructed to handle large aircraft such as the B-17 in an emergency situation. Gholam would have no problem setting down the Flying Fortress there.

Taking additional care to land into the wind, they would abandon the contaminated Boeing and meet up with a part of the support team that would provide transportation back into Mexico. It was about five kilometers to the Rio Grande from the airstrip and only another eight through the state of Coahuila before they would be on Carretera Federal 2, the main highway between Nuevo Laredo and Piedras Negras.

Inside another 24 hours, all of the Hezbollah personnel involved would be out of Mexico along with their new hostages. Most would leave the country by civilian airliner while a few, tasked with the security of their captives, would make their way out on a Cuban flagged freighter.

Meanwhile, the United States would be fighting a growing manmade catastrophe of a magnitude near unheard of in its existence. The persistence of the nerve agent could last for weeks with the cooler temperatures of fall and then winter, while the disruptions to the country's infrastructures would continue for years to come.

Over the next hour, the most sinister plan ever devised by any principal of modern terrorism would reach full engagement, and what occurred then would be completely irreversible. The man called Yahla al-Qassam would go down in history as the greatest practitioner of such terrorism ever, and would finally reach the important destiny for which he had been created for. 'Allah'u Akhbar!' Nothing could stop him now.

CHAPTER TWENTY-FOUR

Ezekiel Templar had been rapidly gaining on the renegade B-17, traveling better than twice the speed as the Flying Fortress was making at this altitude. He kept low to the ground and off the horizon from the Boeing, letting the mottled gray camouflage of the Messerschmitt blend in with the Hill Country landscape below.

As he closed rapidly, Ezekiel formulated a hasty plan of attack that seemed to have the best chance for success. He would come up fast on the right side of the four-engine bomber, zooming up beside as he cut throttle and lowered flaps to match its speed. Opening the small window framed into the side of the 109's canopy, he calculated to close within 50 yards and attempt to put rounds into the flight deck area with the folding stock AK.

It was a plan rife with ifs and maybes, but it was the only plan handy for the circumstances he found himself in. He knew he had to stop *The Uvalde Raider* now, before it got any closer to the populated areas surrounding San Antonio. To do that, he figured he only had about thirty rounds in the AK and the element of surprise to get the job done.

Each one of those rounds would have to be placed out of the danger zone where the VX was stored, or the aircraft would leak the deadly substance over the area overflown. Somehow, he had to bring the bomber down, hopefully in a sudden and uncontrollable manner. There was plenty of highly inflammable aviation gas in the wing tanks of the old bomber and that was how stocks of nerve agent were best destroyed, by incineration.

As he came up fast from behind and below, he could make out the metal tube protrusions angling down and away from the original waist gunner positions on the Boeing. Evidently, these delivery devices were connected to the original .50 caliber machine gun mounts still emplaced in the aircraft. He reasoned that the holding tanks and other apparatus were in the bomb bay area, it was where he had seen the terrorists working the night before. Ezekiel made a big mental note to keep his rifle fire directed away from that section of the airplane.

He was where he needed to be, on the right approach with enough air speed to surprise the bomber's occupants. The colonel started a zoom climb, timing the diminishing distance to coincide with a chopping of the throttle while in the same instant employing the flaps on the German fighter. It was a maneuver that called for an enormous amount of finesse. Once he matched the speed of the slow-moving Boeing, the Messerschmitt would only be a few miles an hour over its stalling speed.

The Me109 Gustav arced gracefully skyward. Ezekiel Templar made his best guess on the throttle and flaps, and cracked back the side window as the splotchy gray German fighter pulled alongside the polished aluminum clad American bomber. A blast of wind through the cockpit greeted him as he struggled to bring the AK into position. The pistol grip of the assault rifle banged hard against his left thigh; its barrel being whipped about by the hurricane force of air. The pain was sharp and intense, and Ezekiel fought against the ensuing nausea that added upon everything else occurring within the cramped confines of the Messerschmidt's interior.

'There!' he thought to himself as he lodged the forearm of the AK into the space created by the opened slot of the side window. He rotated the safety lever to what he thought was semi-auto fire as Micah had instructed, and looked at the huge Flying Fortress that filled the view to his left. Shifting the muzzle toward the flight deck against the shrieking wind, he found himself staring into the saucer sized eyes of a startled Yahla al-Qassam. The old Air Force colonel gripped the assault rifle even tighter and pulled the trigger.

The first indicator for Gholam Javad that things were not going well was when Al-Qassam grabbed the co-pilot's control wheel and steered hard to the left, swearing vehemently in his native Farsi. As the Flying Fortress banked hard in that direction, he heard the sound of impacts on the side of the old bomber as if someone was banging on it with a baseball bat. He knew the sound for what it was, he had been shot at often enough by the Iraqis.

However, Gholam's biggest problem was not the incoming rounds, but in making the corrections needed to keep the staggering Boeing in the air. Yahla's sudden action had upset the balance of the airplane and caused them to lose a lot of speed. He reached over and pushed all four throttles forward, while at the same time working control wheel and rudder to gently bring *The Uvalde Raider* back to level flight. Behind him he heard yet more cursing, this time in Arabic as the two Shi'a Lebanese bounced off the bare metal sides of the Boeing's interior.

"Brother! Do not do that again!" he addressed Yahla with raw authority in their native Farsi. Qassam might be the leader of this team and the golden boy of many but Gholam Javad was the commander of the Boeing while in the air, as well as those who flew along with him.

Qassam whipped his head around and glared hard briefly at Gholam. But as a growing realization set in, the Hezbollah leader's expression changed into a palpable chagrin. He had panicked for the briefest of moments and responded in a way that nearly brought on that one giddy mistake he so feared. If one of those containers of VX had ruptured or if Gholam had not responded as skillfully as he had…

The shooting had ceased and he ordered one of the Shi'a Lebanese aft to check the containers and delivery equipment. Then he began to peer around for the German fighter, wondering where it had gone. How had that old man managed to free himself, get that Messerschmitt in the air and track them down? The same Messerschmitt, by the way, which he had been assured by his men as being rendered inoperable?

And why wasn't Max Grephardt flying the fighter? What had become of Mustafa Abbas, his young champion whom he left in charge of the hostages as well as the other half of his team? What happened to the rest of his Hezbollah men left on the ground? And most importantly, who all knew of his plan now and what was being done to stop him?

The man known as Yahla al-Qassam shook the growing list of questions from his mind, and concentrated on the here and now. Even if the captives had managed to escape, they were still some fifteen miles from the nearest town. Their vehicles were disabled and all communications going into the ranch house had been cut off. Time and Allah were still on his side.

Looking through the windscreen of *The Uvalde Raider* he could plainly see the Guadalupe River below, even if he could not see Ezekiel Templar and the Messerschmitt. Moving his head and eyes all around, he wondered to himself: *Where has that accursed infidel gone and what is his next move?* The terrorist leader found himself wishing fervently that he had put that bullet into the old man's head, rather than his leg.

At that same precise moment, Ezekiel Templar was recovering from several different problems of his own. In handling the unfamiliar AK, he mistakenly rotated the safety lever to full auto. The weapon had proven nearly impossible to control in that mode, twisting and bouncing around in the cyclone-like wind. Most of his shots went wild, and he had wasted precious ammunition as well as that element of surprise.

Most crucially, he had come back too much on the throttle and in the midst of firing felt the right wing begin to dip. The Me109 was starting to stall, and the buffeting turbulence from being so close to the large bomber only added to the Messerschmitt's instability.

In a blur Ezekiel re-engaged the safety lever on the Kalashnikov and yanked the muzzle out of the blasting wind, then rammed the throttle forward. The Daimler inverted V-12 responded immediately but the right wing continued to dip earthward. Ezekiel knew that if he went into a full stall and began to spin, he would never recover at such a low altitude.

Instinctively he worked both stick and rudder, gently angling the control surfaces to go with the increasing bank, and at the same time easing the nose of the Messerschmitt down. With every fiber of both mind and body, he began willing the needed air velocity over the flight surfaces of the little fighter to regain some semblance of control.

The right wing continued to dip and Ezekiel found himself nearly inverted in a clumsy half roll. The empty shell casings from the AK rattled around and bounced off the interior of the cockpit as he fought the assault rifle itself to keep it from doing the same. Still with one hand on the stick, he began pulling back gently as the 109 Gustav went completely inverted and on its back. With the nose still pointed down, all he could see was a lot of way-too-close Texas terrain rushing up to greet him at a frightening pace.

But all 1,475 horses of water-cooled Daimler were pulling hard and combined with his maneuvering to keep the nose down, the gray camouflaged fighter was picking up speed again. Ezekiel kept the pressure on the controls and completed the slow roll with the ground still coming on fast to meet him. With no air speed indicator, he had no measure of how fast he was going, other than his decades of being one with an airplane. He began easing the stick back ever so slightly, and the agile German fighter responded in kind, leveling out in a distance measured in feet above the rock and cedar studded soil.

The colonel closed the flaps as his speed increased and pulled back into another zoom climb, looking every which direction for *The Uvalde Raider*. His left leg throbbed in agony and he had lost the element of surprise, but he was still alive and still in the fight. And for the first time since they had met the day before, Yahla al-Qassam was the one playing defense while having to deal with a growing list of unknowns.

Ezekiel Templar wanted the Flying Fortress downed and he wanted the nerve agent contained. But in a very personal manner he also wanted Qassam and he wanted him in the worst way. The Hezbollah leader was a malignant evil, a rare and supremely lethal kind of human pestilence of high intelligence, personal charisma and almost supernatural zeal. If the Iranian terrorist was allowed to walk away from this, there would be other horrific attacks and untold numbers of other innocent people put at risk.

No matter what else happened, no matter what the cost, Yahla al-Qassam had to be stopped.

Permanently.

Back in *The Uvalde Raider*, all eyes were scanning the skies both high and low for the American colonel in the mottled gray Messerschmidt. The Shi'a Lebanese ordered aft had reported no damage to their deadly cargo, and Gholam was certain there had been no real harm done to the Boeing bomber. The Hezbollah pilot regained their original course and altitude, and was flying just north of the wandering to and fro banks of the Guadalupe.

Dead ahead they could see Canyon Lake and off to the right, on the very edge of the horizon, the higher points of the skyline for San Antonio. The Iranian terrorist leader could also see several population centers scattered about the bomber's present location. He glanced at his map and confirmed their identities for any future reference. They were not only indicators to triangulate the aircraft's position, but would also serve as secondary targets if the need arose.

"Brother!" Gholam yelled over the din of the engines and speed, "He cannot hurt us! The Kalashnikov he has is next to useless against this aircraft, and he cannot accurately fly and fire it at the same time! Do not despair, Allah is still smiling upon us!"

Al-Qassam nodded his head in acknowledgement, but continued to look in every direction in conjunction with the two Shi'a Lebanese to his rear. Grimly he noted that Gholam was also glancing about, the action somewhat belaying the sincerity of his words of solace and confidence. The Iranian pilot banked the Flying Fortress slightly to the right, bringing them on course to close in with the river.

"How far?" Gholam questioned in a loud voice.

"About 40 kilometers to the highway!" replied Yahla over the surrounding noise.

Gholam consulted the flight clock on the instrument panel. "We should start to turn south in about ten minutes, Brother!" He grinned broadly at Qassam with a fiery blaze in his eyes and yelled, "Allah'u Akhbar!"

Their pilot's enthusiasm was infectious. For the first time since they had left the ground, Yahla al-Qassam smiled and lifted up his voice in response. It harmonized with those of the two Hezbollah henchmen standing close behind. "Allah'u Akhbar!"

The two most holy words in Islam had barely cleared their lips, when a series of 7.62X39 rounds began punching up through the bomber's belly beneath their feet. One caromed into the flight deck area, bouncing off the metal insides of the aircraft with the sound of an angry bee in flight. Another one made its way from below to find flesh and bone. The Arab terrorist directly behind Qassam screamed and fell to the hard metal floor plate. He continued to howl in anguish, holding his shin area tightly with both hands as blood oozed between his clasped fingers.

At only seventy-five feet below Ezekiel Templar continued to trigger the Kalashnikov, firing this time in semi auto mode. Having jettisoned the 109's birdcage canopy for a greater field of fire, Ezekiel had brought the Messerschmitt up stealthily under the Boeing from directly behind and below. It was a classic combat maneuver and the cagey Air Force colonel was using it to full advantage. This time he deftly manipulated the throttle and flaps to match the speed of the Boeing exactly, keeping enough momentum going forward to eliminate the chance of stalling the German fighter again.

Bracing the AK as best he could against the top frame for the windscreen and with the unfolded stock under his arm, he actually could sight roughly along the assault rifle's barrel and fire far more accurately. In addition, he had also fumbled around and managed to remove the underslung cleaning rod to get more of a purchase on the windscreen support, which steadied the short barreled Soviet weapon a bit more.

The irony of it all was not lost to him even as he focused on the bomber, the attack from directly behind and below by Me109s had been a favored tactic against the Flying Fortress box formations over occupied Europe. Except then the German fighters had traveled at far greater speeds and heights firing heavy machine guns and cannon. And he had been in the B-17, not the Messerschmitt.

Ezekiel continued to aim along the Kalashnikov's barrel, fighting against the whipping of the wind as he pressed the trigger repeatedly. The 109 wobbled and weaved along its flight path in his improvised style of flying, but the Texan doggedly regained his position of attack and kept shooting. At this distance he could actually see the rounds impact the belly of *The Uvalde Raider*, and could shift his aim accordingly. He knew that all he had to do was to keep it up, and sooner or later one of those rounds would make their way to the pilot or a vital control system.

The bomber started a cautious bank to the left and the colonel followed, staying with the Boeing. He imagined the pilot was trying to be as careful as possible with the hideous payload being transported. That plus taking evasive action in a Flying Fortress, like any other large aircraft of the era, was a matter of measured control input and then the ensuing wait for something to happen.

Ezekiel had them right where he wanted them, above an isolated area and away from any centers of population. *'Qassam'*, he thought, *'you weren't figuring on this, were you? It's a little different when someone is shooting at you, isn't it? Well, welcome to the big leagues, you soulless sonofabitch.'*

Concentrating on the next round, he pressed the trigger on the AK again. He felt the vibration in his hand as the hammer fell and struck the firing pin, but nothing else happened. Instinctively he wedged the stick between his legs and reached up with his left hand to work the bolt. He pressed the trigger once more. Still nothing.

His left leg was burning as if it was on fire from being wedged up against the control stick, but he ignored the pain. Pushing the magazine release on the Kalashnikov, he angled the magazine where he could see inside and his heart sank to the ground rushing by below. The magazine was empty.

For the first time since his wife had died, Ezekiel Templar felt himself wanting to cry. Despairingly, he looked at the now useless assault rifle still clenched in his right hand. Bringing it over and into the shrieking wind outside of the cockpit, he dropped the weapon over the side of the Messerschmitt. The AK tumbled down, smashing on to the rocky terrain on impact. It was not only now useless to him, but the short-barreled rifle could prove to be an impediment in the fighter's cramped quarters for what he had to do now.

Ezekiel Templar had always been a thinking man, or he would never have made it as far in life as he had managed to do. At heart he was also a careful person, the kind of man who preferred to never make a move before thinking it completely through. There was a vast difference between taking a chance and a calculated risk, and he had done very well in calculating the risks that happened to confront him over all these years.

From the moment the Messerschmitt left the tarmac at the Bar JA, he had kept a final option filed away deep within his consciousness. It was not one that any sane human being ever desired to consider in any normal circumstance or mode of thinking. Ezekiel racked his brain as the Messerschmitt drifted away from the bomber, trying to come up with something else. Something, anything, that he had overlooked up to this point.

But there wasn't anything else and time was running out. They were less than twenty minutes from San Antonio. He scanned the horizon in all directions, looking for any kind of sign signaling that help might be on the way. The vast emptiness of the clear blue Texas sky signaled back its message of bitter finality. There would be no help, no last moment outside assistance. It was all up to him and it was now or never. Resignedly, he shoved the Gustav's throttle against its full power stop and shot forward into the eastern beyond.

CHAPTER TWENTY-FIVE

Inside *The Uvalde Raider*, the sudden pandemonium had dissipated with the cessation of the incoming fire. Gholam scanned the instruments one more time and relaxed a bit. They were still in the air, still moving toward their target and with no impending signs of doom noted in the numerous instruments arrayed before him. His uncle had not exaggerated to the small boy about the Boeing B-17. What a magnificent aircraft!

The man called Yahla al-Qassam sat back down in the co-pilot's seat, wiping the blood from his hands on his khaki trousers.

"How is he?" Gholam yelled over the drone of the radial engines.

"Alive!" responded Qassam. "But of no use anytime soon! I will have to help with the pumps!"

Gholam nodded in agreement. "We drifted north during the American's last attack. Our intersection point with the highway will be about eight kilometers off!"

It was Qassam's turn to nod in agreement. He looked through the front and side windows of the bomber.

"Where did he go?" he asked.

"Up ahead!" Gholam pointed to the Messerschmitt streaking away, just below the horizon. "I think he is out of ammunition! Perhaps he is trying to reach an airport to alert the authorities!"

Qassam studied his map once more and leaned over toward the pilot. "He'll never get there in time!"

Gholam kept his eyes fixed on the disappearing Me109. The mottled gray pattern made it hard to see, even when he knew where to look. Watching his defeated opponent race away, the pilot commented, "He is a brave and determined man! I would like to have known him under different circumstances!"

For a long moment, Qassam said nothing in return. Finally, he responded. "He is an infidel and an enemy to Islam! He will burn in the eternal hell!"

Gholam said nothing else. He continued to follow the Messerschmitt's progress, until he had to lower his eyes to check the instruments again. As he did so, he heard Qassam exclaim excitedly.

"What is he doing now?"

The pilot glanced back up and had no trouble picking out the Me109 this time. Its dark silhouette was now above the horizon, going into a steep climb that Ghalom marveled at. He had never seen any piston driven aircraft climb so fast.

His admiration turned into a vague concern as he observed the Messerschmitt execute a perfect Half Cuban Eight, coming right back at them at a blistering rate of speed. Both Iranians watched as the powerful fighter bore in, looming larger by the second in their windscreen.

Ezekiel Templar came out of his inverted angle of flight, performing a perfectly timed half roll and aimed straight at the oncoming Flying Fortress. His hand was steady on the stick and the inverted Daimler V-12 was at full song, nose slightly down with the morning sun to his back. He had never felt any more alive, or in more control of any other aircraft.

He was thinking of where he had been and where might he be going next. Not far away, just over the horizon to the southwest was home, the area of Texas where he has spent his years growing up. He thought of hot, lazy days along the Nueces and the Frio, of weekend trips into Uvalde and of breaking horses that summer below Chalk Bluff with his brother Jeremiah. Those had been shining times and to a young boy in search of adventure it seemed as if they would never end.

In his mind the snapshots of time continued on with his years in the Air Force, of friends no longer around whom he missed so dearly. He thought again of Max and of their unlikely friendship that had spanned languages, nations, continents and wars. *Sorry about your baby here, Max, but I just don't know any other way.*

Then his memories turned to his only son, Jacob, lost in a sudden fireball that had been an F4 Phantom on a mission in a controversial war that had ripped a nation in two. It had not only done so with his country, but it had also wounded his own family in a way that never healed.

Through it all, he thought of Sue. Oh, how much he had loved that woman. Why did you have to take her away from me, too, God? For as far back as he could remember, Sue had been there. She had been the little girl in pigtails and freckles, grinning at him in first grade class. It was his first day in school and the first time he had gotten in trouble, though hardly the last. She had grinned at that, too.

Then she had been the stunning young woman, dressed for their high school prom. It had taken him nearly a week to work up enough nerve to ask her. She had said yes, and then asked him what had taken him so long. She said the same thing when he proposed and was the most beautiful bride he ever laid eyes on.

Sue had literally glowed when Jake was born, even if she was much worse for the wear. The delivery was so difficult they never tried again. Their only child had grown into such an extraordinary young man, so full of so much potential that in the end was never realized.

When they had gotten the word about Jake, all they could do was hold each other tight and hope the hurt would go away. Nights found them talking, trying to reassure each other as they cried themselves into a troubled sleep. It had been during the peak of the moon program, and he had turned to his work with a vengeance to try to fill the deep feeling of emptiness inside. Sue did not have that luxury, all she had was he and Jake.

It hadn't been that much longer when he held her hand for the last time, in that hospital room in Houston. He had taken her to the finest doctors he could find but was told there was nothing they could do. *"Her heart is just played out, Mr. Templar,"* yet Ezekiel knew better. The love of his life did not die from a bad heart, she died from a broken one.

In the world he hoped to find next they would all be there, waiting for him. Ezekiel Templar had tried to live the best and most honorable life he could, though there were times he made his mistakes.

Sometimes they had been big ones. He had also made more than his fair share of hard decisions, then went on and tried to make peace with them.

Ezekiel wondered if Sue would be asking him what took so long this time, too. *'It's all right, Sweetheart, I'm here now and we have the rest of eternity together.'*

His last thought was a final appeal to the All Mighty as well as a closing affirmation for what was to come. *'Forgive me, Father, for I have sinned...many times.'*

The mottled gray Messerschmitt impacted *The Uvalde Raider*, slamming into the flight deck of the bomber with a combined speed of nearly 600 miles an hour. A terrifying clap of man-made thunder echoed through the nearby hills and valleys, as the two aircraft welded themselves together in a deathly embrace. The Flying Fortress paused in mid-air, as if a giant unseen hand had reached up from the ground and stopped it. Then the nose portion of the Boeing, sawed asunder by the hurtling Me109, drooped sharply and dropped away.

The rest of the big Flying Fortress stalled and simply fell over on itself. The fall steepened, the four-engine craft going into an inverted flat spin. Down it fluttered and spun like the last, large leaf of late autumn following the first freeze. It continued falling in such a fashion until the Boeing and what was left of the Messerschmitt exploded on the rock-strewn pasture below. The impact sent up an ugly, tell-tale column of fire and black smoke, and searing flames fed by hundreds of gallons of aviation gas greedily consumed any and all things within their reach.

CHAPTER TWENTY-SIX

Micah had patched up Blue Shirt as best he could, working fast to stop the bleeding and repositioning the Shi'a to rest more comfortably. It was a matter of precious seconds, but he couldn't in good conscience let the man lay there and bleed to death. He also took the precaution of making certain the Hezbollah terrorist was securely restrained, just in case he had enough remaining resolve to try to wander off.

During his first aid work, the former Marine found the keys to the Suburban in the man's front pants pocket. He gathered them up, along with the dropped AK and nearby Czech CZ25 submachine gun, and walked as fast as he could back to the SUV. He tried to recon shuffle again but his ribs simply would not cooperate. Once in the Chevrolet, the engine fired immediately and Micah was headed out.

It was fifteen miles back into town, partly by caliche surfaced road. The highway patrolman flogged the three-quarter ton unmercifully all the way in, hitting speeds that would make a Saturday night dirt track champ a bit queasy. He brought the tan Chevrolet to a smoking, skidding halt under the sally port and headed for the front door of the Sheriff's Office.

Juanita Onofre was working the day shift as dispatch, manning the radio console on what had been a very quiet Friday morning. That was, until being startled by the door flying open and Micah Templar careening through it.

Or at least, she thought it was Micah. His appearance was a double shock for her. Caked blood covered the top of his head while some, still drying, oozed all the way down his neck. His left eye was so badly swollen that all she could see was a mere slit, with the pupil peering out through the narrow gap. His lips were split and puffy and he walked unsteadily, favoring his right side.

The lawman's face was pockmarked with bruises, cuts and abrasions, as were his swollen hands. What was left of his highway patrol uniform had been ripped and torn, and was covered with a filthy mixture of sweat, dirt and blood stains. If there was ever a case of looking like death warmed over, Micah Templar was a still breathing example of the disease.

"Where's the sheriff?" he asked urgently.

"In his office, taking a call from the jail commission." Juanita paused and then added, "Micah, what happened? You look awful! We need to get you to the emergency room."

"Tell him I need to talk to him, right now." Micah responded roughly, never breaking stride. He looked over and saw the apprehension in her eyes and stopped. "I'm okay, Juanita," he spoke in a softer tone. "But I got to talk to Roy. We've got an emergency like never before."

Juanita grabbed the phone and punched the intercom button as Micah walked into his own office and turned the lights on. Making his way to his desk, the trooper half collapsed into the chair and opened the drawer where he kept his important phone numbers. Selecting the one he wanted out of a notebook, he set it down on the desk top and started dialing. Midway through, Sheriff Roy Sharpe stepped into the room.

"Good Lord, Micah..." he began, finding himself stunned at his friend's appearance. The highway patrolman raised his hand and stopped him from saying anything else as the line on the other end picked up.

"Captain Burton, its Micah Templar." Micah spoke into the phone. "I'm fine, sir, but we have an emergency situation and I called you direct to save time. Do you have a paper and pen handy?" He cupped his hand over the receiver. "Roy, I need you to start calling every sheriff between here and the San Antonio area. Ask them if they have any reports about old World War II aircraft flying over their county. Tell them it is an extreme emergency. Also tell them that DPS will be in touch shortly to help coordinate the effort. Probably the feds, too."

Sheriff Roy K. Sharpe had been a peace officer most of his adult life, and had developed the discerning ability to quickly read a situation while simultaneously gauging the seriousness of it. He had worked with Micah for years, even back to when Sharpe was still a deputy. During that time he had been with Templar in a couple of tight spots, and liked as well as respected both the officer and the man. As Micah began to explain to his captain what was happening, the sheriff listened in. Then he turned and started for the phone in his own office.

He was sprinting to get there.

The highway patrolman finished the phone conversation with his captain, who in turn immediately launched his district office into a beehive of frenzied activity. The captain had the position and resources to get the word out rapidly to those who needed it most. Micah looked at the clock on the office wall and realized with a dreadful sinking feeling they had already run out of time. *The Uvalde Raider* had to be in the San Antonio area by now.

And what about Tio Zeke?

Juanita had called the two duty deputies in, as well as a local volunteer EMT. They were all standing in the doorway when Micah looked away from the clock. She brushed past the other three and put a large mug of iced sweet tea in front of him. Micah picked it up and began drinking as only a parched and exhausted man can do.

"Micah, I know you don't have time to go to the ER," Juanita said. "So, I called Jude Thomas in, along with A.J. and Pablo. The sheriff wants them brought up to speed and I want Jude to take a look at you." She turned and started back out the door.

"Okay, Juanita," he responded. Micah took another long swig of the sweet tea before continuing. "And Juanita," she paused and looked back as Micah smiled through his cracked and bloody lips. *"Muchisimas gracias."*

The matronly woman grinned back as the three men gathered in the doorway stepped aside to let her through. Every good department had their Juanita Onofre, exemplary at her job and in her concern for others. She was one of the best dispatchers Micah had ever worked with. No matter what the situation, she did her part and then some, and was fiercely loyal to the officers who depended upon her. Those who had any sense responded in same.

EMT Jude Thomas made his way over, telling Micah to take off what was left of his shirt as the trooper briefed the two deputies on what had occurred. He warned them of the two Hezbollah terrorists still alive at the airstrip, as well as the dead ones and where to find them.

"There is also a body inside the flight shack. He's a German national and was murdered by that terrorist handcuffed to the rail." Micah paused for a moment, lowering his head as an aura of deep sadness weighed upon him. "Fellas, that man saved my life. Please give him the care he deserves. He was my friend, and he died because of me."

Micah looked up at them again, setting his grief aside to be dealt with later. "Remember those two terrorists still alive are *muy malvados*, no matter how bad off they may look. Be real careful." The highway patrolman grunted under his breath as the EMT probed his right side.

"Hurts?" asked Thomas.

"Oh yeah."

"It ought to, I think you got a couple of busted ribs there." The EMT continued to examine Micah.

The highway patrolman turned his attention back to the deputies. "That's about all I can tell you. There should be several troopers in the county within the hour, as well as the rangers. I imagine the feds will show up soon enough, too," he paused again. "Thanks, guys, I really appreciate you."

"We'll get it done, Micah," replied Pablo. "You just take it easy." A.J. nodded in agreement.

The two deputies left quickly, headed for their patrol units. Jude Thomas had finished his poking and prodding, and now stood studying Templar with his arms folded on his chest.

"Well?" Micah asked, taking another long swig of the iced sweet tea.

"You need to see the doc ASAP," replied the EMT. "I've already told you about the ribs and that gash in the head is going to need stitching up. You'll also need x-rays of both areas because there's no telling what's going on inside." He produced a roll of gauze from his crash kit. "I'll wrap those ribs for now, but only if you get yourself over to the ER first chance you get."

"Done," replied Micah.

The EMT worked rapidly with the gauze and white medical tape. Jude Thomas had been an Army medic at one time and knew his business. Within a few minutes he had wrapped and taped the ribs, and was gathering his gear together to leave.

"You going out to the Bar JA, Army?" asked Micah.

"Yep," responded the EMT. "After working on you, I just can't wait to see the other guy." Thomas stood up, bag in hand. "Remember, Jarhead. You get to the ER pronto. Don't make me come looking for you."

Jude lingered for a moment, obviously troubled about what he had heard. "Micah, about these terrorists and their plan. Do you really think?" his voice trailed off.

"That they can pull it off?" Micah finished the question. "I don't know, Jude. As of right now we are beyond out of time and even further out of options. All I know is that if anybody can stop them, it'll be my Uncle Zeke."

The presence of Bob Sharpe drew their attention. He stood in the doorway, looking at some written notes in his left hand.

"Micah," he said. "I just got word from the sheriff over in Kendall County. He says they've been getting reports of a crash involving a large aircraft over the past few minutes. Best location they can give at present is southeast of Kendalia and a bit north of the Guadalupe River."

"Several units from different agencies are responding," he continued. "The area is very near the edge of his territory with Blanco and Comal County. I told him to tell everybody to treat this as an extremely dangerous HAZMAT incident, and to stay the hell away until DPS gets there."

"Roy, if it's *The Uvalde Raider*, they need to evacuate out to a couple of miles from the crash. That VX is supposed to be really bad stuff."

"Yeah, I know," the sheriff shook his head in agreement. "I listened long enough while you talked with your captain to realize that. Look, I met the Kendall County Sheriff during our last association convention. He's a new man, but smart and with an excellent reputation. He'll handle this fine until they can get help to him."

Micah Templar reached for his phone, intent on updating Captain Burton. There was a DPS district office in San Antonio and DPS Austin was not much farther away. The Kendall County Sheriff would get plenty of help out there quickly enough. The main challenge now was to isolate both the area as well as the aircraft's nightmarish cargo. He had no exact idea of how Tio Zeke managed to bring the old bomber down, but he had.

Roy Sharpe's next words made him stop. "Micah," he spoke slowly. "There is something else you should know. Some of these reports are saying the crash was caused by a mid-air collision with a smaller aircraft. One report in particular described it as a smaller gray aircraft with German crosses on the wings." The sheriff added, "Like you see in old World War Two movies."

At that moment Micah knew exactly how Tio Zeke had managed to stop *The Uvalde Raider*. But this was no time for mourning and barely enough for a short, silent prayer. The trooper only nodded, picked up the receiver and began dialing again.

CHAPTER TWENTY-SEVEN

Two weeks later, a black and white Dodge Diplomat turned off Lamar Boulevard and into the parking area for the DPS Headquarters Building in Austin. At the wheel was Trooper Micah Templar, dressed in the Texas Highway Patrol winter uniform with tie and long-sleeved shirt. The brass officially referred to the uniform's color as desert tan, but it looked suspiciously like Confederate gray to the uninitiated.

Wearing his nicest pair of black Justin ropers and with his best uniform freshly dry cleaned, Micah eased out of the driver's seat of the Dodge. Though wrapped tightly in the Velcro secured chest brace, his slowly healing ribs still did not take kindly to any sudden movement. That was why he was driving a Diplomat today, its automatic transmission was a lot easier on those fractured bones than the five speed manual in his Mustang patrol unit.

Gingerly Micah put on his uniform Resistol felt hat, trying to avoid the still tender gash on the top of his head. Carefully, almost reverently, he laid his Ray Ban Aviators on the Dodge's dashboard. They had been a gift from Tio Zeke when Micah graduated from DPS Recruit School, all those years ago. A memento of happier days, he would be buying another pair in order to put these away for safekeeping.

The highway patrolman adjusted the gig line on his Sam Browne belt by habit and pensively eyeballed the massive white building before him. Like many other troopers, he did not like going to Austin and he also didn't like being anywhere near the academy area. Beyond that, he especially didn't like going into the Headquarters Building when summoned by the high brass.

On top of everything else, he was supposed to be meeting with the Director of the Texas Department of Public Safety himself, in his office. That was usually a place where they summoned you when you had really screwed up, or if the brass wanted something really special out of you. Micah did not care for either idea.

He checked his watch and mentally prepared himself for whatever awaited. Up the steps and through the glass doors, Micah soon found himself in front of the area marked 'Director's Office.' Taking in a long breath, he pushed through and walked inside.

At the desk sat a middle-aged woman wearing reading glasses who was evidently the director's personal secretary. The lady looked up from the assorted papers on her desk and smiled one of those professional secretary smiles, the kind that makes you wonder if they are in on the joke while you don't even have a clue.

"You must be Micah Templar," she said.

"Yes ma'am, unfortunately I am," he deadpanned in return.

The secretary laughed politely. "Would you please sit down? The director is expecting you, I'll let him know that you are here."

"Ma'am, I have been sitting for the past 250 miles. If you don't mind, I'd just like to stand a bit."

"Well, of course you can," she responded in an agreeable manner. Picking up the phone, she pushed a button. "Colonel? Trooper Templar is here." There was a pause. "Yes sir, I will."

She put down the phone and spoke to Micah. "He'll be right with you." The secretary smiled again and returned to her work.

Micah looked around the room as he waited, thinking more than anything else about what might be in store for him on the other side of that inner door. He took stock of his situation and what he knew about the DPS's recently appointed head.

The Texas Department of Public Safety was changing rapidly, much like the state which it had served so faithfully for the past half century. The days of Homer Garrison and Pat Speir, when the occupancy spent in the director's chair was measured in decades, had mostly come to a close.

The current director, or colonel as the head of the DPS was traditionally known, was said to be a good enough man and had been in the Department for over thirty years. But the scuttlebutt had it that he was already on his way out to make room for someone else. That was another reason for avoiding DPS Headquarters: much like any other large government bureaucracy it served as ground zero for personal fiefdoms, rumor mills and political intrigues.

Absentmindedly Micah studied the large map of Texas centered on the wall before him. Though covered with a plexiglass shield, it was obvious the area just north of San Antonio had been receiving an inordinate amount of attention. Finger smudges covered the general location, along with small marks and light scratches made from other objects.

Micah knew the crash site was brimming with activity and the list of unanswered questions were growing even as the cleanup continued. As a highway patrolman stationed in a somewhat isolated, rural area he had not been made privy to much of anything by official channels existing within the Texas DPS.

Captain Burton had called on occasion, as well as some of the troopers he knew in the San Antonio area. But no one could tell him much as far as what was going on. All his captain could say was that in his opinion Micah had done an exceptional job, which made him feel somewhat better about the situation. However, he was not to talk to anyone as the investigation was still ongoing.

The fact was most everybody in the DPS had no idea of what was happening. As soon as the Feds moved in, the exchange of information that was supposed to go both ways was shut off and apparently forgotten. As far as Micah knew, no one from the DPS was allowed on scene save at the very highest levels.

Fellow highway patrolmen he had visited with were able to confirm that much. Though they were nominally part of some sort of response force, their duties consisted of nothing more than traffic control to keep the curious away. This was easy enough to do, as their checkpoints were also kept a good deal of distance from the site. Anything closer than their outlying posts was soon nicknamed 'G-Man Land.'

One young troop had brought along a small camera, and was taking photographs of the general area while manning one of the check points. Somebody had seen him do so and the camera was confiscated on order from a federal honcho who showed up minutes afterwards. Then some high-ranking brass from DPS Headquarters came out and reamed the hapless rookie a new one. He was threatened with anything and everything including being fired and filed upon under some sort of obscure federal government statute. Needless to say, nobody brought a camera with them anymore.

Inside G-Man Land, the Feds had their own checkpoints manned by some sort of uniformed troops armed with M16s, M60 machine guns and no sense of humor. There were also patrols out around the clock, both on foot and by vehicle and on occasion a few were spotted in special protective gear. Heavy equipment, some of which no one had ever seen before, was going into the site and then back out.

There were also numerous tractor trailer rigs with some sort of custom-built vans being used. The units would arrive empty and then leave the scene loaded down with whatever. The License & Weight troops were the first to pick up on this, but they weren't exactly sure of their purpose.

Meanwhile, the sheriffs of the counties involved were not real happy either. If the DPS troopers felt like they were being kept out of the loop, these local peace officers were being treated like the proverbial mushroom. Their citizens, concerned about what was happening and rattled by wild rumors, were demanding information from the law enforcement agencies they knew best: their county sheriff's offices. The sheriffs were asking the feds and in turn found themselves summarily ignored, or handed off to public information types who had no real idea themselves of what was occurring.

The maddest of all was the recently elected sheriff of Kendall County. During the critical first minutes of what could have been a major disaster in the making, he and his small department had responded without hesitation to protect their citizens, as well as their county. One of the callers, a nearby rancher, had reported *The Uvalde Raider* going down and stated he was enroute to the crash scene to see if he could be of any assistance.

On direct orders from the sheriff, a responding deputy veered away from his original route. The peace officer ran through a couple of closed gates and fence lines in determined fashion, cutting across country to intercept the rancher. The end result was one thoroughly trashed example of what had been a new Ford Crown Victoria patrol car, but the deputy had succeeded in stopping the could-be dead man before he had gotten into the danger zone.

Now that same sheriff and his department were being treated like diseased pariahs by the federal authorities. Roy Sharpe had relayed to Micah what transpired in the phone conversations shared with his furious Kendall County counterpart.

"I'd be fighting mad too," Roy had declared. "He and his men did a crackerjack job, risking their necks and putting themselves out way beyond what anybody could expect." Sharpe paused and shook his head in admiring frustration. "Not one civilian life lost, not even any injuries."

The plain-speaking lawman then snorted in disgust. "Hell, the whole outfit deserves some sort of official recognition and the feds treat them like they don't even exist. Worst thing is, his locals are scared and wanting to know what's happening out there. But he can't tell 'em nothin' because the feds refuse to say anything to him!"

Bob shook his head again, but this time not for the same reason. "So he's in the dog house with the folks who elected him to office, the same folks he and his deputies busted their butts for in keeping safe. What a deal…"

The sound of the inner door opening behind him brought Micah back to the present and he turned to see the director himself standing there. "Come on in, Micah, we've been talking about you." The colonel was smiling, but Micah did not know if that meant something good or something bad. He decided to play it as if it was something bad, that way he wouldn't be disappointed or unpleasantly surprised.

Moving closer together, the two men shook hands and the trooper noted the director's firm grasp. He also made note that the colonel looked him straight in the eye when he did so. *'At least it's not like shaking hands with a dead fish,'* Micah thought. *'And he don't have that look of one eye on a snake and the other one looking for a stick to beat it with.'*

The head of the DPS escorted the highway patrolman into his paneled office, where three other men sat in different chairs. Micah was introduced to each one in turn and also shook hands with them.

Leading out for the three was a large, overweight man with a receding hair line that swept back to a bald spot at the very top of his head. The thinning hair that remained had turned white and contrasted sharply against his ruddy complexion. The near obese fellow wore horn rimmed glasses and dressed in an ill-fitting suit, which made him look more like a seedy lawyer than anything else.

The colonel introduced him to Micah. "This is Mr. Humboldt, he's in charge overall of the federal recovery efforts where your uncle's plane went down."

"Very pleased to meet you, Trooper Templar. Very pleased." Humboldt smiled broadly and in vigorous fashion pumped Micah's right arm up and down.

"This is Mr. Wadley," the colonel continued. "Mr. Wadley is with the FBI, and was sent in from Washington to head up the law enforcement and security angles for the operation." Micah turned slightly and found himself looking at a thin, pasty fellow who reminded him of an animated caricature of a human ferret.

He instinctively found himself disliking Wadley, a feeling that was only reinforced when the two shook hands. The government bureaucrat had a limp grasp and a clammy feel to the palms, and his hands were too soft and well-manicured to have ever seen much use. '*Like shaking hands with that dead fish*,' Micah thought, '*and with the eyes to match.*' Wadley said nothing, so neither did Micah.

The head of the Department continued the introductions. "And this is Mr. Eggers." From off to the side the third man rose from his chair and walked agilely toward the others. Of average height and an athletic build, Eggers was dark headed with facial features and a skin tone that would allow him to blend in most anyplace. When he grasped Micah's hand it was in a firm, no nonsense manner. He looked the highway patrolman in the eyes intently, as if he was searching for something of a read himself.

"How are you, trooper?" Eggers asked, and meant it.

"Doing all right, sir," responded Templar.

Micah found himself slightly taken aback. There was something truly remarkable about this man and it started with his eyes. They were just as dark as his hair, almost black, and penetrating in their gaze. Behind them Micah could sense the presence of a highly intelligent and capable human being, someone with a warrior's heart. Someone who, given the right circumstances, had the capacity of being a very dangerous man.

Yet it was not only those eyes but the man himself that caused Micah to do a double take. It was as if he had met him before, somewhere else a long time ago. Even his name tugged at Micah Templar's memory. Eggers…where had he heard that before?

CHAPTER TWENTY-EIGHT

"Sit down, gentlemen." The director gestured at the chairs placed around the large office.

Humboldt and Wadley sat back in their previous seats directly positioned in front of the director's sizeable wooden desk. Micah picked a chair over to the side, where he could watch the two in front of the desk as well as his boss who seated himself behind it. He was getting a vague impression that the head of the DPS was not exactly happy with either of these two. It was as if there had been some sort of difference of opinion before his arrival.

Micah Templar glanced over at Eggers, who had selected a chair near the rear of the office that allowed him to watch everyone else. Micah found himself studying the man more as another little fact popped into his head. The colonel never said who Eggers actually worked for. The man met his studious gaze, nodded and smiled a bit.

'Who are you, Mr. Eggers?' Micah questioned himself. *'And why do I keep thinking I know you from someplace else?'*

"Micah," the colonel started speaking and Templar looked back at him. "We called you in today to visit about what happened last month and what is going to be happening in the near future. These gentlemen are asking for the Department's cooperation in this matter, but we as an agency can't fully give it unless you do too.

"As a member of this Department, you were placed in a situation that really has no precedent in the history of the DPS, or the Texas Highway Patrol. At least, not in the modern era of our existence." His colonel paused a moment and looked straight at him.

"I have read your report as well as the statements of those locals you came into contact with that morning. I have also spoke at length with the rangers who did the investigation at the Albright airstrip. What you went through was more like some sort of military combat action, than anything having to do with civilian law enforcement.

"Personally, I want to take this opportunity to tell you in man-to-man fashion that what you did was simply exemplary, and in the highest traditions of our Department. More so, the citizens of the state of Texas owe your uncle and Mister Grephardt a debt of gratitude that can never be adequately repaid."

Micah cut his eye over to the two men sitting in front of the desk. Humboldt looked a little too earnest as he listened in, while Wadley appeared to be impatient and perhaps even a little agitated. Then again, Wadley hit the trooper as one of those types who was always a little agitated about one thing or another.

Intertwining his fingers and placing his hands on his desk, the director leaned forward. "But now you are going to be told something entirely different about all this and these gentlemen are going to be doing the telling." The head of the DPS looked hard at Wadley and added a shade icily "After all, that is the very least they can do."

'Uh oh,' thought Micah to himself, *'so much for the halo routine. Now comes the hammer.'*

Humboldt shifted his hefty weight uneasily in the overstuffed chair and took his glasses off to clean them with a handkerchief. "Firstly Trooper Templar, the Federal Government also wants to commend you and your companions for your courage and bravery. Unfortunately, the three of you were working under some altogether mistaken assumptions."

The partially bald man stopped polishing his eyewear and looked up. "We need for you to understand something that may come as an absolute shock. After thoroughly investigating the crash scene, it is our determination there was no sort of chemical agents whatsoever on that aircraft."

Micah stared at the government official with incredulity as the oversized bureaucrat continued on. "Furthermore, and in regard to this group that tried to take your uncle's aircraft: We have found no evidence of any of them being from the Middle East, or of belonging to any sort of terrorist organization. As far as we can tell those involved were actually members of a South American drug cartel, though we are not at liberty to say much more than that."

Humboldt paused, looking up through his glasses at the overhead florescent lights. Evidently satisfied he placed the horn rims back on his fat, ruddy face. "The reason they wanted your uncle's aircraft was to pick up a shipment of assault weapons purchased illegally here in the United States and smuggle them across the border. From there, the aircraft was going to be pressed into service as a transport to conduct large scale smuggling operations involving controlled substances."

Glancing at Wadley somewhat pensively he finished off by saying, "That's about all there is to it. No nerve agent, no terrorists and no plot to murder innocent civilians. Just common criminals attempting to become wealthy through weapons smuggling as well as narcotics trafficking."

For several seconds, an uneasy silence fell over the room. At first Micah was confused and somewhat stunned, his mind trying to correlate with what he knew as facts and what was being said now. As his suspicions started to take form as to what sort of game was presently being played, he felt a flush of anger rising within himself, causing him to grip both arms of his chair.

The highway patrolman fought to steady his emotions as his eyes widened involuntarily, forcing his eyebrows so high they pulled at the stitches on top of his head. Micah Templar did not like being lied to, and had spent nearly twenty years at a job where people did so on a daily basis. Humboldt was not even in the top fifty percent of the class.

Forcing himself to keep an even tone in his voice, Micah responded in a low, slow manner of speaking to keep his rousing anger in check.

"Let me get this straight," he began. "You want me to believe that Qassam's bunch was part of a Latin American crime cartel, and they went through all of that just to smuggle a bunch of drugs in."

"Not just drugs, Templar, but weapons too," Wadley interjected sharply. "We have a huge problem with our lack of gun laws in this nation and smuggling them south is a wide open business." The FBI supervisor stopped and then added maliciously to put Micah in his proper place, "or perhaps you don't read the newspapers out where you come from."

The highway patrolman eyed the FBI supervisor with a rapidly growing dislike. If there ever was truth to the old adage of buying somebody for what they were worth, and selling them for what they thought they were worth, and making a lot of money? Well, this guy fit the bill to a tee.

"Oh, but you are so wrong there," Micah replied, looking hard from Wadley to Humboldt and back again. "I happen to do a good deal of reading and I notice things, too. After all, noticing things is what the State of Texas pays me to do. Picking up on little stuff like when people are speaking Arabic instead of Spanish, or when I'm being shot at by fully automatic AKs stamped with Russian markings, and not some semi-auto version out of a local gun shop."

"There are the other things I noticed," he continued, "like needing three-quarter ton vehicles to carry in a bunch of spraying equipment, as well as several large blue plastic drums that everyone seemed to have a real healthy respect for.

"And if they were smuggling weapons into Mexico, where were they? They weren't at the airstrip. Also, if they were running guns, why take the scenic route and fly north of San Antonio? When *The Uvalde Raider* went down, she was nearly twice as far from the border as when she took off."

Humboldt tried to reply but instead trailed off as Micah pointedly ignored him and kept speaking, now gesturing from time to time with his hands and stabbing with his right index finger for emphasis. As the trooper made his case, Wadley's face became darker and his eyebrows set into one hard line. But he remained silent.

"Then we have the crash scene itself. It's shut down tight and sealed off, and no one seems to know what's going on or wanting to explain why. There are military troops out there right now, armed with M16s and carrying or wearing protective gear. The same kind of gear designed for nuclear, biological or chemical warfare. If there was no nerve agent found, then why is that?

"Finally, Qassam made it a point to tell us what was in those plastic containers and what they were being used for. I think he did it to either taunt or try to impress my uncle, or maybe both. Or maybe he really did want some kind of historical record as to what was happening. Whatever it was, I also know my Tio Zeke believed him enough to destroy his own aircraft while sacrificing his life to stop him."

Micah Templar paused for a moment, staring fixedly at the two men. "Matter of fact I believed Qassam myself, just like I don't believe you two gents now. We have a saying out in West Texas, 'Don't pee on my boots and tell me it's raining.' Right now, my boots are soaking wet and there ain't a cloud in the sky."

Another long silence followed. The colonel appeared to be slightly amused but not that he would show it much. During his response, Micah had cut his eyes a couple of times to where Eggers sat. Each time the trooper glanced over, the man was grinning a little more. Micah was not sure of what was going on just yet, but he felt as if he had at least one ally in this affair.

Humboldt shifted his ponderous weight again in the protesting chair, looking first at Micah, then the colonel and then to Wadley, then back again. Wadley was trying to stare bullet holes through the former Marine and Micah was responding in kind. The two glared at each other with open contempt, and the room fairly steamed in the rising pall of deep animosity fermenting between them.

"Very well," Wadley muttered ominously. "Since you seem to have such a strong opinion in your recollection of facts, let me fill you in on a few others.

"Trooper Templar, you are in a very precarious situation legally speaking. I read the same reports your colonel did, but I have a completely different take on what happened. There was a great deal of shooting going on at that ranch and you did more than anyone else, as well as more killing.

According to your own admission you shot one man in the back and killed him, shot another from the rear who was just trying to get away and then cold bloodedly executed a third from a concealed position, not to mention killing yet another one with your revolver. Furthermore, all this was after you nearly beat a man to death with your bare hands, and far beyond the point needed in making any legitimate arrest."

Wadley paused, staring at Micah with his peculiarly shaped ferret face. His eyes were calculating, and his body language oozed unshadowed arrogance. In a voice mixed with sarcasm and threat, the FBI supervisor went on. "You say you read a lot. Well, I strongly suggest that you read about excessive force and civil rights violations, because you may very well find yourself answering to both in a Federal court of law."

"Mister," Micah retorted, "if you plan on dragging me into any court of law, I fully expect to see that human rattlesnake they called Mustafa there to testify, along with that other terrorist I patched up."

"By the way," the highway patrolman mused, "exactly what happened to those two? Seems both disappeared about as quickly as your people got involved. It's as if they never existed."

"Templar," replied Wadley testily. "Those two are of no concern to you, now or ever. Believe me, you have far too many other troubles of a personal nature to spend time wondering about what happened to them."

"Says who? You?" queried Micah skeptically. "You talked about Federal law, so let me tell you something about Texas law. Those two are guilty of theft, kidnapping, aggravated assault, attempted murder and murder, among other criminal acts found in our Penal Code. Plus, they would be necessary witnesses in any charges you might bring against me. I think I have a vested interest in their whereabouts for all kinds of reasons."

All of the color began draining from Wadley's face and he scowled with clenched teeth at the defiant trooper. Wadley was the sort of person who was used to having everyone beneath him bow near unthinkingly to his authority, and to kowtow to while undergoing his oft-practiced repertoire of unfiltered intimidation. Micah Templar was of a different breed entirely and his blatant obstinacy was galling the FBI supervisor to no end.

"Look, we are doing our best to help in your situation, Templar," Wadley snapped back. "Asking for nothing in return but a little cooperation. But if you want to play hard ball, you need to run and get your little bat and glove right now and start practicing, because you are going to be playing way out of your league."

There it was, full in Micah's face. He was being herded by Wadley and Humboldt into going along with this absurdity foisted upon him, or else. He had no idea what their reasoning was for doing so, or why. But he was fully aware that he was being threatened and everything within him was in open rebellion because of it.

Emphatically, Micah rose and leaned over with both knuckles on the edge of the colonel's desk. The trooper's face turned to stone, the only sign of life present being in his eyes that blazed with a hot fire from below. "Mister Wadley," he said, "You do whatever you think you need to. But if you think you can change my mind by trying to intimidate me, or that I would actually believe your idiotic story, then you are even a bigger moron than what you took me for."

It was evident that Wadley had not been spoken to like this before, or at least in a very long time. His narrow-featured face turned the tint of just beyond fitful anger, and he sprang to his feet fuming and sputtering. "Why you simple minded, country assed, backwoods bumpkin! I'll have your badge for this! It and everything else you ever hoped to have," the man raged. "No one talks to me like that, no one! I'll…"

"That'll be enough!" roared the director, who had reached his own limit. "Trooper Templar, sit down." Reluctantly, Micah did as his boss ordered.

"Mister Wadley," the colonel turned his attention to the apoplectic official. "You don't do the hiring and firing around here, or any other place having to do with the Texas Department of Public Safety. I do. Furthermore, you don't come into my office and threaten my men, nor do you attempt to belittle them in my presence.

"You had a suggestion for Trooper Templar. Well, I have one for you. There is a door behind you that leads out of this office. My suggestion is for you to use that door and don't let hit you in the butt on the way out."

Wadley remained on his feet, visibly stunned by the director's words. Through the fog of his own blustering ego, he realized things had not gone according to his design. A man who sat in a prestigious office with some political sway within his own organization, the FBI bureaucrat was used to getting his way. But this had transpired into something unexpectedly different.

In that he had badly misjudged both the trooper as well as the DPS Director, and the entire situation in general. He realized the damage done but it was far too late to do much about it. He also knew that anything else he said at this point would probably make matters even worse. His stomach twisted a bit more when he realized that heads were going to roll because of this, and the first one could be his.

"Come on, Humboldt," Wadley rasped and started for the door. The obese man in the ill-fitting suit remained seated, confused by the sudden turn of events and unsure of what he should do next. Wadley reached the door and looked back over his shoulder.

"Humboldt!" repeated Wadley sharply, with some of the prior authority back in his voice. "I said, come on!" Humboldt sprang up quickly for such a heavy man and scurried for the doorway. Wadley then looked over at Eggers, still sitting comfortably to the rear of the office. "Well?" he demanded.

"Well, what?" responded Eggers in an easy, devil-may-care manner. "I don't work for you, Wadley."

Eggers shifted his attention and tone, respectfully addressing the man seated behind the large desk. "I would like to stay a few minutes more if it's all right, sir." The director looked at him carefully for a moment and nodded curtly in affirmation.

Wadley stared at each of the three men remaining in the room, wanting so badly to say something as he exited but deciding against it. He stepped out and closed the door behind him.

The colonel and Micah both looked at Eggers expectantly, who leaned further back in the chair, crossed his legs and folded his hands in his lap. He began to speak quietly.

"I felt that Wadley and Humboldt were going to screw this up, which was a good reason to tag along. Gentlemen, believe it or not, they were trying to do the right thing. However, they just don't know how. One's a bumbling career bureaucrat and the other a pompous, power loving, bully. Simply telling the truth and appealing to someone else's better nature is beyond either of them."

"Then what exactly is the truth, Mr. Eggers?" asked the colonel, "and what's this all about?"

"It's about American lives, sir," responded Eggers earnestly. "It's about fellow Americans being held as hostages a half world away."

CHAPTER TWENTY-NINE

"You were right all along, Trooper," Eggers continued. "So was your uncle. Right about the VX, about their operations plan and about those men being terrorists. They belonged to a fairly new Islamic extremist group calling themselves 'Hezbollah.' Literally, the word translates into 'Party of Allah' and they are about as fanatical and ruthless as they come.

"The man who called himself Yahla al-Qassam was a highly placed operative in this organization, among some others. That was not his real name, by the way. We believe he was actually an Iranian, who was also somewhat of a legend within the Ayatollah's Revolutionary Guard. If they had succeeded in their plan, it would have done indescribable damage to our nation's infrastructure, not to mention leaving us with around a hundred thousand civilian casualties.

"Hezbollah has become the driving force for Shi'a Muslim terrorist activities over the past few years. They have been responsible for numerous bombings and attacks on Israel and Lebanon as well as other places, including that truck bombing at the Marine Barracks in Beirut seven years ago."

Eggers halted briefly in his monologue, gauging if the other two men were comprehending all that he was saying. Seeing they were, he moved on.

"They and their affiliated splinter groups have also conducted a massive wave of kidnappings in that region. Many of these hostages have been held for several years now, some of them our own people. Terry Anderson and Thomas Sutherland are both Americans, and have been held by Hezbollah since 1985. They also kidnapped two American military officers, Army Lieutenant Colonel Buckley in 1984 and Marine Lieutenant Colonel Higgins two years ago.

"There were others. Terry Waite was an Anglican Church envoy we worked with for a time, in an attempt to get a few of our people released. He had some success but was kidnapped himself in January of 1987. He is a subject of the British crown, but he was trying to help us so I count him as one of ours, too.

"Buckley and Higgins were tortured repeatedly by Hezbollah and later murdered." Eggers paused, looking down at his intertwined fingers and speaking in a softer, more personal tone. "They were both good men. Buckley earned the Silver Star in Vietnam, and also received the Bronze Star with a combat 'V' and two Purple Hearts. Higgins had a Bronze Star with a combat 'V' and also a Purple Heart. They deserved a great deal more than what they got."

Eggers raised his head again and gazed steadily at the two other men. "In fact, they all do and that is why I am here asking for your help. Recently one of the other hostages was released, an Irishman by the name of Brian Keenan. This was less than two months ago, and it gives us hope that we might be able to get our other people back alive.

"You see, Keenan was released within days of the Iraqi invasion of Kuwait. Just about everybody in that part of the world is looking to Uncle Sam to kick Saddam Hussein out of there, and for the first time in decades we have some real leverage in the Middle East. There are several sitting governments and opposition groups who wouldn't give us the time of day before this, but now are coming with their hats in their hands and wanting help with the Iraqis.

"Our plan is to put that leverage to good use, and get our hostages freed and out of Lebanon. We're certain that if we can get enough of these different groups to put enough pressure on Hezbollah, it can be done. Even the Syrians are wanting to form an alliance with us against Saddam, and they are major players as far as sponsors for these terrorists."

Eggers contemplated Micah with his hauntingly familiar eyes. "This is where you come in, Trooper, as well as your Department. As I said before, things are finally going our direction and it looks promising in regards to getting those hostages back.

"But if we were forced to admit publicly that Hezbollah was involved in this kind of terror plot against a major city in our country, everything would fall to pieces. The final result could be much the same, as we'd likely get the rest of our people back in pieces. Not to mention how it would adversely affect this forming coalition against the Iraqis."

Eggers paused again, still studying them as he spoke. "Look, there are parts to this deal I don't like any better than you do. If there's anyone who has a grudge against Hezbollah, it's me. One of these days they, or somebody very much like them, will do catastrophic damage to our nation unless we stop them once and for all. And they're already here, Qassam proved that."

He continued on urgently, passionately. "But right now we need just a little bit of breathing room to get our hostages back. We figure it won't take more than about a year to get this done, then we can start taking the fight to Hezbollah and the Iranians in ways we never have before. On behalf of our country I am asking you, pleading with you, to go along with us for the time being. We will make it right for everyone involved, just give us some time. Please."

Eggers stopped talking and let his words filter into the heart and conscience of the other men seated in the room. Micah tried to put his own mind around what he had heard as well as what it meant. There was so much at stake in so many different ways and he was being asked to make a decision that would affect all of it. He found himself desperately wanting some more time to think the situation through, and more so about the possible consequences in how he chose to respond.

It was the director who spoke next, and in his words were the echoes of the same questions and soul searching that his trooper was experiencing.

"Mr. Eggers, you do realize the cover story that Wadley and Humboldt were peddling has huge holes, don't you? What they were proposing would never stand up to any real scrutiny."

Eggers faced the head of the DPS and answered. "Yes sir, we do. But it will take months, maybe even years, for someone on the outside to thoroughly debunk this story and publicize what actually happened. By that time our hostages will be freed, with no remaining need of not making the whole truth known.

"Besides, our media works mostly on a 24 hour news cycle these days, something different is always coming along. Today a mysterious midair collision in Central Texas but tomorrow who knows, other than it will likely be something different. Much of the curiosity in this should die down once the media turns their attention elsewhere."

Eggers hesitated and shifted his attention to Micah. "It could be especially so if we can get the man most closely involved, as well as his organization, to go along with this cover story for the time being."

Micah returned the man's steady gaze, but said nothing. In his mind was a set of scales, one side labeled 'right' and the other 'wrong.' Both ends were having weight added to them rapidly as he tried to think this through. While he was doing so, the DPS colonel asked his next question.

"What about the other people involved who have knowledge of what really happened? Are you going to allow federal officials like Wadley to intimidate and strong arm them like he tried to do Trooper Templar?"

Eggers turned his attention back to the man behind the desk. "Director, we both know that those like Wadley will ultimately hang themselves if given enough rope. This has been coming for a while, and by the time I get through filing reports and placing phone calls, he'll be doing good to keep a job passing out pencils at Quantico.

"There will be no more such tactics used on anyone with knowledge of this. Personally, I was dead set against this method from the very beginning. Now I can go back to Washington and make my case, using what happened today to illustrate why we need to keep good faith and work together. I give you my word, or you can go to every media outlet in Texas with my blessings."

"I might still do that," warned the director.

"Yes sir, you might," replied Eggers. "But I don't think you will, not as long as I keep my word." A quiet fell over the room again. Slowly the colonel's head turned and his eyes fell upon his trooper, who remained deep in his own innermost thoughts.

"Micah?" the colonel queried. It was only one word but it asked so very much.

"What about the sheriff's offices and other elected peace officers involved?" Micah questioned. "How are you going to make things right for them? They did their duty and risked their necks to keep their citizens safe, but now they are being asked questions. Questions they don't have any answers for because you guys ignore them, and their own sworn responsibilities."

"That will change, too." Eggers responded. "Starting immediately, we will begin providing information and enough assistance to those officials and their counties to make a lot of those questions go away. Again, we need your agency to help coordinate in this. You know so much more about the personalities involved than we could ever hope to."

"There are some who were in on this from the beginning," Micah suggested warily. "They are good men, and women, and deserve to know the truth."

"Then you tell us who they are and if need be, we'll go and visit with them together," responded Eggers. "You say they are good people. That tells me they can be trusted once they realize what the stakes really are. Perhaps they can help head off a good amount of the speculation."

"Mr. Eggers", interjected the director. "You are making several promises in several different directions at once. No offense intended but beyond you trying to keep your personal word, what guarantees do we have that you can make any of this happen?"

Eggers never hesitated. "Well sir, how about a phone call from a fellow Texan in the White House, along with a couple from certain ranking members on Capitol Hill?"

The sitting head of the Department of Public Safety raised one eyebrow ever so slightly, betraying the slightest sign of being impressed. He nodded his head in affirmation and commented. "That would be a good start, Mr. Eggers."

Both men looked to Micah who stared quietly at the carpeted floor, still adding weight to the opposite ends of that imaginary scale. Whatever he decided would affect a lot of lives, not least of all his own. His sense of honor and integrity were his most important personal possessions, and Micah realized that only he could ever really do harm to either. Beyond that Tio Zeke and Max were no longer around to defend theirs, and he felt the overwhelming need to do right by them, too.

Yet everything that Eggers said made sense. Those Americans being held would be in far greater peril once what happened at the Bar JA became common knowledge. It would be natural and completely understandable for the American public to be outraged, and to demand immediate action against Hezbollah and their Iranian confederates.

Micah Templar remembered all too well the hatred and cruelty shown by the terrorists at the Albright Ranch, and what they had done and attempted to do. There would be no sense of conscience, no mitigating circumstance, no concept of any sort of mercy that would spare those hostages…

He raised his scrutiny and met the same of Eggers, and found himself looking again into the depths of those piercing eyes that tugged disturbingly at a distant memory. *'I can't remember who you are, Eggers,'* Micah thought, *'but for some reason I know I can trust you. Why is that?'*

The trooper kept his eyes locked with the other man, and watched as Eggers smiled at him again ever so slightly. *'He knows that I am trying to place him,'* Micah thought, *'and that I know I can trust him.'* With that, Micah came to his decision.

"Okay, I'm with you," the highway patrolman said. "Or at least until you give me reason to be otherwise."

Eggers stood and walked over, clasping hands with the colonel who rose from behind his desk. He turned and gave Micah another firm handshake, a genuine gratefulness emanating from within.

"I need to get going to put all this in motion." Eggers looked over at the director. "Expect those phone calls within the next forty-eight hours, sir. You might also pass along that some congressmen will be visiting the area in the next week or so. That should help take the pressure off those local officials."

Eggers faced Micah again. "Trooper Templar, thank you. Your country owes you and your uncle, as well as Mr. Grephardt, a great deal. As for myself, it looks like I owe you another one. I'll see you around." With that, the man turned quickly and made his way out of the room. Micah watched as the door closed behind Eggers, his mind still going through fits in trying to place where he knew him from. *'He owes me another one? What was that supposed to mean?'*

"Micah, would you sit down again?" asked the director. "If you don't mind me asking, do you know him? Because he sure acted like he knew you."

"Sir, I do think I know him. But I just can't remember where or when." Micah replied.

"Well, it will probably come to you soon enough" reasoned Micah's boss. "I don't believe either of us have seen the last of Mr. Eggers."

The colonel seated himself again behind the desk. He brought out a sheath of papers and examined them for a minute or so before speaking.

"Micah, I meant what I said about your report and what the ranger investigation determined. Your actions will bring nothing but pride to every man who ever pinned on a Texas Highway Patrolman's badge, as well as the

DPS as a whole. But I am afraid there will be even more asked of you in the near future, and that your life is about to change in some fairly significant ways. I also think you already realize that, especially after what we just agreed to."

"Thank you, sir, for saying so. And yes, I has a strong suspicion about the other part."

The head of the DPS went on. "You have nearly twenty years with the Highway Patrol, and a good record and reputation. Yet you never tried to promote or even move to another substation. Is there any compelling reason why?"

"No sir," responded Micah. "Other than I like working the road and felt I owed it to my family to stay in one place. After a while, that one place became home. There are some who might not like me because of this uniform or how I do my job, but they always treated my family like their own. I don't think any peace officer could ever ask for anything more."

"Hmmmm," the colonel responded. "I believe I can appreciate that. My first duty station was in a little community in the Panhandle, just about as far north as you can get and still be in Texas." The director paused, measuring the memories of his own past. "I met some of the finest folks I ever knew there, sometimes I find myself wishing I had stayed on."

Abruptly, he brought himself back to the present. "But have you ever thought about trying to promote now? I know your sons are grown and on their own. The Department can always use good men in higher ranking positions, wherever you might choose to go."

"Thank you, sir," replied Micah. "But no, I guess I'm just not geared that way. That would mean moving to a much bigger community and I've always kind of liked my elbow room."

For the first time since Micah had walked in, he saw the colonel smile broadly and shake his head in understanding. "Well, can I ask what your plans might be after the dust settles on this?"

Micah shifted his weight and sighed. "Well sir, I don't have much further to go before I can retire, and I figure the next year or so will be spent on what happened at the Albright's. Plus, Uncle Zeke didn't have any surviving closer kin than Abby and I. According to his will, we are the sole beneficiaries."

The head of the DPS cocked an eyebrow in obvious surprise. "You mean that you are inheriting Templar Aerospace?"

"I don't know about that" replied Micah thoughtfully, "maybe some of the proceeds from it. Running a company like Templar Aerospace is something I know absolutely nothing about, and have no real interest or time to learn. But there are some smart people who worked for Uncle Zeke and they still share his vision, so there is talk about them buying it."

"Then your life is probably going to change in more ways than first thought," mused the colonel.

"No sir, not like you might believe. You see, business slowed way down after the Apollo missions. That was their bread and butter, and after the rest of the program was scrapped Templar Aerospace had to scramble in some different directions. As explained to me, that process is still going on."

"But it still should add a hefty bottom line to your retirement check. Micah, I would say you're a lucky man but I won't, you've paid too high of a price for the privilege." The colonel stopped before adding kindly, "is there anything special you might want to do?"

"Well sir, have you ever heard of a spot called Alamito out in the Big Bend?"

"I know a little bit about the Big Bend," admitted the DPS boss. "But I can't say I have ever heard of… What did you call it? Alamito?"

"Yes sir. If you drew a line between Marfa and Lajitas, and then an intersecting one between Alpine and Presidio, you'd end up real close to Alamito as well as Plata, which some think as being one and the same. Both sites have been abandoned for decades now but there is land available nearby. I've been watching a small place that's come up for sale, bordering Alamito Creek."

Micah explained further. "Most folks don't want something that remote, however it suits us just fine. The ranch house is small, but nice and Abby really likes it. It has some shade trees, decent fencing and good grazing between the creek frontage and when the rains come. If all goes well and the Good Lord is willing, we'll be able to afford that place and what comes with it."

The director looked quizzically at the highway patrolman. "You really do like your peace and quiet, don't you?"

"Just as peaceful and quiet as I can find, and still be in Texas. I want someplace where someone'll have to work to locate me, and after looking around awhile likely not stay for long. Somewhere where I can look in any direction and see nothing but miles and miles of more nothing. And nobody."

"I suspect you have a reason for that," commented the colonel.

"Yes sir. I do, and more than one," revealed Micah. "The world is changing even as we sit here talking, Colonel, and not for the better. I wasn't blowing smoke up Wadley's skirt when I told him that I do a lot of reading, and pay attention to what's happening around me."

Micah paused to better collect his thoughts. "Sir, you heard what Eggers said today and I know what we locked horns with on the Albright. My gut is telling me that was only the beginning, and we as a country are not near ready to meet what'll follow. It's like some gigantic storm brewing, and when that storm breaks loose it won't be anything like we've ever seen before."

The highway patrolman addressed the colonel in dead earnest. "I don't know how many other Qassams are out there, but I reckon more than a few. And every one of them hates us and everything we stand for with a temperament nigh impossible for most Americans to understand. They're going to try again, and as many times as it takes. They're not stupid and one of these days, they're going to get lucky. God help us all when they do."

"So you are going to retire, move out to some remote spot on the map and let it happen?" asked the director bluntly.

"And what can either of us really do to stop it, Colonel?" questioned Micah. "We can both holler and wave our hands and kick dirt until we drop from exhaustion, but it won't make any difference. Like I said, the average American can't understand that kind of evil and don't want to hear about it. It conflicts with all those more pleasant things they'd rather enjoy, and how they want to see this world and their lives in it."

"There are changes coming in our Department, Micah, to meet these challenges. You could stay on and promote, and be a part of them."

"It'll be too little, too late, Colonel" replied Templar, "and we both know it."

Micah Templar eyed the other man, weighing his words before adding. "Let's just say I plan to pick my ground real carefully from here on. So far I've lost an uncle, a good friend, and nearly got myself killed. Both of my sons are in the Marine Corps, and it don't take a genius to figure where they'll be if this coalition idea takes hold. With all due respect, sir, I tend to believe my family has done their fair share in this fight so far, and then some."

"I can't argue that, Micah, and I do understand, especially about those sons." The colonel lowered his head pensively. "My own is a platoon commander with the First Cav at Fort Hood. My best guess is that he'll be there right beside your sons if and when we go into Kuwait."

"Yes sir, there's going to be a lot of sons headed out and it'll be hard for them." In Micah's mind was the image of Jeremiah Templar standing at the bus station, hand held high to that departing Greyhound. Micah swallowed hard. "Sometimes it's just as hard on the fathers, maybe more so."

The man behind the desk studied his trooper, sensing a welling of grief. "You were in Vietnam, weren't you Micah?"

"Yes sir" the trooper responded. "Marines. Two tours."

The colonel was silent for a while and stared out his office window, A lingering sadness came over his features. "I had several friends who went to Vietnam, some were a lot older when they came back. A few came home in a flag-covered box and one of them is still over there, someplace. No one really knows where, not even his own family. It still hurts when I think about them, and I can't even begin to imagine the pain a parent feels."

"Yes sir, I doubt if any of us can unless we've been there ourselves" responded Micah, "and that's one place I don't ever want to be."

The other man's eyebrows knitted together in circumspection. "Wars bring nightmares that never end for those who have paid the most dearly, in one way or another. There are people in our agency with cousins, brothers, even fathers still listed as MIA after all these years…"

Micah did not hear much more of what the director said, but not because he was consciously trying to tune him out. Rather it was at that exact moment he remembered who Mister Eggers was, and why he knew they could trust him to keep his word. The heartbreaking acronym of 'MIA' served as the trigger release for what he had been trying to recall. Micah knew now why Eggers would do everything possible to get those hostages back alive.

CHAPTER THIRTY

During the long drive home from Austin, Micah began to recall events from some three decades prior and belonging to another world entirely. He mentally castigated himself for his inability to remember those events beforehand, and how he first met Mister Eggers. That initial meeting had amounted to something important, even heroic in a time when so much seemed to bring nothing but misery, grief and destruction.

These were the memories of his youth, at least of a youth that vanished near overnight in exchange for a seemingly unending struggle to stay alive. That, and to keep alive other young men whose welfare had been thrust upon him. Too often he fell short of that mark, and perhaps his lingering guilt in doing so was one of the reasons he hadn't recognized Eggers to start with.

Of all of God's Creations, the human mind stands alone as a wondrously crafted complexity beyond compare. It accomplishes numerous vital feats and actions without so much as a single conscious thought. More so, it can actually shield part of itself from the other when seeing and experiencing too much.

Such is what occurs with certain memories. The memories are still there, but buried so well that it takes a strong, willful effort on the other part to bring them again into the light of day. They are seared into one's mind and very being, yet only brought forth and examined on uncommon occasions.

This was one of those rare times…

It was in late January of 1969 in Quang Tri Province, the northernmost territory for what was once known as the Republic of South Vietnam. Quang Tri and four other provinces made up the American military zone called 'I Corps.' Micah Templar had been an acting platoon sergeant in a grunt outfit there, part of Second Battalion Ninth Marines. The regiment was nicknamed "Hell in a Helmet," and for good reason. It had been a tough year for the Marine Corps, the regiment and himself. The Ninth Marines had conducted one combat action after another for the past eleven months running. Those actions had taken a heavy toll on everyone involved.

This had been his second tour, his first in country was in 1966 as a very green PFC. But what had gone on the first time around and what was happening two years later were hardly comparable. The Tet offensive of the January before had sparked a series of bloody, vicious encounters at places such as Con Thien, The Rockpile, Mike's Hill, Vandergrift Combat Base and the Ben Hai River. Elements of the Ninth also fought at the Battle of Khe Sanh and had the casualty lists to prove it. Those following engagements in spots blissfully unheard of by a vast majority of Americans only further sapped the regiment's strength.

But the final months of 1968 had brought a welcome respite, as the North Vietnamese Army was forced back across the DMZ due to the staggering losses inflicted by the hard fighting Leathernecks. Micah had been slightly wounded that August and medevacked to the rear for a hospital stay. During that period both he and the Ninth Marines had time to rest and make ready again for their tough, wily and highly capable foes. That wait would not last long.

As Tet 1969 approached, American intelligence chatter was at a fever pitch concerning a massive NVA buildup in the vicinity of the A Shau Valley, near the border with Laos. Not only was this worrisome fact marked by increasing numbers of enemy personnel and units but also by an escalation in their activities, and it all pointed like the proverbial dagger at the throat of I Corps. When heavy artillery barrages and air strikes proved less than successful against the expanding enemy capabilities, the call went out yet again to 'send in the Marines.'

Thus began the last major offensive of the United States Marine Corps in Vietnam, a two-month long assault that would go down officially in military journals as Operation Dewey Canyon. For the Marine grunts on the ground Dewey Canyon proved to be a tough, sometimes desperate journey up the watershed of the Da Krong River and into Laos itself.

Yet these Marines left their marks at every chancy step, providing the Marine Corps with dominant tactical successes due to their individual sweat, tenacity, spirit and life's blood. Five Medals of Honor were earned by the men of the Ninth Marine Regiment during Dewey Canyon, but only one would survive to receive our nation's highest honor. The other four, along with many another good Marine, would lose his life somewhere along the way.

Early on Micah's platoon had set in on a knoll about two clicks west of Firebase Razor, under construction at the time. Razor was one of the necessary stepping stones toward the Laotian border as well as the enemy contained within, and he and his men were providing a blocking force against any possible NVA reconnaissance or incursion.

Their position had been a good one, not only as an obstacle for any attacking forces but also as an observation point. Some 500 meters to the west down steeply sloping terrain was the Da Krong River, which before the monsoons was nothing more in spots than a rocky stream. That would change in the next few days, when that rocky stream would become a raging beast fed by nine straight days of near continual rain.

For now it served as a clearly defined marker for their area. The wide, open riverbed was a welcome change from the triple canopy jungle that covered their side of the steep, hilly landscape. Across the river the jungle thinned into large, isolated clumps of trees and tangled undergrowth surrounded by large swaths of elephant grass.

The different terrain making up the opposite side allowed their field of view to extend to the west for nearly two clicks. Just south of the knoll, the river took a sudden jag to the east before it continued on south. The ground fell away in a more gradual incline to that general direction, which afforded them even a better view toward Laos and the Ninth's ultimate objective.

It was fairly early in the morning, and Micah had just made breakfast from a box of C-Rats labeled "Beef, Spiced with Sauce." At least that was what they called it for officialdom's sake, but the joke was that it looked and smelled much like a can of Alpo dog food. He was talking with the newly arrived second lieutenant about how the platoon's three squads were employed around their makeshift CP, when Mister Eggers first entered Micah Templar's world.

"Sergeant, Gonzales says we got movement coming in from the west, across the river."

Micah looked up into the earnest face of a young PFC from Third Squad. His boy-like features were belied by dirt and whisker stubbles on his face, mixed with the deeply etched lines of protracted weariness brought on by daily life as a Marine grunt.

"What sort of movement?" he asked.

"Gonzales don't know exactly, said it was something strange and to go get you ASAP."

Micah had met Corporal Enrique "Chapo" Gonzales even before they had both landed in the same platoon. A star linebacker for the McCamey Badgers while in high school, the short, stocky Gonzales was known in the outfit as being a Marine's Marine. When he said he saw something strange and needed Micah immediately, the acting platoon sergeant knew that business was fixing to pick up.

"Lieutenant," he addressed the new platoon commander, "I'd better go take a look." Micah reached down for his M14, the most prized possession he had in country. As per Headquarters Marine Corps all line companies by now had transitioned to the M16 but he still preferred the older, heavier battle rifle due to its far greater punch and reliability. His existing chain of command appreciated his demonstrated skill with the non-standard weapon, and tended to look the other way.

Second Lieutenant Amos A. Johnson had only been assigned as the new platoon commander as of yesterday. A lean, blue eyed, strikingly handsome Cornhusker who had run track for the University of Nebraska, he had only been commissioned six months ago and had seen Vietnam for the first time the week past.

This was his first command and he found himself involved in the steepest learning curve of his young life. To compensate for part of that was the sagely advice from older, more experienced officers: pick out your best NCOs and learn from them. It was advice that he planned to follow.

"I'm going with you, Sergeant" replied Johnson.

The gaunt PFC led the way to a spot above the platoon's improvised CP, an observation point affording a commanding view to the west and south. Micah had personally selected this location as their primary OP and put the best man he had in charge of operating it. That was why Gonzales was here.

"Whatcha got, Chapo?" asked Micah as he crawled next to the dark complected man, who looking through a Bausch and Lomb spotting scope. Lieutenant Johnson wiggled up on the other side.

"I got bad guys. NVA regulars, looks to be at least platoon strength" replied Gonzales, never taking his eye off the scope.

"Where?" asked Templar, picking up a pair of binoculars lying in front of him.

"About 1500 meters out, directly to our west in that low area draining to the river. You probably cannot see them through the binos unless they are moving. Right now they've stopped, and we have beaucoup elephant grass and brush in the way," replied the corporal.

"Okay, so what's so strange about that? Probably doing a little skirting recon to see what's up with Razor" observed Micah.

"No, Mikey. This is not a recon; I think it is a hunting trip. I think they are tracking someone or something."

"Huh," grunted Micah, scanning the area described with the dull green field glasses. At first, he saw nothing, but as Chapo predicted he picked up the motion as soon as they started moving again. At this far out, the NVA troops were only mere specks drifting toward the riverbed.

Micah Templar steadied the binoculars as best he could on a low berm to their front, making certain he was still in the camouflaging shade. They were NVA and far more in number than a standard recon team. Beyond that he couldn't tell much more. Gonzales' far more powerful spotting scope was much better at picking out the details at this distance.

The three Marines watched the enemy movement for some time, trying to determine exactly what was going on. The NVA soldiers came to a clearing and hesitated for a moment, but then pushed on through as tactically sound as possible. Micah continued to concentrate through the twin lenses in total silence, straining his eyes for a better read on the evolving situation.

It was Lieutenant Johnson, looking through his own binoculars, who broke the silence.

"What do you make of it, Sergeant?" the new officer quizzed.

"I'm with Corporal Gonzales, sir. They are definitely NVA and at least platoon strength. Plus, I gotta real itchy feeling there's more of them covering this bunch. And it's not a recon mission, either. If it was, they would have taken the time to skirt that clearing rather than crossing it. Whatever they're after, they must want it awfully…"

"They are tracking someone," Chapo interrupted. "I can see him."

"Where?" responded Micah.

"About 250 meters below the lead NVA, still in that low area. See the huge tree standing by itself in the middle? Look about thirty mils to the right and down the incline a bit."

Micah scanned anxiously with the binoculars, trying to pick up what Gonzales was seeing.

The corporal swore softly under his breath. "Aw shit, Mikey. That looks like one of ours. Not a grunt, but definitely *norteamericano*."

Templar caught the movement in the area Chapo was describing. It was not Marine jungle utes, or any other clothing pattern worn by American ground troops. It looked more like the coloring of some sort of flight suit.

"Navy or Marine Corps flight suit" said the lieutenant slowly, verifying what Micah had been thinking. "You know, I think I know who this guy might be."

Johnson continued on. "Right before I moved up from Vandergrift, there was a briefing on an A4 that had gone down inside Laos. The plane was off the USS Hancock on Yankee Station and was attempting to bomb the same general area we'll be going into."

"Sir, when did this happen?" queried Micah.

"The bird went down around two weeks ago, evidently it broke apart in the air during a night mission. There was a search, but the pilot ended up being listed as missing and presumed dead" replied Johnson.

"Then maybe Lazarus has arisen, Lieutenant" said Micah, "because that's the only thing that makes much sense right now. Whoever the man is, he's probably been seeing the choppers coming and going from the firebase. He figures wherever there are choppers, he'll find Americans."

Gonzales cursed again under his breath, but this time more vehemently. "Mikey, I think they may have seen him. They are picking up the pace and angling toward his position."

"Lieutenant, we're going to have to move fast. What do you want to do?"

"Sergeant, I believe the operative word is 'we,'" replied the second lieutenant. "You have a far better handle on the situation right now than I. What do you suggest?"

Micah thought for a moment. "Sir, I want to go get that man but I don't want to have to cross the riverbed to do it. That's nearly 200 meters of mostly open ground, and this could be bait to lure us out there and into a trap."

Still studying the area through his binoculars, Micah continued verbalizing his thinking process as a plan took shape in his head. "Chapo, how much more distance do you think our guy can make before that NVA platoon catches up with him?"

"Well, Mikey" slowly calculated the stocky corporal, "I think it will all go down right at the riverbed. From what I am seeing now, he must be hearing them coming because he's also moving faster."

"I don't think they want to kill our man as much as capture him," Micah remarked thoughtfully. "But that will change quick if they think he's going to be rescued. They see the choppers, same as he does. If I was in charge of that NVA unit, I'd have it set in my mind to go to the river's edge, no further. They are as leery of that open ground as we are. My plan would go from capture to kill at that point."

The lieutenant nodded in agreement. "I follow you so far, Sergeant."

"Okay Lieutenant, then here is my suggestion. We have a range card already set up for that approach, with preplanned fire missions with our 81mortar section and Fox Battery back at Razor. Now, First Squad is already emplaced about 250 meters below us facing the river. We pull the M60 emplaced with Second Squad and some men from Third to reinforce the First. Still with me, sir?"

"Yes" responded Lieutenant Johnson. "Go on."

"When our man breaks into the open at the river bed, we hit them with everything we've got. Direct weapons fire will engage from the reinforced First Squad, and the 81s at Razor will join in as well as what we can get from Fox Battery. We'll start the mortars at the rear of the enemy positions and walk them in as close as we can, providing cover for him to get cross."

"Do you think he'll still come on at that time?" asked the lieutenant. "He's likely to be plenty exhausted and disoriented as it is. When all that shooting breaks loose, he'll be even more confused and hesitant."

"Not if he sees a Marine on the other side, Lieutenant, waving him on."

"And who would that Marine be, Sergeant?"

Micah put down his binoculars, rubbing his eyes for a moment. He looked at the lieutenant. "That Marine would be me, sir."

CHAPTER THIRTY-ONE

In practiced fashion, the word was passed through the platoon as the Marines shifted about in near silence. Perched on the side of the river valley as they were, any errant sound could echo down and carry to the ears of the oncoming NVA.

Each man took a special care, as they became more aware of what was going on and what was at stake. It was all part of Marine Corps tradition, faithfully taught from the rigors of boot camp throughout generations of Leathernecks. You never leave your dead, your wounded or your equipment behind. And you never, ever abandoned any fellow American beyond the wire.

Second Squad's M60 machine gun was moved down to a pre-dug spot with First Squad, the extra men emplaced, and the 81mm mortars readied up at Firebase Razor. The support fire from Fox Battery was iffy, they were on standby due to the possible need of extracting a force recon team further up the Da Krong. Whatever could be brought to bear would have to be enough.

Micah crouched with the leader for First Squad detailing his ad hoc plan, along with Lieutenant Johnson and Corporal Gonzales. Both had volunteered to go with him as close to the river bed as he dared. Micah had first protested, pointing out to the lieutenant that he was needed at the CP to coordinate what was about to occur.

In turn, the second lieutenant pointed out the Marines in his platoon knew their jobs better at present than he did, and if he was only going to be an observer he would rather do so at the tip of the spear. Micah found himself beginning to like and respect their new platoon commander. His unit could have done far worse than Amos A. Johnson.

As far as Corporal Gonzales, one of his many attributes was as a marksman with few peers. The former high school linebacker came from a very large and poor family living some distance out of town. As a young boy, what he managed to bring down with a single-shot .22 rifle often ended up on the dinner table or as bounty money on predators. The hard options of empty bellies or pockets had given Chapo Gonzales a deadly shooting eye, further sharpened and polished by the Marine Corps.

"You sure your *segundo* can run things up there on that OP?" asked Micah.

"I would not have volunteered if I had any doubts, Mikey. Besides, I need to keep an eye on you." Gonzales flashed a broad grin of white, even teeth and lowered his voice as if not to tempt fate. "Remember, we're short timers now. That Freedom Bird will be here soon."

"Yeah, I know," replied the sergeant. "Just want to make sure this Navy airedale gets a fair chance at his own freedom bird. If he's been out there by himself dodging NVA for two weeks, he deserves it."

"That he does" agreed Gonzales. "He is *muy hombre* to have made it this far." The sergeant shook his head in agreement.

"Chapo, I won't need the M14 on this deal," Micah raised the big rifle and offered it up. "I want you to cover me with it."

"Okay, Mikey, but you set the dope. It's your rifle and you know it better."

"What distance?" queried Micah, placing his fingers on the rear sight elevation knob.

Gonzales examined the area through the undergrowth and across the riverbed. "I figure about 400 meters."

Micah nodded in agreement and ran the sights up. He studied the other side of the riverbed, figuring for wind drift and added a couple of clicks of left windage. Satisfied, he handed the heavy-hitting battle rifle to Gonzales along with his spare magazines.

"You want my Made by Mattel?" asked Chapo.

"Yeah, and the extra mags." Gonzales dug out the twenty round magazines for his M16 and passed them over. By habit, each man checked their respective weapons. After doing so, Micah looked into the expectant eyes of the corporal.

"*Tan listo?*" asked Chapo.

"*Listo, amigo*" replied Micah, and they smiled sardonically at each other.

"*Cuidado*, Mikey. Remember, that freedom bird will be waiting for both of us" Gonzales said, and the two men shook hands. Micah turned and began making his way through the brush and to the retaining bank for the river.

CHAPTER THIRTY-TWO

Micah Templar had chosen his new position from above, picking out a point that offered plenty of cover and concealment. Better yet, there was a clear spot to its front where he could stand and attract the attention of someone on the opposite side. The idea that anyone, be they friendly or hostile, would be able to see him so easily had a chilling effect. This was really putting himself into the mouth of the cat.

But there was no time for second thoughts and Micah put his mind solely to what lie ahead. Cautiously, he moved forward on hands and knees to where he needed to be. Once situated he pulled out the binoculars taken from the OP, making certain the pieces of mosquito netting were secured over the lenses to veil any reflection. With them he began scanning the opposite tree line and nearby contours for the hunted aviator.

The minutes crawled by. From below, the sound of water flowing over rocks took away some of his listening ability. At one point he thought he heard something off in the distance, however he could not determine exactly what it was or even how far away. Micah strained both eyes and ears in that general direction but nothing else developed from it. Mentally, he slid back into the waiting phase.

Sometime later, he was scanning the opposite side for what seemed the thousandth time when he saw movement in the high brush above the river channel. It was the slight swaying of a branch, followed by some sort of stirring from behind the concealing undergrowth. Micah forced his eyes to look through the screen of leaves, branches, and tall grass to determine the source. There, if not for more than a fleeting moment, he caught a small segment of the green material that made up a naval flight suit.

The Marine sergeant continued to watch, and calculated the man was walking a quartering route down to the river. If he continued his general course, he should come into the open a bit upstream and on the opposite side from where Micah was proned out.

A minute or so later he saw movement coming through the edge of the brush line, as the man eased over to an outcropping where he could look both up and down the river valley.

Dark headed and of a slight build, he was indeed wearing a Navy flight suit, or what was left of one. The uniform was ripped and torn, and as filthy a piece of clothing as Micah had ever seen. It hung loosely on the shrunken frame of the downed aviator, who moved unsteadily with the all-encompassing weariness of days on end without enough sleep or food, and mixed with a near overwhelming desperation brought on by the constant presence of danger.

It was time for Micah to make his move.

He clambered to his feet and into the open, yelling as loud as he could and waving his arms about wildly.

"Come on, you glorified bus driver! The Marine Corps ain't got all day!"

For the merest fraction of the following moment, it was as if the second hand on Father Time stood still. The haggard man in the filthy flight suit stared incredulously at the waving Marine sergeant, using language that only a leatherneck would direct towards a commissioned officer of the United States Navy. The missing A4 driver recoiled in that split second, and Micah's heart sank to the bottom of his jungle boots at the prospect of the aviator running back into the underbrush.

But the man stopped himself in mid motion, glancing quickly up and down the river valley one final time. Then he was scrambling, slipping and sliding down the embankment, moving as quickly as the terrain and his dilapidated condition would allow.

Micah crouched down and started to yell again, but several things happened almost simultaneously that stifled whatever words were coming through his throat. The angry crack of a supersonic bullet whizzed by his left ear, so close he could feel the heat as it passed.

The crack was followed almost immediately by the heavy report of a rifle from directly across the valley, which was in turn answered by the unmistakable sound of his own M14 from above and behind. A tan uniformed body covered with leaves and small branches fell through the opposite brush line and off the edge of the embankment, accompanied by the long silhouette of a scoped Mosin Nagant. Micah suddenly realized that an NVA sniper had been watching the whole show up to this juncture, and decided it was the time to take his shot.

In the fraction of the second when the sergeant crouched, the NVA soldier missed. But Chapo hadn't.

The moment after his M14 went off and the body of the enemy sniper landed in the river bed, the jungle behind Micah exploded into a maelstrom of weapons fire, sweeping the opposite tree line to his front. Small explosions created by an M79 blooper gun were intermixed with the controlled bursts of the recently re-emplaced M60 and the sharper, higher pitched staccatos of M16s. A few LAAW rounds streaked by, impacting targeted points above the embankment on the enemy's side. He could also hear the occasional boom of his M14, as it sought out and dealt with perceived threats from across the way.

And there were a lot of them. The sound of small arms fire began to pick up on the opposite side. Some of those rounds were directed at him, and the impacts in his general area sent him scurrying off the open mound and into the background of tangled growth and overhang.

He shouldered Chapo's M16 and began firing at anything across the river that might have something to do with hiding an enemy. Out of the corner of his eye he saw the Navy aviator still coming, moving as quickly as he could across the starkly naked gravel and rock bed of the Da Krong.

Micah grimaced as he watched the man struggle on gamely. He himself had emplaced First Squad above this section of the river, as it offered a wide swath of open ground making for easily defendable real estate. But now it was working against them, and against this one man who had come so far and was now so close.

Templar yelled encouragement at the aviator again, but his words were mostly drowned out amid the whoosh of incoming mortar rounds and the attending explosions behind the opposing brush line. After the first few landed, there was the briefest pause for an adjustment of fire. Then a deadly mixture of high explosive and white phosphorous rounds began to fall like biblical fiery hailstones on to the targeted area, and hopefully upon the heads of the NVA troops it concealed.

The fleeing aviator was now almost half way; walking, jogging, stumbling and sometimes scrambling on all fours when he tripped and fell. It was if he was moving in slow motion, and with every fiber in his mind and body Micah was willing him across the open area more swiftly.

But in reality, the downed Navy pilot was moving still slower, as nearly two weeks of exposure and near starvation was leaving him sapped of any sort of reserve strength. Even with the occasional enemy round impacting around his legs and feet, the man simply could not go any faster.

Taking another chance, Micah rolled to his right and crawled over several feet. He popped up from there, cupping his hands and yelling at the aviator again. "C'mon swabbie! This ain't Happy Hour at the O-Club! *Haul Ass!!*"

The officer in the flight suit halted for another split second and looked directly at Micah before pressing on. He was close enough now that Micah could distinctly see his disheveled hair standing up at odd angles, as well as the two week's growth of scraggly beard framing his grimy, sweat stained face. Micah could also see his dark, intelligent eyes, burning with the internal fire of a man who just won't quit.

He was at the river's edge now, staggering directly toward Micah's position. Keeping his eyes locked on the Marine sergeant, the emaciated aviator continued to come on as enemy rounds struck all about. The cover fire from Micah's side of the river had reached a deafening crescendo and the supporting mortar rounds were marching down to the embankment itself. Any closer and there was the real chance of one ending up in the aviator's hip pocket.

Yet it seemed that even through all this, the enemy fire was picking up in intensity. Micah looked on as the naval officer waded into the waist deep river without pause, still glaring at the Marine sergeant. He was not much more than 30 meters away now. Then Micah watched with horror as the man's body suddenly pitched into the water below, taking those fiery eyes with it.

There are times when a man does things by instinct that he might never consider if he had time to think about his actions. Often enough, it is the wrong thing to do as the animalistic drive for personal survival frequently trumps all else. But in the case of Marine Sergeant Micah Templar along the banks of the Da Krong River, that same instinct overpowered him in whole and propelled him forward.

He did not know why, or even what he was going to do if he reached the other man's side, but a supremely fierce desire to help and defend another launched him out of the undergrowth and into the water below. He found himself screaming with a strange, primal rage and fury that only those who have been to the edge of that particular abyss of the mind can ever understand.

Snapping out short bursts from the M16 in the general direction of the enemy, Micah waded with a physical force that churned and frothed the near hip high water. Paying no mind to everything else happening around him, the Marine strode over to where the flailing aviator was trying to get back up.

Micah grabbed him by the back of his collar, jerking him upright. He found himself surprised at how little the battered man weighed.

"Are you hit?" bellowed Micah above the din of gunfire and mortar impacts.

The aviator shook his head vehemently. "No…I just slipped…and fell" he rasped in reply.

Micah noted a huge bump rising on the side of the officer's head, crowned by an ugly gash caused by some sort of blow. Most likely it had been done by a submerged rock just under the water swirling around them. It was the kind of impact that would have knocked many a man out cold.

"Can you move?" yelled Micah above the gunfire from both directions.

"Watch me!" retorted the aviator in return, the fire now lit again in those dark, penetrating eyes.

Slinging the rifle, Micah draped the man's right arm over his own neck and grabbed him around the waist. Together as one they turned and began the bullet-laced trek back to where Micah had come from.

As they trudged forward Micah looked up and saw Lieutenant Johnson and Chapo standing at the top of the embankment, firing their weapons rapidly toward the other side. Struggling through the water while supporting the extra weight of the injured officer, it came to Micah's mind that just as he had gone after this man who he did not even know, a friend and another man whom he barely knew were in turn risking their own lives to come after him.

He also knew that he could never explain adequately in words why, even if he managed to survive all of this. But they had come and he was not alone. And for as long as he might last, he would always be grateful for that.

The Marine sergeant and the faltering aviator began to slowly climb the steep embankment, finding themselves met more than halfway by strong arms and hands that pulled them up and over the top. Those same arms and hands continued to thrust them past the brush line and into the defiladed cover Micah had found before. Once there, all four men collapsed into a spent heap close beside each other.

Micah and the navy officer could do nothing more than breathe in huge gasps of humid jungle air. Chapo looked at them both, then at his sergeant in particular and just shook his head. Lieutenant Johnson, realizing he had survived his baptism by hostile fire, giggled nervously. The shooting from across the river began to decrease. The cover fire from the Marines above them, along with the incoming mortar rounds, continued to sweep the opposing area with fire, steel and lead as the 105s from Fox Battery finally joined in.

As Micah began to get his breathing back under control, he glanced over at the aviator who lay there with chest heaving, still looking hard at Templar. The sergeant reached into a side pocket of his jungle utes, producing a round chocolate treat saved from his breakfast of C-rats. The grunts referred to them as "shit discs," but the emaciated naval officer gobbled it up like it was a sixteen-ounce Kansas City steak. The Marine reached back on his war belt for one of his canteens, twisted the cap off, and handed it over. The man drank the water greedily, small rivulets running out both corners of his mouth.

Temporarily satiated, the straggly man in the ruined flight suit leaned back and continued to stare bullet holes through the Marine as the incoming fire slacked dramatically. On their side of the river, the sounds of grenade launchers, machine guns and rifles also began to fall silent. Only the shrieks and roars of the exploding mortar and artillery rounds kept on. But they were walking away from the opposite bank, pursuing whatever was left of the enemy back to where he had come from.

Still looking straight into Micah's own eyes, the exhausted naval aviator finally spoke.

"Sergeant, you have a really big mouth," he stated in an emphatic, almost insulted tone through cracked and sunburned lips.

"Yes sir," replied Micah laconically. "And you are?"

"Lieutenant JG Thomas A. Eggers III, lately of VA-164 'The Ghost Riders', off the USS Hancock." The hard look disappeared from the man's face, replaced with a large, beaming smile. He offered a grimy right hand and Micah took it.

"Welcome back, sir" was all that Micah could think to say.

CHAPTER THIRTY-THREE

The four of them laid there under cover for some time. Micah and the two other Marines listened to Egger's harrowing tale of being shot down in pitch blackness and of his long journey in solitude from his crash area, traveling generally north and away from Laos.

But the naval aviator had never really been totally by himself, the unwanted company behind him had pursued doggedly throughout his ordeal. Day and night they played an unending, torturous game of cat and mouse through the unforgiving mountains, valleys and jungles along his escape route. Each time the young LTJG thought he had lost them; they would reappear on his back trail like some mixed breed of human bloodhounds.

The emergency rescue transmitter he was issued had been lost when he punched out of the rapidly disintegrating Skyhawk. His survival rations had given out, and his issued water did the same sometime before that. He ate what little he could find along the way, and drank wherever it looked safe enough to do so. Sleep became a lost luxury, he grabbed small, fitful naps when and where he could. The one time he managed to sleep well, he had come within an eye blink of being captured.

This went on for over ten days, and the young pilot had just about given up hope of ever getting away when he saw the most beautiful sight in the world. It was a Marine Huey chopper off in the distance, and he knew that someone other than his enemies were in the area. On occasion, he also began to hear the far-off sounds of a ground war making its way toward him.

Then he saw more helicopters from afar. They were a variety of Hueys, Sea Horses and Chinooks, like worker bees going to and from a hive. Eggers changed his northerly course to follow those dull green bees of salvation, and to find their hive which turned out to be Firebase Razor. He knew the NVA were hard on his heels that morning, close enough to hear them to his rear. He was searching for a relatively safe place to cross the river and struggling with the rising fear of having to expose himself in doing so, when Micah called out to him.

Once deemed safe to do so, the four men cautiously moved out of the defilade and back through the perimeter set up by First Squad. After a 'well done' for all they continued up the slope, accompanied now by a corpsman who kept a sharp eye on Eggers. While off to the side, the corpsman advised Micah and Lieutenant Johnson the aviator was in far worse shape than he would allow for, and needed to be medevacked as soon as possible.

The lieutenant and his sergeant agreed. A stretcher was brought up despite Eggers' protestations and the corpsman started an IV feed to replace badly needed body nutrients for the wizened, sickly man. Four Marines from Third Squad were assigned to the stretcher by Lieutenant Johnson and stood ready to carry the JG up the ascent to Firebase Razor. Before leaving under the power of his newly acquired 'four by' mode of transportation, he asked to speak with Micah.

"Sergeant Templar, I just want to say thanks for everything" the JG said.

"Well sir, I wasn't the only one. You might say you were a community project from the get-go" replied Micah good naturedly.

"I know Sergeant, thank the others again for me."

"Will do, Lieutenant," acknowledged Micah, "and if you get the chance, you might also thank that 81 section at Razor. Those guys laid down a solid wall of bad juju and it was dead on. Without them, we would have had a really rough deal. Might also thank Fox Battery, too. Every little bit helped."

"I'll do that, Sergeant" said Eggers. The aviator was silent for a moment, lost in his innermost thoughts.

He looked up at Micah. "You know, I never really understood loneliness until that first night in Laos. The things that go through your head and what your imagination can do to you. It's as if you're the only one of your kind left on earth. Everything else around you is either an enemy or simply does not care, one way or the other."

The JG looked away from Micah for a moment, blinking rapidly several times. "Every one of you Marines took that feeling away from me today." Once settled again, he turned back to the grunt NCO.

"But especially you, sergeant. Because you were the one who came for me. I won't ever forget that."

"For whatever I did, sir, you are welcome" replied Micah and the two men shook hands one last time.

"Okay, Corpsman, ready to hit the road," announced the LTJG. The Marines at each corner of the stretcher stepped off as one in the direction of Firebase Razor. The corpsman walked closely alongside, holding the IV bottle above.

As the six men made their way up the trail, Eggers rolled partially over and looked back.

"I still say you have a really big mouth, sergeant" the A4 driver stated in a raised voice. He waved weakly with one hand.

Micah returned the wave and grinned. He picked up the M14, feeling the heartening surge of something really good filling him inside. The Marine sergeant savored it, as he knew that in war such feelings would not last long.

Templar's attention shifted to Lieutenant Johnson and Chapo standing off to the side, in deep conversation. The new lieutenant had learned a good deal today, and was proving to be an eager pupil to his seasoned veterans like Corporal Gonzales. There are all manners of education, what is learned in the classroom as well as the hard lessons of life experience. One dealt by and large in theories in the way the world should work, the other in the facts of pragmatic realities. It was a wise man indeed who sought out the value in both.

Between the promising second lieutenant and his hard-bitten corporal a special bond was forming, a bond that few would understand and even fewer ever experience. Watching them helped Micah to more fully enjoy that uplifting feeling, and let his spirit lap up the sensation for all that it was worth.

Because the bad times would return, in full force and making up for the space gone missing. In less than three more weeks the two men now quietly talking, the young lieutenant and his corporal, would join those other good Marines who never made it back from the Da Krong alive.

CHAPTER THIRTY-FOUR

The outcurved clouds hung low over the southwest Texas town of Uvalde, their slate gray color speaking of the possible chance of rain to come. Already a light mist drifted around in wafts and Micah, like all native sons of this region, silently welcomed the slightest hint of moisture.

It rained most of the time he spent in Germany, attending the funeral of Max Grephardt. Max had requested to be buried by the ruins of a small Lutheran church in a family plot, along the banks of a river called the Werra. It was explained to the Texan this immediate area had only recently re-emerged from under the iron fist of Communist control, and evidently there was an involved process to get the interment done at the site.

But the revered Luftwaffe fighter ace, holder of the Knight's Cross of the Iron Cross with Oak Leaves, had possessed many friends in high places. They saw to it that his wishes were honored, as was the man himself. Max's family mentioned to Micah this was the area where their father grew up and always wanted to return to. They said work was taking place to rebuild the old church into what it once was, as well as efforts to locate a suitable pastor to serve there. Micah well understood their innate need to do so, and why.

Max's family members and many friends were grateful to Micah Templar, and for his traveling so far to pay his respects while so much was happening in his own life. Furthermore, hearing firsthand about some of what had occurred and how Max died meant a great deal to them. His personal knowledge and heartfelt grieving for their kinsman provided solace, and the final defining act proved a fitting eulogy for a man who remained true to who and what he was to the very end.

Micah saw it only as the very least he could do. Like Tio Zeke, Max Grephardt sacrificed himself and all his tomorrows for countless others who had no idea of what these two men had actually done. Nor in all likelihood would much be ever known of their other many heroisms, and just how much was really owed to both of them.

While in Germany, Micah was haunted regularly by the same questions he had asked himself before leaving home. Questions that not only defied any clear cut answers but also evaded any adequate explanations, or any erudite words of wisdom when queried about being saved only by the ultimate, personally witnessed sacrifice of another. More than one night found him staring at a wall well into the wee hours of the morning, wrestling mightily with what recently occurred at the Bar JA as well as what happened all those years ago along the Da Krong.

How can one ever hope to even begin to repay the memory of another for such a selfless act? For Micah the topic went far beyond that of a simple philosophical quandary, for it had been Max who deliberately stepped in front of those bullets meant for him. Much like after his final return from Vietnam, Micah Templar was now spending a good deal of time in his Bible, searching for those answers. They would not come easy and his quest would likely last for a long time to come.

And now he was back on his own soil for another funeral, in a private cemetery west of town overlooking the Nueces River. For this was the day they buried Ezekiel Templar, a native son who had gone out into the world and made good. Though Tio Zeke had not lived in the Uvalde area for many years, he still considered this historic community home and requested in his will placement alongside his wife and son.

They were not the only ones buried in this plot. Standing at graveside in the soft mist Micah looked around at the ranger stars, military headstones, decorative memorial markers and simple crosses that all shared one common bond, the last name of Templar. In this ground was the final resting place for many of his kin over the past hundred and fifty years. Not too far away on a solitary low rise stood a weathered stone that read 'Blackstone Templar,' his dates for living and dying and a simple inscription that read '*Land worth dying for.*'

Blackstone was the first Templar who had come to Texas, at a time when it was called *Tejas* and under Spanish rule. There were stories still told about him around campfires and in the history books, and he set a high mark for those descendants bearing his last name. Each one in turn remained true to those same qualities, and many carried them to faraway places and into events that Blackstone himself might never have envisioned. But when their time came, one by one they returned here to take their place alongside him.

Micah's father, Jeremiah, rested close by, waiting with the others for the sound of that final trumpet. His was a stone inscribed with the Marine Corps emblem and the likeness of a pair of gal leg spurs.

Tio Zeke was the latest. Of course, there was no real body to be buried, just a small jar of ashes emplaced inside a casket. It had to be that way, as his body had been part of a hazardous materials operation without parallel. What could be recovered was systematically incinerated and reduced to ashes to avoid any possible contamination.

The rest burned at the scene, other than those fragmentary remains gathered up while being mixed in with Texas Hill Country dirt, sand and rock. There were many who might have been bothered by this, who in this situation probably wanted more to place in that freshly dug grave. But Ezekiel Templar would have understood, and Micah and the rest of his family knew that what was left was more than enough.

Faith ran strong in the Templar blood. Each one in his own way or another had realized that no man, no matter how proud or self-reliant, ever stood so tall as when on bended knee before His Maker. Some of them, like Jeremiah, had ridden a dark trail and suffered great loss to get to that realization. Then there were those like Gideon Hood Templar, whom no one was really sure about except maybe for himself.

In his own faith Micah learned the body of a man is only a temporary shell in which the spirit resides. His father had taught him that early on and as he grew older, Micah held fast to that belief for all the years of his adulthood. He knew he would see Tio Zeke again, same as he would see Max Grephardt, Amos A. Johnson, Enrique 'Chapo' Gonzales and so many others who had meant so much to him during his life's journey on this earth.

Because each in their individual walks shared that same core system of beliefs, so much so that in the end they proved willing to die for them. A man wasn't just a lump of soil and clay that went away when his body returned to whence it came. He was far more than that, especially a good man and he lived on in ways that stretched on through the eternities. That was the way it was, you either believed or you didn't.

As those who had come to pay their last respects gathered round, Micah and the other pall bearers took their places behind the hearse. Once the casket was put in place at graveside, he made his way to where his immediate family waited. His two sons, both in their Marine blues, stood on either side of Abby adorned in a black dress. Behind them were Solomon and Kate Zacatecas, with Jamie Zacatecas beside his mother in his midshipman's winter uniform. Other family members, both close and distant, flanked out into the swirling mist.

The aged Baptist preacher had spoken over Templars before and had known Tio Zeke for most of his life. His words were simple and direct, reflecting the intimate knowledge of a man whom he both respected as well as admired. Micah reflected that when his time came, he hoped that whoever spoke over him was as knowledgeable on the subject. Be they words good or bad, a man deserved honest ones when this chapter of living was done.

After the pastor was finished there was a short pause. The honor guard was called to attention and three crisp volleys of rifle fire echoed out toward the Nueces. Seconds later the slow, sad notes of Taps filled the air. The mournful lament of the lone bugle carried something that ventured far beyond what words alone could ever convey. Micah had heard those same melancholy notes too many times before. As he grew older, they only seemed to grip harder down deep inside.

Following the woeful tune, the Air Force honor guard stepped forward and folded the American flag draped over the casket. With practiced care, the officer in charge came up to Micah and presented the triangled colors. As Micah accepted the proffered symbol, the young first lieutenant spoke softly. "On behalf of the President of the United States, the Department of the Air Force, and a grateful nation, we offer this flag for the faithful and dedicated service of Colonel Ezekiel J. Templar."

The Air Force officer took one step back, then saluted slowly and reverently. Doing a smart about face he joined his detail and they quietly marched away, the only sound breaking the silence being that of his whispered commands and their obeying footsteps.

As Micah's eyes followed their progress, he was distracted by a haunting pair from his faraway past looking back. They belonged to the former LTJG Thomas A. Eggers, standing inconspicuously at the rear of the crowd. Eggers raised a hand and lowered his head slightly in acknowledgement. Micah stared back for a moment, then nodded in response.

CHAPTER THIRTY-FIVE

Some hours later found Micah alone on a bit of high ground to the east side of the Nueces, behind the family place that Blackstone Templar had pioneered nigh a century and a half ago. Amid so many who wanted to speak with him after the funeral he had been unable to locate Eggers again. The man vanished from the cemetery site like an imagined apparition who had never really been there to begin with.

Micah sat quietly on a large rock, deep in thought while surrounded by ghosts of other times or places. He gazed up and down the river, both directions away and as far as he could see. It was at the low point of the year but soon the spring rains would come, turning what presently looked like no more than a stream into a raging, churning monster.

Today the hoped-for rain had recast itself into little more than a sparse drizzle, but as in all things important the hope never goes away. Hope and faith, patience and prayer. Most every man who has ever accomplished anything worthwhile understood the paramount importance of those words.

Seeing Eggers again had carried his mind back to the Da Krong. From where he sat, the nature of the terrain and the positioning of the Nueces itself assisted in his personal journey into the past. Just below his rock outcropping, the river made a sharp jag to the east before it continued on south. The ground ahead sloped down to the river bank, making for similarities to where his platoon had been situated all those years ago.

Micah studied the gravelly, rock-strewn river bed as he pursued the erstwhile wanderings of his mind. It was about two hundred yards across, very close to the distance Eggers had to negotiate and the water was about waist deep. If you could cover his side of the river with jungle, and the other side with clumps of trees and overgrowth separated by stands of elephant grass, it could be the Da Krong during the dry season.

But this was Texas, not Vietnam. There was no jungle and no LTJG Eggers trying to get across. Nor was there an Amos A. Johnson or a Chapo Gonzales ready to risk their lives to cover him. No sound of rifles or machine guns, no mortar fire and no NVA sweeping down from the other side. There was nothing but the peaceful quiet of a southwest Texas winter evening. He wondered if it was this quiet along the Da Krong now.

The sound of footsteps coming from behind brought Micah back to the here and present, and he turned to see Abby walking silently down the dirt path to him. In one hand was some sort of small package, and she smiled tenderly at her husband as their eyes met.

"Evening, Hon" he said. Micah reached up and took her free hand, and she leaned down and kissed him on the forehead.

"Not interrupting anything am I?" she asked.

"Not anything that hasn't been thought through before," he replied. Micah moved over a bit to let her sit down beside him.

"In fact, I'm glad you walked down," he continued. "The seating ain't much but the view sure is nice."

For a while they sat in silence, just soaking up the comfort of each other's company.

"Solomon and Kate are headed on to San Antonio, they need to get Jamie on a flight back to Annapolis" she commented.

Micah nodded in acknowledgment before adding a reply. "That young man is going places, Solomon and Kate have done well by him."

"Solomon said that after things settle down some more, the two of you need to get lost in the Sierra Quemada for about a week," added Abby.

Micah allowed a flicker of a smile along one corner of his mouth and nodded again.

"That would be good," he replied thoughtfully. "Really good."

"He's a good man" Abby confirmed, "and I think the world of Kate. Living closer to them is something I'm looking forward to."

"Still ready to head for the sticks with a retired speed cop and bona fide crazy man?" Now he was smiling.

"I'd go most anyplace with you, crazy man" Abby murmured as she moved closer to him. "And to that little place along Alamito Creek most of all."

Once more the quietness enshrouded them as they stared off across the river. The cloud layering was still there but the sun was peeking underneath as it set in the southwest. The ensuing effect was one of those magical golden hours, the time of the evening when the land takes on that certain tint that only accentuates its natural contours and colors. Even the clouds themselves were lit up as the refracted light took their normal shades of gray into hues of yellow, red, pink, purple and that ever-present sheen of gold.

"That is…beautiful," Abby breathed.

"That it is," agreed Micah.

Not another word was shared as they watched the brilliant orange orb slip below the horizon, taking the golden tint and the rainbow of other colors with it. Abby let out a sigh as it all disappeared before them and the chill of dusk began to set in.

Glancing down at the small package Abby had set at her feet, Micah asked her about it.

"Well, I meant to give it to you before you left the house," Abby admitted. "A very nice man approached me after the funeral and asked me to give it to you. He said his name was Eggers and that you would understand."

She looked questioningly at her husband. "That's the man you helped rescue in Vietnam, wasn't it?"

Micah slowly dipped his head in affirmation as Abby handed it to him. He examined the small package that was wrapped in plain brown paper. On what he judged to be the top was the inscription "To Micah Templar," handwritten in a neat, precise prose.

Curious, Micah removed the packaging that enclosed a cardboard box. Removing the lid, he started examining what was inside. There he found an evenly folded sheet of white paper and a smaller, dark blue box with gold edging. Unfolding the paper, he found himself reading a copied commendation for the second highest medal of valor in the military services of the United States of America.

THE SECRETARY OF THE NAVY
WASHINGTON
The President of the United States takes pleasure in presenting the

NAVY CROSS

to
THOMAS AARON EGGERS III
LIEUTENANT
UNITED STATES NAVY

For service as set forth in the following

CITATION:

For extraordinary heroism during the month of January, 1969, as a pilot in Attack Squadron ONE HUNDRED SIXTY-FOUR (VA-164), embarked on U.S.S. HANCOCK (CVA-19). While conducting night time bombing operations against heavily defended enemy positions in the A Shau Valley area, Lieutenant (j.g.) Eggers' A4E was struck by opposing ground fire. Though his aircraft was critically damaged, Lieutenant Eggers completed his bombing run and only then ejected over the enemy held area. Demonstrating the courage and alertness of a well disciplined fighting man, for the next two weeks Lieutenant Eggers successfully evaded ongoing enemy attempts in capturing him before making contact with friendly forces along the Da Krong

River. Alone, with scant food and water while being pursued relentlessly by enemy ground troops, he exercised outstanding professional skill and resourcefulness, and displayed great courage as well as fearless devotion to duty. His indomitable perseverance and conspicuous gallantry were in keeping with the highest traditions of the United States Naval Service.

For the President
John H. Chafee
Secretary of the Navy

Micah handed the copied citation to Abby. With respecting fingers, he gently lifted the lip to the small dark blue case. Contained within was the unmistakable gold cross with the sailing ship displayed in the middle, suspended by a dark blue and white center striped ribbon. There were also two additional slips of paper folded inside the case. Micah picked up the first. It read:

"It would be an honor for you to consider this on loan to your family until your uncle receives the just recognition he deserves.

From a grateful nation as well as myself,

Thomas A. Eggers III
Da Krong River Valley
'Class of 1969'"

Somberly, Micah handed this slip of paper also to his wife and opened the third one. It was a quote from the award-winning book *These Good Men* by Michael Norman, another Marine who had served in Vietnam.

"I now know why men who have been to war yearn to reunite. Not to tell stories or look at old pictures. Not to laugh or weep. Comrades gather because they long to be with the men who once acted their best, men who suffered and sacrificed, who were stripped raw, right down to their humanity. I did not pick these men.

They were delivered by fate. But I know them in a way I know no other men. I have never given anyone such trust. They were willing to guard something more precious than my life.

They would have carried my reputation, the memory of me. It was part of the bargain we all made, the reason we were so willing to die for one another. I cannot say where we are headed. Ours are not perfect friendships; those are the province of legend and myth. A few of my comrades drift far from me now,

sending back only occasional word. I know that one day even these could fall to silence. Some of the men will stay close, a couple, perhaps, always at hand. As long as I have memory, I will think of them all, every day. I am sure that when I leave this world, my last thought will be of my family and my comrades.
    ...such good men."

As his vision began to blur from the tears forming in his eyes, Micah passed the quote over to Abby. He sat there, staring off into nothingness as she read the note to herself. Then she wrapped her arm around Micah's waist and held on tightly, never saying a word.

They sat together in this manner for some time. Micah thought about the events that had occurred over the past two months and not that far away, and of others that occurred decades ago in another place and life entirely. To be certain, there were differences but so much more was the same. Both had called for the same fidelity, the same love for another, the same sort of sacrifice.

Those connections also extended into the past, bound tightly with the history of his family in Texas and long before. To the very birth of a nation that promised so much, but demanded those same qualities and grit to fashion fine words and philosophy into hallowed ground ready for all comers.

That was when it all came together for Micah Templar, and when he understood with a defining clarity what made the crucial difference in the lifespan of all men, all families and all nations.

"Hon, do you remember the story in my family about Blackstone Templar's last words before he died?" he asked quietly.

"You mean those inscribed on the tombstone?"

"Yeah. They are the last four words of the last sentence he uttered. The complete quote was 'It's a grand country, boys, and it's land worth dying for.' It was something my father had me memorize as a child, I guess every Templar has done so since that tombstone has been there."

"I know our sons did," she replied. "You saw to that, and so much more."

"We both did," he corrected gently. "You were there with me every step of the way, and often enough by yourself because I was headed out the door putting on a hat and a gun."

"And I was wondering if I'd ever see you again," she added. "I prayed for you each and every time you went out that door."

There was a delicate pause between the two. "Sorry," Abby started. "I should not have said that, at least not now. It's just with all that has happened over the past two months, I am still working through it myself."

Micah turned his head and scrutinized his wife of twenty plus years. They had married before his last deployment overseas, and it was Abby who helped him out of the despair of so much unvented anger and pain when he came home. In that and from then on, both realized how much stronger they were as a team than they would have ever been if left to themselves.

Abby looked up and met his gaze, smiling again. "Why did you ask me about the inscription?" she asked.

"Well" he began, searching for the right words. "Because I don't think ol' Blackstone finished that final thought. Either that, or he didn't see it the same way I do now."

The puzzled look on her face beckoned him to explain further.

In response, Micah reached over and took his wife by her other hand. "Much like you, lately I've been thinking through a lot of things. About the war, Tio Zeke, Max, my family and why we are who we are."

He halted for a moment, sighing heavily. "Right on down to our two sons and whoever follows after them. Abby, what happened out at the Albright's was not the end of what's to come, it's only the beginning. Our world is changing into something different than either of us ever wanted or expected."

His wife remained absolutely quiet, her eyes searching his.

"Blackstone spoke of the land," continued Micah. "But it's not just the land, nor is it really the people. It's the beliefs they carry with them, those things they hold sacred and are willing to fight for. Once they lose that will to fight, they lose everything else. Their land, their homes, their way of life, even their souls. Somehow, we have to hold on to our will to fight, otherwise the evils of that changing world will destroy us and all we believe in."

He studied her expectantly, hoping she would somehow understand what he was trying to say. For a long moment, Abby just looked back at him.

"Micah," she finally said, "I think you have known that for a long while now. It's just you never took the time to put to words what you already knew in your heart. Not only that, but you also managed to pass that same will along to both our sons."

"Who are very likely to find themselves right in the middle of what's to come," he interjected.

An impassioned blaze lit in Abby's eyes, yet it softened itself in scale as she responded. "They would not have it any other way, nor would I. They are Templars, and are chiseled from the same rock as their father and those who came before him. As their mother I will keep their safety in the hands of the Lord and be proud of them for the men they have become, and for what they stand for."

Micah nodded, feeling something down deep for the woman seated beside him that mere words were never fully capable of describing. It was a fiercely strong and glorious feeling, of the same sort of fierceness which spawned that generational will to fight. But this was even stronger and more resilient, for it was the power to love.

Now it was his turn to kiss her on the forehead, and hold her just as tightly.

Around them, the dusk of evening was falling rapidly. A slight breeze picked up from the north, carrying the dry leaves of winter along with the growing chill. They huddled together ever closer, his left hand and arm wrapped around her and protectively holding her left shoulder.

"Guess we had better get back to the house, Hon. It's beginning to get colder."

"Just a minute more, Micah," Abby replied wistfully. "Just give me one minute more, before we have to go back and face down that changing world."

THE END

AUTHOR'S NOTES:

As mentioned in context for historical background, this story takes place in 1990 on the eve of the First Gulf War. The basic scenario was something that came to my mind during those weeks, a decade before the morning of September 11, 2001.

By my retirement from the Texas Highway Patrol in 2008, a very rough first draft had been laid out. Later an old friend of mine and someone whom I have a good deal of respect for, Major Stan Waters, THP, was asking what I had been up to as a civilian. I explained the concept for the book and plot surrounding it, and sent Stan a short excerpt.

Stan responded almost immediately, first complimenting my effort and then asking a very pertinent question; "Ben, how much of this is actually doable?"

I stated it would have been completely doable, given proper training and timing during the era in which the novel takes place. However, after 9/11 that window for opportunity was drastically reduced due to the ensuing War Against Terror.

Stan was still not quite convinced and questioned if I might be giving the bad guys some good ideas.

I replied: "Stan, if they haven't already thought of this, then they're not near as smart as I already know them to be. They only need the right opening to make it happen."

Though the American public remains blissfully ignorant on such matters, it is well known in various intelligence circles that Saddam Hussein was working on chemical weapons in the beginning of the 1970s. Furthermore, he was to repeatedly use those weapons against both the Iranians in the 1980s, as well as the Kurds in the early 1990s, who in actuality were his citizens.

In the same time frame the Assad regime in Syria was also producing chemical agents such as Sarin, Yperite and the hyper-deadly VX substance highlighted in this novel. Theirs was a far more successful program than Hussein's. Not that long ago, reliable sources listed Syrian stockpiles as being the third most prolific in the world, by measurement in tons.

To complete this intertwining loop and connect the dots to the abominable triad alluded to in the book, it is also common knowledge that the Iranians worked closely with the Syrians in pursuing these weapon technologies.

The group Hezbollah has a long history of committing unconscionable acts of terrorism. They first came to prominence in the early 1980s when striking against assorted peacekeeping forces in Lebanon. Their most well-known scheme of those years was the bombing of the Marine Barracks in Beirut, which took the lives of 241 U.S. Marines and sailors.

From its inception Hezbollah has depended on Iran for finances, training and leadership. Again, and as described in this novel, these needs are funneled through the Iranian Revolutionary Guard (IRG). In time this relationship has become almost symbiotic and continues on to this day. Whenever Hezbollah makes headlines in yet another heinous crime against humankind, you can just about bet their Iranian benefactors were somehow involved.

As for the many other historical events serving as backdrops to this story I strongly encourage you, the reader, to do research into whatever sparks your interest. History does repeat itself, mainly due to the unchanging corruptibility and innate wickedness of human nature. A knowledge of history, along with an understanding of those inseparable human vices and frailties, allows one to peer into the future with a certain discernment.

We as a people should become more involved in doing so. It is essential to our basic civic responsibilities in ensuring a stronger, safer nation for future generations of Americans. Just as importantly, it also allows us to pay proper homage to those who gave all their tomorrows for us.

Some of those were the men at the Marine Barracks in Beirut on the morning of October 23, 1983. A lot of good Marines died that day, more than a few whom I knew personally.

Two of them were members of my old counterintelligence team.

One of them took my billet there, the one I was slotted to fill before leaving the Marine Corps after my second hitch.

And yes, there is such a thing as survivor's guilt.

"The first duty is to remember" ...

Ben H. English
Alpine, Texas
September 11th, 2020

ABOUT THE AUTHOR

Ben H. English is an eighth-generation Texan who was raised in the Big Bend Country of the Lone Star State. He attended schools in Presidio, Marfa and later, a one room school house in Terlingua. During this time his family had several ranching and business interests in the area, including the historic Lajitas Trading Post which was run by his grandparents.

Mr. English served seven years in the US Marine Corps and upon returning to civilian life, graduated college with honors. He joined the Texas Highway Patrol in 1986, where he served until his retirement in late 2008. He spent the following two years working part time as a Criminal Justice teacher at Ozona High School.

Mr. English has spent much of his life prowling about in the lower Big Bend. His first book, Yonderings, detailed just some of those journeys and was published by Texas Christian University Press.

Presently, Mr. English and his wife live in Alpine, Texas so they can be closer to the land they both love so much. To this day, he likes nothing better than grabbing a pack and some canteens, and heading off in a direction he has never been before.

THANK YOU FOR READING!

If you enjoyed this book, we would appreciate your customer review on your book seller's website or on Goodreads.

Also, we would like for you to know that you can find more great books like this one at www.CreativeTexts.com

www.ingramcontent.com/pod-product-compliance
Lightning Source LLC
Chambersburg PA
CBHW050316110726
47899CB00007B/2262